DEVIL IN THE
WIND

Also by Chuck Barrett

Jake Pendleton Series

The Savannah Project
The Toymaker
Breach of Power
Disruption

Gregg Kaplan Series

Blown
Last Chance
Devil in the Wind

Stand Alone

Dead Ringer (eBook short)

Non-Fiction

Publishing Unchained: Revised

DEVIL IN THE
WIND

A Novel

CHUCK BARRETT

SWITCHBACK
PRESS

DEVIL IN THE WIND is a work of fiction. Names, characters, places, and incidents are products of the author's imagination or are used fictitiously. Any resemblance to actual events, locales, or persons, living or dead, is coincidental.

Edited by Debi Barrett
Cover by Chuck Barrett

FIRST EDITION

ISBN: 978-1-7365098-0-7 (Trade Paperback)
ISBN: 978-1-7365098-2-1 (Hardcover)
ISBN: 978-1-7365098-1-4(Digital eBook)
Library of Congress Control Number: 2021900777

Barrett, Chuck.
        DEVIL IN THE WIND / Chuck Barrett
        FICTION: Thriller/Suspense/Mystery

Published by Switchback Press
www.switchbackpress.com

As Always,

For Debi

The worst lies
are the lies we tell ourselves

PROLOGUE

Reykjavik, Iceland

6:45 P.M.

September, Present Day

Matthew Wolfe smirked every time he thought about what he had done.

It wasn't that difficult.

People saw what they want to see, and he used that to his advantage.

In the past six years he hadn't missed a day of work. He did his job, kept to himself and resented that his superiors never gave him enough credit. Nor did they appreciate all the unpaid overtime he'd worked. And for what? Nothing. No promotion. No recognition. Not even a damn pat on the back.

Now, they would wish they had.

He understood the risk. Yet, the opportunity was too tempting for him to resist.

He knew the tricks of the trade—how to disappear, go off the grid and stay there. How to cover his tracks, change his identity and meld into the crowd. In his job, he'd learned from the best...by locating and tracking those who went dark. He'd learned from the best all right—from their mistakes. He knew what *not* to do and how to evade capture.

When he put his plan together, he dismissed any doubts. He was confident in his planning.

His only regret was the country where he chose to live.

The brochures, research, and coworkers' vacation ramblings did not live up to his expectations. Vacationing in a foreign country was one thing. Living there was another.

The honeymoon stage with Iceland was over. He hated living here.

Mostly cold.

Mostly damp.

And, so far, mostly foggy.

Stores were never open. It was either light winter or winter. Skies dreary and on top of that, it was outrageously expensive.

"Iceland's green and Greenland's icy," he'd heard his coworkers say.

Idiots.

He should never have paid any attention to them. All they cared about were hipster parties and drunken debauchery.

And there was plenty of that in Reykjavik.

He yearned to live in a better environment, but where?

His options for asylum were limited. Many countries without extradition to the U. S. Government were unpalatable in his mind. Third world countries—out of the question. Here, if his location was discovered, he could make his case against extradition.

Although Iceland technically had an extradition agreement in place with the United States, it had been known to refuse extradition requests of high-profile figures despite that agreement. His government knew he had the advantage, but they'd never know he was here. He'd covered all his avenues and the flunkies he worked with were too stupid to see through the convoluted maze of misdirection he'd left for them. Even if one of them got lucky and stumbled onto his location, after his identity was known, he believed he'd be safe from extradition.

Lebowski Bar was a ten-minute walk from his girlfriend's rented basement apartment. It was named after the movie *The Big Lebowski,* starring Jeff Bridges among others and had become a big tourist draw. The bar featured four different *themed* sections. A '50s diner, a '60s Playboy lounge bar, a Southern-style porch, and a bowling alley.

He came here often. The vibe made him feel more at home, more relaxed. An escape from reality. Not to mention the hordes of beautiful women from all over the world who liked to hang out here, getting drunk and taking selfies.

A DJ played most nights at Lebowski's from 9 to closing. He made a point to be long gone before those crowds herded in for the music. He came for happy hour. Usually with his latest girlfriend, but tonight she stayed home studying for tomorrow's exam in her Psych class at the University of Iceland.

He straddled the barstool and ordered his third drink while he waited for his hamburger and fries. Normally he ate before he came to the bar, but Serena wanted him out of her apartment so she could study without distractions. He didn't argue and left early for Lebowski's.

He'd met Serena shortly after his arrival in Iceland. *Self-imposed exile* was the better term. She was ordinary in looks. Not a woman who stood out in a crowd. Perhaps he was drawn to her youth. Or the fact she seemed impressed by his maturity and experience. Good for his ego. But most important was the fact she was single and unattached—critical prerequisites. He didn't waste time letting her know he was interested. His motives went beyond sexual. She had her own apartment and he needed a place to live that allowed him to stay off the grid. Why rent and waste one of his aliases on a lease when he

could run his con job on an unsuspecting ingénue? He knew
what to say, how to say it, and what to do to make her feel he
cared about her. After he got bored with her, he'd move on and
disappear without a trace. Maybe to another town. Maybe to
another country. One with better weather.

His drink and food arrived. Good, he thought. He already
had a buzz going from the alcohol. The food would help
absorb some of the third cocktail. He ate and drank in silence
while his eyes wandered over the chesty brunette sitting next
to him at the bar. Beside her was a woman in a short skirt, both
speaking a language that sounded Italian. At times they leaned
against each other and giggled too loud. The chesty woman
cupped her hand and whispered something into her friend's
ear. The other woman caught his eye and smiled. Easy targets,
he mused, for someone like him. The pickup was his forte.

The thought of making a move on them was interrupted
when the bartender placed a to-go bag and his tab in front
of him on the bar. The to-go food was for Serena. He ate his
food and drained the last of his drink, left enough cash on
the counter to cover his order plus tip, grinned at the drunk
women, grabbed the bag and headed out the door.

The night air was cool and damp. Another foggy night he
thought in dismay. *Always the same shitty weather.* Halos had
already formed around streetlights. He paused outside the bar
entrance to clear his head and try to sober up before he headed
toward her apartment. Serena would be pissed if he came back
drunk. Even though it was her fault for shooing him out of the
apartment before he could eat supper.

He started the slow walk when he noticed a man he'd seen
earlier in the bar waiting down the street. Moments like these
made him question himself. He had taken meticulous measures

to arrange his escape to this God-forsaken country. Sometimes he worried he'd missed something. Some small detail. Not an important detail, but enough to lead somebody to him.

He waited, contemplating returning to the bar until the coast was clear when a woman appeared from around the corner and embraced the man. After a long kiss, the two clasped hands and strolled out of sight.

He let out an audible sigh. *I've got to quit being paranoid.*

He had learned a few tradecraft skills by hacking some of his former coworkers' 201 files and agency training manuals. He used what he'd gleaned as extra precaution. He reminded himself of everything he'd put in place.

They would never find him here.

Holding the bag of food with one hand he shoved the other hand into his coat pocket, and headed toward Serena's apartment, stumbling a few times on the cobblestone streets, catching himself once on a lamp post. Perhaps that third drink wasn't the best idea. He chuckled. Hopefully Serena would be in the mood for a break from her studies to have sex.

When he was a block from the apartment he did another scan—a *dry clean* the agency called it in the manuals. The cold damp fog had thickened obscuring his view down the eerily quiet street. He listened for footsteps. Damn, he thought, *I'm safe but I can't shake this uneasy feeling.*

He hurried the rest of the way to the apartment maintaining a constant vigil of his surroundings. A subconscious habit now since he'd been doing it for so long.

From the street, he took the steps down to the basement apartment and noticed the inside lights were off. Serena must be in the back bedroom studying, he thought, which she did from time to time. Still, she could have at least left a light on for him. *What a bitch.*

One last scan up and down the street ensuring nothing was out of the ordinary. Convinced it was safe, he fished his keys out of his pants pocket. His keys jangled and he dropped them. Twice. Grumbling, he placed the bag of food on the ground while he steadied his hand and jiggled the key into the keyhole.

The door slid open.

It was unlocked.

Shit, she did it again. How many times had he fussed at her for not locking the door? She was too trusting and told him it was safe in Reykjavik. He picked up the bag of food and stepped inside.

The apartment was dark. Perhaps she had gone to bed, he thought, most likely with the plan of getting up early in the morning to study. So much for sex tonight.

He closed the door and turned the lock. He tiptoed toward the kitchen to put her food in the refrigerator when he kicked something soft. Something that shouldn't be in the middle of the floor. He retraced his steps back to the front door and swatted at the wall until he found the light switch.

When he flipped on the lights, his world shattered.

He froze. Brain unable to process what his eyes had just seen. The bag of food fell to the floor. The soft thing he ran into wasn't a thing at all.

It was Serena.

Face-down on the tile floor in a puddle of dark red blood. Skin ashen.

Every muscle in his body tensed, his heart rate accelerated, his breathing labored.

They found him.

Instantly he spun around wondering if the killer was still in the apartment. The place had been searched. The only sound was the pounding of his heart against his chest.

He eased around her body toward the bedroom when something caught his eye. He noticed what looked like letters smeared, barely legible. Serena had scrawled something with her blood across the tile floor.

What had she tried desperately to tell him?

It took a second.

Then he saw what she had written.

A single word.

In all caps.

RUN.

CHAPTER 1

Grass Lake, Michigan
January, Four Months Later

L ife was completely different now, yet in many ways, still the same.

Grass Lake was a quaint town he'd become accustomed to over the past few months, although this winter was harsh. Biting wind gusts blew through the town's streets, barren of pedestrians braving the elements. The leafless trees, dead grass covered by patches of snow and dark gray skies in this small Michigan town fed the dreary feeling he already had. If only the sun would come out, but it looked like it had decided to hibernate with the bears.

Gregg Kaplan was a man who preferred to keep mostly to himself. Introspective, but not really in a philosophical way. He was a patriot. His sense of right and wrong was his moral compass, guiding his actions and decisions in life. Strange for a man whose occupation sometimes required killing. And he had killed many, but none without cause. His targets were bad actors—terrorists, assassins, heads of state, dictators, corrupt politicians...the list went on and on. He recalled his motto from Special Forces, he did bad things to bad people.

But that was a past life. A not too distant past. A life he'd given up. It had been over a year since he told the CIA to kiss his ass. Over a year since his last official assignment. Over a year since he'd heard anything from McLean, Virginia. A past now overrun with pompous, power-hungry wannabes, where government politics and in-fighting seemed to have become the norm.

A norm he wanted no part of.

He wasn't forced to walk away from the CIA, but after his last confrontation with the current Director of Central Intelligence, Lucas Reed, he wasn't going to give the DCI the satisfaction of tossing Kaplan out with the trash.

One downside of having a job as a trained government operative was the training never left him. He was always alert to potential danger. An occupational hazard for CIA officers. As much as he'd like to click the *OFF* button, there wasn't one. And he knew there never would be.

His new life perpetually unsettled. When he wasn't in Grass Lake, he was on the road with no clear destination in mind. But he couldn't shake the feeling that Grass Lake was now a rut with no means of escape.

His rut.

Isabella was here. Yet not the Isabella he had fallen in love with. As the months passed, so did his expectations. The grim reality of her recovery slipping away, leaving him with a void.

He'd rented a furnished apartment above a garage in Grass Lake and the owner was kind enough to give him space in the garage to park his motorcycle. The apartment was all he needed when he stayed there. He owned a home in Tysons Corner, Virginia, but he hadn't spent much time there lately. Minimal, actually. When he bought it many years ago, it made perfect sense. Only seven miles from the George Bush Center for Intelligence—aka CIA Headquarters.

The owner of Roaming Goat lifted an eyebrow when he walked in her coffee shop. "The usual," she said referring to a coffee with one shot of espresso.

"Long night," he answered. "Make it a *black eye.*"

"Okay, two shots it is." She placed her hand on his arm. "Be right back."

He knew what she was thinking, that he tied one on last night. In reality he hadn't had a drink in weeks. It was the ostensible futility of his current situation that kept him up nights. He hated giving up on Isabella, but there was a restlessness inside him that just wouldn't let go. If there was one thing he couldn't stand, it was being idle, especially with no hope in sight. The monotonous routine of his visits to see Isabella left him feeling purposeless in life.

And this was his current rut.

Roaming Goat had been open fifteen minutes and the coffee shop was already half-full of patrons. Locals, who he was now accustomed to seeing on a regular basis. And whom had grown accustomed to seeing him. The air filled with a mixture of fresh brewed coffee and baked goods.

On this cold morning, the coffee shop was warm and inviting with its eclectic decor. Condensation had collected along the windowsills. The industrial look—exposed ceiling joists and ductwork—seemed to be in vogue these days and Roaming Goat was no exception. Behind the counter, a wall covered with corrugated metal roofing tin. A small seating area, with its mustard walls, designed with relaxation and quiet conversation in mind featured a plush couch and chairs. Next to it, tables, where a young couple had already set up their laptops and connected to the free WIFI. Kaplan came here most mornings when he was in town. It was a warm and inviting way for him to start each day.

Except today.

There was a time and place for everything.

Now was not the time and this was not the place.

Not for the confrontation Gregg Kaplan was going to have with the stranger sitting next to the window. He had seen the man briefly yesterday and now the man had followed him into Roaming Goat.

It was only a gut feeling that he was being targeted, but as he'd learned years ago from his old handler—*Never buck your gut.*

The stranger sitting at the table next to the window was just north of six feet and lanky. His thinning gray hair still askew from the blustery wind. A scruffy beard not much more than a stubble made him look tired.

He dressed like the locals. Heavy wool sweater and jeans. His boots looked like a recent purchase. No scuff marks, still shiny. What didn't fit were the reading glasses perched on the end of his long thin nose. Bright blue.

The stranger was studying Kaplan. He made a lame attempt to avert his gaze a few degrees out the window, but it was obvious to Kaplan.

A man with something on his mind.

Or a job to do.

But what?

Many people, perhaps most people, might get rattled by a stranger's relentless examination, but all it did was piss Kaplan off.

This man was a stranger in this town. Kaplan had been in Grass Lake long enough to know the man didn't belong.

After his long search for Isabella Hunt had ended here, Kaplan never really left. Not for long anyway. He rode his

Harley back to his home in Tysons Corner long enough to take care of a few details and make arrangements to be away for even longer periods.

What he was going to do and where he was going were questions to which he still had no answers.

So he returned to Grass Lake. Not in search of answers, because there were none to be found here. But because he truly had nowhere else to go. Isabella's condition hadn't improved... nor, as he'd been told numerous times, would her memory. The brain aneurysm had all but erased that. And with it, any memory of Kaplan.

Why return, he'd asked himself over and over? Another question he couldn't answer. A question Isabella's childhood friend and now full-time caregiver, Clara, asked him on an almost daily basis.

Clara and Isabella grew up next door to each other. Isabella had clear memories of Clara and of Isabella's sister, Christine. She even remembered Clara's husband, Jerry, with whom Kaplan had now become good friends.

The doctors said memories were erased in reverse. Older memories were the last to go.

He spent a lot of time with the couple, but the sting of Isabella not having any recollection of their past together was hard to accept. Especially in the beginning. Even though he tried not to let any emotion show, the despair burned deep inside like molten lava. As with many things in life, reality had a cruel way of breaking through and grounding the soul.

It wasn't the norm for the owner of Roaming Goat to work this early, but times were tough in this small town. Over the past few months, the two had talked numerous times about his situation with Isabella. She was a couple of years older than Isabella and remembered her from high school. She was friendly and chatty and seemed to sense the right moment to stop asking about Isabella and change the subject.

She delivered a cup of something to the stranger along with a bagel and then made her way toward Kaplan with a carafe to refill his coffee. "Another *black eye?*"

He shook his head and pushed his cup toward her. "Regular will be fine, Britt. Don't want the shakes."

While she topped off his cup Kaplan asked, "Ever see that man sitting by the window before?" He motioned with his head.

She knitted her brows. "He looks ordinary, maybe he's just passing through or visiting. You're the first stranger most of us noticed. Especially Beth over there."

When his gaze met Beth, she smiled and whispered to her friend.

"Beth has let it be known she wants to run her hands through your thick head of hair...among other things." Britt let out a chuckle. "Sylvia sitting next to her joked she'd leave her husband if she had a chance with you. She said she could get lost just staring into your big brown eyes. I must say, you've been good for business. Those two have become regulars since you arrived."

Kaplan at 6'1" never considered himself handsome. He didn't fuss about his appearance. Days he spent working out, lifting weights, cardio were to stay fit for his job. Or the job he once had.

"Seriously, those two must be in their seventies," he emphasized.

"Older women like to look, too, you know. I'm not old and I agree with them." She winked. "Besides, everybody 'round here knows you're devoted to Isabella."

Most townspeople knew Kaplan…or who he was. He was the man who came to see Isabella and never left. Isabella was well known in Grass Lake, the closest thing to a celebrity the town had ever had. Champion athlete in college turned CIA officer, however the latter was supposed to be a secret. News traveled fast on this small-town grapevine.

Kaplan didn't know how to respond to the red-headed owner, so he didn't. He felt the heat in his face.

Britt's eyes let him know his stubbled beard didn't hide how he felt. She left his table and when he glanced back at the stranger, the man diverted his eyes—again.

This might not be the place, but it *was* time to put an end to this. If this man was going to start trouble, no cause endangering everyone in the coffee shop.

Kaplan drained his coffee, folded a $10 bill and tucked it under his empty mug.

He slipped on his leather riding jacket, which was draped over the back of his chair and ambled out the door. He turned left on South Lake Street followed by another quick left into the alley behind the Roaming Goat and several other establishments that lined Michigan Avenue, the main thoroughfare through Grass Lake.

In the alley he ducked behind the rear wall of the Copper Nail, a thrift store on East Michigan Avenue. He waited, listening. Nothing. Maybe he was wrong about the stranger.

Then he heard footsteps plodding in his direction.

As the sounds grew closer, Kaplan readied himself. This type of confrontation was second nature for him, not just from years of experience, but over two decades worth. He listened as the footfalls lightened and the steps stopped. He removed his weapon from its holster and readied himself.

"Mr. Kaplan?" The voice hoarse and broken. The man cleared his throat, spoke louder, "My name is David Pearson, I've been hired to find you."

CHAPTER 2

After hearing the man call his name, Kaplan stepped out from behind the wall, holding his weapon out of sight.

As expected, the man from Roaming Goat.

Standing face to face he realized the stranger was taller than Kaplan had first realized. David Pearson was easily 6'3" and not as thin as he looked in the coffee shop. But now, he was wearing a dark overcoat that made him look like he'd just stepped out of the Cold War.

"Who hired you?"

"I can't say," Pearson replied.

"Wrong answer."

Pearson's voice rose in intensity, "I was paid to find you and hand deliver this." He slipped a hand inside his coat.

Before Pearson could withdraw his hand from his coat, Kaplan had drawn his weapon and pointed it at the man's head.

"Whoa," Pearson shouted raising his other hand in the air. Kaplan saw the flash of fear in the man's eyes. "I'm not armed. I was only going to get the envelope I have for you."

"Slow and easy, Mr. Pearson," Kaplan warned.

Pearson nodded and carefully pulled out an envelope from inside his overcoat. "You're not an easy man to find, Mr. Kaplan. I've traveled to D.C., some one-horse town in Wyoming, Chicago and this is my second trip to Grass Lake. I only took a chance this morning when I saw someone riding a motorcycle in this weather. I remembered your dossier said you ride year-round regardless of weather. I gambled it might be you and followed you to the coffee shop."

"My dossier? Who the hell are you, Mr. Pearson, and what

do you want?"

"I'm a P.I. out of Seattle. Normally I only handle skip-tracer jobs. I'm getting paid extra to locate you." He held out the envelope. "And give you this."

"You have credentials?"

"In my other pocket."

His weapon still trained on Pearson, now center chest, Kaplan took the envelope. "Turn and lean against the wall with your hands and legs spread wide."

Pearson did as he was instructed.

"Feet farther back."

After Pearson was in an awkward off-balance stance against the wall, Kaplan tucked his handgun behind his belt buckle and reached into Pearson's coat pocket. He pulled out a folded leather wallet. Inside were Pearson's P.I. license along with his other personal effects...driver's license, credit cards, money, etc. Could be pocket litter to support a false ID, he surmised. Plenty of time to vet Pearson's credentials later. He patted Pearson down to make sure he didn't have a weapon.

Next, he tore open the seal to the envelope. Still keeping his peripheral on Pearson, Kaplan removed the contents and unfolded the small stack of papers.

Kaplan held up a photo and glanced down at the papers. "Who's Curtis Benoit?"

"Do you mind if I turn around now that you know I'm unarmed? My hands are going numb," said Pearson.

"Slow. Do anything I don't like and you'll regret it."

Pearson stood straight, lowered his arms, rubbed his hands together and faced Kaplan. "Mr. Benoit is the man you're supposed to locate."

"You said you're a P.I., why aren't you taking the job?"

"Because my client specifically requested you, by name, and even suggested locations where I might find you. She said this is the type of thing you do and you're the best. She's willing to pay you a lot of money."

Kaplan paused. "What's your client's name? Does she live in Seattle too?"

"Mr. Kaplan, my client wishes to remain anonymous. I'm not at liberty to discuss anything about my client with you or anyone else."

"Uh-huh. I'm supposed to locate Mr. Curtis Benoit and then what?"

"Then you call me," Pearson said. "My business card is in the envelope."

Kaplan rifled through the pages. "Says here Mr. Benoit was last seen in France. Your client wants me to go to France and look for this man?" Kaplan held up the picture again.

"Is that a problem, Mr. Kaplan?"

Traveling to France was not a problem, he thought, leaving Grass Lake was the problem. The job was tempting and that was his problem. He would have to leave Isabella to take it. A rush of guilt coursed through him for even considering the offer. "Sorry. You'll have to find somebody else," Kaplan replied.

Pearson looked bewildered. His hand hastily reached inside his coat, producing another envelope.

Holding the envelope up for Kaplan to see, Pearson stated, "Expense money. Twenty thousand cash. Ten thousand in U.S. dollars, ten thousand in Euro. Plus, two round-trip first-class tickets from Chicago to Paris. You leave tomorrow night."

"Two?"

"I was told you have a partner."

"What partner?"

"I have no idea. My client said you would know."

"Your client seems pretty damn sure I'll take this job. Does your client, or you for that matter, think I'm going to accept a business deal with the sketchy details you've offered. When I take a job, I know who I'm working for and why I'm doing the job." Kaplan lied. Most of his assignments with the CIA were with as little or less information than Pearson and his client had provided in the packet. "To even consider what you offer, I need to know what I'm getting into."

"I told her you would balk."

"She should have listened."

"As a last resort to convince you, she agreed to let me explain the gist of her issue."

"I'm listening."

"My client is an estate and inheritance attorney. She's trying to locate the sole beneficiary of an inheritance—"

"Curtis Benoit?"

"Yes. You are to spare no expense in locating Mr. Benoit. This is a time sensitive situation."

"Spare no expense, huh?"

"Within reason." He held up the envelope. "This expense money should cover everything and then some."

"Where'd she get my name?"

"I have no idea, Mr. Kaplan. Suffice to say she is *well connected* if you know what I mean."

"Not really, Mr. Pearson. Well connected to whom?"

"Apparently she was once legal counsel for some high-ranking politician on Capitol Hill. Perhaps someone who knew of your skillset. Like I said, she is well connected."

"Sorry. Still too many questions that need answering. I'll have to think about it."

"Now that I've located you," Pearson explained. "I'm authorized to give you four hours, then I'm afraid I must insist on an answer."

"What about payment? I'm not doing this for free."

"Ten thousand each, up front, and another ten thousand each when the job has been completed." Pearson hesitated before continuing, "And as a binder of good faith on our part, I'm authorized to give this to you now. If you accept, I can have your first installments wired to you and your partner's bank accounts first thing Monday morning."

"A hundred thousand up front and another hundred when the job is done." Kaplan placed emphasis on the next word. "Each."

Pearson's eyebrows furrowed. "Ridiculous. That's nearly half a million dollars. Fifteen thousand is high as I can go." He added, "each."

"Seventy-five," Kaplan countered. "Each."

"Twenty. And I keep this." Pearson held up the cash envelope.

"Fifty. And you keep that." Kaplan gestured at the envelope. "No."

"Thirty-five and I get the cash. Take it or I walk."

Pearson paused. "Thirty-five it is." Pearson handed the envelope to Kaplan.

"Your client must want to locate Curtis Benoit pretty badly, Mr. Pearson."

"She does. Says time is of the essence. It is a sizable inheritance and I was told the will is very complicated. This amount of money is literally not an issue. Like I said, spare no expense."

Kaplan pulled Pearson's business card out of the envelope

and held it up. "I'll call you with my decision." Kaplan stuffed the two envelopes inside his black leather coat and walked past Pearson toward Roaming Goat and his motorcycle.

"Mr. Kaplan, please remember you only have four hours before the offer is off the table," yelled Pearson as Kaplan rounded the corner out of the alley.

Kaplan shrugged knowing nothing was ever what it seemed.

CHAPTER 3

After Kaplan warmed his black Harley-Davidson Fatboy, he mounted the bike, revved the engine, and took off to the place he needed to go—the only place he ever went—to see Isabella.

The roads were still spotted with patches of ice from the seven inches of snow dumped by the winter storm three days ago. A slower, more cautious ride, but conditions he'd ridden in many times.

Even though Clara and Jerry told him he could just come and go at his discretion, he still rang the doorbell. Every time. Or knocked. This time it wasn't Clara or Jerry who answered the door, it was Isabella. She greeted him with a kind smile. The same kind smile she'd greeted him with since he'd been visiting on a regular basis. "Hello, Gregg Kaplan," she said, always using his full name. She was wearing matching sweatpants and sweatshirt from her days at Amherst College along with the fur-lined slippers he gave her several Christmases ago— before her aneurysm. Her thick brown hair was pulled back in a ponytail.

As he gazed into her brown eyes, the eyes that had always mesmerized him, the eyes that used to sparkle when he told her he loved her, the pit in his stomach returned. His partner— former partner—was not the woman she once was and never would be again. The hemorrhaged aneurysm had wiped out much of her memory like cleaning a chalkboard with an eraser. Any memory of him gone with it. Now she only knew him as the man who came to visit, the man Clara had told her used to be her boyfriend a long time ago. Her eyes revealed nothing. No recognition of what they once had.

Boyfriend. Wasn't that an understatement?

The doctor explained that it wasn't in Isabella's best interest to reveal the depth of their relationship. Best to omit those details. It would only confuse and upset her. As much as he wanted to tell her, explain to her all the love they had once shared, all the passion they once had for each other, and all the danger they'd encountered while partners and operatives of the CIA's Clandestine Service, he honored the doctor's request and kept those feelings to himself. Perhaps not to himself, but he never said anything to Isabella.

"Good morning, pretty lady," he replied and pulled a red rose from behind his back. "I brought you something. A beautiful rose for a beautiful woman."

She took the rose. "Thank you." She shuffled off to the kitchen without another word.

Jerry came to the door, opening it wider and waving Kaplan inside. "Not a good day I'm afraid," he said. "Isabella woke up crying again."

Jerry was a few inches shorter than him, around 5' 10" with thinning blond hair and a blond mustache. He was wearing shorts and a short sleeve shirt, both of which revealed a lot of blond body hair.

"Aren't you the least bit cold?"

"With all this fur? No way," Jerry replied in his usual jovial manner. "It's only in the thirties for crying out loud. Besides it's warm in the house. I'll put on long pants when it gets below freezing."

Kaplan shook his head and stepped into the foyer. "Got a minute? I want to run something past you."

Jerry nodded and motioned to the couch in the living room. "Sure. What's up?"

Kaplan recounted the morning's events and his encounter with the stranger, aka David Pearson, and the prospective job offer. "What do you think?"

"Wow. That's a lot of money. And a trip to France to boot. I'm not seeing a downside, but what do I know? I just do what I'm told around here. You should talk to Clara, she's better at giving advice than me."

"Fat lot of help you are."

"Hey...who you calling fat? Don't make me box your ears." They both laughed.

Kaplan cut his eyes toward the kitchen. "Clara in the back?"

Jerry nodded. "Yep." His friend sat in a recliner and pulled out his new-to-him iPad. Good for three things in Jerry's mind—reading news, checking email and playing Solitaire.

Kaplan walked toward the kitchen and caught a glimpse of Isabella down the hall arranging the rose he gave her in a vase with all the other roses he had given her. A new one every day. All red. She looked up when he passed by and smiled. An empty smile, like an obligatory smile to a stranger.

Clara was in the back room curled up in her favorite chair located next to the largest Christmas cactus Kaplan had ever seen. Clara once explained how old it was and how many generations it had been handed down. He didn't know house plants lived that long.

"Morning, Gregg," she said when he walked in. "Jerry tell you about this morning?"

"He did. Same dream?"

"Yes."

"Isn't that a sign her memory is coming back?"

"No, Gregg. We've been over this before. It means nothing."

He heard the strain in his own voice, "I know. But maybe her dreams are of our past missions together. That could be a start."

"The doctor believes anxiety and her medications are likely the culprits. Gregg, you need to face the truth, Isabella will never remember what you want her to."

"But what if she was told about some of the things that happened? That might trigger something in her memory."

"You know what the doctor said, in all likelihood it would do more harm than good. It would increase her anxiety and there'd be more mornings like this morning. Don't be selfish, telling Isabella will never bring her back to you."

She straightened in her chair and her expression changed. Her brow creased downward. "Gregg, Jerry and I like you. A lot. And Jerry enjoys hanging out with you. You two are like mischievous kids. It's been great getting to know you, so I don't want this to sound harsh, but you need to move on. Not for our sake, not even so much for Isabella's...for yours."

"Can we talk? I want your opinion on something." There was something about Clara's raw honesty he appreciated.

"You're leaving?" she said with no particular look.

"No. Well...maybe. That's my dilemma. This morning we got a job offer."

"We? What do you mean, we?

"Me and my partner, Isabella and me."

"Isabella?"

"Yeah. I thought it was strange too, but I believe the client must not know about Isabella's condition."

"What kind of job offer?"

"Travel to France to locate someone. This P.I. from Seattle

tracked me down. Said his client, specifically requested me
and my partner. Said she heard we have a reputation with this
kind of work. Pays well, too."

Clara was silent for a few seconds then burst out laughing.

Kaplan felt the heat rise up his neck. "What's so funny?"

"You mean like tracking down a fugitive who is being
hunted by the mob? Or going up against a criminal family
empire in Wyoming? You mean that sort of reputation? This
anonymous client doesn't want you and Isabella. She wants
you and that friend of yours from Chicago. The retired WitSec
Marshal with the funny name."

"Moss?"

"Yeah, that's him, Pete Moss. The friend who went to
Wyoming when you located Isabella's sister."

As soon as she said it, he knew she was right. That was
who Pearson was referring to, Moss, not Isabella. At the time
Pearson mentioned it, he assumed either Isabella or his first
partner, Jake. He never even considered Moss as a partner. In
reality, Moss had been more of a partner than either of the
others. Since it was never *official*, he just considered Moss a
friend and ally.

"Gregg." The tone in Clara's voice serious. "You should
take this job. You *need* to take this job. It'll do you good. Take
your mind off things here for a while."

He started to interrupt but Clara raised her finger.

"I know what you're thinking, the job will take you away
from Isabella. Perhaps for a short time, perhaps longer. I think
it would be for the best. Better for Isabella. Better for you.
You both could use a break. If you're gone two weeks or two
months…or two years, she won't really know the difference.
Mornings like this morning became more frequent after you

showed up. Take the job. Go to France. While you're there, try to relax and have some fun. When you come back, if you come back, we'll still be here. Nothing is going to change."

"What do you mean *if?*"

She shrugged her shoulders.

He knew she was right. Yet this was the hardest decision he had ever faced.

"Thanks, Clara," he said and then he walked out of the room.

CHAPTER 4

Gare de Rennes — 10:30 P.M.
Rennes, France

The TGV came to rest at the train station. The assassin checked the time, one hour 25 minutes to travel the 365 kilometers, roughly 225 miles from Paris. Not too shabby. The assassin's home country of the United States could learn a thing or two from European rail service. To make the claim of being the most advanced country on Earth, the United States had allowed its infrastructure to fall into grave disrepair. Congress was at an all-time standstill with no light at the end of the tunnel, bickering over partisan issues, stalemating any funding to fix the problem.

Reasons enough for the assassin to stay away as long as possible. That, and a few dozen outstanding arrest warrants. All under assumed names. With today's technology and advancements in facial recognition software, it was getting harder and harder to get through security even with a disguise. TSA in the United States was becoming increasingly difficult to beat, but not impossible. Disguises now required more than just hair. It involved the literal reshaping of the face. Noses, jawlines, foreheads, chin features—all changed and hidden by precisely the right makeup. Traveling in Europe was much easier. The rules more relaxed, especially away from airports. Rail transportation in Europe made getting from job to job so much easier. And safer.

The assassin's job in this region of France wasn't in Rennes, this was just a good place to hole up for a while. A hideout of sorts. A place for planning and preparation. The actual job itself was on a small island about an hour to the north.

The assassin's rented apartment was a 25-minute walk from Gare de Rennes. Lugging a heavy backpack and pulling a suitcase on wheels over rough brick and cobblestone streets made it feel even longer. It was necessary. The backpack contained tools of the trade. In short, everything needed to kill a person in several different ways.

From the road, the apartment building on Rue d'Antrain looked the way it was advertised on the internet. The studio apartment the assassin rented for two weeks was satisfactory for one person. A double bed in a loft overlooked the kitchen and sitting area. Clean and comfortable. Tomorrow the assassin would locate a rental car, a mainstream brand, compact, and suitable for the ground floor apartment building's covered parking. The ability to come and go without parking on the street was a necessity. Another reason this apartment was chosen.

There was a market within a five-minute walk up Rue d'Antrain. Perfect to slip out and back without drawing unwanted attention.

This contract hit had to be planned down to the last detail since there were many moving parts. A lot could go wrong. The target would be protected by law enforcement and private security, both seen and unseen. High-level targets were challenging. Where was the best place to execute the mission? And more important, the escape route.

Fortunately, the assassin had a few days before the target would arrive. Plenty of time to scout the locale and investigate all ingress and egress options. A wrong decision could blow the mission and cost the assassin everything.

The internet information showed that there was one way on and off the tidal island where the assassination would take place. A long road to walk as no personal vehicles were allowed. Or take the shuttle from the parking lot. The island, a high-profile tourist attraction, religious in nature, was soon to be visited by the largest conspirator of them all. The man who, along with his predecessors, had allowed heinous crimes to go unpunished by decades of denial. And now, the worst sin of them all, blaming others, including victims, of trying to bring about his establishment's downfall. It could have been stopped decades ago but instead, the perpetrators were shuffled in secrecy from location to location without repercussions. The administrators of this cover-up even went so far as to keep secret logs of the so-called transfers. Men who were held in the highest regard were the worst sinners of all. Men who had violated others with total disregard for the laws of Man or the laws of God. They weren't just sinners, but criminals. Men who did not deserve another breath and would no doubt be condemned to Hell.

As much as the assassin wished the man at the top to be the target, he was not.

The target was a smaller fish, but still a man of great power and stature within the organization.

A man who had gone to great lengths to minimize and abate the organization's liability. A man who had single-handedly devised a system that avoided the mounting legal complaints against the organization and averted the blame from the victims. And in the process, he tried to cover his own tracks and eradicate any incriminating evidence against himself. Clever. He almost got away with it.

Until now.

It was time for this boys' club to end.

His secret was out.

CHAPTER 5

Grass Lake, Michigan

Kaplan killed the engine to his motorcycle after parking it in his landlord's garage. He climbed the stairs to his apartment and opened the door. Inside he headed to the kitchen, opened a cabinet and claimed a bottle of whiskey and a glass. After pouring himself a drink, he turned to move toward the only comfortable chair in the place. Then he stopped, reached back and snagged the bottle off the counter.

When he sat in the chair, he placed the bottle on the end table and began to nurse his drink. He thought about his conversation with Clara. Then he felt his mind being hijacked by his emotions. He relived his last mission with Isabella, their first kiss and the last time he made love to her. The taste of her lips, her smooth skin, her moans. Afterwards she fell asleep, but he laid awake studying her, never wanting to leave.

Ever.

After draining the glass, he started to pour himself another and stopped. Setting the bottle down, he put the empty glass next to it. The guilt of leaving Isabella was there. But so was the futility of staying. And now the lure of having an assignment to do something he was good at.

He slipped his phone out of his shirt pocket.

He was ready to make the call.

† † †

Moss answered on the first ring.

"Kaplan, how the hell are ya?"

"Hanging in there."

"Good to hear from you, Bro."

"How's Christine?" Kaplan asked.

Christine was Isabella's sister, a sheriff in a small Wyoming town. During his long search for Isabella, he located Christine and attempted to get her to reveal Isabella's location. She was in the midst of a battle with a corrupt land and cattle baron who felt he ran the town. She cut Kaplan a deal—if he helped her then she would tell him where Isabella was. Moss showed up in Wyoming thinking Kaplan was in trouble. It didn't take long before Christine and Moss began a relationship. They had been seeing each other since.

"I'm back in Chicago...alone, if that tells you anything. Have been for a few months."

"I thought you two couldn't get enough of each other."

"Seemed that way, didn't it? Maybe we got a little too much of each other."

Kaplan asked, "What happened?"

"Nothing happened, *per se*. Christine felt we needed to take a break. She said a few weeks apart might do us good. That was nearly three months ago and nothing has changed."

"Sorry to hear that. I know you really liked her." He paused while he drew the similarities of their situations. "Let me run something by you." Kaplan explained his encounter with the stranger at Roaming Goat, the job offer from the anonymous client and his conversation with Clara. "What do you say, you in?"

"I have been getting a bit antsy lately." Moss waited a beat. "How much money we talking about?" He added, "A man of my talents ain't cheap, you know."

Kaplan told him about the back and forth negotiations with David Pearson and what amount was agreed on.

"Holy shit. Who is this guy? Must be somebody damn important."

"That's the catch. Don't have a lot of background on him. Just last known location and a photo."

"That kind of money can buy this kind of talent. Sure is tempting."

"Couldn't hurt, right?" The line was silent for too long. Kaplan figured he might be thinking the same thing he thought.

"Wait a minute," Moss said. "This job sounds too easy. There's gotta be more to it than simply locating a missing person in France. Nobody's gonna pay that kind of money for such an easy job. What's the catch?"

"I don't know, Moss, but you're right, there's always a catch."

"Always? You mean this is some of your cloak and dagger spy shit?"

"This has nothing to do with the *Company*...that I know of anyway. Although, I imagine that might be how my name got tossed out there. Actually, our names. They want me *and* my partner...and I don't think they had Isabella in mind. You're the only other person I've worked with in a long time."

"What about that first guy? The one you told me about? The NTSB turned secret ops guy?"

"Too long ago. It's you and me they want. And Moss... there are two things you need to know before you jump in and agree to go with me. Number one, finding this guy might not be easy. We don't have a lot to go on."

"Finding fugitives was my job. So, what's number two?"

quizzed Moss.

"Number two, I haven't figured out yet. But with everything I've ever been involved in, there is always a number two."

"That's clear as mud. You thinking it might be dangerous? More than the first time we met? More than Wyoming?"

"Maybe. Hard to tell about these assignments. We won't know what number two is till we get there. But I'm sure there's more to this than simply locating this guy. And in addition, we'll be in a foreign country that really frowns on what we'll be doing."

He thought he heard Moss grunt. Moss was a smart man. Smart enough to say no to his offer.

"Moss?"

"What the hell, Kaplan." Moss finally said. "I got no better place to be. Count me in."

† † †

GRU Headquarters
Khoroshovskoye Shosse, Russia

Igor Nevsky had been head of the Second Directorate for a year and a half and his job was already threatened. He thought it was unfair that the failures of his predecessors should reflect badly on him, but the Russian President still held him accountable. And there had been many failures prior to and leading up to his appointment with the Main Directorate of the General Staff of the Armed Forces of the Russian Federation or GRU. Most notably, the electoral interference failures in the elections in the United States. Not that his predecessor hadn't interfered, he had, but it was Nevsky who got blamed. In retaliation, the White House sanctioned nine Russian entities and individuals, including the GRU and the Federal Security Service of the Russian Federation or FSB for their activities to spread disinformation during the 2016 elections and were now investigating the 2020 elections.

Ultimately, the United States State Department revoked diplomatic privileges of 35 Russians and expelled them from their country. In addition, the U.S. denied Russian access to two Russian owned installations. One in Maryland and one in New York. Then, a year and half later, indictments were handed down against several GRU staffers charging them with conspiring to interfere in the American elections.

Now, with the latest news of a U.S. intelligence officer stealing secrets from his government and on the run, the pressure was on him and the GRU to capture this man and bring him in before another country got to him. If Nevsky failed, his career was over. Perhaps even his life.

Sitting across from Nevsky was his second in command, Dmitry Gagarin, a man who had made a name for himself in the field as one of the best operatives and operative trainers in GRU history. And the most successful. Since the Second Directorate was geographically responsible for the Western Hemisphere, it was his job, their job, to bring in this man.

"Dmitry, who is your best asset in the United States right now? Someone who won't fail us. Someone we can trust to finish this task at any cost."

"That would be Tatyana Kazakov," Gagarin said. "She has a perfect record in the field with only a few minor scrapes. She has been based in the United States for nearly a decade. Fluent in English and manageable in five European languages.

A perfect match for this mission."

"What about family?"

"No living family in Mother Russia." Gagarin passed a file across the desk to him. "Orphaned at age six. Raised and trained at *The Academy*. Top of her class. A year after we planted her in the States, she married an American man, like she was instructed. No children, again as instructed. As far as her husband knows, her job requires extensive out-of-country travel, therefore he is used to her being gone. As far as we can tell, she has never been suspected of anything. She has a recruit in training who she claims is ready for his first field trial. I am confident, between the two of them, she will be successful with any assignment she is given."

"Very well, Dmitry, activate her at once…and her recruit." Nevsky returned the file on Tatyana Kazakov and opened a drawer, pulled out a dossier and passed it to Gagarin. "This contains everything we know about the target. And Dmitry, I want our assets to know that under no circumstance is this man to fall into the hands of a foreign hostile. Extreme measures are authorized." He paused and then, "And ensure she understands failure is not an option."

Dmitry dipped his head in respect, turned and started for the door.

"One more thing, Dmitry," Nevsky called out. Gagarin spun to face him. "Personally see to it extra layers of backup are in place behind Kazakov. Like I said, failure is not an option."

CHAPTER 6

Chicago O'Hare Airport

Kaplan and Moss had settled into their first-class seats as soon as they boarded the B767 to Paris's Charles de Gaulle airport. It was an 11:50 p.m. departure from Chicago O'Hare and Kaplan had suggested they review the files in several hours, after the flight crew served them breakfast. Gave them both a chance for a few hours of sleep. Fresh minds and rested bodies, clearer thought processes.

Earlier, when he met Moss at the airport, he almost didn't recognize his friend. Since he'd last laid eyes on Moss, the big man had grown a full beard. Wisps of gray flanked his chin. The bushy beard and bald head gave him a Shaquille O'Neal look.

Moss acted nervous and although the former Deputy U.S. Marshal didn't seem the type, Kaplan knew from experience Moss had a fear of flying. Or perhaps he was uncertain of the danger involved in their upcoming assignment. Either way, it was a done deal.

The eight-hour, ten-minute nonstop flight wouldn't arrive in Paris until 3:00 p.m. Paris time. As much as it seemed that making the time-change adjustments going east might be difficult, Kaplan's experience taught him traveling west through time zones seemed worse.

Kaplan had made prior arrangements to meet Moss at security in Chicago at 9:30 p.m. or 2130 by the 24-hour military clock ingrained into his psyche. That gave them two and a half hours to clear security and get to their gate before their flight was scheduled to depart.

Scheduled, being the key word.

The current snowstorm battering the Great Lakes region gave him expectations of a delay.

Moss showed up thirty minutes late, at 2200 hours. He looked like he hadn't slept in days.

Kaplan, however, had a more pressing matter on his mind. Like the man with the modestly spiked blond hair who lingered outside security until Moss arrived and was now sitting at their gate. His facial structure suggested Eastern Slav. Wide forehead, pale skin, and deep-set narrow eyes. He'd seen the look before. It was uncanny how often he was right. However, something about the man's body language made him suspicious. The man sat too stiff and had nervous eyes. The man's mere presence put Kaplan's instincts on alert. Just like David Pearson did in the coffee shop in Michigan yesterday.

He positioned himself with his back to the strange man but giving him a clear view of the man using the reflection in the large airport window. He knew better than to assume he was simply being paranoid.

He sat across from Moss. "Did you tell anyone about this trip?"

"I mentioned it to Christine on the phone, but she didn't seem all that interested. Too concerned with that *we need some more time apart* bullshit. Why?"

"Just wondering. Did you give her specifics?"

"You do remember I was a Witness Security Deputy U.S. Marshal, right? I know not to give away too much. Just told her that we were going to France to look for someone. Sadly, I think it made her day that I was leaving the country."

Kaplan studied the reflection of the stranger. He was glad Moss was coming with him. There was no doubt that Moss had been a good U.S. Marshal, but he didn't have the skills Kaplan had. Mainly hunting down terrorists and eliminating them.

To most people it might seem odd to instinctively know things about people. Like who was the biggest threat in a crowd of people, whether they were right-handed or left-handed, their weight and be accurate within a few pounds. CIA training he had received many years ago at *The Farm* were skills he'd perfected over the years.

He sized up the stranger and had an uneasy feeling.

† † †

Somewhere Over the Atlantic Ocean
Red Eye Flight

As good fortune had it, their flight departed on time since the snowstorm eased up about an hour before departure time. It had now been six hours since they left Chicago and the interior lights in the cabin had been turned off for five of those. He took a short slumber, maybe four hours and felt rested. The cabin crew was stirring, and he could smell breakfast wafting from the first-class galley. His stomach growled.

Curtains pulled closed behind him cordoned off first class from the remainder of the aircraft cabin. First class did have its perks. Wider seats that reclined 180° into makeshift beds, more legroom, and the cabin crew treated them like royalty.

They should be treated like royalty, he thought, especially after paying nearly $10,000 for roundtrip tickets. Apiece.

The date for the return trip was left open-ended. A simple call to Pearson when the job was done, and he would handle scheduling the flight back to Chicago.

The blond man that was on his radar at the gate was seated somewhere in the back of the aircraft. He hadn't mentioned the stranger to Moss. Not yet anyway. He'd wait before he shared those suspicions.

As the cabin lights slowly brightened, he leaned over and poked Moss in the arm. "Time to rise and shine. They'll bring breakfast soon."

Moss twisted in his seat. "Leave me alone."

"Didn't get your beauty sleep?"

"Shut-up, asshole."

"Somebody needs coffee." Kaplan unbuckled his seatbelt, stood and stretched his arms above his head. "Time for a head run."

When he returned Moss was sitting upright, his tray table in front of him. A flight attendant was taking breakfast and drink orders. Another was pushing a cart from the galley. The aroma of freshly brewed coffee filled the first-class cabin. His stomach growled again. He sat and leaned toward Moss. "I don't know about you, but I'm starving."

"Damn straight," Moss agreed. "And I'm going to need a pot of coffee to wake my ass up. I hate long airplane rides."

"Seriously, you hate all airplane rides."

Before Moss could reply, one of the flight attendants wheeled the cart between them and handed them a glass of orange juice and a cup of coffee. "Cream or sugar?" he asked. They both declined.

There were two flight attendants working the first-class section of the flight, both men were in their twenties. Not bad duty when first class had a grand total of six seats.

After breakfast, one of the attendants took their trays while the other was passing out hot hand towels so each passenger in first class could freshen up.

"Man, I could get used to this kind of life. Glad I came." Moss took the hot towel and rubbed it all over his head and face.

"Don't get used to this. We got our work cut out for us in France," said Kaplan.

Kaplan picked up his backpack and retrieved the file David Pearson gave him. He passed a copy of the file across the aisle to Moss. "Don't say I never gave you anything." He stuck his hand out. "Let me have your phone."

"What for?"

"If in Paris, or anywhere else for that matter, we get separated or need to separate, I want the *Find My* app set up on our phones so we can locate each other."

"So, you can locate me if I get lost is what you're really saying, right?"

"Hell yes. You have no sense of direction. If we need to separate or something happens to one of us, the other can find him.

Moss's meaty hand passed his phone to Kaplan. "Knock yourself out."

While Kaplan was configuring the apps, Moss asked, "You been to France before?"

"Uh-huh. That's where I broke my leg a few years ago. I told you about that, remember? On the rocky shores of Saint-Jean-de-Luz."

"Yeah, yeah. That's right. When you swam all night after your boat got shot up. That's when you and that former NTSB guy parted ways."

"More or less." He opened his folder. "To the business at hand."

"Think we can go to the Eiffel Tower tonight?"

"We aren't here to sightsee, Moss, we're here to do a job."

"Aw come on, I've never been to France before. And I've always wanted to. Besides, there's nothing we can get started on until tomorrow."

He glanced at Moss. The big guy's face held the excitement of a child headed to Disney World. "We'll see."

"We'll see, my ass. I've already checked out where we're staying. It's not that far from the Eiffel Tower."

"Paris is a big town. It's not as close as it looks."

"According to Google Maps, it's only a mile walk. I might never get another chance to see the Paris skyline at night." He raised the folder Kaplan gave him. "Finding this Benoit guy isn't a life or death situation. It's a find and return assignment. Hell, we don't even have to return him. Just tell your client where he's living. I get a vote and I say I'm going with or without you. Besides, we might not get another chance after tonight."

"Okay, okay, we'll go after dinner." He rubbed the stubble on his chin. "Most places don't start serving food till 6:30 or 7:00. Before then it's usually just drinking."

"Drinking is good."

Kaplan shook his head. "I'm going to regret this, I know."

CHAPTER 7

Wolfe surprised himself with how quickly he'd gotten over the murder of Serena, although at the time four months ago, he'd gone into a full-blown panic knowing *they* had found him.

A bullet meant for him.

But who was after him? Was it his own country? Perhaps the CIA or some other agency within the U.S. Intelligence Community? Or perhaps a foreign operative sent to retrieve information with orders to kill anyone who got in their way?

The reality of what might happen to him shook him up. He knew the government would try to find him and extradite him back to the States. At first when he saw Serena's body, he thought it might have been a random killing. She always left the door unlocked. It could have been a bungled robbery. Then when he saw what she scrawled in her own blood, *RUN*, he knew it was him they were after and that they would stop at nothing to get what he had.

Including murder.

He had grabbed his go-bag from its secure hiding spot in the basement crawl space and executed his escape plan. At the time, he was certain Iceland was the safest place to hide out. Not anymore. His next hideout was mainland Europe with a new identity. To a country he'd visited numerous times and a language he spoke fluently.

He departed Reykjavik in the middle of the same night on a sea-going freighter that took him to Dublin, Ireland where he boarded a second freighter to Lisbon, Portugal. In Lisbon, he cleared customs under his new identity, Curtis Benoit, and boarded the first available sleeper-car train to Paris, a city where he knew he could meld into the crowd. Blend in with the population in relative anonymity. Just another face in the crowd.

His train left Lisbon at 9:30 p.m. and arrived in Hendaye at 11:33 the next morning. Hendaye was on the French border with Spain. He paid the €150 for a private grand sleeper car with a shower and toilet.

The Hendaye rail station earned its fame as the October 23, 1940 meeting place between Adolf Hitler and Francisco Franco. The purpose of that seven-hour meeting was to resolve ongoing disagreements over conditions for Spain to join the Axis Powers in the war against the British Empire.

From Hendaye, Benoit boarded a TGV Duplex to arrive at Paris Gare Montparnasse five hours later. During the trip, he spent most of his time in the cafe car. The s-shaped bar extended lengthwise down the car, behind it a bartender/waiter/short-order cook. Although the extent of the cooking was merely reheating pre-cooked meals.

That's where he met Sophie Bouquet.

And everything changed.

Sophie was dressed in all black. Tights, a loose sweater that hung off one shoulder exposing a black bra strap. The long sweater draped across her narrow hips. She wore boots with chunky heels. Her thick hair was a shade of brown that matched her eyes. An oversized leather bag slung on her shoulder.

She sat next to him and exchanged a courteous smile. The whiff of her perfume kicked his testosterone into overdrive. His roving eyes continued to check her out. Early thirties, maybe.

Her makeup made it hard to tell. His eyes traced the black bra strap against her tanned skin down to her large breasts. She was a very desirable woman.

She spoke French and some broken English. They talked for hours while the train hurled down the track toward Paris. She shared her passions and he shared his—only his were all prepared lies backstopping his new identity. His life was a fabrication. A web of lies. He could never reveal the truth about who he really was. Thank goodness he'd never told Serena the truth.

When the train slowed on its arrival to Gare Montparnasse, he didn't want the encounter to end. He didn't want to part ways with Sophie. He learned she was single and had no boyfriend. "That is so hard to believe," he told her. "You are so beautiful." Actually, that was the truth.

The lie he told her was he had broken up with his girlfriend after she cheated on him. A good way to garner sympathy. He omitted all the grisly information that his girlfriend was tortured and murdered in her apartment because of him. Privileged information.

His con appeared to be working, covertly leading it to a predetermined end. That was his challenge here—not to let their chance meeting come to an end at the Paris Gare Montparnasse train station. He was good at his ever-changing disguise to get what he wanted.

He wanted Sophie.

It was simple for him to gain women's trust. Get what he wanted from them only to leave them with no explanation when he got bored. Yet this time he felt different. There was more than chemistry with Sophie. She was smart and witty and passionate about life. She had a light-hearted sense of humor and a flare for sarcasm that he liked. During the course of their conversations, he learned she traveled extensively inside the borders of France as director of an advocacy group. She gave speeches at rallies around the country, championing the cause of many who were abused as youth.

When the train stopped, he made his move.

He asked her in French, "Do you live nearby?"

"Oui."

"Wonderful. Perhaps you could recommend a good hotel? Not too expensive though."

She fired off the names of a few. Not what he was hoping for. He was thinking maybe the *Hotel Sophie Bouquet,* but that was pushing his luck. Although, he was determined to get there. Eventually.

"You've been so helpful," he said. "I want to thank you by taking you to dinner, would that be acceptable?"

She hesitated. "I don't know. I really should get back home."

"I understand," he said with as much sincerity as he could muster. "Traveling can be tiring. Perhaps another night?"

When they walked outside the train station, he noticed a luggage storage vendor across the street. *Bag Sitter Luggage Storage.* Looked like a good place to store his emergency go-bag. Just in case.

She lowered her head then raised it and smiled. "I live five blocks from here. Why don't we drop our bags at my apartment and go to this wonderful place around the corner?" She paused and then said, "Your treat." She laughed softly.

"Deal." He liked the way she sounded when she laughed.

After dinner and a bottle of wine, she invited him to stay over on the couch. He didn't refuse.

That was four months ago.

He had not spent a single night in a hotel since except when he traveled with Sophie.

Now, her passions had become his passions. He traveled with her from rally to rally, town to town. He had infiltrated her world, become an integral part of her life.

And the best part of all, no one had been able to track him down. A moving target was hard to hit.

That's why he kept moving.

CHAPTER 8

Hotel Waldorf Trocadero
Paris, France

The limo dropped Kaplan and Moss off in front of the hotel. Check-in was quick and easy. Each man had a Deluxe room on the same floor across the narrow hall from one another. By the time Kaplan got settled in, he felt tired and hungry. Mostly hungry. Food would him perk up.

On the airplane after breakfast, Kaplan reviewed the files with Moss, and they came up with a loose plan of action for tomorrow. Too many variables. Too many possibilities. Tracking down this missing person was the epitome of the cliché *needle in a haystack*.

At 1700 hours on the button, Kaplan knocked on Moss's door. "Let's go Inspector."

The hotel door opened. Moss had changed clothes. He wore khakis, a button-down shirt with a sweater tied around his neck. A tweed cap covered his bald head

"What the hell is this?" Kaplan tugged at the sweater.

"I wanted to look French. And stop calling me Inspector."

"You figure you'll blend in dressed like this?" Kaplan chuckled when he said it.

"Exactly."

"Couple of problems, big guy. First off, you'll never blend in. You're what, six-six? Most French men are short."

"Like you?"

"Funny. Shorter than me…by a good bit. And second, that

look went out with the eighties. Go get your coat. The sky's clearing, so it'll get cold before we get back."

"Good idea, let me grab my coat." Moss darted back in his room and reappeared with his coat in hand. "Where're we headed?"

"To the Latin Quarter. I know a great place to eat."

"Then the Eiffel Tower?"

"If that will shut you up, sure. Tonight, you're gonna see the Paris skyline."

†††

The taxi pulled to the curb in front of a bistro on Rue des Grande Degrés. After they got out of the taxi, Kaplan pointed out Notre-Dame across the river. "Shame the fire destroyed the cathedral." He turned and pointed at the bistro. "Best place in town."

"Looks kinda small," Moss protested.

"Sometimes the best things come in small packages. Let's head inside." Kaplan walked through the door. Moss followed. Kaplan was greeted by the owner with a hug and a kiss on each cheek. He noticed a smirk stretched across Moss's face.

"Bonjour, Monsieur Kaplan. Cela fait longtemps que je ne vous ai pas vu." *I have not seen you for a long time.*

"Bonjour, Phillipe," Kaplan replied. "Comment allez-vous?" *How are you?*

"Très bien, merci. Et vous?" *Very well, thank you. And you?*

"Bien." He motioned to Moss. "Ceci est mon ami Pete Moss." *Fine. This is my friend, Pete Moss.*

Phillipe stepped to Moss and stuck out his hand. Moss shook it.

"Enchanté," Phillipe said. *Pleased to meet you.*

Moss nodded.

Kaplan said, "Deux pour le dîner." *Two for dinner.*

"Très bien." Phillipe gestured. "Suivez-moi, s'il vous plaît." *Very good. Follow me, Please.*

Kaplan noticed the bewildered look on Moss's face.

Moss whispered, "You speak French?"

Kaplan shrugged. "I learned the language a long time ago."

"Guess it was a spook requirement, huh?"

Kaplan ignored him.

"Phillipe, les deux menus, s'il vous plaît," Kaplan said. *Both menus, please.*

"Bien sûr, monsieur Kaplan. Comme prévu." *Of course, Mr. Kaplan. As expected.*

"What are you saying to him?" Moss queried.

"I just told him to bring the menus."

"Good, cause I'm starving."

"What is it with you and food?"

"I'm always thinking a meal ahead."

"I've noticed."

Phillipe had a head full of light brown hair, blue eyes, and a goatee. He walked briskly, guiding the two men to a back room with a single table—away from the main dining area and closed off by a heavy curtain.

"What's this?" Moss asked.

Kaplan looked at the big man. "Precaution."

"Precaution from what? We just got here. Is this the number two you weren't sure about?"

"Not yet. It's just you can never be too careful."

Phillipe returned with two menus and an iPad. He handed one menu to Moss and the other menu and iPad to Kaplan.

"What's the iPad for? Moss asked.

"Shopping list." Kaplan winked at Moss who was about to speak when Kaplan cut him off. "Later."

Kaplan tapped the iPad screen a few times and handed it back to Phillipe. "Merci, Phillipe."

Phillipe handed Kaplan a small silver key. "Comment ça sonne six heures du matin?" *How does six in the morning sound to you?"*

"Parfait." *Perfect.* He slipped the key in his front pocket.

Kaplan opened his menu and saw the confused look on Moss's face. "What?"

Moss held up his menu. "This is in French."

"Yeah. That's right. We're in France and they speak French."

"Yeah. Well I don't," Moss said sharply, dropping the menu and leaning back in his chair.

Kaplan spent a few minutes telling Moss what was on the menu until he finally said, "Why don't you let me order the food and drinks?"

"Oh, hell no. First off, I want a beer. And I don't want you ordering me snails or that sushi shit. I want something manly, like steak."

"Glad you decided to fit in. Beer and steak sounds about right."

† † †

After dinner, Kaplan led Moss to the St. Michel subway stop where they boarded Line 4 to the Montparnasse stop. When they surfaced, they were looking at the tallest building in Paris.

"I thought you said you were taking me to the Eiffel Tower."

"That's not what I said. I said I would take you to *see* the Paris skyline."

"But—"

"How 'bout you trust me? I promise you won't be disappointed."

Kaplan paid their admission and took Moss to the top of Montparnasse tower. He could tell his friend was impressed and pleased with the view of the Paris skyline and the Eiffel Tower.

While Moss stared out at the lighted Eiffel Tower, Kaplan made sure he kept a visual on the stranger standing off to his left on the viewing platform. When they left the hotel, he saw a man who resembled the blond man from the Chicago airport last night. He didn't get a good enough look to make a positive ID. Same height, build, general appearance. But right before he and Moss took the stairs to the outside viewing deck atop Montparnasse tower, he saw the same man get off the elevator in the lounge. Plenty of light. No mistake this time. It was him.

What were the odds of this being a coincidence? Once in Chicago, now twice in Paris?

Zilch.

That's what the odds were.

No coincidence.

He and Moss were being followed.

He nudged Moss. "We have a problem." Moss looked at him in the darkness. It was cold and a breeze was blowing. But the sky was clear, and the Paris skyline couldn't have been more spectacular. Every time he spoke, he could see his breath cloud. "Behind you and to the left. Blond man, spiked hair, brown leather jacket." Moss started to turn. Kaplan clutched his arm. "Don't look. He was at the Chicago airport last night.

He was on our flight. I thought I saw someone who looked like him earlier tonight but blew it off. Now, I'm positive. My guess is Eastern Slav. His physical features suggest that part of the world."

"For crying out loud, it's dark as hell out here. How could you possibly tell?"

"Because I saw him downstairs in the light of the lounge. He followed us up here."

Moss raised his hand, lifted his cap with one hand and swiped the other across his bald head while he turned. Spike must have known he was made and darted toward the stairs leading down.

"Dammit Moss, I told you not to look." Kaplan hooked Moss by the shoulders. "Stay here. I'm going after him."

"Ain't happening." Moss's voice deepened. "You go, I go."

By the time Kaplan and Moss made it back down the stairs to the lounge, Spike had stepped in an elevator and the doors were closing. He locked eyes with Kaplan and smirked. Kaplan tried to push through the line, but the security guard held him back. "Fin de la ligne, monsieur." *End of the line, mister.*

He and Moss looked at each other.

Kaplan finally said, "There's always a wrinkle."

CHAPTER 9

Mossad Headquarters
Tel Aviv, Israel

Marla Farache gave her uncle a hug when she entered his office. Eli Levine was Director of Mossad and had been for almost three decades. Most of her lifetime. Almost as long as she could remember. She was an only child and after her father's death, Levine took over his role. According to Levine, she was the last chance of continuing the Levine family's bloodline. Her mother, Levine's sister died last year, leaving only Marla and her uncle.

Levine had been revered in Israel as a director who was firm and fair. Marla had been recruited by Levine as an operative when she was much younger. During her training, he demanded high standards of excellence, pushing her harder than other recruits. He refused to show her favor. She excelled at the skills necessary to become one of the top operatives Mossad had ever put in the field. Something her uncle had been in his younger days.

"Sit down, Marla," her uncle said while pointing to the sofa next to the large plate glass window overlooking Tel Aviv. "I'm sorry to summon you at such a late hour, but I have an assignment I need you to consider. It will put you back in the field as you have requested numerous times since your injury."

Her injury came several years ago when she was shot in the leg by an Al Qaeda terrorist while attempting to exfiltrate an Israeli tourist who had been kidnapped by the radical faction.

She was rescued by an American spy. Just the mention of her injury triggered memories.

Fear.

Pain.

The American.

After that mission, her uncle removed her from the field and designated her as Mossad Deputy Director of American Affairs. A job she knew he gave her to keep her safe. She saw it in his eyes when he told her she would no longer be an operative. Eyes full of concern that he might have lost her during the mission. She almost quit that day, but what else could she do? What she wanted was to return to the field as an operative. To do what she loved. Until now her uncle had refused her pleas to be given another mission. Why now? Why the sudden change of heart?

Levine handed her a folder. She opened it and understood immediately. She flipped through the pages, closed the folder and placed her hand on top. "I understand choosing me, Uncle, but why now? After all this time of shielding me from harm for the sake of your bloodline—."

"You wanted back in the field, I am giving you what you want. I have chosen you because you are best suited for the task."

She patted the folder. "Because of Gregg, right?"

"No, Marla, because I know you are the best operative for this job. The target is in France. You are fluent in French. France is a melting pot of cultures. Why not you?"

She stood and tossed the folder on the sofa. "Do not lie, Uncle. You want me on this because of *him*. You've been playing matchmaker for years. How many times do I have to tell you he is not interested? Why can't you see that? You want me on this job because you know I will most likely run into him."

"I have upset you. I am sorry. But this assignment is not open for discussion. I am sure you will realize this after you read the full dossier. The limo is waiting downstairs, your go-bag is already on the jet and a flight plan filed to Paris." He tapped his finger on the folder. "Everything you need to know is in this file."

This wasn't the first time her uncle had flustered her about settling down, getting married, and starting a family. The older she got, the more persistent he became. He was old school with an outdated thought process when it came to marriage and tradition.

She had done her research. She knew the situation and where she stood. Gregg Kaplan was still in love with his ex-partner, even though Isabella had no recollection of him and never would. But Gregg couldn't seem to let go. She admired his dedication to Isabella. Marla hoped one day she might find someone who would be that committed to her.

Her uncle was right about one thing she would never admit to him. She still cared for Gregg. They had slept together several times but that was history. Yet it was a passion she'd never forget. During their brief time together, Isabella wasn't in the picture. Marla's hidden desire to have a future with Gregg could never compete with his feelings for Isabella.

She picked up the folder. "You win. I see I have no choice in the matter." She headed toward the door.

"Marla," Levine called out. She paused. He walked over, put his arms around her and kissed each cheek. "You are all the family I have left. I love you."

"I love you too, Uncle."

She opened the door and heard, "If you run into Mr. Kaplan, please give him my regards."

CHAPTER 10

At 0630 hours the next morning, Kaplan slipped down to the hotel lobby and stepped up to the front desk. The young man at the desk last night was still there. His bleary eyes bloodshot, a large energy drink sat on the counter next to him. "Chambre trente at un. Gregg Kaplan. J'attends un colis." *Room 31. Gregg Kaplan. I'm expecting a package.*

"Oui, monsieur Kaplan." The young man reached behind the desk and pulled out a silver metal attaché case. "C'est ici." *Here it is.*

"Merci." He took the aluminum case and headed for the lift. His plan for the day required an early start, which meant Moss needed to get moving. Breakfast at 0700, check out by 0800, and to the train station by way of the subway. Followed by a two-and-a-half-hour train ride to the town listed in the dossier as the location where Curtis Benoit was last seen.

Moss opened the door after the first knock. He was up, dressed, packed and ready to go. Kaplan walked past him and tossed the briefcase on the tussled bedspread. Out of his pocket he pulled the silver key Phillippe had given him last night in the restaurant and unlocked the case. Behind him, he heard Moss move closer.

"Let me guess, this is what you ordered on the iPad last night."

"I've worked with Phillippe for a long time, he's never let me down." Kaplan removed a handgun from the foam insert inside the case. A Beretta Px4 Storm .45 caliber, his handgun of choice. He attached the sound suppressor, picked up one of the pre-loaded magazines, inserted it into the butt of the Beretta and racked the slide, loading a round in the chamber. He removed the suppressor and shoved the gun under his jacket behind his back.

He pocketed the suppressor and picked up the other handgun and handed it to Moss. "Glock 37 G.A.P. 45. A weapon I believe you're familiar with." He handed Moss a suppressor and a magazine, again pre-loaded, and watched the big man rack a round into the chamber and pocket the suppressor. He sorted the remaining ammo, giving Moss his and lifted a small box from the briefcase. "Comms for later."

Moss opened the box containing a miniaturized voice-activated communications system. "You thought of everything," he said. "You think that guy from last night is gonna be trouble?"

"Guess we'll find out soon enough, won't we?"

"Just when I was beginning to like this place," replied Moss.

"One more thing, Inspector…we can't get caught with weapons in France. We can't afford to arouse suspicions among the locals or police while we track down Benoit. Not an outcome either of us would like."

"Gotcha," Moss followed Kaplan's lead and tucked the Glock under his jacket. "I'm retired, you can stop calling me Inspector." Moss patted his stomach. "I'm hungry, can we go eat now?"

After a quick breakfast, they checked out of the hotel and made their way toward the subway. Kaplan scanned the area for any sign of surveillance from the stranger who slipped away from him last night at Montparnasse Tower.

Nothing.

After changing subway lines, he and Moss arrived at the train station, Gare de Lyon, where Kaplan approached a kiosk and printed their tickets for the TGV high-speed to Dijon. There, they would connect with a regional train to Beaune, a small town in the heart of the Burgundy region and, according to the file, the last known sighting of Curtis Benoit.

On the forward bulkhead in their TGV car was a monitor displaying the train's speed. Moss elbowed Kaplan. "Damn, man, look how fast we're going. 300."

"Nice, huh? That's like 180, 190 miles per hour. We need this kind of transportation in America."

Moss had focused all his attention on his open iPad. He had connected to the TGV's WIFI and was searching wineries in the Beaune area.

"You know, Moss, this isn't a vacation. We have a job to do, not play tourist."

Moss threw back his head and snorted. "I sat in a plane for over eight hours to get my fat ass here. We can kill two birds with one stone. So why not have some fun *and* find Benoit?"

Kaplan shook his head.

"This one looks cool." Moss's attention was back on his iPad . "It's called Patriarche...we *gotta* check it out." He leaned toward Kaplan and pushed his iPad forward. "Look at these caves filled with wine bottles. And they offer wine tasting tours."

"Maybe we can work it in," Kaplan stipulated. "Provided we have time."

"Damn, Kaplan, don't be such a kill-joy."

Moss's lack of commitment to the task at hand was quickly getting under Kaplan's skin. France was a country easy to fall in love with. He had explored the possibility of buying a *gite* in the region they were headed to now. He had looked online at many small, furnished vacation houses in the rural Burgundy region of France. Once again, though, life got in the way and he abandoned the idea. But now, listening to Moss's excitement, that urge to buy had struck again.

Beaune, France

The connection in Dijon was too tight and they missed their transfer and had to take the next regional train to Beaune, which came along 30 minutes later. Kaplan grabbed his backpack and duffel as the train pulled into the station and beckoned Moss to do the same.

Gare de Beaune was two blocks east of the city wall. A smaller train station in comparison to Dijon, and minuscule when compared to Gare de Lyon in Paris. Kaplan had already mapped out the walking route to the two-bedroom two-bath Airbnb he had rented for the next three nights. The apartment was on the northern edge of town, inside the city wall and just south of the medieval city gate arch, Porte St. Nicolas, on Rue de Lorraine.

Clear skies and balmy air greeted them, unseasonably warm temperatures for this time of winter. A sign next to the train station alternated between the time and the temperature—12:23 and 13° C. After running the conversion in his head, it correlated to roughly 55° F. He stripped his coat and jammed it in his duffel. Moments later, Moss followed suit.

"Whew," Moss said. "A lot different here than Paris. No crowds, warmer and no rain."

Immediately upon entering the city wall from the east near the train station, Kaplan motioned to a walking path leading to the top of the old city wall, Rempart de la Comédie. "This way."

"You sure? Seems like we should go in the other direction."

"That's one reason I installed the *Find My* app on your phone. We go this way."

Moss blew out a breath while they walked. He pointed at a street sign. "*Rue* must mean street. What else should I know?"

"*Rue* is road. *Place* is plaza. *Pont* means bridge. *Porte* means gate. Just ask if you see something."

Rempart de la Comédie dropped them within thirty feet of the apartment at the Porte St Nicolas arch. The keys to the apartment were located in a lock box to the left of the large blue door. It was 1240 hours on a Sunday afternoon and the streets were quiet—few pedestrians and virtually no cars. No sounds at all.

Kaplan punched in the code sent to him in an email and opened the lock box, retrieved the keys, and he and Moss climbed the narrow staircase to the third-floor apartment.

Everything was as advertised, neat and clean. He pointed to the first bedroom on the right. "That's your room. It should be quiet. I'll take the room overlooking the street."

"Sounds like you've stayed here before." More a question than a statement.

"Nope. Never have. Just did my homework when I booked the place."

Moss sat on the bed and bounced a few times like he was checking to see if it was comfortable. "I think we should figure out…" Moss stopped mid-sentence like he'd lost his train of thought.

The peace and quiet of what seemed like a sleepy little Burgundy village erupted in a madhouse of noise. Sirens. Both men rushed to the windows to see what was happening. Wailing klaxons pierced the quiet as police and Gendarmerie cars raced down the street, heading in the same direction—toward town center. One Gendarmerie car followed by another and another and then a seemingly endless stream of emergency vehicles. Fire, rescue, ambulances, and more law enforcement.

"Whataya think, Kaplan? A lot of excitement for such a small town. Should we check it out?"

Kaplan kept his thoughts to himself while he surveyed the growing swarm of activity down below. "Why not?" he finally said.

They followed a small group of locals scurrying down Rue de Lorraine. More small groups joined in, chattering in hushed voices like they were sharing a secret. Some spoke loud enough for him to hear.

"What are they saying?" Moss broke in.

"I can only make out bits and pieces but sounds like someone died during Mass at Collégiale Notre Dame."

"Notre Dame? I thought that was in Paris."

"Common misperception. Notre Dame literally means *our lady,* meaning the *Virgin Mary* or *Mary, mother of Jesus.* There are many Notre Dame cathedrals in France, not just the one in Paris. You'll see one in almost every town and village. And at least one cathedral I know of is physically larger than the one in Paris."

"Must not be much happening for so many in town to turn

out because somebody died," suggested Moss.

"Small town. Everybody knows everybody. Probably just curious to see who died."

"How many times did you say you've been to France?"

"A few." Kaplan pointed as most of the pedestrians turned west on Rue Marey. "Follow the crowd."

"Have you ever been to Beaune before?"

"I have."

"I thought you just said in the apartment that you hadn't."

"No, you asked if I had *stayed* in the apartment we rented. I have not. Yes, I have been here in Beaune before…a few times."

They turned on Rue Marey, passed the clock tower and rounded the corner onto Rue Notre Dame where in front of them was the backside of a large gothic cathedral. Rue Paul Laneyrie ran along the west wall of the cathedral, which was now barricaded by police.

"Turn here." Rue Maizières. The small street wrapped around to the west until it came to a dead end at Avenue de la République. They took a left then left again at Place du Générale Leclerc where he saw the front façade of the Collégiale Notre Dame and a preponderance of emergency vehicles. They pushed through the crowd as far as they could. Police were in charge of crowd control while the Gendarmerie was handling the area around the victim.

The crowd had fanned out around the barricade. Some were distressed and emotional. Women sobbing, hugging their bewildered children and making the sign of the cross on their chests. Many men, shaking their heads in disbelief, crossing themselves as well. There was a lot of chatter amongst the growing horde of onlookers.

"What are they saying, man? Don't keep me in the dark."

Kaplan leaned close to Moss keeping his voice low, "Sounds like a priest had a heart attack while giving an outdoor prayer after Mass."

Moss stretched to see over the people gathered around the barricade. "Yep. Looks like a body under a sheet at the foot of the steps to the church."

"One man said he clutched his chest and collapsed to the ground. Another said he tripped on the steps and fell." He looked at Moss. "You know how unreliable witnesses can be? Two people see the exact same event but see it in a different way. It's all individual perception."

Moss nodded. "Perception is reality." He elbowed Kaplan. "Holy shit."

"What?"

"There." Moss pointed in the direction of a tall silver cylindrical object. "See what I see?"

"An outdoor projection system?"

"A what? No. Look to the left of it. Between the projector and the wall. Isn't that the dude we chased in Paris?"

Kaplan's focus moved to where Moss directed. He immediately recognized Spike. The same man who gave him the uneasy feeling in Chicago at the airport. The same man he saw outside the hotel in Paris and then again atop the Montparnasse Tower. And here he was again, over three hundred kilometers from Paris, in Beaune. In the midst of the crowd at a church Mass of all places.

And Spike was staring right at him.

CHAPTER 11

The unidentified stranger with the spiked hair complicated things. Kaplan hadn't planned on being followed to Beaune and now he needed to know why.

"He's on the move. I'll go left," Kaplan said to Moss, who understood the strategy. Without a word Moss went right. Spike recognized their ploy, pulled his hoodie over his head and pushed deeper into the horde of people.

Suddenly Spike bolted right, ahead of Moss, shoving his way through the crowd as he made his way toward Rue d'Enfer, a side street leading away from the plaza. Kaplan wished he and Moss had taken an extra minute before leaving the apartment to grab the comms.

Moss rushed after Spike down Rue d'Enfer. Knowing where the street led, Kaplan decided to pull back and head toward Avenue de la République hoping to cut off Spike's escape route.

As soon as Kaplan cleared the crowd he bolted into a full sprint. He rounded the corner, east onto Avenue de la République, ran past three parked cars when he spotted Spike fleeing through an archway and down several steps to his left about 20 meters in front of him. Spike picked up his pace toward Place Fluery and shot a quick glance over his shoulder.

When Kaplan was even with the archway, Moss came bounding down the same steps from where Spike appeared, taking them two at a time. Moss angled onto the street behind Kaplan while they ran after the stranger.

Spike was slim and fit.

And fast.

Kaplan told himself he couldn't let Spike get away. Not again. He picked up his pace. Moss lagged behind.

Spike turned right at Place de la Halle down Rue de l'Hôtel Dieu, which led by the entrance to Musée de l'Hôtel Dieu, a famous museum and former hospital noted for its colorful roof tiles. Kaplan shot his hand out signaling Moss to go left while he continued to follow Spike. The short cut might allow Moss to close the gap and cut off the man's escape.

Spike took a left on Rue Nicolas Rolin then into Place Carnot where another group had gathered. From the southwestern corner of the plaza, Kaplan saw Moss approach from the opposite side and signaled him to stay on the north side of the plaza. Place Carnot was full of vendors and kids gathered around the carousel, all taking advantage of the unseasonably warm and sunny weather.

To his right, Kaplan noticed a string of cafes with patrons seated at with tables outside on the sidewalk. Spike's head snapped back to check Kaplan's position and when he turned back around, he plowed over an older couple standing in line to get a table at a café. The woman fell landing on the concrete next to a table with patrons. Spike almost went down with the woman but managed to regain his balance. The elderly man shook his fist in the air and yelled obscenities in French at the fleeing stranger.

Spike's stumble after knocking over the woman let Kaplan narrow the gap. Kaplan was breathing hard forcing his legs to keep up the pace. *Too close. Can't let up now.*

The narrow cobblestone road made a slow bend to the left. He galloped past three more cafes and a wine bar. He was closing in on the target when he saw Moss had the angle on Spike as Place Carnot ended at the five-points intersection.

Moss was closing in…the big man's hand reached grabbing the target's arm.

It appeared Moss had Spike at the entrance to Rue Vergnette de Lamotte, but Spike twisted his arm, wriggling loose and out of his hoodie.

Spike took off racing up the road. Moss, hanging on to the hoodie, chased after him. Within a minute, Kaplan was running side-by-side with Moss who was breathing too hard. Moss slowed, shook his head and waved his hand for Kaplan to keep going.

Spike rounded the corner at Rue Félix Ziem and disappeared out of sight. When Kaplan reached the corner, he regained sight of the blond man turning at the next street. That next street was Rue Carnot, a name he recognized from earlier when he and Moss were following the crowd to Collégiale Notre Dame.

Spike was slowing and grabbed his side. *Cramps.* Now was Kaplan's chance to catch him.

Spike maneuvered through the crowd and turned west on Rue Marey at Place Monge. The crowds had waned. Kaplan yelled, "Stop," causing the target to swing his head around. He tripped on the uneven cobblestones, nearly falling as he moved toward the clock tower door. His hand twisted the knob and then he kicked the door in. Vanishing inside.

Kaplan remembered the clock tower from his prior visits to Beaune. The Romanesque Beaune Clock Tower was once an important landmark in the town, visible for many kilometers outside the walls. During the Summer Festival of lights, this was one of the many landmarks illuminated by projectors, like the one they had just seen in front of Collégiale Notre Dame.

Kaplan approached the tower door Spike had entered. He

reached back and withdrew his weapon. Moss was headed toward him in a slow jog, trying to catch his breath. Kaplan stuck his head inside and heard footsteps pounding up the stairs. Spike was trapped.

He waited for Moss to catch up. "He went up. Stay here."

"Like hell," Moss struggled to say. "You go, I go."

He stared at Moss and knew better than to argue. "You okay?"

Moss gave two nods.

Kaplan gestured upward with the barrel of his weapon. "Let's get this bastard."

Moss nodded again, not able to speak.

Kaplan, with Moss only a couple of steps behind, gripped his Beretta, holding the barrel up and ahead as he climbed the stairwell. Moss followed his lead and pulled his weapon out. Flight after flight of stairs passed beneath them. He counted the floors from below and recalled a total of seven to the top. They kept climbing. He could no longer hear the sound of footsteps above. If he was wrong that the tower had no open exits and Spike managed to find an escape, they might never catch him.

During the climb they passed two doors, both apparent accesses to the clock tower from the adjacent building. He passed them by as he could hear Spike on the stairs above him.

Standing on the last floor there was no sign of the stranger only a metal spiral staircase leading to the spired top of the tower. Kaplan and Moss eased up the staircase, weapons readied, through the door on the back of the tower and onto the balcony at the top.

Spike was trapped.

He had crawled onto a dormer. Grasping the roof with

one hand and holding the other out as a warning not to come closer. Kaplan studied the man. Spike's face tight with tension. Eyes tight.

"Not another step," his voice warned with a heavy accent. His exhaustion evident by his winded speech.

Kaplan was right. Spike was indeed Russian. He assessed the situation. Spike didn't appear to be armed. And with both hands grasping the dormer, he wasn't likely to be able to draw a weapon. The balcony wrapped around the apex of the clock tower. Several small spires surrounded a single taller spire. Gargoyles ornamented the smaller spires.

"Why are you following us?" Kaplan asked, keeping his weapon trained on Spike. Although he knew the answer, he still asked, "Are you Russian?"

Moss had navigated around the balcony in the opposite direction and now he and Moss flanked the dormer.

Spike's eyes cut back and forth between him and Moss.

Kaplan lifted his weapon slightly, taking aim at Spike's head. "I asked you a question. Why are you following us?" He clicked the hammer back on his Beretta. "Answer now."

"You stupid Americans," Spike mocked. "I'm not the one you want."

"What makes you think I'm searching for someone?"

Spike glanced below and then back at Kaplan.

"Let me shoot the bastard, Kaplan. I hate Russians." Moss pointed his Glock at Spike.

Spike stared at Moss. He cut away from Moss and locked eyes with Kaplan and spit. "You get nothing from me."

"How 'bout I shoot your skinny ass off this tower?'" Moss's voice rising in intensity. "Now, answer the man's question."

Kaplan interrupted, "I think you better answer my friend.

He gets trigger happy if you try to mess with him."

Spike was sweating profusely. And the longer they stayed in the open, the more anxious he became. Something else was going on with Spike and it wasn't sitting well with Kaplan. "Why are you following us?"

Nothing.

"Seriously Kaplan, let me shoot him." Moss said as he raised his weapon at the Russian's head.

Spike scanned the rooftops. *Was he thinking of jumping?*

"Come down and let's talk." Kaplan motioned for Spike to return to the balcony.

Spike shook his head. "Nyet." He peered down and then focused on Kaplan.

Kaplan saw it on Spike's face. Desperation. A feeling that might cause Spike to do something stupid.

Moss moved closer to Kaplan on the catwalk. He saw it too. "I don't think he's coming down till we're gone."

"Don't be foolish. Come down and we'll talk." Kaplan said again.

Kaplan eased a step forward. Spike's head exploded. Blood and brain matter created a pink mist in the air and splatter stained their clothes.

The lifeless man fell to the courtyard below.

Kaplan and Moss leaned over the balcony rail to see the fallen man when more bullets pinged the wall behind them. He and Moss scrambled off the balcony and back inside the protection of the clock tower.

"I didn't see that coming," Moss said.

"That makes two of us."

CHAPTER 12

Tatyana Kazakov had given her protégé every chance to complete his assignment. But he failed. His attempts to follow the Americans undetected from Chicago showed a lack of comprehension of the stealth and disguise skills she taught him.

This was his first field trial. And his last.

Her skills far excelled his as evidenced by her following her protégé *and* the Americans without being detected by either. She taught him the skills of disguise, but he ignored her lessons and as far as she could tell, Gregg Kaplan knew her protégé had been following him from as far back as the Chicago airport. Now it was up to her to complete the mission or meet the same fate as her protégé.

Death.

As much as she'd like to think no one was watching her, she knew better. The Director of the Main Directorate of the General Staff of the Armed Forces of the Russian Federation never allowed operatives from the GRU to operate without at least two layers of backup. Trust was not in the GRU dictionary.

She was there in case her protégé failed. There was certainly someone watching and waiting to ensure she didn't fail either.

Or try to defect.

Although rare, defection was something that had happened in the past. An operative sent on a mission only to take the opportunity to elude the GRU in an attempt to escape the brutality of life in Russia and that of the Russian president's regime.

Her protégé was young and impetuous. He thought he

knew better than she did about the art of surveillance, but he didn't. His cavalier attitude allowed the Americans to recognize him for what he was and chase him through the small French town.

Her task was simple on paper, but difficult in practice. Find the man going by the alias Curtis Benoit before anyone else and put him in a secure location so GRU's extraction team could steal him away and obtain the secrets the man stole. Her mission had one caveat, since there were several actors on stage after the same prize, if it looked like one of her competitors might get to Benoit first, especially Russia's SVR, she was to kill Benoit. It was vital to the Director of the GRU that he present Curtis Benoit to the Russian president and not let the man fall into the hands of a foreign country.

She could not take the chance that her protégé would talk to the Americans. Hopefully she killed him before he said too much. When the Americans leaned over the balcony, she tried to kill them but missed. They ducked back in the tower too fast. She ran over to the dead man lying on the pavement and checked his pockets.

She had a bigger problem.

Her protégé's cell phone was missing.

CHAPTER 13

Once again, things had gone from bad to worse.

Just when Kaplan thought his luck had changed, bad luck and trouble found him again. This time in a country familiar with him and his past. He pondered his next move. *Their* next move. Wait for the Gendarmerie or get the hell out of Dodge.

Moss interrupted his introspection.

"We can't just stay here, man, we gotta move."

Moss started down the stairs. "I'm not waiting around for the cops to show up." He reached behind his back and tucked his weapon away. "Like you said, this isn't a country that looks favorably on us being in possession of these."

Kaplan fell in behind Moss while they made their way down the stairs, their pace increasing with every step. Even if they could prove they hadn't done anything wrong, it would cost them time. And their weapons would ensure the French Gendarmerie would lock them in jail for an indeterminate amount of time.

Ultimately, he knew they would both be exonerated from the shooting, but they would still be held in violation of French law for possessing two unregistered, unlicensed, and untraceable firearms. Furthermore, he had no idea what a ballistics report might turn up about the history of their weapons. For all he knew, one or both firearms might have violent histories that could potentially land them both in French prisons for the rest of their lives.

Moss was right.

Time to leave Beaune.

Before Spike died, he didn't give them much to go on. Actually, he gave them nothing. He was rebellious and scared. It was in his eyes. As it turned out, rightfully so. Someone was watching him and that someone ensured Spike wouldn't talk.

A thought struck him while he followed Moss down the stairs. It would be rather simple for him to disguise himself and blend in for a day or two, but Moss was a different story. How do you get a six and a half foot plus, two-hundred-seventy-pound Black man to blend in with the crowd in a small town in France?

Moss stood out in a crowd.

Hell, he hovered over a crowd.

Even leaving the clock tower and getting back to the apartment without drawing unwanted attention might prove to be a daunting task.

His observation skills were turned on as he retraced their steps after they had followed Spike into the clock tower. The building next to it was attached, like most of the buildings were in Beaune. On the bottom floor next to the tower was a coffee shop. During their ascent, he remembered passing two doors in the stairwell—one on the second level and one on the fourth level, both presumably leading to the building adjacent to the tower. What was behind those doors, he had no idea, but it was a sure bet to be a more sound escape plan than out the clock tower door leading to the street, which by now would have attracted quite a crowd around the dead man's body.

"Moss, stop." He commanded as they reached the fourth level door. He twisted the doorknob. Locked.

"Good thinking," Moss said. "Probably not a good idea to

go out the way we came in."

Kaplan placed his hand on the door. "How's your shoulder?"

Moss understood.

Kaplan held up three fingers and counted them down. After he balled his fist, both men slammed their shoulders into the door. It budged but didn't give way.

They looked down the stairwell and heard the clock tower door open on the ground level.

Without hesitation, they rammed their shoulders into the door again. This time it swung open into an attic-like room with dormers overlooking the street below. The room was full of discarded old church furniture. Old pews, broken pulpits, several chests.

They entered and Kaplan pushed the door closed behind him.

Without speaking, each seized a chest and moved them in front of the door. Then, they wedged two pews, one on top of the other, against the chests.

"There," Moss said. "That should keep everyone out for a while."

"And us till we find a way out of here."

At the far end of the attic was a staircase. They moved with quiet steps, down the flight of stairs to the door at the bottom. This one was unlocked. Kaplan eased it open an inch at a time.

No noise. No one in sight.

It opened into a large office. There were stacks of bibles and hymnals in one corner. He could only assume the Mass and subsequent turmoil at the Collégiale Notre Dame had emptied this place on a Sunday afternoon. He stepped into the hallway, saw another stairway that descended to the second floor directly beneath the stairwell they just came down.

There was no door at the bottom of that level, just another stairwell. Odds were, Kaplan surmised, this final flight of stairs would end facing the street on the first-floor landing.

It did.

Kaplan and Moss froze in synchrony.

Voices coming from behind a partition. Female. Two of them.

Kaplan listened while Moss tapped him on his shoulder.

Kaplan kept listening. Moss kept tapping.

He turned to Moss and whispered, "What?"

"What are they saying?"

"Sounds like it was a Cardinal who died in front of Collégiale Notre Dame."

"A Cardinal? You think that Russian did it?"

"What? Gave him a heart attack?" Kaplan continued listening to the women talking. Then he said to Moss, "Okay, sounds like both women are going outside to take a look at why a crowd is gathering."

They heard the door open and close. They waited a few more seconds. No sounds.

Kaplan poked his head out of the stairwell and sure enough, looking through the window he saw the street was straight ahead with people flocking toward where he knew the Russian had fallen.

Moss said, "There's gotta be a back door, don't ya think?"

"Hope so."

Kaplan's eyes scanned the back of the building. It looked like a maze of cubicles and partitions. They needed to get out of the building and far away from the murder scene because, sooner rather than later, this building would be searched.

They split up looking for an exit anywhere but the front

street.

Kaplan heard Moss's low whistle and found him standing next to a set of double doors that he remembered led to a side road. The back would have been better, but there didn't seem to be another option.

The front door opened. The women were back. One crying. They had no doubt seen the dead man at the base of the clock tower. Kaplan unlocked the door and pulled it open. A door chime rang.

"Oh shit," Moss grumbled.

Kaplan looked right, toward the street entrance to the clock tower. He pointed left and both turned to see the back side of Collégiale Notre Dame.

Kaplan said, "Keep up. He heard Moss grunt.

The side street was Rue Notre Dame, the same street they had followed the crowd down earlier…when they were just curious and before they witnessed a man's head explode in front of them. A quick glance at his watch. They had been in Beaune just under an hour. Kaplan picked up his pace. So did Moss as a sense of urgency seemed to strike them at the same time.

They passed an open courtyard to their left behind the clock tower where Spike fell. Then Kaplan noticed something that unnerved him. Mounted on a pole just inside the courtyard wall were two security cameras. One pointed toward the back of the clock tower and the other pointed down at them.

Not only would the cameras have captured he and Moss on the tower when the Russian was killed, it captured their escape route also.

"Moss," Kaplan commanded. "Keep your head down and follow me. Don't make eye contact with anyone and don't stop regardless of what you see or hear."

At this point, Kaplan's training took over. The town and its streets were a maze, which helped his escape. He knew where they were in relation to the apartment, so he led Moss due east. He had a plan. One he didn't share with Moss in case it didn't work out. After twenty minutes of zigzagging through the streets of Beaune, all the time getting farther away from the clock tower, he saw what he was looking for—the city wall. They were on Rue Armand Gouffé and the city wall at this point was called Rempart Saint-Jean.

"We split up here," instructed Kaplan. "This ramp will take you back to the apartment. Just like when we first arrived."

"And if it doesn't?" Moss challenged. "When we got on the wall earlier, the sign said something Comédie."

"Just stay on the wall and you'll get there. I promise."

"But—"

"Trust me on this, Moss. I'll meet you back at the apartment. Have everything ready and we'll leave as soon as I get back.

† † †

An hour later Kaplan returned to the apartment. When he opened the door, Moss was pointing his weapon at him.

"Where the hell have you been?" Moss lowered his gun.

Their backpacks and duffels were by the door.

"Taking care of business."

"What kind of business?"

"You'll see. You ready?"

"You know where we need to go?" asked Moss.

"No. Not a clue. Just away from this place for now."

Moss stretched a grin across his face. "How bout we check

out Bourges?"

"You still want to sightsee? Get your gear. We need to get out of here. Now."

Moss held up a cell phone. "I think our guy Benoit is in Bourges."

It took a second to register. Kaplan asked, "Is that the Russian's phone?"

"It is. I found it inside the pocket of his hoodie."

"It wasn't locked?"

"Nope. Took me awhile using my translator app to figure out the Russian texts from someone with the initials T.K., but looks like our best bet is to head to Bourges."

"Damn. I could kiss your ugly face right now. You can fill me in on everything you found later."

They walked through a courtyard and out a side gate onto Rue Charles Aubertin and to a small car made by Toyota. "Throw your stuff in the back and get in."

Moss did as instructed and then folded into the passenger seat after pushing the seat as far back as it would go.

Kaplan put the car in gear and drove out of the city.

"Moss asked, "Where'd you get the car?"

"You don't want to know."

CHAPTER 14

The only sound inside the car was the whirring noise of the four-cylinder engine. Moss kept his head down typing on his iPhone.

Kaplan left Beaune behind in his rearview mirror over twenty minutes ago. He was glad Moss had found the Russian's phone. Moss didn't glean a lot of info from the text messages on the phone. Spike's last text told him to leave Beaune and head to tomorrow's *dispute* in Bourges to locate the target. Hopefully that target would lead them to Curtis Benoit. It was a long shot, he knew, but it was all he had to go on at the moment. His instinct told him that the reason Spike was following him must have something to do with him being hired to locate Benoit. But what was the connection?

He had weaved through the remainder of the *outside the wall* portion of Beaune until the road led them into rural wine country. He marveled at how beautiful the Burgundy region of France was. Sunny skies and warmer than average temperatures made today's earlier events seem somewhat surreal. But they weren't. There were blood stains on his dark shirt to prove it. Moss had changed out of his blood-stained shirt before Kaplan returned to the apartment.

As Moss had hinted, he couldn't help but wonder if the Cardinal's death outside Collégiale Notre Dame was somehow connected to the dead Russian.

The silence was pierced by an electronic voice on Moss's phone.

"In one point three kilometers turn left on highway D23."

"What the hell? Where are you trying to take us?"

Moss smiled. "Bourges. Took me a while to find it, but I got it plugged in. All back roads. Google Maps says it will take three hours seven minutes."

"Back roads are good." Kaplan checked his watch. 1615 hours. Not even four hours had passed since they had arrived at the train station in Beaune. "It'll be getting dark soon. That should keep us inconspicuous until tomorrow."

"Then what?"

Kaplan turned his head toward Moss. "We worry about that tomorrow. First, we need to find a place to crash for the night. Preferably *not* in the city *and* somewhere with private parking. Something like a B&B outside of town…or along the way. Since you've become so technologically savvy, why don't you find us a place?"

Moss held out his hand. "No problem. Give me your phone."

"What for?"

"I don't want to mess up Google Maps. Took me a long time to figure out our route."

Kaplan slipped his free hand in his pocket and pulled out his phone. "Have at it."

Moss took his phone and began punching the phone's keypad. There weren't a lot of cars on the rural road and several of the small towns they passed through were nothing more than a crossroads with a few rows of stone houses and a cafe. They had long since left the valley and were on the curvy roads of the low-rolling hills.

After fifteen minutes of grumbling and swearing, Moss

said, "Dammit Kaplan, you'll have to do this. All these websites are in French."

"Can't you use that translator app you used to translate the Russian texts?"

"No. A few foreign words is one thing. Navigating a website is another. We'll be in Bourges before I get all of this translated."

Kaplan pulled the Toyota to the side of the road. He and Moss swapped places.

Moss snapped his seatbelt and eased the car back onto the roadway. Kaplan, phone in hand, went to work. Within a few minutes, he was on the phone speaking to the proprietor of a bed and breakfast south of Bourges in a small town called Saint-Just. He reserved two rooms and told the man on the phone they would arrive shortly before 1900 hours

Kaplan ended the call and plugged the B&B address into Google Maps on Moss's phone. Kaplan's guess about their arrival time was close—1849.

"Sounds like we got a place to stay."

"Yep. And after today we need a good night sleep. We'll be there in a little over an hour," I got us two rooms. Sixty euro each. Plus, a terrace and a lounge."

"What about food, Kaplan? I'm getting *hangry*."

"Thinking a meal ahead again, I see. Restaurant on the ground floor, B&B above."

✝ ✝ ✝

The drive took longer than he'd expected, and they arrived at the B&B at 1910. As it turned out, the place he booked wasn't a B&B at all, it was a hotel that included breakfast at the restaurant located below the hotel. The terrace was out front by the parking lot and overlooked an open field to the east.

Kaplan had Moss park the Toyota on the side of the building in a parking spot that was masked by shrubs and another parked car.

After they checked in and put their bags away, they agreed to meet downstairs at 1930 for dinner. His room was modest at best, but for 60€ he didn't expect much. At least it was clean with an ensuite bathroom.

When he reached the terrace, Moss was already waiting. Mention food and Moss was always on time or early. Kaplan was surprised how crowded it was. Appeared everyone came out for the warmer than normal January night.

Moss found a table inside away from smokers. After they were seated, Kaplan scanned the room making mental notes of everyone around them. A young man behind the bar was taller than the average Frenchman, over six feet, body of a long-distance runner with thick brown hair scooped up in a man-bun. He had on a bright yellow t-shirt with 'P.A.P.A.C.Y.' printed across the chest in bold black letters. Kaplan made the presumption that it stood for some sort of religious organization.

"What do you make of the bartender?" he asked Moss.

"I dunno, but his shirt matches that flyer on the wall over there."

Moss directed Kaplan's attention to the wall. Sure enough, there was a yellow flyer taped to the wall that matched the bartender's shirt. A young waitress showed up, took their order and disappeared into the kitchen. Actually, she took Kaplan's order as he had to order for Moss since the waitress spoke no English.

"What's the plan for tomorrow?" Moss asked.

"Go into Bourges and see if we can get any information on some kind of *dispute* like the text message on Spike's phone said. I'm betting the word she meant was protest or march or something like that."

"What kind of protest do you think it could be? Clean air? Clean water? Climate change? Fight against a corrupt politician?"

"Yes."

Moss smiled. "Right. Could be anything."

The waitress delivered their food and beverages promptly to the table.

"Smells good," said Moss. "Tell her that for me Kaplan. Also tell her if she doesn't mind bringing me some more bread. I could eat a horse right now."

Kaplan rattled off some French to the waitress. She put her hand over her mouth, giggled, winked at Kaplan, pivoted and returned to the kitchen.

"I'm sure I won't like what you said to her but right now I'm too hungry to give a damn." Moss picked up his fork and dug in. In short order the plates on the table were empty. The basket of bread had a few more slices left. When Kaplan reached for the basket, Moss jerked it away.

"Sorry. I think these are for me."

"All I told her was we would like more bread."

"Yeah...I bet that's what you said." Moss took both slices and slathered them with butter.

They stayed in the restaurant another twenty minutes and ordered another drink before Kaplan decided to call it a day. What a long trying day it had been. First, the train trip from Paris to Beaune. Followed by the death of a Cardinal in Beaune where they spotted the mysterious Russian man from the Chicago airport. Then a chase that resulted in Spike being shot from the clock tower…as well as he and Moss being shot at by a sniper. And now, an escape from Beaune in search of a *dispute* in Bourges. Could this day get any crazier?

Before they left the restaurant, he headed to the wall with the yellow flyer attached. The translation read:

P.A.P.A.C.Y.
Join the revolution!
Rally begins at 10:00 a.m.
Saint Etienne Cathedral - Bourges

It was scheduled for tomorrow.

Small print near the bottom of the page in English:

Parishioners Against Priests Abusing Catholic Youth.

There it was.

Their first real lead.

His luck had finally changed.

CHAPTER 15

The room might have been clean, but the bed was uncomfortable. He'd slept on worse over the years. In Special Forces, he'd adapted quickly and learned to catch sleep whenever he could. Rocky ground, snow, sand—it didn't matter. He slept when possible, knowing it might very well be days before he got another chance.

It wasn't the bed that kept him awake, it was his mind racing over the possibilities and ramifications of what was printed on the poster in the restaurant. What if there had been the same kind of protest in Beaune yesterday? That didn't explain the shooting of Spike on the clock tower. If so, was it coincidental? Was he missing something?

It didn't take much imagination to understand what P.A.P.A.C.Y. was doing. They were protesting one of the most controversial topics in today's world regarding religion. A systemic problem the Catholic Church had been dealing with for some time. Decades. Worse was the fact the Vatican had repeatedly refused to take a hardline stance against it and its abusive Catholic priests, which was reported to be 5.3% of the over 400,000 priests worldwide.

It had become a media-sensationalized account of fraternal lenience and silence. Something a good portion of the world's population felt the current Pope and his predecessors had merely paid lip service to victims and problems in the Church. *Never apologize, never explain, never admit* had been the bureaucratic guidelines of the Church for decades.

Kaplan's cell phone rang. It was Moss.

"What's up?"

"I don't know about you," Moss said, "but I was awake most of the night. Who sleeps in these beds? Midgets? My feet froze hanging off the bed all night. And that damn poster from downstairs bothered me, too."

"That makes two of us."

"It would be nice to know if P.A.P.A.C.Y. held a protest in Beaune yesterday, wouldn't it?"

The things that had kept him awake during the night also bothered Moss. "What I want to know is who shot Spike on the clock tower. and why was he shooting at us."

"I'd like to wrap my paws around that person's neck," Moss added.

"That person?"

"Yeah. After what happened to us in New Jersey, I make no gender assumptions."

"Right. Valkyrie."

"That bitch. My leg still hurts when it rains," Moss complained.

"She could've killed you, you know, if she hadn't taking a liking to you. I mean you two did spend a lot of quality time together alone in your car, right?"

Moss disconnected the call.

Kaplan stared down at his phone and smiled.

†††

They met downstairs for breakfast at the prearranged time. Moss was over his apparent ire at Kaplan's taunting and ordered a large American style breakfast. The waiter this morning spoke English well, which allowed Moss to order for himself.

Either last night or this morning, Moss had shaved off his beard and his dimples rose to their former prominence. It was a clean look on Moss. No head or facial hair at all. It was the way Moss looked when they first met in Lexington, Virginia in what seemed liked ages ago. In reality, it had only been 18 months. They weren't partners but they teamed up together for a common purpose. A day later Moss was shot in the leg by the assassin Valkyrie. Moss wasn't her target back then, it was Kaplan.

He had already mapped out the route from the B&B to Bourges including parking and walking time to Saint Etienne Cathedral in order to arrive at the protest by 1000 hours. Kaplan felt the strange familiarity in his pre-planning. He liked that feeling. He was once told by his handler that the unknown was fear. To overcome it was preparation. In his mind, one could never do enough preparation for a mission. A skill taught in Special Forces and then reinforced as a clandestine officer with the CIA. Unrelenting preparation and four operational imperatives—keep it simple, provide for every contingency, never panic no matter how much the plan goes awry…which it will, and exploit the fact that most people are fools when it comes to things that actually matter…like their own survival.

They checked out of the B&B, loaded the bags into the car and headed into Bourges. It was another beautiful day in France. Sunny and just like yesterday, unseasonably warm. When Kaplan checked his weather app this morning, the forecast high was 15° C or roughly 60° F. The wind had picked up from the southwest. A balmy January day like this meant only one thing—an approaching cold front and an almost certain impending change in the weather.

"Remind me again why we are only staying one night?"

Moss asked.

"Never stay in the same place twice."

"We were staying several nights in the apartment in Beaune, why not here?"

"In Beaune, we were simply tourists raising no suspicion. That all changed with that security camera aimed at the back of the clock tower *and* the alley. We must proceed from now on with the understanding that we might have been identified and are now wanted men. With all the checks and balances... and inconveniences that come with it. If they pulled the video of us from that courtyard camera, they'll have our pictures and will be on the lookout."

"Inconveniences?"

"Better to be inconvenienced than thrown in jail."

Moss conceded, "Guess you're right."

"Of course, that could still happen if we let our guard down."

"Riddle me this, Kaplan, how will we get out of France if we're wanted men?"

"If push comes to shove, the same way we got our weapons."

"Same guy?" Moss queried.

"No. I've made quite a few trusted contacts over the years. Several of them are cobblers."

"Cobblers?"

"Someone in the business who provides fake identification documents like passports, called shoes."

Moss shook his head. "Of course."

"Worst case scenario, we travel to another country, like Italy or Spain, and leave from there."

"What about Germany?"

"Not a chance," Kaplan snapped back. "Germany is too rigid. We'd probably have better luck just prancing into the Charles De Gaulle airport in Paris with the passports we flew in on rather than try to leave Europe from Germany."

"Security that tight, huh?"

"Among other things," Kaplan acknowledged. "Always have a backup plan, Moss, but let's be optimistic. This will all work out. *Mostly* as planned.

Kaplan drove into a parking lot called Parking Centre Historique. *Historic Center Parking.* At the south end of the parking lot was Le Château d'Eau. *The Water Tower.* It wasn't a water tower at all so much as a round building with a decorated facade. Built in 1865, it collected water in two super-imposed basins. It was decommissioned in 1940 and added to the list of Historical Monuments in 1975.

At the north end of the long narrow parking lot was a traffic circle. Beyond that, he could see the spires of the cathedral.

Kaplan backed in a parking space against the west wall between two similar looking vehicles. A *hide-in-plain-sight* kind of thing, but with a little discretion. "No sense announcing our presence, right?" Kaplan smiled at Moss.

Standing outside the car Moss asked, "What about our stuff?"

"Leave nothing in the car that can identify us, like passports and IDs. Bring your weapon and ammo like we did in Beaune. And your comms."

"Basically prepare as if we aren't coming back to the car at all?"

"Yep."

Kaplan and Moss zigzagged their way from the parking lot using the massive spires of the cathedral as their guiding star. It was a short walk. Seven and a half minutes according to Kaplan's internal clock. As they passed the L'euro Café on Rue Moyenne, the number of protesters caught him off guard. So did the number of law enforcement officers, ranging from *Police Municipale* to *Gendarmerie Nationale*. He made note of armed officers on several rooftops and terraces overlooking every angle of the cathedral—Gendarmerie.

The majority of the protesters near the stage wore the yellow P.A.P.A.C.Y. shirts. He figured those in the yellow P.A.P.A.C.Y. shirts were part of the organized group and the rest were simply outraged protesters chanting and holding signs.

The crowd started shuffling toward the front entrance of the cathedral where the stage was located.

He could hear a woman speaking through a loudspeaker trying to get everyone's attention. A clear sign the protest was about to begin.

Everyone packed in tight, including him and Moss. Wafts of body odor and cigarette smoke filled the air. There was a makeshift stage set up in the plaza next to the cathedral wall surrounded by a swarm of yellow shirts like bees on a hive.

The Cathedral of St. Etienne was one of Europe's great Gothic churches. The design was inspired by Paris's Notre Dame cathedral, yet its footprint was actually larger. It took 55 years to build and was regarded as one of the three churches that made up the *High Gothic Style* in France. Paris's Notre Dame, Chartes, and Bourges. Having been spared the ravages of the French Revolution and both world wars, Cathedral of St Etienne was one of the best preserved, if not *the* best.

A familiar face stepped next to the stage, the young bartender with the man-bun from the hotel last night.

The woman introduced Man-Bun as her brother. The

young man promptly stepped onto the stage.

He felt Moss jabbing him in the ribs. Not soft trying to get his attention jabs, but rib pounding jabs.

"Holy shit," Moss blurted. "You see him?"

"Stop it, I'm not blind."

Kaplan wasn't a hundred percent it was the man they were after. The man had his head lowered staring at something in his hands. Probably his phone.

The woman who introduced Man-Bun left the stage walked over and stood next to him. The man raised his face and smiled warmly at the woman and kissed her on the forehead.

Kaplan double-checked the photo on his phone.

It was the man they were sent here to locate.

Curtis Benoit.

CHAPTER 16

"That's our guy, Kaplan, that's our guy," Moss said.

The man standing by the stage fit the description and matched the photo of Curtis Benoit in the profile given to Kaplan in Grass Lake.

Benoit was maybe 5'8", slender with graying brown hair covering the tip of his ears. His face was in the beginning stages of growing a beard. He didn't have a beard in the photo. A yellow P.A.P.A.C.Y. t-shirt was pulled over a long-sleeve white thermal top. Slim-fit jeans like most of the French men in the crowd.

Kaplan saw a swarm of uniforms penetrating deeper into the crowd.

"What's up with all cops?" Moss asked.

"Seriously? After what happened yesterday you have to ask?"

"I don't know, Kaplan. I thought about it a lot last night. I'm not convinced what happened in Beaune has anything to do with what's happening here."

Kaplan explained the differences in the uniforms. "Those with assault rifles blocking the doors to the cathedral along with the snipers on the rooftops, they're part of French law enforcement called the Gendarmerie Nationale. Their responsibility is policing smaller towns, rural areas, the armed forces, and military installations. They also police airports and shipping ports." He directed Moss to another set of officers. "These men and women are Police Municipale, basically local cops. Their responsibility is pretty much like local cops in the

U.S. The Gendarmerie has been known to run roughshod over the locals, like our FBI does local cops. But mainly, they work in synchrony and with a cooperative spirit...until something major happens."

Kaplan surveyed the crowd again. "We should split up and work our way closer to the stage. I don't want Benoit to get away." He indicated to Moss, "Work your way to the right side of the stage and I'll go left. We're too close to let Curtis Benoit slip through our fingers now. Turn on your comms."

"Wait a minute," Moss objected. "Our job is over. We were only hired to locate. Not catch and deliver. Isn't that what he told you? Call him when you locate Benoit?"

"He did. But things are more complicated now."

"Like a dead Russian?"

"For starters." He paused while he watched the stage and his target standing next to it. "I want to talk to Benoit first. Maybe he can shed a little light on all this. For some unknown reason they're paying us a lot of money to simply *locate* this guy. I'm not buying the heir to a fortune story. Something isn't right about this job we're hired to do."

"Agreed," Moss said as he activated his comm system. And without another word the big man started weaving through the crowd toward the stage.

Kaplan did the same.

Man-Bun held the microphone close to his lips and began ranting about how the Catholic Church, at the condoning of the Pope, was harboring criminals, child molesters, and sexual predators. He used the same phrases that had been plastered all over the national and international headlines for several years. With each new accusation, the crowd roared. Protest signs bounced up and down. Fists balled in the air as the volume of yelling increased exponentially with each levied accusation.

Next, Man-Bun started sharing his own experience of abuse at the hands of his childhood priest here in France. His shame, embarrassment and subsequent debilitating bouts of depression. And his anger, not only toward his abusive priest, but the Catholic Church as a whole.

Man-Bun's plan was obvious, work the crowd into an anti-Church frenzy.

It was working.

A loud beeping sound captured Kaplan's attention to his left. A white truck with red and blue police markings rolled into sight from around the northeast side of the cathedral. It was a tanker-like vehicle with two men posted on top. A riot-control vehicle with a water cannon. Its intent was clear, blast the crowd if the protest got out of hand and became a threat. He guessed P.A.P.A.C.Y. had already earned a reputation for its protests in France.

Kaplan eyed the mob in search of Moss. His partner's bald head towered above the assemblage making him an easy target to pick out over the multitude of heads. He also noticed something disturbing. Very disturbing. Two uniformed Gendarmerie officers' attention was on Moss.

Kaplan's muscles tensed.

"Moss," he warned through his comms. "Get out of there Moss, the Gendarmerie—"

"Wha—"

Then Moss's comm system went dead.

"Dammit." Kaplan lowered his head. *Think.* He viewed two armed officers and a blonde woman escorting Moss away from the cathedral toward a white Gendarmerie van now parked in front of the tourist information building.

He had to get away and regroup. Forget Benoit. Getting out of here and figuring out a plan to rescue Moss was now his number one priority.

He turned around to make his way back through the crowd and saw a familiar face stare up at him.

"Monsieur Kaplan," the man said. "It has been a while, has it not?"

"Lieutenant Heuse." Kaplan recalled their previous encounter from several years ago. "I'd like to say it's a pleasure."

"It is Capitaine now."

Heuse was dressed in faded jeans, a wrinkled white button-down shirt and a tweed sports coat. Necktie pulled loose leaving a two-inch gap below his collar. Late fifties, maybe older. Gone was the unfiltered cigarette that used to dangle from his lips with its long ash precariously hanging on. Replacing it was a plastic straw tucked in the corner of his mouth. He wore suede chukka boots and had a thin mustache that matched his salt and pepper head full of hair.

"Moving up in the world, I see. I believe you once told me you had reached the pinnacle of your career," said Kaplan.

"Things change." Heuse shrugged his shoulders. "I must say, I am quite surprised to see you back in France so soon after your unfortunate accident on our lovely northern coast."

"Things change." Kaplan shrugged his shoulders mimicking Heuse.

Heuse smiled. "Touché. And your limp, it too has disappeared."

Kaplan instantly glanced at his leg. "A lot of physical therapy and exercise."

"I must inquire. Why are you here, monsieur?"

"Just a tourist, Capitaine, who happened on this protest by

accident."

"Aah. I sincerely wish that were the case, monsieur, but we both know it is a lie."

"What do you want, Capitaine? I've broken no laws."

"That remains to be seen, Monsieur Kaplan. That remains to be seen."

Kaplan stared at the short Frenchman, wondering how this encounter was going to end. "If there will be nothing further, Capitaine, I'll be on my way."

He tried to push past Heuse but felt his arms restrained. Flanking him with a tight grip on each arm were two of Heuse's uniformed officers.

He knew nothing good would come of this.

Heuse stepped close to Kaplan's face. Too close.

"Monsieur Kaplan, I hope for your sake you are not armed."

† † †

Dalton Palmer had been sent to observe the Americans. A recon assignment to begin with, later it would change, but not until the time was right. *Track and report.* Those were his orders. And track he had. The man he had been assigned to follow and his friend had just been detained by French law enforcement.

Interesting, but baffling. As far as he could tell the two men had done nothing wrong. They were just working their way through the crowd when the large Black man, Pete Moss, was escorted away by two uniformed policemen to a Gendarmerie van. Then the other American, Gregg Kaplan, was seemingly arrested as well.

This added an unexpected complexity to his mission, but nothing he couldn't overcome.

CHAPTER 17

Gendarmerie Headquarters
Bourges, France

Kaplan didn't pretend he could predict the future or pick up the scent of trouble blowing in the wind, but he knew enough not to ignore the warning signs tapping him on the shoulder. What was going on here was more than tapping. More like a gut punch. Something wasn't right. The thing was, how to stop it.

Of all the scenarios he'd anticipated, this was the worst case...short of being killed. The man he and Moss were after was almost within their grasp. So close. And now, Kaplan was in custody in France by French law enforcement with an unauthorized weapon. The exact situation he'd warned Moss about had happened to him.

He sat alone in an interrogation room, wrists cuffed to a table, staring at the two-way mirror while waiting for Capitaine Travers Heuse or someone else to enter and read him the riot act.

The room had an institutional look and feel. Concrete block walls painted stark white. Video cameras mounted in the corners, their beady red eyes staring at him. The room warm, almost uncomfortably so and the sticky particles of heavy nicotine use clinging to the walls and ceiling made his wait for Heuse even more uncomfortable. But that was what they wanted. It was part of the design. Intimidation and discomfort. An interrogation technique he was accustomed to and one seemingly employed around the globe.

He knew from past experience with Heuse that the man was with the GIGN, or the French National Gendarmerie Intervention Group, an elite police tactical unit whose mission included counterterrorism, hostage rescue, surveillance of national threats, targeting organized crime, as well as an assortment of other duties. Based out of Versailles, Heuse's presence in Bourges puzzled Kaplan. Why would Heuse be here in Bourges? And why was he at the protest? What possible interest could this protest be for the GIGN? Could there be a connection between the GIGN and Curtis Benoit?

He let the earlier events of the day run through his memory banks, checking to see if he remembered something he might have overlooked that could have prevented he and Moss from being taken into custody.

He came up empty.

No indicators.

No warning signs.

Nothing.

The loud demonstration was peaceful. Certainly law enforcement was there, but that was to be expected.

He thought about what had happened in Beaune the day before. Could the Gendarmerie have known about him and Moss in Beaune? It was unlikely a connection had been made this soon. Besides, other than the unauthorized weapons he had done nothing wrong. Neither had Moss.

Perhaps that was it.

Moss.

His friend was a standout everywhere they went. How hard was it *not* to notice such an imposing man of his stature? In this country especially, where Moss was at least a full head size above most people. And spotting Moss in a crowd made it easier for someone to find Kaplan.

After another few minutes of introspection, the only possible and quite unsettling scenario hit him hard. He and his partner had been sandbagged. And if so, it had to be David Pearson, the man who hired him. Pearson sent him to France under the ruse that Curtis Benoit's last known whereabouts was Beaune. He knew…or leaked…that Kaplan and Moss were there, probably armed. He gave the French authorities their descriptions. Set them up. That explained Heuse's presence. Right or wrong, it was the only explanation he could come up with at the moment. But why? What was Pearson's motivation?

He was angry. At himself. He should have seen this coming. He had done his homework, though. David Pearson checked out to be a registered private investigator in Seattle. But from the beginning, he and Moss believed the whole thing was too easy to be true. That was a lot of cash just to track down a missing person. He now knew it for what it was, an irresistible carrot waved in front of him at a time when he needed something like this in his life. Something to tempt him out of his rut.

The worst part was he'd dragged his best friend into this mess and wasn't sure he knew how to get either of them out of trouble.

† † †

Capitaine Travers Heuse stood in the monitoring room watching Gregg Kaplan through the two-way mirror. The video monitors were on and recording. As was the audio feed. On a small table in front of him was a small duffel containing the handguns confiscated from Kaplan and Moss in front of

Saint Etienne Cathedral. He had removed the magazines and emptied the rounds from the chambers. He knew Kaplan and of his past. He knew who he worked for. He recalled their previous encounters when tracking terrorists in Paris, the explosions at the Louvre, and saying his final goodbyes to Kaplan after the man was injured at the end of a long swim to shore in the cold Cantabrian Sea. The *then* Director of Central Intelligence, Scott Bentley, retrieved Kaplan from a French hospital and flew him out of Fuerte de Socoa, Saint-Jean-de-Luz, France. That was the last he'd seen or heard about Kaplan until yesterday.

The man standing next to Heuse was an American who worked for the United States Government. He also used to work for former DCI Bentley. Now, he was the CIA Deputy Chief of Station in Paris.

The American was medium build and height. The receding hairline emphasized his deep-set eyes and dimpled cheeks. His amicable smile displayed his straight teeth. The man was smart and well-versed...in both English and French. He wore khakis, a blue button-down shirt, no tie and a navy blazer. A *VISITOR* badge on a lanyard draped around his neck, his U.S. Government credentials tucked inside his left jacket pocket. In many ways, he was forgettable, which fit the profile for what he was.

A spymaster.

Heuse had no idea Gregg Kaplan was in France, nor did he care for that matter. It wasn't until the American showed up at his superior's office in Versailles and insisted Heuse get involved. The reason still not clear. The American wanted Kaplan detained by French authorities and brought in for questioning as a favor. He claimed Kaplan was illegally armed.

How he knew, he would not say.

As a favor, Heuse's superior obliged knowing that someday they might need a favor from the U.S. Government. And goodwill went a long way in this business. Quid pro quo. An IOU from the CIA was not a bad thing to have tucked in one's back pocket. The request was still a mystery to Heuse. The American knew exactly when and where to locate Kaplan and his friend, so why didn't he just handle it himself? Or better yet, have his own men handle it. But Heuse did as his superior ordered and arrested Kaplan and Moss.

"Monsieur, how much longer do you wish me to detain Messieurs Kaplan and Moss with this charade?"

"Not much longer. Look at him," the American said while staring at Kaplan through the glass. "He looks like a man who just had an epiphanic moment. I think Gregg Kaplan is struggling to figure out who is responsible for him being here in France. He's angry for getting suckered."

"Suckered? Is American phrase, yes?"

"Yes, Capitaine. It means he has been taken advantage of and sent here under false pretenses."

"Ah, oui. Do you wish to talk to him?"

"At some point but not here," the American admitted. "After you release him, Kaplan will track me down, but first I want you to lay a little groundwork."

"I do not understand."

"You don't need to. Here's what I need you to do and say, Capitaine."

CHAPTER 18

The door to the interrogation room opened and Heuse walked in with a small black duffel bag in his hand. He sat down across the table from Kaplan, back to the mirror and locked eyes with him as if he wanted to say something but didn't. Then he reached into the bag and removed Kaplan's Beretta Px4 Storm .45 caliber and laid it on the table in front of him. Next he pulled out Moss's Glock 37 G.A.P. 45 and set it next to his. The magazines had been removed. Lastly, he removed two sound suppressors and placed them upright next to the handguns.

"You and your friend have broken many French laws having these in your possession," Heuse said in a stern tone. "Offenses France does not take lightly. What were your intentions with these weapons, Monsieur Kaplan?"

"I can assure you Capitaine these were only for protection."

"You told me earlier you are in France as tourist. Let me *assure you*, Monsieur Kaplan, tourists have no need for such weapons in France."

"Not my experience the last time I was here.

Heuse picked up the suppressors, one in each hand. "If you are here on holiday like you claim, you would not have smuggled these into our country."

"I've made a lot of enemies over the years."

Heuse placed the suppressors on the table. One rolled a few inches before coming to rest near Kaplan's hand. Then, he picked up Kaplan's Beretta, pulled back the slide and peered into the barrel. "Unauthorized possession of this, especially by foreigners, carries with it stiff prison terms, monsieur. Are you aware of this?"

Kaplan remained silent. He wasn't going to be baited.

"Well, monsieur? Do you understand how much trouble you and your friend are in?"

"You know damn well I'm aware of French law, so why ask such a stupid question?"

"Because Monsieur Kaplan, I do not think you have grasped the gravity of your situation."

The badgering continued for another few minutes before Heuse appeared to be running out of threats against Moss and him.

Something about this was off. Way off. He'd been in too many interrogations not to recognize a farce when he saw it.

"Okay Capitaine, enough of this bullshit. How about you tell me what the hell is going on?"

The door opened and a man summoned Heuse to the door. "Capitaine, would you come here, please?" He was American, his attire and Southern U.S. accent gave him away.

Kaplan didn't recognize the American, but the voice sounded familiar. As much as he tried though, he couldn't place where he'd heard it.

The two men talked in low voices. Then the American backed out of his line of sight after he handed Heuse a manila envelope. Heuse's demeanor changed slightly and after a few more seconds of what appeared to be a rapidly escalating discourse, Heuse nodded, closed the door and returned to the table.

"Who's your friend?" Kaplan asked?

Heuse blinked his eyes and widened them. "That man does not concern you, Monsieur Kaplan."

"If what's in that envelope has anything to do with me, it

does."

"What is in this envelope was provided to the French government."

"Handed to you by an American? What is it?"

"You Americans lack the quality of patience."

"Yeah? Maybe I'd be a lot more patient if I wasn't being jerked around. I'm done talking. No more pretext, Capitaine. What's going on?"

Heuse looked conflicted. The Frenchman twisted and looked back at the mirror. Beads of sweat formed on his temples and one ran down his cheek.

The door to the interrogation room opened and a woman entered. Same woman who escorted Moss to the Gendarmerie van at the protest. Heuse stood abruptly. "Colonel."

The tall slim woman had shoulder-length blonde hair. Her fair skin accentuated by her blue plastic-rimmed glasses. Behind them, striking blue eyes. She crossed the room with purpose. It was clear by the vibe change in the room Heuse was intimidated by her...or her authority. As she approached the aroma of her perfume wafted over him, pleasant yet a tad overpowering. Mid-forties and well maintained.

"Monsieur Kaplan." Then in English. "We should talk."

"You're not French," Kaplan asserted.

"Danish." She placed a business card on the table and pushed it in front of Kaplan. It indicated her rank with the GIGN was Colonel. That made her Heuse's boss.

"How do you pronounce this?" He pointed to her name on the card.

"*Pear* like the fruit, *knee* like the joint. *Pernille*."

"Colonel Pernille Skouboe?"

"Correct, Monsieur Kaplan."

"Tell me Colonel, how does someone from Denmark become such a high-ranking officer with the French GIGN?"

She didn't answer, kept her face rigid. She sat in Heuse's chair while the Capitaine took a few steps back and propped against the wall next to the door. She opened the envelope she took from Heuse when she entered and slid out a paper and several photos, placing them face down on the table. She leaned in and looked him in the eyes. Her eyes now steely, hard and serious. "Let's cut to the chase, as you Americans are fond of saying. I am willing to overlook certain...indiscretions by you and your friend in exchange for some information."

"I'm listening."

"What is the nature of your business in France?"

"What makes you think I have *business* in France?"

"First," Skouboe said as she placed her hand on his unloaded weapon. "There is the matter of your possession of this...and your friend of his. It is not the first time individuals in your line of work have been caught with firearms in their possession. A violation of French law."

"Is that it?" Kaplan asked. "Because one quick phone call can make that charge disappear."

"Perhaps at one time, Monsieur Kaplan. No longer I'm afraid. Your over-confidence might be your undoing. Besides, I have more." Skouboe flipped over one of the photos. It was a picture of he and Moss standing in a crowd of people in front of the Collégiale Notre Dame in Beaune. Next she flipped over a photo of them running down the alley behind the clock tower in Beaune. Without explanation, she flipped over a third photo of the dead Russian's body face down at the foot of the clock tower. "Starting to understand?"

"You know as well as I that we had nothing to do with the

shooting of the man at the clock tower," Kaplan explained. "As a matter of fact, someone shot at us too."

Skouboe displayed no emotion, just a serious stare. Then she smiled and leaned back in her chair. "Perhaps you are correct. But of course our investigation into this matter might drag on for weeks, perhaps even months and all the while you and your friend will be sitting in a jail cell until you are officially exonerated...or convicted." She again put her hand on Kaplan's weapon. "And then there is the matter of this."

"Why me? Why us?"

"You must know by now Monsieur Kaplan that I am fully aware of your past, shall we say, adventures in our country. I am aware of your employment and your employer—"

"Former," Kaplan asserted. "Former employer."

"If you say so, Monsieur Kaplan. That issue is quite frankly irrelevant and between you, the CIA and the United States Government. I ask again, what is the nature of your business in France?

Kaplan didn't answer at first, contemplating the ramifications of his answer. Guarding his words, he said, "We're here to locate a missing person."

"What is this person's name?"

"Is that relevant?"

"It is if you want to leave here without being thrown in jail."

He paused and then said, "His name is Curtis Benoit. He's the heir to a large inheritance in the United States. We are trying to locate him and have him contact an attorney to claim his inheritance."

"I see," Skouboe said. "And he has gone missing?"

"He was last seen in France. He has gone incommunicado.

He's not responding to his family's urgent requests to contact them, so Moss and I are here looking for him."

"And your need for these weapons?" She placed her hand on Kaplan's gun. "Is Monsieur Benoit a dangerous man?"

"Not that I've been told. But, you know my history. You know very well why I have a weapon. And as you've already seen, not without justification. My odds are better if I'm armed."

"Monsieur Kaplan, I am aware of your contribution several years ago in the arrest of several terrorists in Paris. A debt of which we at the GIGN are still grateful. As a token of goodwill for your service to France in the past, I will forget you and your friend were ever in Beaune plus I will go so far as to overlook your possession of these illegal weapons and ammunition. However, I will not give them back. In return, I request you and Monsieur Moss leave France immediately. Do we have a deal?"

He head-nodded at the door. "What about the American? The one who gave Capitaine Heuse this package? What's his role in all this?"

"A simple courier from Paris. Nothing more."

And there it was—her tell. An ever so slight twitch and the twirling of her wedding ring.

She was lying.

He knew it but opted to play along with her ruse. Anything to get him and Moss out of here as soon as possible.

"Colonel," Kaplan said. "You have a deal."

CHAPTER 19

Ministry of Intelligence and Security (MOIS)
Prime Ministry Intelligence Office
Tehran, Iran

Intelligence Minister Qasem Khatami read the direct communiqué from Iran's Supreme Leader handed to him personally by the Islamic Revolutionary Guard Corps (IRGC) Major General Majeed Sattar who was standing in front of Khatami's desk. Attached to the document was the bio of an American who had fled the United States Government. An American the Supreme Leader had taken a great interest in having brought to Iran. An American who had single-handedly cost the Iranian government millions and set their nuclear weapons program back years, if not decades. The IRGC Major General never moved while Khatami read.

After finishing the communique, Khatami removed his glasses and set them on top of the small stack of papers. He massaged his upper nose between his forefinger and thumb. He knew the pressure, a silent and unspoken one.

The man standing in front of him knew what the communique said and was clearly trying to restrain a smirk. He was in the driver's seat on this one. If Khatami's MOIS failed, then Sattar and his QUDS Force would be tasked to complete the mission and Khatami would be swiftly removed from office and replaced by someone else of the Supreme Leader's choosing. Khatami's fate would be sealed.

Adding to the insult was the two-decades-long professional

and now personal rivalry he had with Sattar whom he'd attended the military academy with many years ago. That was where the rivalry began. As both men ascended in the ranks of the Iranian hierarchy, Khatami invariably came in a disappointing second. Never besting the now Major General.

Khatami knew why this mission had landed in his lap. His long-time rival had instigated the assignment with the Supreme Leader. Another test where if he failed, his rival would gloat like he always had.

But the stakes on this one were much greater—for both of them. If Khatami was successful he would no doubt be promoted to a rank above his rival.

"Well Qasem?" his rival said with his balled fists propped on his hips. "The Supreme Leader wants your assurances that you will succeed or the IRGC-QF will take this assignment from you. And I can assure you, I will be successful."

"Majeed, you were an asshole at the Academy and you are an asshole now. You can tell the Supreme Leader that MOIS will take this assignment. And we *will* succeed." He tapped the stack of papers with his glasses, folded them and put them in a case. "Now, take your leave of me and get out of my office."

Sattar stepped closer, put both hands on Khatami's desk and leaned forward. "Qasem, I am looking forward to your failure. MOIS will be better off without you. As will all of Iran."

Khatami stood and pointed to the door. "Get out now...or I'll have you thrown out."

Sattar laughed, turned and headed for the door. "You are a fool, Qasem."

After Sattar left the room, Khatami eased his way to the window and watched as his rival walked to his chauffeured limousine, a level of status only a privileged few had attained.

Certainly, something he had not. Good riddance, he thought, as Sattar's car drove out of sight.

He walked back to his desk and sank in his chair. After a few moments of concentration, he put on his glasses and pulled a folder from his right drawer. Inside were the names of his best and most trusted operatives. The assignment from the Supreme Leader could not be handled by any run-of-the-mill operative, no, it must be a top tier asset.

Top-tier *team*.

That was something else he needed to ensure. He needed a strong team with an even stronger leader.

He reread the communique and noted something peculiar about his target. The man loved women. Mostly exotic women. He flipped through the operatives' files and stopped at one in particular. Her reputation had preceded her. An operative with a perfect track record. Willing to do anything for Iran. At any cost. A woman more ruthless than most men. Cold, brutal. He smiled.

He punched a button on his phone and a voice answered through the speaker. "Yes, Minister Khatami," the voice said.

"Summon Jasmine Habibi to my office immediately."

† † †

Curtis Benoit sat quietly in his seat on the train next to Sophie.

She was busy working on her laptop, something she did after every rally. She made notes about the day's event, attendance, overall success, or lack thereof. Then she'd turn her attention and focus to upcoming rallies, primarily the next one on the calendar and update the website. She'd make phone calls and send emails as necessary to ensure all preparations were in place. Then she would focus on logistics and scheduling future rallies with an emphasis on spreading the P.A.P.A.C.Y. message to as many French people as she could reach, including media interviews and appearances.

Something had happened at the rally in Bourges that troubled him. He couldn't quite place his finger on it, but it rattled his usual confidence.

There was a heavier than usual presence of French law enforcement at this rally. Not just local Policia like before, but the Gendarmerie Nationale. Along with a water cannon vehicle. Odd, since all their other rallies had been peaceful. That was part of the message—combat the evils of the Catholic Church in a peaceful manner. A rally with chanting and yelling was one thing, any semblance of violent behavior was another. It would be a distraction to their cause and would give P.A.P.A.C.Y. a bad reputation and the Church a reason to have them banned, something Sophie Bouquet wanted desperately to avoid.

He'd heard news reports that there was a Russian murdered in Beaune the previous day but had yet to confirm it. And a Cardinal had died of a heart attack while giving Sunday Mass. Were those events somehow related? How could they be? P.A.P.A.C.Y. had no rally in Beaune. Not yet anyway. The Beaune rally wasn't scheduled for another week, although he and Sophie had been in Beaune the week before last acquiring permits to hold a P.A.P.A.C.Y. rally in that city.

Something else at the Bourges cathedral had bothered him. Two men on opposite sides of the stage were detained by the Gendarmerie. One was impossible to miss. A large towering Black man with a bald head approaching from his left. The man was stopped and escorted by two officers and a blonde woman to a Gendarmerie van and driven off. He had never seen the large man before that day, he was certain of it.

With all the excitement from the protesters he almost missed the other man advancing from his right. His face unfamiliar, but something about this man and his purposeful stride was familiar. This man was not as tall as the Black man, had thick dark hair and an unshaven face. He wondered if the two men were at the rally for the same reason. Perhaps he thought this because even though they were approaching the stage from opposing angles, they were doing it at the same time as if zeroing in on a target. But what target?

He had kept an eye on the two men while they slowly yet methodically worked their way through the horde of people toward the stage. There were eight potential targets near or on the stage. Unfortunately, he was one of them. Not knowing troubled him. Was he the target? Or was it one of the others? It was not unusual for the leaders of the rally to get death threats. The young man on stage was railing forcefully about the sins of French Catholic priests' abuse of youth. A story mentioned in the news nearly every day, not just in France, but around the world. The media had proven to be the Church's worst enemy.

The young man speaking on the stage was the reason Sophie Bouquet got involved in the first place. He had been abused by a priest when he was a young altar boy. Pierre Bouquet, Sophie's younger brother was the one on the stage speaking to the protesters. Sophie and Pierre grew up in a suburb of Paris. It was there in their local parish that Pierre was abused. When he reported it to his parents, they silenced him and refused to let him expose the priest, stating it would be an embarrassment to them and the Church. Pierre was told some things were best kept secret.

Pierre quit as altar boy and ultimately distanced himself from the Church entirely. As Pierre grew older he suffered from anxiety and depression. He left home when he was eighteen and moved away from the city. A failed suicide attempt that resulted in Pierre's prolonged hospitalization and rehab was the catalyst that prompted Sophie to become an activist for his cause.

Initially a volunteer for P.A.P.A.C.Y., an American founded activist group, Sophie advanced to become director of the France division of P.A.P.A.C.Y.

When the black-haired man in the crowd was confronted by two Gendarmerie Nationale uniformed officers, he chatted with a Frenchman in a tweed coat for a few moments before being led away. What did the man want? Was he there to stop Pierre from speaking? Or was he after something...or someone else entirely? Or nothing at all?

As much as he and Sophie were on the go he knew it was unlikely his new identity had been breached. Something else was going on. Sophie and P.A.P.A.C.Y. had certainly garnered unwanted tension between them and the Catholic Church. He was sure the Church saw her as a thorn in their side. But however unlikely it might seem, deep down he felt this had something to do with him and not her.

No proof, just a gut feeling.

One that had kept him alive so far. And one he had learned to trust.

And then there was Sophie.

He liked her—a lot. But he wasn't in love with her. At least that's what he kept telling himself. She was smart, fun and dedicated to her brother's cause—traits he admired—but he'd been living with her for four months and that was nearing his maximum involvement time with any woman.

By now he would have grown tired of a woman and ready to move on. It was different with Sophie. Not only was he not growing tired of her, he longed to be with her. Stay with her.

In the past, he never cared for anyone. Even his parents were emotionally uninvolved in his life growing up. He spent years building an emotional wall to keep anybody from hurting him. He didn't want anyone caring for him. Yet he knew Sophie did. She'd already started slipping in the quick little *love ya* every now and then, like at night before bed or when getting off the phone. He thought they had made an agreement to keep it non-committal. Now he felt like she was changing the rules and a part of him didn't want that to happen. But a part of him did want it to be different with Sophie.

For four months they had seen each other almost every day, spending most of their days together while he helped her with her job planning and attending rallies. It had allowed him to see many of the sights France has to offer and experience them with a local who knew much more than tour guides. But at what cost?

Serena's death had shaken his confidence. Something he thought he'd regained until the incident in Bourges.

This had his inner voice rattled.

It screamed *run.*

And he wasn't one to ignore that voice.

CHAPTER 20

Gendarmerie Headquarters
Bourges, France

Colonel Pernille Skouboe ordered Heuse to uncuff Kaplan from the table. She said to Kaplan, "If you ever return to France, I advise you to remain within the law. If you will follow Capitaine Heuse, he will return your belongings." She placed her hand on his Beretta. "Except for your weapons, of course. I assume you have a vehicle in town, correct?"

"I do," Kaplan replied while rubbing his wrists. "Le Château d'Eau parking lot."

"Very good." She spun on her heels and exited the room.

Heuse motioned for Kaplan to follow. Moss joined them in the hallway within a minute. He seemed confused with the buzz of activity as the GIGN began treating them cordially.

"What the hell's going on?" Moss whispered to Kaplan.

Kaplan grunted. "Later."

As they were being escorted to an exit where a waiting GIGN vehicle was to take them to their car, Kaplan saw the American again, leather messenger bag hanging on his shoulder. He was talking with Colonel Pernille Skouboe at the opposite end of the long hallway. Their body language appeared amicable, unlike what he witnessed with the American and Heuse or Heuse and Skouboe.

Courier my ass.

Skouboe handed the American the small black duffel bag.

Something strange was going on and he vowed to get to

the bottom of it.

† † †

Ten minutes later, the GIGN vehicle dropped them off at the water tower parking lot. Kaplan looked at Moss and said, "Let's go."

"Where're we going?"

"Back to Gendarmerie headquarters."

Moss snapped, "What the hell for? You trying to get us locked up? Again?"

"I got a feeling they don't want to arrest us."

"Funny it felt like we were arrested sitting in that smelly interrogation room. You gonna tell me how you got us busted loose?" Moss asked.

"I cut a deal."

"A deal?"

"Actually, they cut us a deal. Leave France immediately and they forget we were ever here."

"How'd you pull that off?"

"Repayment of a debt they owed me from years ago, I guess."

"In case you forgot, we won't get paid if we can't tell that P.I. where to find Benoit. And now you want to give up and leave the country?"

"I didn't say that."

"If this conversation is headed somewhere, how about getting to the point."

"There was an American at the station. I want to talk to him."

"An American?"

Kaplan explained, "Right before the Colonel came in to question me...or whatever her role really was. That whole interrogation thing, it's a ruse of some sort...orchestrated. A show. I'm sure of it. By whom and for what reason, I don't know yet. Certainly not Heuse...maybe not even Colonel Pernille Skouboe. Farther up the food chain, perhaps."

"You said it might get messy," Moss said. "And you believe this American is involved?"

"Maybe. Heuse was called to the door by the American. The guy handed Heuse a manila envelope. I got a good look at the guy. To my recollection I've never seen him before. And I never forget a face."

"But?" Moss interrupted.

"But I recognized his voice."

"Don't keep me in suspense, Kaplan. Who was it?"

"I don't know. The voice was familiar...very familiar. The Southern cadence. It belongs to someone I know...someone I should know. I just can't place it."

"So, let me see if I got this right. A guy whose face you've never seen has a voice you recognize but you can't figure out who."

"Yeah. Something like that."

"That's clear as mud. I can't wait to see how this turns out." Moss patted his hand on the dashboard. "Alrighty then, let's go find your mystery man."

After they arrived back at Gendarmerie building, Kaplan made a 180 in the street so the car was facing toward town center. He parked the car by the curb within easy sight line of the front of the Gendarmerie building and let the engine idle.

"Hey, nothing like another tour of the police station?" Moss joked. "What does this dude look like?"

"Little shorter than me. Balding with a fringe of brownish-gray hair on the sides and back. He's wearing khaki pants, blue shirt and navy sports jacket. Probably has a messenger bag hanging on his shoulder."

Moss pointed out a man walking out of the Gendarmerie Nationale building that matched Kaplan's description with a trench coat draped over his arm. "Is that the dude?"

"Yep." Kaplan put the car in gear. "That's him."

The man strolled out the front gate to a parked car in a side lot right behind the bus stop. When the American drove off down Avenue da Saint-Armand, Kaplan accelerated onto the road and started the tail. He kept a safe distance. Easy since the American had not made any turns. Yet. Making the same turns was where he might be made. At N151, the American turned right, so did Kaplan. Kaplan kept up with the flow of traffic not losing sight of the target. He followed the American along Rue d'Auron which emptied into town. The city street was narrow and one-way. This might be easier than he thought. Kaplan let another car get between him and the American for safe measure. The American turned on Rue des Arènes. The car between them went straight. Kaplan fell behind about a block's distance between them. At Rue du Marché, the American made a left. So did Kaplan but, after noticing a large parking lot ahead at the bottom of a small incline, he veered down Rue Emile Deschamps hoping he could circle around and reacquire the American near the parking lot.

Moss broke the silence. "Don't lose him. Right now, we could use that *eye in the sky* like you had in New Jersey, remember?"

It hit Kaplan with sudden epiphany. Like a bucket of ice water had been thrown in his face. "What'd you just say?"

"I said—"

"That's it, Moss. You're a freaking genius. That's the voice."

"What voice?"

"The American's voice. I'm absolutely positive. The man at Gendarmerie HQ, the man who gave Heuse the envelope." Kaplan rounded the corner in time to see the American pull his car into the parking lot. "That man right there." Moss looked where Kaplan was pointing. "That's the voice in my ear…Alan, my CIA controller. No mistake about it."

"Controller?" Moss queried.

"Handler."

† † †

Kaplan parked in the first available parking space on the side of the road. Now on foot, Kaplan saw Alan heading back up Rue du Marché and instructed Moss to backtrack the route they had just driven while he tailed his handler up the hill. His handler turned the corner on Rue de Arènes walked a block to Place Gabriel Monnet, up the steps to Rue Jacques Cœur where he turned right again. He was walking at a leisurely pace, messenger bag over one shoulder, black duffel in his opposite hand, coat draped over his arm. Kaplan held back until his handler disappeared from sight. After a quick glance back to see where Moss was, he bounded up the steps for fear of completely losing sight of where Alan was headed.

He reached Rue Jacques Cœur and spotted his handler walking down the middle of the empty street as if he hadn't a care in the world. Kaplan was surprised his handler paid such little attention to his surroundings. Kaplan kept his focus on Alan while waiting for Moss to catch up.

Winded, Moss asked, "Where'd your handler go?"

Kaplan watched Alan nearing a crossroads. "There, seemingly oblivious he's being followed."

"Or doing it intentionally."

"Or that."

His handler rounded a corner and disappeared from sight.

"Come on," Kaplan said. He sprinted down Rue Jacques Cœur to the spot his handler disappeared. It was an intersection with four streets coming together at odd angles. Three streets created a 'Y' shape while the fourth veered due west from the fork. No visual of his handler on any of them. Gone. He must have ducked into a building. But which one?

Moss lumbered up to where Kaplan was standing. "Where'd he go?"

Kaplan turned and noticed a hotel at the north side of the fork.

Hotel D'Angleterre.

"My guess is here," Kaplan said as he pointed to the hotel. "It's the only hotel in sight."

"Makes sense." Moss replied. "What are you going to do now? Go in after him?"

"Pretty sure that's what he wants us to do. We go find him. He's got a lot of explaining to do."

Side by side, they walked quickly along the cobbled road toward the double green hotel doors and entered. To his left were the lobby's sitting areas. Two of them. One open, the other private.

The entrance had pale yellow walls, green carpet with matching drapes on the windows held apart by corded tie backs. A long multi-patterned tile hallway was adorned with oriental rugs. To his right, the reception desk where a young woman was standing behind a green marble counter. She smiled. "Bonjour Monsieur."

"Bonjour Madame. Did you happen to see a man walk in here right before we did?" He asked her in French. He gave a quick description.

"Oui, monsieur."

"I'm an old friend and haven't seen him in years. I'd love to surprise him. Could you kindly tell me what room he is staying in?" he asked.

She leaned back, a guarded look on her face. "Oh no, monsieur, we take our guest's privacy seriously."

He glanced back down the hall, trying to think of a way to find his handler. All he knew now was his handler did come in the hotel.

Moss stepped next to him. "We can always wait him out."

"That won't be necessary, Inspector Moss." Kaplan heard the familiar voice call out. "Gregg, we finally get a chance to meet face to face."

† † †

Dalton watched Kaplan and Moss enter the hotel. They had been following another man, presumably American but in reality, he hadn't gotten a good enough look at the man's face to know for sure. The two men were released from Gendarmerie custody and were escorted into town, only to return to the Gendarmerie station in their own vehicle in order to follow another man.

This was indeed a curious turn of events.

As instructed by his superior, track and report.

CHAPTER 21

His former handler was standing in the doorway of one of the hotel's two lobby sitting areas—the private one. He extended his arm inviting them in. "Let's talk."

"Funny, you don't look like your voice," said Kaplan.

"Really? And what did you think I would look like?"

"I don't know. Taller. Nerdier. Pallid from working in the Ops Center all day, every day. Certainly not like you just flew in from some Caribbean island."

"Interesting," Alan said. "I play a lot of golf."

"Figures."

"Gregg, the agency once labeled you *difficult,* not a team player."

"And why is that?"

"They're pencil pushers, politicians and bureaucrats. They could never grasp your full potential."

"If that's the way the Agency felt, then why did *you* want the headache?"

"I like a good challenge. Besides, I saw something others at the Agency couldn't see."

Kaplan grunted. "I'll bite, what's that?"

"Everything I wasn't."

"Okay Alan, why don't you tell us what this is about?"

"Still impatient, I see."

Alan gestured for Kaplan to lead the way into the small private room. Alan closed the door behind them and approached Moss. "Inspector Moss, my name is Alan Welch. I'm the Deputy Chief of Station in Paris."

"Deputy COS? When did that happen?" interrupted Kaplan.

Welch ignored him and extended his hand to Moss.

Moss shook his hand. "Call me Pete, if you don't mind. I thought you were Kaplan's handler." Moss gave a chin nod toward Kaplan.

Welch said with a hint of a smile, "Gregg and I have history. I feel I know you too, Pete. I've kept tabs on you and Gregg ever since you two met in Virginia."

"Wait. What?" Kaplan interrupted again. "You've been spying on us?"

Welch wrinkled his forehead. "Not spying, really. Just staying informed. It's my job, remember?"

"*Was* your job, Alan. I don't work for you anymore...nor the Agency."

"Actually Gregg, you do. You're getting a paycheck. You should be thankful too. It was at my insistence that Director Reed put you on extended administrative leave and not separation from service like he wanted. I convinced him we had too much invested in you to let you go and that you would eventually come around." Welch motioned to the chairs. Moss sat. Welch sat. Kaplan remained standing and folded his arms across his chest. "I explained to the Director you needed a cooling off period. Time to wrap your head around things with Isabella. He squawked at first—"

The mere mention of Isabella's name sent a pang of guilt through Kaplan.

"Reed's an asshole. He never liked me."

"I won't disagree with either thing you said. He never did like you, but our agency isn't a popularity contest. And you're too good an operative to lose."

"Don't do me any favors, Alan. I'm done with the agency."

"Sorry, Gregg, it's not that simple. Have a seat, please, and let me explain."

He was reluctant at first, finally relenting and taking a seat across from Welch. Best to look the man straight in the eyes. "You know, Alan, your tradecraft skills suck. I expected better, especially when I figured out who you were."

"Breadcrumbs, Gregg. I expected you to track me down."

"What makes you think Moss and I wouldn't just leave France like the GIGN told us to?"

"I know you. That's not your nature. You weren't going to rest till you got to the bottom of what was going on."

Moss nodded. "Man knows you well, Kaplan."

"Okay, Alan, I'll bite. Why did you want me to track you down?"

"Because I want to brief you on your next assignment."

Kaplan's tone hardened, "I'm not doing it. Find someone else." Kaplan felt the heat in his face. He looked at Moss. "Besides, we already have a job we're working on."

"Yes, you do," Welch agreed. "For me. And technically you've already accepted your new assignment." Welch directed his attention at Moss. "You both have. And received partial payment, I might add."

"What the hell's he talking about?" Moss asked Kaplan.

Kaplan realized he'd been played. "I knew it was some bullshit like this when Skouboe let us go. Alan, you sandbagged me. You knew if you approached me with this crap in the States, I'd never come to France. So, you conned me...and Moss."

"I did, Gregg. I'm not apologizing for it either. Your country needs you on this assignment."

"Come on, Alan, don't blow smoke up my ass. You hired David Pearson, that P.I. out of Seattle to offer me a job. I checked Pearson out, he's legit. He's a licensed P.I. and lives in Seattle. Is he on the Agency's payroll?"

"No," Welch admitted. "He's just a P.I. I had one of our analysts pose as an attorney and hire him to track you down. But, since you're such a moving target, it took him longer than I'd anticipated...than we'd anticipated. I had her fully backstopped just in the case Pearson got suspicious and started snooping."

"Why me, Alan? And why drag Moss into this?"

"I need the best on this one."

"First off," Kaplan said. "Moss doesn't work for the company."

"No, he doesn't, but you do. Besides, Moss can tolerate you, which few people can. You two make a good team. I checked Pete's security status, his SCI-TS clearance in still valid, all I did is raise it some. Remember, I've seen you two in action. But I had to do this on the down low. Reed would have my ass if he knew I'd activated you without his knowledge." He paused, glanced at Moss and continued, "and brought in a civilian to boot.

"This is bullshit," Kaplan growled.

"I needed you here, period. For reasons I'll explain later. The deception was my doing. When the Paris station was alerted, I knew what had to be done. I needed someone who can do this mission without the director finding out. I don't think Reed grasps what we're dealing with. Therefore, it's imperative you two stay off the radar."

"Maybe Reed just doesn't care," Kaplan said.

"Perhaps." Welch turned toward Moss. "Pete, sorry for the

misdirection, if you want to bail, I'll make all the arrangements for you to return to the States. I can't *legally* force you to stay. But Kaplan stays."

Moss scratched his head and waited a beat. "One question, Mr. Welch. If I stay and keep Kaplan from screwing up this assignment, do we still get paid the amount agreed upon with that P.I. dude?"

Welch didn't appear surprised by the question, probably anticipated it. He held a tight grin and answered, "Right now, Pete, I need Kaplan and would prefer he had you as his partner. Since I'm not in a position to negotiate, the answer is yes, I will pay the agreed amount." He paused a beat and focused on Kaplan. "To both of you. Expect the balance upon completion of the assignment."

Moss rubbed his hands together. "Perfect, then let's get down to business."

Kaplan spoke up, "Moss, don't be an idiot. Take him up on his offer and go home. Remember when I told you there would be a number two to this assignment? Well this is it. It's gonna be dangerous."

"Not a chance, pal, you're stuck with me. I gotta make sure you don't go and get yourself killed."

Kaplan clenched his jaw, narrowed his eyes and studied Welch. "How'd you find us, Alan? How did you know where we were? Where to send the GIGN?"

"Simple, really. You let your guard down with my misdirection. You kept your personal phones active. Welch looked at Moss. "You both did…I sent you to Beaune, yet you ended up here."

"You tracked our phones?" Moss scowled at Welch.

"Had to, Pete. If I hadn't then we couldn't have this

conversation."

"How?" Moss asked.

"I reauthorized the agency's wiretap of Gregg's personal phone when I was handed this operation." Welch shifted his eyes to Kaplan. "Good thing I kept you on the payroll, Gregg, or I couldn't have done it." Welch turned back to Moss. "As for you, Pete, our analysts simply used travel pattern analysis to ID a phone that traveled nearby Gregg's and that enabled us to track your phone. That way I could keep tabs on both of you."

Moss looked at Kaplan. "Just like the techies at the Marshal's Service do to track fugitives."

"Meaning Alan's been spying on us all this time," Kaplan added.

"No," Welch argued. "I did it to track you while we were working together. You know this already, Gregg. You agreed to it years ago. You signed the official documented permission. Standard ops to track operatives in the field. Just like we do certain government officials in cases where their lives are threatened with kidnapping or in the event of emergencies. Never know when something might come up and I need to locate you. Besides, all I can do is track. I can't read your traffic. I didn't exploit your burner phones. I trust your judgement. If you felt the need to disable your personal phone so I can't track you, then I assume you don't want others tracking you either for the sake of the mission."

"Why not come to me directly?" Kaplan asked. "After we arrived in Paris."

"I wanted your interest piqued. Wanted you to do what you do best—get to the bottom of things."

Kaplan said nothing for a few moments. It was a lot to consider. It was one thing that he'd volunteered before he knew

Welch had deceived him, it was another to drag his friend into what he now knew would likely be a dangerous mission. He knew Moss could handle himself.

Putting aside Welch's trickery, he and Moss did accept the job. In reality, the terms were still the same. It's just now he knew who he was actually working for—the CIA. And now, Moss was too.

The truth was he missed the secret world he had worked in. Ever since they stepped foot in France, he felt the strong pull to work in it again.

"We're here." He glanced back at Moss again. "Might as well give us a mission brief and explain why there are other actors involved trying to find this guy. You can start by telling us exactly who Curtis Benoit really is. After we get all the facts, I'll let you know if we'll do it."

† † †

Gendarmerie HQ
Bourges, France

Capitaine Travers Heuse had been waiting for Colonel Pernille Skouboe in an empty office for nearly an hour when she returned from her teleconference with the Générale. She sat in a chair at a desk and took off her glasses. With elbows on the desk she propped her head in her hands and massaged her temples. Her thick blonde hair draped down obscuring her face from Heuse's view.

"Sorry you had to wait so long Capitaine," Skouboe said in French. "The Générale has brought us an impossible case

I'm afraid. One that demands our immediate and unfettered attention."

Skouboe raised her head and swiped a wisp of hair from her face. "Do you remember a few months ago when we received a burn notice from the CIA about Matthew Wolfe?"

"Oui, he's living in Iceland last I heard."

"Apparently not anymore." She passed a folder across the desk. "According to this intel, he is in France."

Heuse studied the files inside. "What does the Générale want us to do?"

"He wants us to pull out all the stops to find him. Search every city, town and village. No stone unturned."

"That's a lot of manpower. Does the Générale understand what a logistical nightmare this will be?"

Skouboe sat up straight and put her glasses back on, ran her fingers through her hair and tucked it behind her ears. "I tried explaining it to him but he basically said if I couldn't do what he wanted, he'd find someone who could."

"No pressure, then?" Heuse gave a brisk smile.

She smiled back. "Right."

Heuse slid the papers around, stacked them on top of each other and started reading. "Hmm."

"Speak your mind, Capitaine."

"Says here Matthew Wolfe's last confirmed location was Beaune. I know it might sound a little far-fetched, but what if the reason Welch wanted Kaplan and Moss detained was to order them to track down Wolfe. Welch *did* know Kaplan's location, so he's obviously tracking him."

She steepled her fingers, her eyes serious. "Under normal circumstances, I'd say your theory was a stretch, but I'm not so sure. And Beaune is one hell of a coincidence."

"Why don't you just ask Welch?"

"And how do you suppose that conversation would go? The CIA likes to hold their cards close to the chest. They don't share information until they need us for something."

"You mean like making an arrest under false pretenses?" Heuse leaned toward Skouboe. "Don't you find it a little bit curious? Or perhaps troubling?"

"Capitaine," Skouboe answered. "I have dealt with Alan Welch since he arrived in Paris last year. He has been nothing but forthright when dealing with us. I believe him to be an honest man. He explained in great detail why he needed us, and specifically you, to bring in Monsieur Kaplan. I owed him a favor from last year's attempted terror attack on our subway in Paris. If it weren't for one of his Paris operatives stopping the suicide bomber on the Metro, we would have had mass casualties instead of the one lone dead terrorist."

"Now he owes us." Heuse closed the folder and pushed it back across the desk to Skouboe. "And why me? In reality, I hardly know Monsieur Kaplan. Why come all the way here from HQ just to perform a false arrest and then let the man go? Perhaps we should be keeping an eye on Messieurs Kaplan and Moss because I'm certain they aren't leaving France anytime soon, despite your instructions. Why were they at the P.A.P.A.C.Y. protest in the first place? Furthermore, who is this man Kaplan and Moss are looking to find?" He pulled out his notepad. "Curtis Benoit? I checked out the name, he's not on our radar. Does Welch know something we don't about this man? He didn't make Paris Deputy Chief of Station by being a Boy Scout. After your meeting with the Générale, I don't know how you feel, but I think there is something dishonest about this whole thing. It has the smell of a sewer rat."

Skouboe intertwined her slender fingers and clenched them tight. When she was sure she had Heuser's full attention she began, "I understand where you are coming from, Capitaine, but I trust Alan Welch." She raised a finger before he could interrupt. "And I share your concern. You make a compelling argument. Welch told me why Messieurs Kaplan and Moss are here. I'd like you to dig deeper into the man they are after, this Curtis Benoit. He has a French name. I want to know who is he and what they want with him. I'm not sure I buy the whole heir to a large inheritance thing either. I also want to know everything about Monsieur Kaplan. Perhaps you can handle that personally and quietly, Capitaine, if you don't mind."

Heuse nodded. "As a matter of fact, I've been keeping an updated file on him ever since our encounter several years ago. You know, he was one of the two men who helped stop a terrorist attack at the Louvre."

"Not stop it, Capitaine. That attack happened. Rather those attacks happened. The Louvre and the Eiffel Tower. All he did was mitigate some of the impact and help us take down the associated terrorist cell, but make no mistake, those attacks did occur." She paused. "I'd like to see that file, Capitaine."

"Certainly Colonel. It's in my office in Versailles."

CHAPTER 22

Hotel d'Angleterre
Bourges, France

Kaplan watched Welch unlatch his leather messenger bag
and retrieved a file folder. Then Welch took out another,
thicker folder. On the outside, he recognized the familiar CIA
dossier label with *TOP SECRET* stamped across it. He also
recognized the name on the folder and all the pieces fell into
place—*OPERATION TURNCOAT.*

The name was not Curtis Benoit, but a code name now
spoken only in the dark recesses of the CIA in McLean,
Virginia. He'd read about the man and his treasonous acts from
the CIA brief sheets. Never seen a picture. The man was a self-
proclaimed whistleblower, although most in the Intelligence
Community, or I.C. as it was called on the inside, saw him
as a traitor. The United States officially labeled him a traitor
and had filed charges of treason against the man under the
Espionage Act of 1917 along with theft of government property
and revoked his passport. Very similar actions were taken
against Edward Snowden. But this man was a bigger threat
to national security than Snowden ever was. He knew more,
had stolen more. In the CIA's opinion, Snowden was a small
fish compared to this man. His name was Matthew Wolfe, aka
Turncoat as coined by the CIA's enforcement division.

Before Welch could speak, Kaplan pointed to the dossier
and said, "Word on the street is Wolfe sought asylum in
Iceland."

"You knew who you were after then?"

"Wait. Time out," Moss interrupted making the time-out hand signal. "Who's this Wolfe dude?"

Kaplan raised a *wait a second* finger at Moss and said to Welch, "I've never seen Wolfe before, just know his reputation." Kaplan opened the dossier and showed the picture to Moss.

"That's Curtis Benoit," Moss said. "This guy is really someone named Wolfe?"

"Matthew Wolfe," Welch explained, "is a traitor not unlike Snowden. The Intelligence Community has gone to painstaking measures to keep this out of the press. Especially his picture. He's considered an HVT."

"What's an HVT?" Moss asked.

"High value target," Welch replied.

Kaplan chimed in, "If he was in Iceland, how'd he get to France? Why didn't you just nab him in Iceland?"

Welch continued, "We tried to covertly detain him, but Iceland exercised its autonomy and sovereignty with regard to Matthew Wolfe and refused extradition after our government's request. We have it on good authority he secreted away to France after the woman he was living with in Iceland was murdered by foreign actors. We don't know who but have our suspicions. We have credible intel he's here. In France. Problem is, so do a lot of other interested countries. And they all want to get to him first. He stole top-secret information that we can't allow to fall into our adversaries' hands. Not to mention the money he pilfered from black offshore accounts and stashed away with such deep concealment we might never recover all of it. Turncoat has a *Capture Alive* order on him issued by Director Reed."

"He's here, Alan," Kaplan said. "He doesn't look quite the

same." Kaplan tapped the picture. "Hair's longer, grayer and he's growing a beard—"

"You've seen him?" Welch interrupted.

Moss was nodding.

"This morning," Kaplan admitted. "At the P.A.P.A.C.Y. protest in front of the cathedral. He was standing next to the stage."

Moss interjected, "Right before that blonde woman dragged me off in her paddy wagon."

"Wait," Welch shouted. "He's here? In Bourges? And you're just now telling me this?" Welch's face turned red. "What the hell, Gregg?"

"This is on you, Alan. I couldn't tell you what I didn't know." Kaplan put his elbows on his knees and leaned toward Welch. "If you hadn't been playing this bullshit game with us, we'd have him by now and I would've called it in to David Pearson. But worst of all, you involved the GIGN in this matter. Do they even have a clue who we are after or did you lie to them too?"

"We have to go back to the cathedral," Welch insisted not answering Kaplan's questions. "We have to try to locate Wolfe."

"Do you honestly believe Wolfe is still hanging around after watching the Gendarmerie haul us off?" Moss asked. "I guarantee he's long gone."

"We have to try," Welch said.

"You know Alan, you really screwed the pooch on this one."

Welch nodded. "I should have brought you in sooner. I know that now."

"Damn straight. And not played this bullshit shell game."

"Shell game? Maybe if you'd faced the truth about Isabella from the beginning and stayed active with me, I wouldn't have had to play games to get you here to do your damn job. You know she'll never recover."

Kaplan came out of his chair and moved toward Welch. "You piece of…"

Moss jumped up and stood between Kaplan and Welch. "Whoa. Taking a punch at your handler won't help us catch this asshole."

"Look Gregg," Welch said. "I know you loved Isabella. I apologize."

Moss kept his stare on Kaplan. "You okay?"

It took a couple of minutes for him to calm down. He'd been with Alan Welch for many years and Welch had always been a straight shooter. The callousness of his remark caught Kaplan off guard. It hit a nerve. He recalled something the man who recruited him into the CIA many years ago, Admiral Scott Bentley, had said to him, *the worst lies are the lies we tell ourselves.* He knew Welch was right. He'd already been facing that reality. He had been lying to himself or stuck in some state of denial. It just didn't sit well coming from someone else.

Moss sat back down. Kaplan stood unsure of what to say next.

Finally, Kaplan looked Welch in the eye and said, "Just stay out of my way, Alan. We'll find Wolfe."

Welch gave a sharp nod. "Whatever support you need, it's yours." He picked up a small nylon duffel from the floor next to his chair and tossed it to Kaplan. "You'll need these."

Kaplan unzipped the bag.

Inside were their weapons.

Before he and Moss walked out, he cautioned Welch, "Don't ever mention Isabella's name to me again."

CHAPTER 23

A fter Kaplan and Moss left Welch at the hotel they walked the short distance to the Cathedral of St. Etienne.

The plaza was empty except for a few wandering locals and tourists. Nothing left behind that a protest ever took place.

No random flyers strewn about.

No trash in the plaza.

Nothing.

Almost as if it never took place. But it did take place, he was there. He saw Wolfe, aka Curtis Benoit, aka Turncoat, with his own eyes.

Moss rotated 360 degrees with his palms up and said, "What gives?"

"Hell of a damn clean-up crew."

"Got any ideas how we can pick up Wolfe's trail again?" Moss asked.

"I have a few," Kaplan said. "Well, one."

"Okay, you gonna to tell me or keep me in suspense?"

"Since we aren't on the run from the law we have the luxury of taking our time. I say we go back to the B&B where we stayed last night."

"Right," Moss jumped in. "And wait for the bartender with the man-bun to return. Good idea."

Walking back to the car, Moss asked, "Why is this whistleblower so important? Is he more of a security threat than Snowden?"

"One of Wolfe's specialties was his knowledge of the global satellite and nuclear picture. He wasn't just your ordinary hacker geek. Ever hear of Stuxnet?"

"Vaguely."

"Wolfe was instrumental in Stuxnet, it was a joint U.S.-Israeli cyber-attack on Iran's nuclear program. It was just a small part of an overall nuclear hacking operation known as *Nitro Zeus*. The targets of it were power plants, transport infrastructure and air defenses. Wolfe was able to get the Stuxnet virus implanted in the computer system of Iran's uranium enrichment plants which in turn destroyed several of their centrifuges. In so doing slowed Iran's progress toward their nuclear weapons program. Also, Wolfe is *the* authority on Saudi Arabia's secret nuclear weapons program, thus Iran has an even larger interest in Wolfe. And if Iran wants Wolfe, you can bet Israel's Mossad will go to great measures to ensure Wolfe never falls into Iran's hands. I'd bet Mossad's interest is strictly *kill on sight* if the Iranians get close. And we already know first-hand the Russians are involved. And why wouldn't they be? Getting Wolfe would escalate Russia to the forefront of nuclear weapon domination."

"Holy crap," Moss said. "Who doesn't want this guy?"

"This is that top-secret shit our government doesn't want anyone to know about. Wolfe apparently feels like we're treading on dangerous territory with our nuclear program. He has a theoretical doomsday outlook and wants to expose all the nuclear powers."

"So, Wolfe's a good guy?" Moss interjected.

"Depends on your point of view. Some admirable ideals I guess, but naive methods that to me seem questionable. Plus, what he has done is still classified as treason by our government."

They reached the car and both men folded into their seats. Kaplan started the car. He noticed the weather was changing.

A high cloud cover had rolled in and the temperature was dropping.

He continued, "But they are his ideals and not shared by the Intelligence Community. Or the DoD. He's viewed as a threat to national security. There's something else." He paused for effect. "Something that makes him more of a threat...and more desirable for our unfriendly foreign actors."

"What's that?"

"He was an integral part of the secret operations of the NRO."

"The NRO? You mean like in National Reconnaissance Office? The operators of your *eye in the sky* network?"

"Yeah. And Wolfe has intimate knowledge of not only our satellite system, but all the world's satellites. Seriously. Everything anyone has put up there in orbit. All trajectories. All orbits. He knows owners and orbital locations. And their capabilities. Which are communications, which are commercial, and which are military. Between his work with the NSA, CIA, and most recently the NRO, his brain is a treasure trove of top secret, classified intelligence. Can you imagine what would happen if Russia got hold of the knowledge he possesses? Or China? Or even North Korea?"

"Or Iran?" Moss chimed in.

"Exactly. Speaking of Iran, as I mentioned Wolfe is *the* authority when it comes to the secret Saudi nuclear weapons program. It is a commonly held belief he knows as much or perhaps more than most Saudi officials or engineers about their own program. And, according to the file Alan gave us, the Crown Prince has gone so far as to put a contract on Wolfe."

"That complicates matters."

"Right. I doubt China or North Korea care too much about

Wolfe, but I could be off about that too. North Korea's dictator is too focused on his own nuclear program. You know, harassing South Korea and the U.S. with all those nonsensical missile shots into the ocean. It's nothing more than political taunting. And who really knows what China might be interested in but it's doubtful they would send anyone after Wolfe."

"Why is that?"

"There's an old joke that goes like this—if the mission was to steal a ton of sand from a particular beach, the CIA would devise an elaborate scheme including a submarine to sneak in and steal it all at once. China on the other hand, would send a million people to bag a handful of sand and return to China."

Moss snorted.

"What makes Wolfe even more dangerous is he has an ax to grind. Similar to Snowden, he feels the world should possess the same knowledge. Level the global playing field. He believes if every citizen of every nation on Earth possesses the same knowledge then that's the first step to world peace. What he's done, though, is create a race for global superiority. If one country is able to acquire Wolfe's secrets then they could dominate the world."

"You're right about him being naive."

"More like the first step toward M.A.D."

"M.A.D.?"

"Mutually assured destruction. I think that's why Alan went to all this trouble to keep Wolfe away from our enemies. As smart as Wolfe is, he has his faults and weak spots. And that is what these other foreign nationals will use to get to him. And get what he has."

"What does he have?"

"He downloaded top-secret data from the NSA, NRO and

CIA servers. Many terabytes of sensitive data. I don't know, maybe it's stored on a hard drive he tucked away for safe keeping. I just know he stole it from the U.S. Government."

"Then we have to get to Wolfe first," Moss added.

Kaplan pointed to the folder Welch had given him. "Look in the file Alan gave us...the thick one. Read his profile. Wolfe spends a lot of money on women, that's his chink in the armor—women. He's a whore dog. And although he likes all women, he really has a thing for foreign women. His profile shows whom he chose on those dating apps back in the United States. His reputation is that of a womanizer. Been his pattern since his college days. Twenty years later, he's still as bad as he ever was, maybe worse."

Moss flipped open the folder and scanned the pages with his index finger. "You're right. You think some of our enemies have sent honeypots to get close to him?"

Kaplan laughed. "Honeypots aren't used anymore like you might be thinking, but it is possible, perhaps quite probable that our enemies have sent women to get close to Wolfe. Our allies too."

"Our allies? Seriously?"

"Sure. Germany, France, Britain, Israel. I'm sure they all have interest in Wolfe's knowledge. How aggressively they would pursue him remains to be seen. Any hesitation to get involved would be to avoid jeopardizing their relationships with the U. S."

While Kaplan drove toward Saint Just and the B&B where they stayed last night, Moss was silent reading Wolfe's file.

He closed it and said, "Is it true what Welch said? Are you still on the CIA payroll?"

"I've been on the federal payroll for well over 20 years

in one capacity or another and have rarely taken sick leave. Needless to say, I've accumulated a lot of leave. When I left last year, I gave instructions to burn my sick leave then process my retirement papers. Yes, I'm still on the payroll. But in the same way you were with the Marshals Service until your retirement."

Moss said nothing, but Kaplan could see him in his peripheral vision. Staring at him.

"I guess when I said I quit that was a little misleading. I am still technically employed. Is that a problem for you, Moss?"

"Hell no, not by me." Moss laughed. "One question though. With what we now know after talking to Alan, do you think the Russian's presence in Beaune, Spike I mean, has anything to do with Wolfe?"

"It has everything to do with Wolfe," Kaplan answered. "And whoever took shots at us is still out there looking for Wolfe."

"As I said Kaplan, we better get to him first."

CHAPTER 24

"Didn't think we'd be coming back here," said Moss.

The B&B was the same one they stayed in last night. Same one where Man-Bun worked as a bartender, thus the reason for their return. Man-Bun was their only lead, their only remaining link to the P.A.P.A.C.Y. protest from earlier today. And Kaplan thought their last chance to pick up the trail of Matthew Wolfe, aka Curtis Benoit.

Kaplan and Moss approached the desk in the downstairs lobby. The old innkeeper's face gleamed with recognition.

"Ah, messieurs, you have returned," the man said to Kaplan. "Would you care for the same rooms?"

Kaplan ignored the man's request. "The young bartender from last night—"

"Pierre Bouquet," the man injected.

"Yes, Pierre," Kaplan smiled pretending he knew the bartender. "Last night he invited us to the protest in Bourges, but—"

The old man cut in again. "Oui, such a sad thing that happened to him when he was a child. Can't say I blame him for his anger toward the Church. So many demons haunt him every day. Demons he struggles to deal with."

"I'm sure," Kaplan said in agreement. Although it didn't take much imagination to figure out. Probably something Pierre was saying on stage while Kaplan was being escorted away by Heuse. "Like I was saying, Pierre promised to meet with us at the protest, but we could never locate him. Will he be working tonight?"

"Sorry monsieur, Pierre called a few hours ago. He had another episode after the rally and his sister has already moved on to the next venue. She is director of the French Division of P.A.P.A.C.Y."

"His sister?" Kaplan's interest was piqued. "Was his sister the woman who introduced him at the protest yesterday?"

"I do not know, monsieur, I was not there. She has many who work for her, a team of volunteers and paid staff. But since the rally was here it is likely Sophie did introduce him."

"Does his sister live around here?"

"No monsieur, Sophie lives in Paris where she runs P.A.P.A.C.Y. from her home office near Montparnasse. Pierre lives not far from here." He paused. "Those demons I mentioned. Never know when they will raise their ugly head. Pierre won't be back in until tomorrow night." The man pulled out a tin box filled with index cards. "I was about to call another bartender in for tonight."

Kaplan knew better than to ask the innkeeper for Pierre's address but he had a plan he was pretty sure would work.

"Perhaps I can catch Pierre another time." Kaplan reached in his front pant pocket for his wallet. "Same rooms as last night would be perfect."

Moss shot him a sideways glance.

He handed the innkeeper enough cash to pay for another night's stay in the two rooms. The man handed him a key and held one out for Moss. The two men took the stairs to their rooms.

Kaplan followed Moss into his room, went in the bathroom, unrolled way too much toilet paper for the commode, tossed it in and flushed. As expected, it clogged.

"What the hell, man?" Moss grumbled.

Kaplan explained his plan.

A moment later, both men were again standing in front of the man behind the counter in the lobby. He explained the situation to the innkeeper and then turned to Moss. "I'll get our bags while you handle this."

He walked out the door and threw a glance over his shoulder, the innkeeper was following Moss up the stairs.

Perfect.

When Kaplan returned with the luggage, the innkeeper was walking down the hall toward the stairs with a plunger in his hand. Kaplan nodded. "Merci," he said. *Thank you.*

"De rien," the man replied. "I told your friend you can't use a lot of paper in these old toilettes."

Moss swung open the door when Kaplan knocked. He stepped inside and tossed the big man's bag on the bed.

"You get it?" Moss asked.

Kaplan held up his phone with a photo of an index card. "Let's go pay Pierre Bouquet a visit."

† † †

Pierre Bouquet lived in an older apartment complex just west of the Bourges airport. Two quadraplex buildings per block. Kaplan checked his note, comparing it to the address on the wall next to the single garage door. A red Mini Cooper was parked outside the garage. Next to it, a black Mercedes. In front of the Mercedes, a six-foot gate leading to a patio which, as far as he could tell, was the only access point to the apartment unless there was a rear door leading from some sort of common space behind the single-level units.

On the wall below the unit number was a doorbell with an

attached speaker.

He decided to drive around the complex, if for no other reason than to get the lay of the land and perhaps gain some insight as to the apartment complex design. He drove to the end of the street and turned left.

It was a dead end.

The last apartment unit had a low gate and he found himself peering down a long greenway back in the direction of the entrance to the complex. It appeared the greenway served as every unit's backyard. He made a U-turn and headed back toward #5, Pierre Bouquet's apartment. He was caught off guard when he saw a Middle Eastern woman opening the driver's door to the Mercedes at Pierre Bouquet's apartment.

"Shit," he muttered. He held his hand against the rearview mirror to shield his face when the woman looked in their direction. She was lean, bordering on skinny, with long black hair, olive complexion and big dark eyes. She was dressed in black jeans, white blouse and a short black leather jacket.

Kaplan cruised past Pierre's apartment, turned left and out of sight of the Mercedes.

Moss asked, "Who was that woman? You look like you just saw a ghost."

"A ghost I didn't count on. That's Jasmine Habibi, she's a MOIS agent."

"MOIS?"

"Iran's Ministry of Intelligence and Security."

"A spy?"

Kaplan said nothing. He whipped the car around, pulled to the corner and stopped.

"Dammit Kaplan, talk to me."

"Yes, she's a spy. An Iranian honeypot, like you called them, sent here to find Wolfe no doubt. She totally fits his dating app profile of preferred woman types. But she's no ordinary spy. She's one of the world's most ruthless spies." He inched the car forward and saw the black Mercedes turn away from them and exit the apartment complex. He hit the accelerator and headed for Pierre's apartment. "If she paid Pierre a visit and he was home then he's probably dead."

"Body count's going up."

"Jasmine never leaves witnesses. And if she's here, then Pierre is somehow connected to Matthew Wolfe, aka Curtis Benoit."

"Or his sister is," Moss added.

Kaplan parked in the spot vacated by the Mercedes. Both men jumped from the car, weapons drawn and headed for the gate. It was unlocked. In tandem, both men hustled into the patio and through the door to unit #5.

Pierre Bouquet, aka Man-Bun, was unconscious on the floor with an expanding puddle of blood around his chest.

"Shit," Kaplan muttered as he rushed toward Pierre. He knelt down on a knee and felt Pierre's neck for a pulse. He looked up at Moss who was standing next to him. "Weak, but alive." He ripped open Pierre's shirt. A gunshot wound to the chest. "Missed his heart, but not by much. Grab me a towel or something."

Within seconds, Moss threw him a hand towel. Kaplan used it to put pressure on the wound. "Look around, Moss, see if you can find what Jasmine was after."

"Isn't *he* what she was after?"

"Maybe," Kaplan answered.

Less than a minute later, Moss returned. "Must be my luck in France for finding phones. Found this under the sofa." He held up an iPhone. "But this one's locked."

Kaplan picked up Pierre's right hand. "Start with the thumb, then forefinger. See if either of those unlock it."

Moss checked both. "Nope, still locked. Says it doesn't recognize the fingerprint."

"Do his other hand, maybe he's a lefty."

Ten seconds later Moss called out, "Got it, left forefinger. Uh oh, this is not good."

"What?"

"His contact list was open...to this address." Moss held up the phone for Kaplan to see.

It was an address in Paris.

And it belonged to Sophie Bouquet.

"Take over for me," Kaplan said. "I need to make a phone call."

Kaplan and Moss swapped places. Now the big man was holding pressure on Pierre's chest wound. "That Jasmine bitch made a mistake assuming he was dead," Moss said.

Kaplan took out his phone and thumbed in the number.

"Gregg," the voice on the other end said.

"Alan, listen carefully and do exactly what I ask." He talked to Welch for two minutes, then texted two addresses to his phone. He grabbed Pierre's phone and texted Sophie's address to himself. He found two belts in Pierre's bedroom, linked them together end to end. He snatched a bath towel, folded it four times and returned to Moss. "Here put this on top of the rag and lift Pierre."

Moss lifted Pierre's unconscious body while Kaplan slipped the belts underneath. Next, Kaplan strapped the belt over the towel and pulled the belts tight, notching it as tight as he could.

"That'll have to do," he said to Moss. "Welch called an

ambulance. Come on, we need to go."

Before Moss stood, he said to Pierre, "Hope you make it, buddy."

Inside the car Moss asked, "Where we going in such a rush?"

"Paris. And I hope we get there in time."

CHAPTER 25

Avenue du Maine
Montparnasse, Paris, France
Three hours later

Kaplan had tried numerous times to contact Sophie Bouquet by phone but there was never an answer. He tried with his phone and with Pierre's, which he had slipped in his pocket before they left Pierre's apartment.

He explained everything to Alan Welch before he and Moss left Bourges for Paris. Welch dispatched a team to Sophie's apartment. Kaplan was certain Jasmine Habibi would go there. Sophie's life was in danger. It was a distraction from finding Matthew Wolfe, but he couldn't allow himself to sit idly by when he knew Sophie Bouquet might meet the same fate as her brother. Welch had called emergency services to Pierre's address. He was still alive, now unconscious at a Bourges hospital. Welch informed him he had not been able to contact Sophie either. Welch put a tracer on her phone but it couldn't be located and his men didn't get an answer when they knocked on her door, so he instructed them to wait until Kaplan arrived.

He understood why Jasmine Habibi was looking for Pierre, simply the same reason he and Moss were. But why drag Sophie into it? What was her connection? Unless Wolfe's presence at the protest had something to do with P.A.P.A.C.Y. And since Sophie was director of France's division of P.A.P.A.C.Y., maybe there was a connection he was missing.

When he and Moss arrived at Sophie's apartment, two of Welch's agents were waiting downstairs with another two men posted at her door. The team leader informed him Welch had given them strict instruction not to enter explaining it was a matter for the local police.

"You and your team can leave now," Kaplan said in no uncertain terms. "We'll take it from here."

Kaplan approached the door and checked to see if it was locked. It was. He stepped back and kicked it open with one blow. Wood splinters flew as the lock broke through the door jam.

They entered and did a rapid search of the apartment.

No Sophie Bouquet.

Somebody got here before them as the apartment had been ransacked. Drawers emptied, bookshelves cleared, furniture overturned. Someone was searching for something. He wondered if they found it. He and Moss continued to search through the mess in the third-floor apartment while Welch's men remained outside in the hallway. In the bedroom Kaplan discovered Sophie had a live-in boyfriend. Men's clothes in her closet. He wondered where Sophie Bouquet and her boyfriend were.

Were they here when the intruder arrived?

Walking around an overturned chair something caught Kaplan's eye, a small book with a folded yellow piece of paper stuck in the pages as if used as a bookmark. He recognized the shade of yellow. It was the same shade as the P.A.P.A.C.Y. flyers he'd seen at the B&B and the protests. He retrieved the book from under the bed and placed it on the mattress. He pulled out the paper and opened it. It was another flyer, like all the others except the date and location was different.

P.A.P.A.C.Y.
Join the revolution!
Rally begins at 10:00 a.m.
La Cathédrale de Bayeux

Then in small print near the bottom of the page in English:

Parishioners Against Priests Abusing Catholic Youth.

Exactly the same as the one in Bourges, except for two major differences. This one was to be held in Bayeux instead of Bourges.

And the date of the protest was tomorrow.

CHAPTER 26

Hotel d'Argouges
Bayeux, France

They were back in the car heading from Paris to Bayeux in darkness. As Kaplan had anticipated, the balmy January weather of the past two days was a precursor of things to come. The wind had shifted from the north and increased in intensity before they left Paris. Cloud cover was thick and the sky dark well before sunset. The farther west and northwest they drove, the temperature dropped. By the time they reached Bayeux, it was snowing. A light snow, but snow nonetheless.

He briefed Welch on what he'd found at Sophie Bouquet's apartment and that he and Moss were almost to Bayeux. Welch said he was on his way back to Paris and should be there before Kaplan made it to Bayeux.

"I can't be of much assistance to you unless I'm in the Paris command center," he explained.

Kaplan could hear the road noise through the phone.

"I should be in the office in forty, check in when you get to Bayeux."

"I'm pulling into town now."

"Argouges?"

"Where else?"

"Great. Say hello to Frederic and give me a heads up when you get moving in the morning."

"Roger that."

Kaplan pulled into a hotel he'd used in the past, simply

because it had once been used as a CIA safe house and he knew the proprietor. A family business handed down after the man's father passed. Although it currently functioned as a five-star hotel, it had also been used by the American Intelligence Community since the end of World War II. A debt the father felt he owed to the United States and remained passionate about until his death.

Hotel d'Argouges was named for its builder—Lord d'Argouges. The hotel had a small chateau ambiance with private gardens and upscale public spaces originally serving as an 18th century residence.

Kaplan and Moss climbed the steps to the main entrance. Each step in the new fallen snow squeaked under their shoes. Kaplan knew the owner who was manning the check-in desk. A personal touch his father had instilled in him.

Kaplan greeted the owner in French. "Things haven't changed much around here. Still working the desk at night, I see."

Frederic's eyes showed delight in seeing an old acquaintance. "Ah, Monsieur Gregg," Frederic said in English. "What has it been, four, five years? What brings you to Bayeux?"

"Business. We need a couple of rooms, Frederic. Got any vacancies?"

"Hmm." Frederic studied his guest log. "I have a large tour group staying here for a couple of nights, just got here today from their tour of the Normandy beaches. Tomorrow their tour guide has them going to the Tapestry Museum, among other things. The only rooms I have available are the basement rooms in the Garden House around back. You know the ones I'm talking about, right?" Frederic gave Kaplan a wink. "They haven't been used in a while, but they're clean with fresh linens for, um…unexpected guests." He lowered his voice to a whisper. "And since you're here on *business*, can I assume I'll be billing at the McLean rate?"

"Never miss a chance to make an extra buck, eh Frederic?" He reached into his pocket and held out Alan Welch's card. "Take a picture of this with your phone. That's to whom and where you'll send the bill."

"Merci." Frederic held his phone up. "Latest and greatest from Apple. Has three camera lenses. Takes great pictures at night too."

Kaplan shrugged.

"Wait, let me guess," said Frederic with a chuckle. "You still have that archaic flip-phone like old people carry."

Moss laughed. "Got you pegged."

Kaplan laid his flip-phone on the counter. "It works. Oh yeah, and I have one of these, too." He slid a hand in his coat jacket, pulled out a phone and placed it next to his flip-phone. "Latest and greatest from Apple."

Frederic smiled and said, "Touché. You should always have backup."

The proprietor placed two keys on the counter. "Off the books as usual?"

"Please," Kaplan replied.

"Any, *special requests*?" Frederic asked.

"Not at this time, we came well equipped."

Kaplan swiped up the keys in one hand and said to Moss, "Let's go."

Walking down the stairs Moss said, "Special requests? You sure got a lot of connections in this part of the world."

"Comes in handy, especially with these assignments."

"I've got a special request."

"What's that?"

"I'd like a clean change of clothes. These are beginning to stink. All our clothes are in our duffels back in Bourges at the B&B."

Kaplan stopped. "Shit. Guess I'll have requests after all."

He drove through the archway beneath the hotel to the parking lot in the back. He pointed to a separate building with the front facade covered in green ivy outlining the windows as it crawled up to the roof. "This is us, the Garden House." Kaplan glanced at his watch—2100 hours—no wonder he was hungry. "What do you say we find our rooms then meet back at the car in ten and go find some food."

"Thank goodness. I thought you were on a diet or something. I'm starving."

† † †

The restaurant was crowded even at this hour of the night. Most patrons were drinking although a few were still dining. They were seated at a table with a clear view of the packed bar. Kaplan ordered food again for both he and Moss since the waiter spoke no English. Nothing exciting, just enough to tide them over until morning when Frederic would prepare a gourmet breakfast guaranteed to sate even the hungriest of appetites.

The food came fast and they ate fast. Moss ordered Duyck Jenlain Ambrée, a French beer and Kaplan ordered his drink of choice, Jameson Irish Whiskey and ginger ale with a wedge of lime. He was tired. It had been another ordeal of a day, like yesterday, but longer. They got lucky finding Wolfe the first time. But he knew Wolfe would be more careful now.

And complicating the search, he and Moss needed to locate Sophie Bouquet before she met the same fate as her brother. He didn't know if she had been notified her brother had been attacked and was in a hospital. There was still no answer on her phone and Welch informed him thirty minutes ago that his techies haven't seen it come back active. There could be a basic explanation for it, such as a lost or broken phone, dead battery or there could be a sinister explanation—she had already been captured...or killed. All he knew was she was supposed to be at the protest tomorrow morning. He'd find her, tell her what happened to her brother and keep her safe from Jasmine Habibi.

It appeared Habibi was following the same trail as he and Moss. Pierre Bouquet spoke at the protest in Bourges. Matthew Wolfe, aka Curtis Benoit, was seen at the protest wearing a P.A.P.A.C.Y. shirt. Habibi obviously collected Sophie's address from Pierre's phone the same way Moss did. She must have had a team in Paris since Sophie's apartment was ransacked before Welch's team could get there. According to Welch, no one had gone in or out of Sophie's apartment for at least two hours prior to Moss and Kaplan's arrival. Therefore, someone got there first.

The big question in his mind was whether or not the person who ransacked Sophie's apartment had found the flyer for the Bayeux protest. Another thought occurred to him. P.A.P.A.C.Y. was an organized protest group therefore their schedule was probably posted on the internet. He did a quick search on his phone and there it was, the entire rally schedule including dates and locale. If someone wanted to find Sophie, they'd be at the protest in Bayeux.

He tucked his phone in his pocket and made his usual

instinctual sweep of the restaurant and bar when he spotted a familiar face at the bar. An unsettling familiar face. She was red headed, a long thick mane, in her thirties with a chiseled jaw, jutting chin and long neck. It wasn't her face that captured a man's attention, it was her strong well-built body. She sat with her typical broomstick posture, shirt cut low displaying her firm breasts.

She was Russian and she was dangerous.

Moss gave him a funny look. "Kaplan. What do you see?"

"Trouble." He reached in his pocket, got his phone and called Welch.

Before Welch could speak, Kaplan started in. "Game's up. I want to know what you aren't telling me. Why am I staring at Tatyana Kazakov?"

"Damn," Welch said. "The Iranians and now the Russians? You sure it's Kazakov?"

"Come on Alan, you know as well as I she's not someone I'd forget. Not after our run-in in Budapest. She looks exactly the same, right down to the scar on her neck. We came here to find Sophie and now this. What's Sophie Bouquet got to do with Wolfe? I want to know what's going on and why do other actors have better intel than us? Habibi and Kazakov both seem to be one step ahead of us. How can that be?"

"I'm not sure," Welch said. "I have a feeling someone is deliberately feeding me bad intel."

"Not good enough, Alan, what aren't you telling me?"

"A few months ago Langley was hacked. Our IT guys said even though Wolfe did an excellent job of removing his trail, he didn't completely erase his digital footprint. That's how they found out about Iceland. Then he disappeared. We all assumed we might never hear from him again. Two weeks ago, he slipped up. He logged onto the servers at Langley, get this, using the director's log-in. As careful as he usually is, we were able to trace his IP address to a specific area of France."

"Beaune?"

"Yes. He used an internet café outside the city wall. That's why you were sent there first. Of course, we had no idea about Sophie or her brother's involvement until you figured it out. Even though we knew about P.A.P.A.C.Y., we didn't connect the dots. As far as the CIA is concerned, P.A.P.A.C.Y. is just another non-violent special interest group. Not our concern nor jurisdiction."

Kaplan could see Moss getting antsy. Then he whispered, "I gotta make a head run." Kaplan nodded. Moss got up and left the table.

Kaplan let his eyes wander back toward Kazakov. She was now staring at him. "I need to go," he said and hung up.

Tatyana Kazakov tossed her head back, licked her lips and smiled at him. She raised her drink glass as if to toast *may the better man win*. She winked.

He stood.

She placed her glass on the bar and stood.

Behind her he saw Moss returning from the bathroom. Kaplan made a move toward Kazakov and nodded to Moss. Moss understood. He saw Moss reach his hand out for Kazakov's shoulder when a blade appeared in her hand.

Kaplan yelled trying to get louder than the raucous crowd. Tatyana Kazakov spun, wielding the knife toward Moss's torso. Kaplan's cell phone vibrated.

When Tatyana arced the knife toward Moss, the big man's arm came down to block. The shiny blade slashed across his left forearm. Across the room Kaplan could see red gush from

Moss's arm. Moss's right fist connected a glancing blow to the side of Kazakov's head as she moved to duck his attack. Kaplan saw her head recoil from the blow and he bolted in their direction.

Several patrons saw what was happening, some screamed, most just backed away, one man tried to stop her. The man seized her arm. She swung toward him thrusting her blade into his midsection near his navel. He let go of her arm, doubled over and fell to the floor, both hands clamping his gut.

Panic and terror erupted causing chaos. He never slowed his sprint toward Moss and Tatyana. Cell phone still vibrating.

Kaplan started to reach for his weapon but stopped. Too many bystanders could get hurt. Kazakov picked up a bottle from the bar and threw it in Kaplan's direction. He ducked. Another bottle flew over his head.

Kaplan stood and pushed his way past patrons as he saw Kazakov execute a quick right punch-kick to Moss's chest and then launched a jumping roundhouse kick to Moss's head. Kaplan heard the crunch of Moss's nose from five feet away. Moss's head wobbled—face covered in blood.

Tatyana bolted to her left, narrowly escaping Kaplan's grasp, sliced her way through the crowd and into the streets.

By the time Kaplan made it outside, Tatyana Kazakov was gone.

CHAPTER 27

Dalton had logged it all in his notebook. After he summarized his thoughts, he would compile his report of today's events as his boss had ordered.

Kaplan and Moss were on the move a lot today. From Bourges to Paris to Bayeux. A lot of driving, but not without incident.

Near the airport in Bourges, he entered a home. Shortly after that he left and then the police and an ambulance arrived. But that wasn't the interesting part for the man to log in his notebook, it was the three women who had been in the same home before Kaplan.

Two of the women he recognized as foreign assets. One Russian and one Iranian. The third woman was a mystery. Coincidentally, Kaplan and Moss had a run-in with the Russian woman here in Bayeux. But she got away albeit with a bloody face. By the time Kaplan made it outside, the Russian woman had escaped into the night.

He held his notebook to the light.

Time to report his observations of the day.

CHAPTER 28

When Kaplan went back inside, Moss was sitting on a bar stool. He had a towel wrapped around his left forearm and held a smaller towel to his nose.

"Who the hell was that red-headed, knife-wielding, crazy-ass bitch?"

"Tatyana Kazakov. A GRU asset."

"T.K. from the text on Spike's phone?"

"Good bet."

"Great. First the Iranians and now the fucking Russians. Or really, the Russian, *then* the Iranians, and now the Russians again. You weren't kidding about this thing getting ugly, were you?"

"Nope."

"Maybe I should've taken Alan up on his offer." Moss tried to laugh but instead winced.

"Not too late."

Kaplan called Frederic and explained what had happened. Frederic insisted Kaplan and Moss return to the hotel immediately and he would make arrangements for Moss to receive medical attention.

"Time to get your ass to a doctor."

After he squared with the restaurant and talked with the police he drove Moss back to the hotel. Frederic had arranged for a doctor to stitch up and bandage Moss's arm. His nose had almost stopped bleeding and the good news was it wasn't broken. The doctor stuffed some gauze inside each nostril and told him to leave it there until the bleeding had completely stopped.

Kaplan's phone started vibrating.

Welch.

Again.

Sixth call in thirty minutes.

He didn't want to deal with him right now, but he knew Alan Welch. If the man was anything, he was persistent. He'd keep calling till Kaplan answered, regardless of the hour.

He answered, "Now's really not a good time, Alan."

"What the hell happened in Bayeux? My team in Paris picked up police chatter about a woman stabbing a couple of people then escaping. Tell me it wasn't a repeat of Budapest with you and Tatyana."

"Not me and Tatyana, no," Kaplan reassured. "This time it was Moss and some innocent bystander who felt the wrath of a scorned Russian asset."

"Moss got stabbed?"

"A gash across his arm and a busted nose. A few stitches and he'll be good as new."

"Who got stabbed? I was told someone was taken to the hospital."

"Just some guy at the bar. Tried to step in when Tatyana knifed Moss. He took it in the gut." Kaplan paused. "I think the police bought my story. Claimed we'd never seen the woman. Said she was acting like she was high on drugs."

"Did you have weapons on you?"

"Yeah, but we didn't use them. Too many innocents in the bar."

"And Tatyana Kazakov? What happened to her?"

"Not much. Moss got in a blow to the side of her head. Probably has a headache and black eye."

There was a long awkward silence. He checked his phone to ensure the connection wasn't lost. "Still there, Alan?"

"Gregg...you and Moss need to be careful."

"I need to get back to Moss, Alan. So, if there isn't anything else—"

"There is one more thing. We tracked an inbound aircraft to Caen, a town about twenty minutes or so east of Bayeux. It's a Mossad jet."

"Not unexpected, is it? I mean, if Iran is involved, stands to reason Mossad has a vested interest."

"It's Eli Levine's jet, Gregg. He sent Marla Farache."

† † †

It was hard for him to describe his feelings for Marla Farache. She was Eli Levine's niece. The Mossad director's niece. He liked Levine and knew the old man liked him. They'd had several encounters in the past, some business, some pleasure, all friendly. More than likely, he'd found favor with Levine after he rescued Marla.

Several years ago she had gone into Egypt to exfiltrate an Israeli tourist who had been captured by Al Qaeda terrorists. During the attempt, Marla was shot. Kaplan was there on another mission, stepped in and pulled her and the tourist to safety after mounting what was, in effect, a one-man rescue mission that resulted in the deaths of their captors. He performed a field triage on her wounds and then carried Marla on his back five kilometers to safety.

That act earned him what had become unending favor with Mossad, and more specifically, Eli Levine. On more than one occasion, he'd felt like Levine was playing Cupid with him and Marla. But the timing had never been right. Looming over him was Isabella. First with her disappearance, and now her lingering medical condition.

What was he thinking?

Deep down he knew whatever there was between him and Isabella was gone forever. She was not now nor would she ever again be the woman he fell in love with. He'd spent the last year of his life hanging on to the past. He had always heard the old phrase *you can never go back*. Nothing could be more true in his case. He couldn't go back. Like Clara had repeated to him so many times over the past few months, it was time for him to move on. It had just been hard for him to see it...or accept it...until now.

He wondered why Levine would send Marla to France and involve her in the search for Wolfe. Last time he saw Marla, she told him Levine had named her Mossad Deputy Director of American Affairs.

He and Marla had had sexual encounters in the past. Brief liaisons. His memory of her still fresh in his mind. Smooth skin, a supple body like a dancer. Wide brown eyes full of mischief and black hair that draped down over her shoulders. Making love to her had left him wanting more. The first time was before she was shot and captured. The second time was a little less than a year later while traveling on the same jet Welch said had just touched down in Caen, France.

He couldn't honestly say he wasn't looking forward to seeing her. He just hoped it wouldn't be under adversarial circumstances. She was here to find Wolfe. His dossier was quite clear about the exiled man's affinity for exotic women. Marla fit that description well. A true definition of exotic beauty.

Now there were at least three foreign actors in play. Iranians, Russians, and the latest, the Israelis. All after the same target. Some with perhaps different motives than others, but albeit after the same person. Mossad would kill before allowing Wolfe to fall into Iran's hands. And the reciprocal was true as well. Russia and the GRU wanted what Wolfe stole from the U. S. Government. That's why they sent Tatyana to get close to Wolfe. He found it amusing that all the foreign assets so far were women sent to capitalize on Wolfe's weaknesses. Not stupid. Always go after your target's weakness. Kaplan knew there were probably others out there lurking in the shadows. Russia never sent an operative in the field on a mission like this without at least two or three layers of backup. A second and third tier of defense. Iran likely sent a team of which Jasmine Habibi would run point. And MOIS might even have backup in place too in case Habibi failed.

Tomorrow could prove to be an interesting day.

CHAPTER 29

The next morning Kaplan awoke early, checked his watch—a little before 0600. The sun was still on the other side of the world. When the sun did find its way overhead, it wouldn't change things much. It would stay hidden behind the thick blanket of winter clouds. He dressed and headed for the front desk of the hotel. He knew Frederic would have fresh coffee in his office and he needed to talk to him before the other hotel guests started making their way to the dining room for breakfast.

He zipped up his leather jacket and raised his jacket collar. It was cold and each breath came out as tiny clouds. Three inches of fresh snow fell overnight and the temperature dropped into the lower twenties. What a contrast from the two previous days. Cold weather and fresh snowfall put an added element of complexity to his task of locating Wolfe.

Last night he called in a favor with Frederic. Actually two. He and Moss needed clothes since theirs were still at the B&B in Bourges. And he needed new *spook kits*. One for each of them. Something Frederic had provided in the past.

A spook kit was usually tailored for specific missions. In this case it would contain a few hard-to-acquire items an operative might need in a foreign country. Essentials, like foreign cash, sterile SIM cards, trauma kit, tracking dots, burner phones—at least two each, folding knife, firearm, ammo, suppressor, and a Leatherman multitool. Optional items he passed over were a taser, pepper spray, and handcuffs, instead opting for Tuff-Ties since they were lighter and easier to pack and carry. He also requested two comm packages with hideaway earbuds—no sense announcing the fact he was an undercover operative. Besides, the others were in the hotel room in Bourges.

He returned to his room, a brisk one-minute walk from the office, and found Moss leaving his room.

"Do you ever sleep?" Moss asked. "Where'd you get the coffee?" A cup in Kaplan's hand, wisps of steam rising from the mug.

"I talked to Frederic. Checked on a few things." He motioned for Moss to follow him into his room.

"I need coffee and food."

"Frederic's bringing breakfast over and more in about ten minutes."

"Clean clothes? Cause these have blood stains on them and…" He tucked his nose into his armpit. "They're getting a little ripe."

"That. And other essentials as well."

"I can hardly wait."

"How's the arm?" Kaplan asked.

"Achy. Sore to the touch." He placed his hand on the bandage. "What is it with you and these crazy women? You coulda warned me, you know."

"No time. And the nose?"

"Hurts worse than the arm. Bleeding stopped and I can finally breathe out of it again."

Frederic arrived and had another man with him. Frederic was holding a tray with two platters of breakfast food. Kaplan's stomach growled.

Frederic faced the other man and said, "Francois, go ahead and get started. I'll be right back with coffee and juice."

Moss took several steps back when Francois approached

him.

Kaplan spoke first. "Francois brought us clothes, Moss. I guessed at your size. Extra tall. Extra wide."

"Oui, monsieur, I have many sizes in my van." Francois pulled out a tailor's tape measure. His English broken, but good. "In a few quick moments, I have you sized. Do you mind, monsieur?" He held up the measuring tape.

Moss turned around and held his arms out to the side.

"Monsieur, that not necessary. Hands down, s'il vous plait."

Francois measured across Moss's shoulders, back, waist and leg length. "Perfect," he said. "I have everything in van for man your size."

The man left when Frederic returned with an urn of coffee, cups and two nylon duffels over each of his shoulders. He gestured to the food tray. "Just leave this when you are through. I'll have housekeeping pick it up later." He dropped the duffels on Kaplan's bed. "Bill to the same man?"

"Yes, Frederic, that'd be great."

Frederic nodded and left.

Moss grinned. "Alan's going to flip when he gets this bill."

"You heard what Alan said, Moss, 'Whatever support you need, it's yours.' His words, not mine. And we need these."

Moss wasn't looking or listening as far as Kaplan could tell. He was seated in a chair stuffing his mouth with food and washing it down with coffee.

† † †

At 0830 sharp, Kaplan knocked on Moss's door. Moss was in his new clothes. Decked from head to toe in tactical clothing and gear. Frederic had his contact equip them both with three days' worth of clothes and undergarments. The tactical clothing came from the same manufacturer that made tactical wear for military and law enforcement. Fortunately for them, the special street-styling would allow them to blend in and not look military or law enforcement. Tactical pants, plenty warm for today's cold weather. Each man was outfitted with a tactical parka, different colors, again not obviously tactical but very utilitarian in function. Plenty of hidden pockets with quick access to weapons. One of those hidden pockets housed the voice-activated comm system Kaplan had requested with a hidden microphone sewn into the collar of the parka. No push-to-talk button. No speaking to your sleeve.

"Now this is what I'm talking about," Moss said.

"Yep, Frederic knows how to deliver."

Kaplan's tactical pants were dark green, Moss's black. The parkas were deliberately unlike the pants in color. Kaplan wore a tan parka while Moss's was a mid-range blue. Kaplan was given a tweed Irish Touring cap while Moss was given a wool beanie to cover his bald head.

In Kaplan's mind, they were ready for work. Both of them packed the small trauma kits in a zippered pouch in the back of their jackets. Firearms secured to their waists with quick access through the parka by a side quick release zipper. A small zipper on the left forearm concealed a foldable quick-open knife.

They looked at each other and smiled.

"Let's do this," Kaplan said. He reached into a hidden pocket. "Turn on your comms."

Moss activated his comms and said, "Showtime.".

Both men walked out into the cold morning air.

CHAPTER 30

La Cathédrale de Bayeux
Bayeux, France
0845 Hours

The cathedral was a massive building as large as the Notre-Dame in Paris. It dominated the small town of Bayeux with its two dark Gothic spires, originally Romanesque in design. It was the seat of the Bishop of Bayeux and Lisieux as well as the original home of the Bayeux Tapestry, which was now housed in its own separate museum just a few blocks away.

Originally built in Norman-Romanesque style architecture, it suffered major damage in the 12th century and was later rebuilt in the Gothic style.

The cathedral was less than a fifteen-minute walk from the hotel, Kaplan noted, even in the snow and cold. The clothing Frederic's contact supplied them with was warm and comfortable. Suitable for today's adverse weather conditions.

On the walk to the cathedral he saw proprietors clearing the sidewalks of snow and ice in front of their businesses, some used shovels, most used brooms. A couple had foresight and had sprinkled the sidewalk with salt pellets.

When the two men arrived at La Cathédrale de Bayeux, P.A.P.A.C.Y. had already begun setting up the stage for the protest on the snow-covered southeast lawn of the cathedral. There were no exposed yellow t-shirts in this weather since every one of the volunteers wore heavy coats and jackets. It was too early for the demonstrators to start assembling, which was the main reason Kaplan wanted to get there early—a chance to speak with Sophie Bouquet alone, tell her about her brother and warn her that others would be looking for her. Also, to see if she had any idea who Matthew Wolfe was…or in this instance his alias, Curtis Benoit.

There weren't many cars on the road at this hour in this weather. A van was parked on the south side of the cathedral along Rue L L le Forestier. The rear door open and two young men were unloading sections of a portable stage while two others were assembling the stage adjacent to the south facade of the chapel. The sky was clearing to the distant north and the wind increasing, meaning dropping temperatures during the day and another cold night ahead.

Kaplan discreetly surveyed the area, memorizing everything from faces to license plates. Sophie was nowhere in sight. He had committed her likeness to memory although Moss had her photo up on his phone while he helped Kaplan scan the area.

"Why don't you just ask one of these dudes where Sophie is? They should know," Moss said.

"Good idea."

Kaplan shuffled through the snow to the stage. Both young men's cheeks and noses were rosy from the cold. Heavy clouds of exhale puffing from their mouths like exhaust from a tailpipe in cold weather.

"May I help you?" One of them asked in French.

"Do you think Sophie will be along soon?" Kaplan made it sound as if he and Bouquet were friends.

The young man held up his gloved hand and pointed down the street to the west. "She went to the coffee shop for coffee and pastries."

Kaplan turned in the direction the young man indicated.

He could see the sign for the coffee shop from where he stood.

"Merci."

"De rien." The man returned to his work.

He and Moss started west on Rue L L le Forestier toward the coffee shop. Although it had snowed three inches during the night, the stone-laid, single-lane road was relatively clear of any snow build-up and almost devoid of icy patches...and pedestrians.

While they approached the corner, he saw two women entering the coffee shop. One with a child on her hip, the other holding the hand of a toddler. A red BMW wagon passed the two women and continued down the street.

To his immediate right, the entrance to the cathedral. Caddy-corner across the intersection was a small plaza.

At the coffee shop, one of the women held the door open for someone to exit. A woman holding a coffee cup carrier in one hand and a paper bag in the other. She wore a knee-length wool coat, light brown with a herringbone pattern. A wool cap pulled over her long brown hair. Late-thirties.

He recognized the face.

Sophie Bouquet.

"That's our girl," Moss said to Kaplan in a hushed voice.

The two men stepped off the sidewalk to cross the street.

Sophie turned to thank the woman just as a white van cut in front of Kaplan causing him and Moss to jump back out of the way. The van stopped abruptly in front of the coffee shop blocking his view of Sophie.

He heard a scream, then the sound of the sliding side door slamming shut. The van sped off, tires squealing as it barreled down Rue des Chanoines.

On the pavement in front of the coffee shop were the

decimated remains of what Sophie Bouquet held in her hands. Smashed coffee cups spilling onto the cobbled stone street and a bag of pastries.

Sophie was snatched right in front of him.

He and Moss ran toward the fleeing van. It was a futile attempt but he had to try.

Rue des Chanoines made a shallow bend to the left as it snaked toward the south.

Then, without warning, a red BMW wagon appeared from a side road to his right and smashed broadside into the van. The same BMW that had just driven past the coffee shop moments earlier.

The BMW kept grinding at the side of the van, tires spinning and smoking, pushing it toward a building in what looked like an attempt to pin the van against the wall.

The van struck a white pylon, the only thing protecting the building from certain major damage. Grinding metal sounds filled the air as the side of the van scraped across the front end of the BMW. The van inched forward, cleared the pylon on its left side, slipped slightly to the right and escaped the force of the BMW.

Steam rose from the front grill of the BMW. It didn't move.

The van accelerated and was soon out of sight.

When he and Moss reached the BMW, he saw the side-curtain airbag was still inflated. Yelling and cursing came from a woman's voice inside the car. Flailing arms beat at the airbag.

He yanked the door open, retrieved his pocketknife from the sleeve of his parka and sliced open the side-curtain airbag releasing the air inside.

Behind the steering wheel, an olive-skinned woman with black hair and rich brown eyes.

Marla Farache.

CHAPTER 31

L ike a scene from a bad dream.

Matthew Wolfe was drinking coffee at a table inside the warm coffee shop while Sophie was getting coffee and pastries for her volunteers on this cold morning. He offered to help her carry the drinks and food, but she refused. "No sense both of us freezing. Stay inside where it's warm and join me right before the rally starts," she told him. And then it happened.

Sophie was taken right in front of his eyes.

Kidnapped.

He saw two people jump from a white van that slid to a stop as Sophie left the coffee shop. A man and a woman. The man could fit in any crowd and be forgettable. But not the woman. She had long red hair and a protruding chin. She looked well defined in her tight-fitting cold-weather outfit. And she had a black eye. The two captured Sophie, knocking the coffee and pastries from her hands, shoved her into the van through the sliding side door and sped out of sight. The entire incident was over in seconds.

He stood to chase after them when he saw two familiar men race after the van. The same two men who were taken by law enforcement at the rally in Bourges yesterday. *What were they doing here and why were they after Sophie?* He walked outside the coffee shop using the other patrons as cover and watched as the two men ran after the van. Then the van and another car were involved in an accident a block down the street. But the van fled the scene and disappeared around the corner.

The two men sprinted down the street and rescued a dark-haired woman from the BMW. From this distance she appeared to be okay. The woman gave the dark-haired man a hug. He saw the two men and the woman engaged in conversation.

Panic set in.

All this time in France and nothing suspicious. Almost boring, which was what he wanted. What he needed. But over the past two days, he had a déjà vu of Iceland and what happened to Serena. Was the same thing happening here? Was he the target or was Sophie? As controversial as P.A.P.A.C.Y. was with all the rallies targeting the Catholic Church, it seemed unlikely anyone would take such extreme measures to stop a peaceful rally.

Or maybe not?

As much as the Church had engaged in sinister practices of silencing critics in the past, this was the 21st century, it would be a stretch to think they were responsible and had kidnapped Sophie.

They had to know a kidnapping would get several law enforcement agencies involved. Not only would an exhausted search be conducted but they wouldn't want all the publicity that came with it.

As much as he tried to rationalize that it had to do with Sophie, deep down he knew it had nothing to do with the controversy that P.A.P.A.C.Y. was protesting at these rallies. They were after him.

He was conflicted. Should he try to find Sophie or take this opportunity to disappear? He knew the location of the next rally scheduled for the day after tomorrow. Perhaps his best course of action was to leave this hotbed and get to the next rally site quietly and covertly. He did have unfinished business there. Or maybe he should just go back to Paris, pack up his belongings and disappear for good.

A tough decision, but he finally made one.

He only hoped whoever took Sophie would do her no harm.

† † †

Kaplan pulled Marla Farache from the wrecked BMW. The impact with the van had bent both front fenders into the tires. Until the fenders were pried away the front tires wouldn't budge.

After he deflated the side-curtain airbag he reached inside and unbuckled her seatbelt. Before he could speak she climbed out of the car and embraced him, squeezing tight around his waist, burying her head into his chest.

"Marla, are you hurt?"

"No, Gregg, I'm okay."

"You two know each other?" Moss asked.

Kaplan nodded. "We go back a few years. Moss, Marla. Marla, Pete Moss."

"Nice to meet you," Marla said to Moss.

"Likewise."

Kaplan added, "Marla is with Mossad."

"Of course she is," Moss said.

When her grip lightened, Kaplan pushed her back. "Marla, what the hell were you thinking? You could've gotten hurt."

A slight smile crept across her face, then quickly faded. "I was trying to stop her from getting away."

"Stop her? Stop who?"

"Tatyana Kazakov. That was her team. Tatyana took Matthew Wolfe's girlfriend."

"What?" Moss exclaimed. "Sophie Bouquet is Wolfe's girlfriend?" He gave Kaplan a puzzled look. "Why didn't Alan share this intel with us?"

"That's a damn good question. He and I need to have another chat," Kaplan said. "But first." He faced Marla. "How did you know Tatyana was going to kidnap Sophie Bouquet?"

"I didn't. When I rode by the coffee shop, I was checking to see if Wolfe was in there with his girlfriend. Then I spotted you and Mr. Moss walking up the street. I went to turn around. That's when I saw the commotion and you chasing after the van, so I tried to intervene and stop them from getting away. After I rammed the van, I recognized Tatyana in the front passenger seat."

"That was a dangerous stunt, Marla."

"All in the line of duty. Isn't that something you once told me?"

He didn't answer at first, trying to process everything. Then he said, "How many players are involved, Marla? And how did you know Sophie and Wolfe were a couple? We didn't get that intel."

She chuckled. "The CIA really let this one fall through the cracks, didn't they?"

It was a rhetorical question. Kaplan knew it. But there was more truth to it than he cared to admit. Alan and his minions had definitely dropped the ball. "Come on Marla, who else is involved?"

"The Russians, Iranians, and an unknown player. As far as I know that's it."

"Chinese?"

"Could be, I guess. We don't know yet."

"And the Israelis," Moss added.

"Mossad is involved merely because the Iranians are here."
She turned to Kaplan. "Have you seen them?"

"You mean Jasmine?"

She wrinkled her forehead. "Yes, Jasmine.

"She was in Bourges, at Sophie's brother's apartment. She
nearly killed him. He's in a hospital in Bourges. Alan reported
he's in bad shape."

"Jasmine didn't do that to Pierre Bouquet, Tatyana did. I
got there as Tatyana was leaving. I found him already beaten
and shot. He wasn't responsive. I found his phone in his
back pocket, pulled up Sophie's address, tossed his phone on
the floor and left. I wasn't in Pierre's apartment more than a
minute."

"Why didn't you take Pierre's phone?" Moss asked.

"Too much activity. I didn't want the phone traced back to
me. Can't be too careful. Jasmine was coming in the apartment
complex when I was leaving. Now Tatyana has Sophie and
soon she'll have Wolfe."

"That red-headed bitch sure gets around." Moss grasped
Kaplan by the arm and pulled him aside. In a low voice he
said, "How come we're the last to know what's going on? Even
Mossad knows more than the CIA and Wolfe was one of ours.
We should be leading the pack, not last in line. I don't know
about you, but last place is not somewhere I want to be."

"I don't like playing catch-up either, Moss." He eyed Marla.
"Keep her company while I call Alan. Our top priority now is
finding where Tatyana took Sophie."

CHAPTER 32

Sophie Bouquet's wrists were strapped to a chair in the middle of a musty cold room. The only furniture other than her chair was a chair facing hers and a small table about three meters to her left. On the table she saw a handgun. Two large men with their arms folded stood like sentinels next to the table. Both men armed.

Her mind couldn't comprehend the whirlwind of what had just happened to her. She had been abducted when she walked out of the coffee shop. A man and a woman shoved her into a white van. Her mouth duct taped, and her hands and feet tied with some rough woven twine that cut into her skin. Within seconds, something crashed into the side of the van. All three people in the van were yelling something in a language that she could only guess was Russian. The van pitched sideways and railed against something, grinding as it inched forward. Both sides of the van caved in toward the interior. Finally, the van lurched forward and sped away. To somewhere, not far. The ride was short. Maybe three, four minutes at most, then she was dragged out of the van, into a vacant house, shoved into this chair and strapped to it.

The large men were intimidating, but not as much as the red-haired woman with a black eye. She was in command, pacing the floor while she talked to someone on her cell phone. The conversation sounded heated. Russian, if that's what the language was, was a harsh language.

Too many questions and thoughts filled her mind. Why was she taken? *Kidnapped* was the better word. What had she done to deserve this? Did this have something to do with her advocacy group, P.A.P.A.C.Y? And what about Curtis, was he okay? He must have tried to come after her. She was sure he'd already called the police. Hopefully they would rescue her soon.

The red-haired woman slammed her phone on the table and stomped in her direction. "Oh merde," Sophie whispered to herself. *Oh shit.*

The woman pulled up a chair, spun it around so the back was facing her and sat down, resting her arms on the seat back. She pushed up her sleeves. A tattoo on her right forearm of a snake biting the head off a man. The woman sat erect in the chair, forearms strong like a gymnast. She had man hands. Her icy blue eyes scorched Sophie to the core causing her throat to tighten. A large scar on her neck couldn't go unnoticed. A dangerous woman, she thought. The woman ripped the duct tape from her mouth. Sophie trembled uncontrollably. Tears welled in her eyes.

When the woman finally spoke, her French was minimal at best, with a strong accent. "Tell me where I find Matthew Wolfe."

"Who?"

"Matthew Wolfe."

"I've never heard of Matthew Wolfe."

The woman reached out and hooked a handful of Sophie's hair, then leaned in close. "Do not make me hurt you. I do you like I do your brother."

"My brother? Pierre? What did you do to Pierre?"

"He refuse talk. I hurt him very bad. Much pain. Hurt you worse if not talk. Now, tell where Matthew Wolfe is?"

"I am trying to tell you, I don't—"

The woman smashed her fist into Sophie's jaw. "I have not

patience. Answer now."

Sophie wailed, "I...I don't know...Wolfe," she struggled to speak through the sobbing.

The woman got up and retrieved her phone from the table. She held up a picture of Curtis in front of Sophie's face. "Matthew Wolfe. Where he is?"

A fleeting moment of hope. She sucked back her tears. "There must be some mistake." She tried to keep her voice calm but couldn't. "That's Curtis, not someone named Matthew Wolfe. It is a mistaken identity. You are looking for the wrong man."

The red-haired woman raised her hand and slapped Sophie. It stung. "No," she yelled. "This Matthew Wolfe." She tapped her forefinger against the phone's screen several times. "Last chance or I hurt you. Where is this man?"

Sophie was paralyzed by her emotions. She couldn't tell this crazy woman where Curtis was.

The woman stood, kicked her chair to the side and buried her fist into Sophie's face again.

Sophie head snapped back, blood oozed down her cheek.

Her ears rang.

The lights grew dim.

Darkness took over.

CHAPTER 33

Kaplan's call to Welch didn't last long. Welch already had his people in Paris with eyes on the situation in Bayeux. The white van had been located a few minutes ago. Tatyana had driven it a short distance to a house on Rue Pierre Trebucien, across the street from a large cemetery named Cimetiére de l'Ouest. The van had backed into the garage. He redirected the call to his comm system and walked back to where Moss and Marla were waiting.

"Tatyana and her team are only two minutes away by car." He studied the red BMW. Steam still rose from the hood and fluid had pooled beneath the front end.

Moss weighed in, "We're not going anywhere in this thing."

"700 meters. Eight minutes walking, four if we run," he said to Moss and Marla. He eyed Marla. "You up for it?"

She cinched her coat. "What are we waiting for?"

He keyed up the Paris station on his comm system. One of Alan's men issued instructions. "Head west on Rue Bourbesneur for one block, then cut through the park.

The trio ran, following instructions. They reached the park only one block away. Kaplan pointed out a walkway leading into the park. "That way."

The park was empty and covered in snow. No tracks on any walkways. As the three approached a statue, he saw it was actually a fountain. Alan's voice crackled in his ear. "Pass the fountain then turn west thirty degrees. You'll exit the park looking directly down Avenue Conseil."

"Roger that," Kaplan said. He yelled to Marla and Moss

who were running two steps behind him, "This way."

They ran down the road, careful not to slip on the snow-covered surface. Alan's voice stayed in Kaplan's ears. "Second road to the left, Rue Pierre Trebucien, seventh garage on the left."

Turning the corner Kaplan said, "Target acquired."

"Gregg, listen carefully," Alan said in a forceful stern voice. "You're to take Kazakov and her team alive. I don't want to deal with the Russians or get embroiled in an international incident."

"Can't hear you, Alan. You're breaking up." Kaplan disconnected from Welch.

"We're not going in easy, are we?" Moss asked.

"Hell no, but we aren't going in guns blazing either. If we have to defend ourselves, so be it. If Tatyana or any of her team goes down in the process—"

"So be it," Marla interrupted. She already had her weapon out and ready. Both men smiled.

They drew closer to the house, it looked like nobody lived there. The exterior was yellow, faded from age and moldy in places. A *For Sale* sign in the front yard. The white van with the caved in sides backed in the garage. Red paint transfer along the right side of the van from Marla's BMW.

"Marla, take the garage. Moss front door. I'll crash the back door. Wait for my signal." He cut across the lawn and into the back yard. Found the back door and never slowed. "On my mark," he said into his comm.

"Now, now, now."

He and Moss crashed through the front and rear doors simultaneously catching Tatyana and her two men off guard. He saw their confusion when ingress came from two directions.

Her men were typical Russian goons— no brains, all brawn. Trained to protect and maim. They were bulked up and slow.

He assessed the room as he entered. Two goons slightly to his left standing next to a table, Tatyana in the center of the room, unarmed and facing Sophie who was strapped to a chair, head hanging down. Moss entered the room to his right.

The goons simultaneously went for their weapons. Kaplan yelled, ordering them to stand down to no avail. Both Russians moved away from each other taking aim at their intruders. Kaplan's peripheral registered two things, Moss dropping to his knee and Tatyana spinning toward the door behind her.

Two shots rang out at the same time. Moss and Kaplan got off the first shots. The goon closest to Kaplan fell to the floor, half his skull missing as the pink mist splattered the wall behind him. The other goon, clutching his chest, went down. Not dead...yet. Moss rose from his kneeling position and walked toward the fallen Russian with his gun trained on him. The man said something in Russian, one hand clutching his chest the other still gripping his weapon.

"Don't do it," Moss warned the Russian.

The Russian raised his gun. Moss unloaded two more shots into the Russian. One in the chest and a final shot to the head.

Meanwhile, Tatyana had yanked open the door only to find Marla standing on the other side with her weapon aimed at Kazakov's head. Marla marched her backwards into the room. Kaplan saw Marla was too close but couldn't relay the message to Marla fast enough. Tatyana grabbed Marla's weapon pivoted to the side and turned the firearm outward until Marla had to either release the gun or Tatyana would break her wrist. Now, Tatyana Kazakov had Marla's weapon, using her as a human shield and pointing the weapon at Kaplan.

"I should have known I'd have to deal with you again," she said to Kaplan. She looked at Moss. "How is arm?"

"How's the eye, bitch?" Moss fired back.

"Let her go," Kaplan ordered.

"No." She pulled on Marla and marched her backward, gun still trained at Kaplan. She reached the doorway leading to the garage. Then Tatyana made her move.

She fired a bullet into Sophie, shoved Marla to the floor and stepped into the garage. She took aim at Marla. Kaplan's bullet struck Tatyana in the shoulder before she pulled the trigger, knocking the weapon free. Kazakov clutched her arm and fled through the garage.

CHAPTER 34

Cimetiére de l'Ouest

Kaplan pointed to Sophie. "You two take care of her wound and call for help." Then he raced out the door. Tatyana was at least fifty feet ahead of him and running toward the wall of the cemetery across the street. He'd been in foot pursuit with her many years ago. She was fast. But this time, she was injured and bleeding. Although only a shoulder injury, she was losing blood and eventually it would cause her to slow.

He hoped.

She reached the wall and cleared it with relative ease, leaving only bloody handprints on the top as she scaled it and disappeared on the other side. Kaplan reached the wall three seconds later and pulled himself up and over. He spotted the redhead weaving through the headstones. He hadn't made up any ground.

The cemetery was large considering the size of the town, but then again, it had been here a very long time. It was divided into sections delineated by gravel roads throughout. Clearly some sections were much older than others and it appeared the oldest section was at the far western wall. And that was the direction Tatyana was running. But she wasn't running in a straight line, something he could use to his advantage. From what he could discern at first glance, there was only one way in or out of the cemetery without scaling the wall again and that was the general direction Kazakov was headed. He knew how he could close the gap substantially or perhaps completely.

He turned down the first road and cut behind her while she kept weaving through the plots of tombs, headstones and crypts. By the time she made her turn toward the exit, he had cut her lead to fifteen feet and she was slowing. Her wound leaving a trail of blood. Then she stopped and spun around wielding a knife. He'd been in this situation with her before.

Many years ago.

Same woman.

Different location.

Knife fight. Part two.

Not this time.

He reached into his parka and pulled out his Beretta. "We're not going to do this again," he said tapping his neck bringing her scar to mind. "Remember Budapest? You lost, but I spared your life. Now you're coming with me."

"This time, Gregg Kaplan, you lose. Unlike Budapest, I kill you," she said in her strong Russian accent.

"Don't be stupid. I have a gun, you have a knife."

"You lucky before." Her eyes wild like a trapped animal. "Put gun away, get knife. Fight like man."

"It doesn't have to end this way, Tatyana. Surrender to me now, let my people talk to you. After that, we'll let you go."

"Never. I do not surrender."

"You're injured. Drop the knife and let me help you." Kaplan pulled the slack out of the trigger.

He never heard the sound.

No bang.

No pop.

Nothing.

Tatyana Kazakov's chest exploded in a sea of red. She crumpled to the snow-covered ground.

He spun and ducked, searching the wall and rooftops behind him and saw nothing. No people. No vehicles.

The GRU had been known to stack layers upon layers behind operatives to ensure failures were dealt with swiftly. If they took Tatyana out of play, their top operative, then the GRU might be finished with their attempt to capture Matthew Wolfe.

They might have officially bowed out.

Although he wasn't ready to bet on that.

† † †

Kaplan backtracked his steps to the blood-stained wall. Up and over where he and Tatyana had scaled it earlier. And to the house where the two Russians were dead on the floor exactly where they fell. Marla was tending to Sophie. She had laid her flat on the floor. She was in bad shape.

A large pool of blood had gathered beneath the empty chair.

Moss was nowhere in sight.

"How is she?"

"Fading in and out. As you can see, she's lost a lot of blood."

"Where's Moss?"

"He went to find Curtis Benoit at their hotel."

"We know where Wolfe is?"

Sophie muttered something unintelligible. Marla cut her eyes at Sophie then to Kaplan. "Benoit."

"Right. Where is he...are *they* staying?"

"Hotel d'Argouges."

"That's where we're staying."

"That's what Mr. Moss said too, then he took off out of here without another word."

Sophie made an abrupt sound then her head fell to the side, eyes wide open.

Marla put her fingers on Sophie's neck. She shook her head.

Sophie Bouquet was dead.

CHAPTER 35

While Kaplan and Marla headed back to Hotel d'Argouges, he contacted Alan and explained what had happened.

"You were instructed to take them alive," said Welch. "I told you I needed somebody who could operate under the radar in France. I can't have Director Reed getting wind of this. I can't have this turning into an international incident."

"And I told you that'd I'd do this without you running interference. I can't do my job if I'm dead." He could hear Welch blowing out his breath. "Besides, someone else took out Tatyana. That one's not on us."

"I'll send in the janitors. Now find Wolfe." Welch disconnected.

It was a short but brisk sprint back to the hotel. Marla matched her pace with Kaplan's. It brought back memories when Isabella was his partner. Everything had been a competition with Isabella. Who was the fastest runner, who could locate the target first, who could take the best shot. He missed that rivalry.

Standing on the front steps of Hotel d'Argouges was Moss and Frederic.

"How is Miss Bouquet?" Frederic asked.

"She didn't make it." He looked at Moss. "Wolfe?"

"Gone. Cleared out his stuff from the room. Neither Frederic nor any of his staff saw him leave."

He activated his comm to Alan.

"You got him?" Alan asked.

"Turncoat's in the wind."

† † †

A lot to report today, thought Dalton. He had observed more than his mind could piece together.

A woman was kidnapped in front of a coffee shop in broad daylight by the Russian woman. Kaplan and Moss showed up too late to stop it. Then the getaway van got in a wreck down the street. Kaplan pulled a woman from a wrecked car and then the woman, one he didn't recognize, stayed with them, as if they all knew each other.

Now, at another house, several gunshots followed by the Russian woman running out of the house, jumping a wall into a cemetery where she was shot and killed...but not by Kaplan who was chasing her. By a sniper. Confusing was an understatement. But his job was not to analyze, his superior would do that for him. His job was to track and report.

After Kaplan and the unknown woman left the house, a team of men showed up and hauled out several bodies. This team was not law enforcement, it was a clean-up crew.

He picked up his phone and called it in.

CHAPTER 36

Gendarmerie Nationale
Versailles, France

Colonel Pernille Skouboe looked up as Capitaine Travers Heuse soft knocked on her half open office door interrupting her from reading an email. She was startled when she saw him. His disheveled appearance made him look like he'd been on an all-night drinking binge. His usual tweed jacket gone. As was his tie. His face in need of a shave. This was unlike him to meet with her unannounced looking like this.

Heuse had reached the end of the line, career-wise. Capitaine was the highest rank he would ever hold with the Gendarmerie Nationale. Not because he wasn't qualified, just the opposite. He excelled in his job. But he was *old-school* in a law enforcement agency determined to change its image. He was a casualty of modern and changing times.

Skouboe had recognized the need to reinvent herself years ago and made the adjustments necessary to advance her career. Especially as a woman. And as a Dane. This was something Heuse could never grasp. He was, as she had once heard, the architect of his own downfall. Plus, he was reaching that magic age where he would start receiving pressure to take his hard-earned retirement. Not pressure from her, but from higher up the GIGN food chain. She didn't agree with the new direction the Gendarmerie Nationale was taking, but she didn't disagree either. It *was* time for change, time for a new direction. She just wished it wasn't at the expense of valued and loyal officers like Heuse. And there was something irreplaceable with old school experience in law enforcement. Something many of her superiors couldn't grasp because they were the fresh young faces of the improved GIGN.

"Come in, Capitaine. Please have a seat."

He sat, leaned forward and placed the folders he had carried in on her desk. "Like I mentioned before, I have kept an updated file on Monsieur Kaplan since our encounter several years ago. When Monsieur Moss entered the picture, I started a file on him as well."

"Do you keep files on everyone you encounter, Capitaine?"

"Not everyone. Foreign government assets like Gregg Kaplan, I do."

"I see." She picked up the files, rummaged through them and started reading. Kaplan's file was quite thick. Eight years in the Army after his parents were killed in a traffic accident involving a logging truck. Six of those years in Special Forces. Numerous commendations and medals. He held a civilian federal government job until he was recruited by Admiral Scott Bentley, the then Director of the CIA, where he had been employed ever since. Recently though, he had been classified voluntarily inactive due to personal reasons. According to Heuse's research, Kaplan went AWOL after his CIA partner's sudden disappearance. Apparently he spent well over a year searching for her only to find out she had suffered a severe medical incident that had rendered her with virtually no memory of her past. Some sort of brain aneurysm.

Retired Deputy U.S. Marshal Pete Moss and Kaplan met a couple of years ago while Moss was handling a Witness Protection case that had been breached. While trying to recover his witness, who Kaplan had stepped in to save, Moss and Kaplan joined forces to bring the witness to safety and take down a New Jersey mobster while doing so. The two had been friends ever since. More to the point, they seem to have become crime-fighting partners of sorts. The former WitSec Inspector was a large man at a towering six feet six inches plus. His prominent stature made him easy to pick out of the crowd in Bourges. And that allowed Heuse to locate Kaplan.

"Seems like an odd pairing to me." Skouboe closed the folders and set them to the side.

"As far as I can tell Colonel, it works for them. They appear to function well together." Heuse fished out a small notepad from his shirt pocket. "I have more intel for you," he said. "I did some investigating into Curtis Benoit. That name is an alias. He is not French. His real name is Matthew Wolfe."

"Wait, what?" Skouboe was taken by surprise. "Matthew Wolfe?"

"One and the same."

"I thought he was in Iceland and America was going to extradite him."

"They tried. Then he disappeared."

"Hmm. Seems your hypothesis was correct. Any idea how he got into France without our knowledge?"

Heuse flipped a few pages in his notebook. "The details are sketchy but it appears he might have come in by freighter to Portugal and entered France on false identification via rail service."

"That explains Alan Welch's interest in Kaplan and Moss."

"It also appears Colonel, that Mr. Welch has not been forthright with you about Wolfe."

"He certainly kept this vital piece of information to himself, didn't he?" She opened the next folder in the stack. "What's this about? Who are Pierre and Sophie Bouquet?"

Heuse sat upright, eyes serious. "Alan Welch called in an emergency in Bourges. The report states one of the P.A.P.A.C.Y. volunteers was beaten in his home and left for dead. My guess is Kaplan and Moss found him at his apartment while they were looking for Wolfe."

"So, Messieurs Kaplan and Moss didn't leave France."

"Did you think they would?"

"Not really. Were Pierre and Sophie Bouquet P.A.P.A.C.Y. volunteers?"

"Yes. Pierre is the one in the ICU unit."

"Do we know who did this?"

"The Russians or Iranians are good guesses. Apparently, there is a connection between the P.A.P.A.C.Y. group and Monsieur Wolfe. I believe there are many countries, not just the Americans who would like to find Wolfe."

"And Sophie Bouquet? Wife?"

"Sister. She's the French director of P.A.P.A.C.Y. Her brother lived near Bourges and she recruited him to organize and speak at the Bourges rally."

She tapped on the top page of the file. "How did she get to Bayeux?"

"P.A.P.A.C.Y. just finished a rally there this morning. Our intel has it that the Russians, specifically Tatyana Kazakov, abducted her before the Bayeux rally."

"Tatyana Kazakov? Merde." *Shit.* "What happened to her?"

"An anonymous tip called emergency services, but Sophie was dead when they arrived."

"Kazakov and her team? Where are they?"

"No one knows, Colonel. They have vanished."

"What does the intel say?"

"There is no more intel. Almost like Kazakov and her team never existed."

"But they were there, right? No mistakes with our intel?"

"Our intel was specific. Kazakov and her team were in Bayeux. She went after Sophie Bouquet to get to Wolfe, aka Curtis Benoit."

"Do you think they got him and took off?"

"I wouldn't think so. Everyone else is still looking for him. CIA, Mossad, MOIS…and obviously the Russian GRU."

"I've heard enough." Skouboe stacked three folders and handed one back to Heuse. "Capitaine, I am going to pay a visit to Alan Welch." She pointed to the folder in Heuse's hand. "You are going to Mont Saint Michel. If this P.A.P.A.C.Y. rally gets too worked up, disband the rally and send them away. I want you to personally see to it the Pope's visit is uneventful. Do I make myself clear?"

"Oui."

CHAPTER 37

Wolfe was in the wind.

That was all that mattered.

There was nothing left for Kaplan and Moss in Bayeux. Kaplan knew picking up Wolfe's trail again could prove difficult, especially now that he'd decided to take Alan Welch out of the loop. The CIA had bungled this op from the beginning. Their intel was lousy and that was giving the CIA a lot of undeserved credit. Having intel after the fact made his job impossible. It was time to go rogue.

"What's our next move?" Moss asked.

Before Kaplan could respond Marla interrupted. "Where do you think Wolfe has gone?"

He looked at Frederic. "What type of vehicle was he driving?"

Frederic furrowed his brow. "There was no vehicle. I picked Madame Sophie and Monsieur Benoit up at Gare de Bayeux yesterday. I was supposed to take them back this afternoon to catch the train to their next stop."

"Do you know where they were headed?" Kaplan asked.

"Southwest of here to a town called Rennes," Frederic said. "I heard them mention a day off before the rally at Mont Saint Michel day after tomorrow. It's supposed to be a big event. The Pope will be there. Big security deal. Helicopter in and out. Access road to the island will be closed for a full twenty-four hours. This is a massive event for the French."

Kaplan processed what Frederic had told him. Where would Wolfe go next? He had a few ideas, none of them good. He reached into his parka and disabled his comms. He looked at Moss. "Turn off your comms and your phone."

"What for?"

"Frederic," Kaplan said as he stuck out his hand. "Thank you for all your assistance. I'm sure we'll see each other again someday." He turned to Moss. "Let's get our gear and go." Kaplan walked down the steps toward the Garden House.

Moss yelled to Kaplan, "Just a sec." Kaplan caught what Moss said to Frederic, "Thanks for everything. Next time I'm back, I'll leave him at home so I can relax and just be a tourist."

Kaplan shook his head and grinned.

He waited for Moss at the bottom of the steps. When Moss reached him, they headed toward their rooms. He heard light footsteps running behind them.

"Gregg, wait." It was Marla, but the two men didn't stop.

She ran around in front of him forcing Kaplan to stop. She poked him in the chest with her right hand. "Where are you going? Are you planning on leaving me here after I helped you with Tatyana?"

"You have something else in mind?" Kaplan said.

"Yes, I'm coming with you."

"Tell her Kaplan," Moss said. "We don't need her."

"Not sure we don't need her, Inspector," Kaplan admitted to Moss. "To catch Wolfe, we need to go dark and I'll take all the manpower we can get."

"What do you mean go dark?" Marla asked.

"Disable our phones." He glanced at Marla. "If you come with us, you follow my orders, not Mossad." Marla nodded. "Then disable your phone too. And we only use burner phones from this point forward."

"One more thing," Moss said. "Call me Moss, call me Pete, asshole, whatever, but stop calling me *Inspector.* It sounds condescending when you say it and I don't like it." Then Moss mumbled, "I hope to hell you know what you're doing."

CHAPTER 38

"Okay, okay," Kaplan said. "I didn't know how you felt. I didn't mean to sound condescending. You should have told me before now it bothered you."

"Seriously Kaplan, I've told you like a hundred times, yet you keep on saying it."

"Point made." Kaplan paused. A rough day already. And he knew it would only get worse. He had to decide how to handle Marla. Should he have agreed to let her tag along? He wasn't completely honest when he said they needed all the manpower they could get. Bottom line was, Marla was a talented spy. He didn't *need* her as extra manpower so much as he *wanted* her with him. He didn't realize he was staring at her until she spoke up.

"Gregg." Her voice snapped him back to the present. "We should check out the train station since we're so close, don't you think?"

"Good idea," Moss interjected. "Come on Kaplan, let's get our gear."

Moss and Kaplan loaded the duffels in the small trunk of the car. Marla sat in the backseat behind Kaplan giving Moss plenty of room to push his seat all the way back.

The train station was less than a kilometer from the hotel and the drive took them past the cathedral. P.A.P.A.C.Y. had already broken down the stage and were putting the final pieces back in the van. He checked his watch, 1040. Kaplan stopped the car on the side of the street, got out, and ran over to the volunteers. After a couple of minutes, he returned, got in and started driving toward the train station.

"What was that all about?" Moss asked. "Did you tell them Sophie is dead?"

"No. Just wanted to see where they were going next and if anyone had seen Curtis Benoit."

He drove in silence, offering nothing more.

Moss was staring at him when Marla spoke up. "Well, what did they say?"

"Apparently Wolfe, or Benoit, was to meet Sophie at the coffee shop this morning. Neither of them ever showed. If Wolfe was inside the coffee shop and saw Sophie get abducted, that could explain why he vanished. He must know they weren't after her but using her to get to him."

When they reached Gare de Bayeux, Kaplan wheeled in the lot, parked and the three of them walked to the depot. As they approached the tan building with gray doors, he observed a young man in a red baseball cap trying to manage his luggage and the young child he was holding. Next to the main entrance was a young woman in a yellow coat leaning against the wall, her backpack on one shoulder, red purse on the other, Air Pods in her ears, iPhone in one hand and a cigarette in the other. When he passed by, he could hear her music.

One of the first things he took note of when they reached the entrance was the lack of security cameras on the exterior of the building. And inside, only two. One capturing footage of the ticket counter and the other mounted at the opposite end of the depot. There were a handful of people in the station, two at the counter and five others milling around waiting for the next train, preferring to wait inside rather than stand in the cold. Marla got in line behind the couple at the counter. Kaplan went train-side, no one waiting by the tracks. Wolfe wasn't here.

He waved to Moss. "Mind checking the men's restroom?"

Moss shot him a thumbs up. Kaplan stepped next to Marla as the couple in front of her left the window. Marla bent forward and talked to the attendant behind the counter.

Moss walked up behind Kaplan. "Empty. No sign of Wolfe."

Kaplan moved away from the counter with Moss and pointed to a security camera above the ticket counter. "Wish I could get my hands on that video footage. Make sure he was even here."

"You could call Alan."

"Not an option. If I call Alan and our intel is somehow being compromised then we won't be the first to the party."

"Gotcha. Why don't you show his picture to the attendant."

"Damn, Moss, you are good for something."

Marla cut him off. "Trains only go in two directions from here. West and east. The westbound train will be arriving soon, he couldn't have made the earlier one. Eastbound goes to Caen and then onto Paris. The only train he could've taken was the 0940. That would get him to Paris at 1202. Gives him an hour head start."

"It's a two-and-a-half-hour drive, so there's no way to beat him there. I guess now I've got no choice, I'll have to call Alan and take a chance nobody else gets this intel."

Marla said in a low voice, "I have a jet twenty minutes down the road. We can't beat him to the train station in Paris, but we can beat him to Sophie's apartment."

"Provided, of course, that's where he's headed," Moss added.

"Come on, gentlemen, let's move it," Marla said abruptly.

CHAPTER 39

Capriquet Airport
Caen, France

He remembered the jet from a few years ago. It was still in pristine condition. Something he was certain Eli Levine insisted on. He knew the door in the back led to a bedroom. He'd slept there before, once, at Marla's insistence, when he'd been awake so long, he could barely function. He also remembered Marla slipping in bed with him on the same flight.

Marla went to the cockpit and spoke with the pilots then returned and sat next to Kaplan. Moss sat across the small aisle. "We are going to Aérodrome de Toussus-le-Noble," she said. "It is the closest airport to Paris. I've arranged a driver to pick us up with instructions to get to Montparnasse as fast as possible. Wheels up to wheels down is only thirty minutes. Wolfe will have to take the subway from Gare St Lazare to Montparnasse. It'll be tight, but we should beat him there by a good fifteen minutes."

"Nicely done, Marla," Moss said.

"Thank you, Pete." She turned to Kaplan. "See, Gregg, I can be useful."

"I never said you weren't useful, I just—"

"Bro," Moss interrupted. "Stop while you're ahead."

"I think it was you who said we don't need her."

"I never said that." Moss winked at Marla. "Besides, that was before I knew she had this fancy jet."

The flight was even shorter than anticipated, only twenty-five minutes from takeoff to landing. The ride into town every bit as long, but they still arrived at Sophie Bouquet's apartment before noon. Marla, or rather Mossad, had a team permanently stationed in Paris, just like the CIA did, with a driver who knew how to expeditiously negotiate the heavy Parisian traffic.

Now the wait for Wolfe had started.

At Kaplan's behest, the trio went up to Sophie's apartment. The door wasn't locked, it couldn't be since Kaplan kicked it in the day before. The apartment was still in shambles like it was yesterday. After a quick search of the bedroom it was clear Wolfe had not yet returned to claim his belongings. "Someone needs to stay on the street and keep a lookout for Wolfe."

"I'm not waiting outside, it's cold and windy," Marla said.

"Count me out, too." Moss chimed in.

"Gimme a break people. How about we rotate every hour? He should be getting here within the hour anyway, right?" Kaplan directed his remark toward Marla.

"I'm not doing it," she replied.

"Moss, you and I take shifts? Hour on, hour off?"

Moss hesitated.

"Seriously? You're going to let the cold stop you from doing your job?" Without waiting for a response, he said, "I don't even know why I brought either of you. I'll do it myself. Just keep your comms on for my call when Wolfe gets here."

Kaplan left the apartment without another word.

† † †

In a disappointing turn of events, Dalton lost the trail of Kaplan, Moss and the woman when they boarded a private jet outside of Bayeux and flew off. He used his binoculars and wrote down the tail number of the aircraft. When he called it in, he finally found out who the unknown woman was. She was Mossad. And since the jet was registered to the director of Mossad and reportedly his private jet aircraft, the woman must be his niece, Marla Farache.

The identity of all the players now known. Two American men—Gregg Kaplan and his large Black friend Pete Moss. The dead Russian Tatyana Kazakov. The Iranian Jasmine Habibi. And Marla Farache.

And now, all of them were whereabouts unknown. He had to rely on his superior to provide further details before he could proceed ahead with his mission.

All he could do was sit around and wait.

CHAPTER 40

CIA Station
Paris, France

After showing her credentials, Pernille Skouboe waited for security to announce her arrival to Deputy Chief of Station Alan Welch. Within a minute the door buzzed, and she was allowed through the massive security door behind the desk in the lobby. She'd been here numerous times and was familiar with the routine. The GIGN had similar procedures and precautions in place at their headquarters. A small frame man escorted her to Welch's office. Welch stood when he saw her.

"Come in, Colonel, come in. You must have been reading my mind. I was about to call you when they announced your arrival."

Skouboe ignored his greeting and marched over to his desk. She wagged her long slender finger at him. "I don't like being lied to, Alan."

He looked stunned by her aggressive confrontation. "Wha—"

"You know very well. The ruse you had me pull on Mr. Kaplan. Curtis Benoit? Or is it Matthew Wolfe? I thought you were an honest man. Someone I could actually trust in this business of lies and deceit. How many lies have you fed me?"

"Please, Colonel, have a seat." He waved to the man standing by the door. "Privacy please." The man closed the door and remained outside. Skouboe hesitated then sat facing his desk.

"Technically, I didn't lie. But I haven't been completely forthcoming with you either. For that my sincere apology. Curtis Benoit is the alias Matthew Wolfe has been using in France."

"I know that already, Alan. Obviously. It's been months since we received your government's *Burn Notice* on Matthew Wolfe. Why didn't you inform me he relocated to France? We would have worked in concert with the CIA to apprehend him."

"It's more complicated than that I'm afraid. We've only known ourselves a couple of weeks. It has taken my superiors a while to come up with an action plan. One I'm sure you won't like. I received this communique this morning."

He reached into an open drawer and removed a folder. He handed it to her. She opened it and scanned the pages while Welch remained silent.

When she got to the last page, her head snapped up. "Is this what I think it is?"

"Yes, Colonel, it's a Black Ops sanction authorization on Matthew Wolfe."

CHAPTER 41

"Mr. Deputy Chief, this is inexcusable." Colonel Pernille Skouboe's voice was harsh. "You used the GIGN and our resources to do internal CIA business. Covert Black Ops in France…by the CIA? A sanctioned hit? Shit, Alan. What the hell were you thinking? And I trusted you to be honest with me. That will never happen again. You have betrayed the cooperative spirit of our agencies. When my superiors find out what the CIA is doing—"

"Colonel, I implore you not to elevate this matter. I admit, I should have been up front with you on our investigation but as you might imagine, this is a sensitive matter. One that should never leave this room. If this were to get out…suffice it to say it is more than our jobs we'd need to be concerned with." There was a warning in his eyes.

She held her tongue. Part of her wanted to throw the file at Welch, storm out of the room and call her superiors. But she saw an opportunity gleaming on the horizon. One, that if she played her cards right could come in handy one day for her own career enhancement. It was painfully clear Welch owed her more than a small favor. She nor the French intelligence agencies have much use for Wolfe or the information he allegedly stole. With few exceptions, the United States and France shared information openly. But the French I.C. also wouldn't take kindly to a sanctioned hit of a whistleblower on French soil. No, she could use this to call in a favor. Get the CIA to do her dirty work. Every intelligence agency had broken protocol and skirted the law at one time or another.

Necessary to keep their country safe. Secrets had to be kept. Standard operating procedure with a multitude of matters within the Intelligence Community. France was no exception. The GIGN had plenty of dark secrets. She had a few skeletons in her closet that needed to stay buried.

Finally, she said to Welch, "Do Messieurs Kaplan and Moss even know about the sanction? Or did you mislead them as well?"

Welch tilted his head slightly and she knew the answer before Welch spoke.

"That order arrived from D.C. this morning," Welch explained. "I haven't told Kaplan. That might prove counter-productive."

"Why is that?"

"How much do you know about Gregg Kaplan?"

"Very little, actually. I know he works for the CIA and has for many years. I know you used to be his handler. Some other basic background and work history. After that, not much more. Capitaine Heuse had some dealings with him a few years ago. I understand he was instrumental in mitigating some of the fall-out from a terrorist attack here in Paris and the subsequent break up of a terrorist cell."

"First and foremost, Kaplan is a dangerous man. He's a trained killer who allows his sense of right and wrong to dictate his actions even if that means not following orders or breaking laws. Other than with Isabella Hunt, his first and only CIA partner, he is a loner. He works mostly off the grid. Then he met Pete Moss a few years ago and they have formed... shall we say, an informal partnership. Kaplan is crafty, hiding in plain sight and at one time his name sent fear into the hearts of terrorists. I'll admit he can be difficult, but he gets the job done. I've never had an operative as good as him. He has an uncanny ability to think like the enemy he is hunting. Albeit sometimes in an unorthodox manner."

"You make him sound a little like a—"

"Patriot," Welch finished the sentence for her. "Kaplan is a patriot to the core."

"Actually, I was going to say a killer with a conscience. A bit ironic."

"Our agents must feel what they do is their duty to the country they serve when they pull the trigger. It's easy for us to make life and death decisions behind a desk. Not so much in the field."

"My government and the French people won't take it well if this operation is leaked. You must understand the risk I'm taking by not reporting this."

"I do," Welch agreed.

"And you can guarantee me that your agents, Kaplan and the man working with him, will take care of this problem without making headlines in the paper?"

"Kaplan is by far the best operative to track down Matthew Wolfe. We should have this issue resolved and wrapped up neatly within a few days. And then you will forget he was ever here."

She sat silent and thought about what Welch had said. She knew what she should do but knew advancing in this line of work was cut-throat. This decision could not be made lightly. But she sensed he had not shared everything with her about the sanction on Wolfe. "Okay, Alan, I'll give you a pass on this one, but I want to make myself clear, if anything like this ever happens again and you withhold even an iota of critical information from me, I'll take it straight to the top of my agency and yours. Is that clear?"

"Yes, Colonel, understood and reasonable."

"One more thing, Alan. You owe me. And when I cash in my chip, I expect your full and expeditious cooperation. Also, you're to let me and only me know when this sanction goes down. And you had better make sure it goes down quietly or I'll deny we ever had this conversation. You alone will take the fall." She paused, recalling what he said to her as she walked in his office. "Now, what were you going to call me about?"

Welch reached into his center desk drawer and pulled out a folder marked *TIME CRITICAL*. He reached across his desk and handed it to her. "We have received credible intel that an assassination attempt will be made on the Pope during his visit to Mont Saint Michel."

CHAPTER 42

After an hour of waiting in the coffee shop across the street from Sophie Bouquet's apartment building, Moss showed up to relieve him. "Thought you could use a break."

"How'd you know where I was?"

"I watched from the window. Knew even a tough guy like you wouldn't stand in the open if he didn't have to." He shook his head. "No sign of Wolfe?"

"Nope. Matter of fact, no one has even gone into the building since I've been sitting here."

"What about a rear entrance? We didn't even talk about that," Moss said.

"Already checked before I headed out. Couldn't find one."

"Doesn't mean there isn't one, though, right?"

"No, I guess it doesn't. Just means I couldn't find one from inside the building. I didn't physically walk around back. Maybe I'll do that now." Kaplan stood.

"Hold up," Moss said. "I have something I want to talk to you about."

"I should get moving. I don't want to leave Marla up there by herself for very long in case Wolfe shows up."

"That's what I want to talk to you about...or rather who. And this won't take long."

Kaplan sat back in his chair. "Make it quick."

"I don't really know how to put this delicately so I'm just to come out and say it."

"Today would be nice."

"It's Marla. She's got the hots for you."

Kaplan laughed. "The hots, really? And that's putting it

delicately?"

"Okay, she more than just likes you, if you get my drift."

"What the hell, Moss. We aren't in high school for crying out loud. What made you feel like you needed to tell me this?"

"She was telling me about how you rescued her when she got shot." Moss added reluctantly, "I think the girl's in love with you."

Kaplan stood, slapped some cash on the table. "See you in an hour."

He walked around the back of the apartment building in search of a rear entrance and found a freight entrance to the restaurant next door that actually did connect to the apartment building through a side door. It could have been used by Wolfe to slip in and out undetected from the road. And he could've done it while he and Moss were in the coffee shop across the street and Marla was alone in the apartment.

He worked his way through the apartment building from the freight entrance to Sophie's apartment. He reached the door, drew his weapon and pushed the door open.

When the door flew open, Marla was crouched in a firing stance, weapon trained at Kaplan's chest.

"Dammit, Gregg," she yelled. "I almost shot you. Why didn't you knock like we agreed?" She lowered her weapon.

"I found a rear entrance to the building. I thought he might've tried to slip in the back way undetected. Precautionary measures."

She checked her watch. "He's late. What should we do?"

"Wait a little longer. If he doesn't show in an hour, we reassess our options."

His evaluation was interrupted when his comms went active. It was Moss. "Heads up, we got company."

"Who?"

"That Iranian chick we saw at Pierre Bouquet's. The one you said doesn't leave witnesses."

Not now, he thought. He had enough on his plate without dealing with Jasmine Habibi. "Is she alone?"

"No such luck. She has two oversized goons flanking her. Just like that Russian bitch did."

"Get up here ASAP."

"On my way."

CHAPTER 43

"Moss said we have visitors," Kaplan relayed to Marla. "Who? You look worried."

"More annoyed than worried. Jasmine Habibi and two of her men."

"How do you want to handle it?"

"Moss is on his way up. He'll slip up behind them. We'll take cover and be ready for them when they get here."

"Gregg, I know it's a bad time, but I have a confession."

"If it's about what you said to Moss, we can talk about it later."

"What? Moss? All I did was tell Pete about the time I got shot and you carried me out." Her face looked bewildered. "What did he say?"

"He said…basically the same thing."

"Then what are you talking about?"

"Nothing. Doesn't matter." He averted her gaze. "Back to your confession?"

"I haven't fired a weapon in years except at the range to pass my quals. Not since I got shot have I fired at anything other than a target."

He ignored her.

"I didn't want you to worry or think I shouldn't be back in the field," she said. She took several deep breaths. "I can do this."

He wanted to give her words of encouragement, when he heard footsteps outside in the hall and saw shadows beneath the door. "Targets outside door," he whispered into his comm.

"Coming up the stairs now," Moss said. "Less than a minute."

He faced Marla and saw the concern in her eyes. "Marla, you *can* do this," he said softly. "Just like the old days. You're still the same badass you've always been." He signaled for Marla to crouch behind the sofa for cover. He did the same.

That was all he had time for just as someone twisted the doorknob.

The door swung open. It was Habibi's men filling the doorway. Both armed with handguns, but neither had their guns trained ahead when they entered the room. They could have passed for twins except for the stark age difference. Same large build and height. One with a few extra pounds. Dark hair, dark eyes. Both light bearded. Definitely Middle Eastern.

"Freeze," Kaplan yelled. The two Iranian men were not expecting a confrontation. Both men started to raise their weapons. "Don't do it."

One looked back at Habibi, then at Kaplan.

"Don't be an idiot, Jasmine. Tell your men to stand down."

She was wearing nearly the same outfit as yesterday. Black jeans, pale blue blouse and the same black leather jacket. Her long black hair was pulled back into some kind of bun. Her dark eyes piercing.

"Or what?" She stepped into the doorway behind her men and scanned the room. Recognition flashed across her face when she spotted Marla. "I should have known Mossad would team with the Americans." She returned her glare to Kaplan. "Give us Wolfe and my men will let you live.

"Again, don't be an idiot, Jasmine." He trained his weapon on her chest. "You and your men have ten seconds to leave.

Both Iranians raised their weapons. This could get ugly

fast, he thought right before he saw a large shadow appear behind Jasmine.

"Don't fucking move," Moss ordered, voice deep and penetrating. His hand reached out and shoved Jasmine into the room next to her men. "Tell your men to drop their weapons or you're the first to die."

It was a standoff. The Iranians had two weapons drawn to their three. Moss held his weapon at shoulder height aimed at Jasmine's head. "Go ahead bitch, call my bluff," Moss said with a hint of a smile.

Seconds ticked before Jasmine relinquished and signaled her men to drop their weapons. The men did as commanded.

"Tell them to kick their weapons over here," Kaplan instructed. "And Jasmine...slowly remove your weapon and do the same."

"I'm not carrying."

Kaplan eased the slack out of his trigger.

"I don't have—"

"Do it now, Jasmine."

She reached behind her jacket and removed a handgun, bent down, placed it on the floor and kicked it across the room to Kaplan.

He pointed to her leg with the barrel of his Glock. "And the knife."

She clenched her jaw and removed her knife from the calf sheath and kicked it across the floor.

Moss shoved her out of the way when he entered the room. "What is it with these crazy women and knives?" He collared each Iranian man and shoved them face first against the wall, kicking their legs out in the frisking position. One man resisted and Moss slammed the man's head into the wall so hard it caved in the plaster. The man's knees wobbled. "Fuck with me again asshole, and you'll end up in the hospital," Moss growled. "Or the morgue."

Kaplan told Marla to gather their weapons while he walked over to Jasmine. "I should have killed you when I saw you in Cyprus a few years ago, but you weren't my target."

"Then why don't you kill me now?" Jasmine tested his resolve. "You won't because you Americans are cowards."

"Coward? No. Disinclined, yes. Why kill three unharmed foreigners when I need to make my bullets count. You don't count."

She spit in his face.

He wiped the spit with his sleeve. Then slammed his fist into her jaw. She fell to the floor, lip bleeding. He signaled with the barrel of his gun for Jasmine to stand. "I'm going to let the three of you go. Leave France. Return to Iran."

She spit blood on the floor. "And if I don't?"

"Make no mistake, Jasmine, if I see you in France again, I won't give you a warning. I will kill you first and then your two thugs. Now, take your men and get the hell out of here."

Moss released his grip on the two men and shoved them toward the door. Jasmine said nothing, just motioned with her arm and the three Iranians left Sophie Bouquet's apartment.

"Now what?" Moss said. "You know she won't leave, right?"

"Yeah, I know. But she's out of our hair for now."

Marla checked her watch. Kaplan could tell something was off. "What is it, Marla?"

"It's been way too long," she said, her voice rising in intensity. "Wolfe should have been here by now. Something has happened."

Moss shoved his handgun in his waistband. "Wolfe's been

in the I.C. long enough to know a few tricks of the trade."
He was directing his analogy to Kaplan. He waved his hand
around the room. "There isn't anything in this apartment he
really needs that he can't replace. Maybe when he caught that
train out of Bayeux he didn't come to Paris. Maybe he stopped
off along the way."

"And gave anyone looking for him, like us, a little
misdirection," Kaplan suggested. "Even though Alan said he
would suppress the news of Sophie's death, maybe Wolfe got
the news somehow and made a run for it."

"I would if I were in his shoes," Moss added.

"As much as I hate to do it, I guess I'll bring Alan back in
the loop."

"There is another alternative," Marla offered. "I can have
Mossad pull video footage in Bayeux and Caen. If he got off
in Caen, we'll know. That should give us somewhere to start
looking again."

"And then I'll owe Eli a favor? No offense to your uncle,
Marla, but I'll pass."

"No, Gregg," she said. "This time, you'll owe *me* a favor."
An impish smile curled her lips.

CHAPTER 44

He acquiesced to Marla's insistence she use her Mossad analyst to locate and track Wolfe's location. As much as she complained, he refused to let her turn on her phone. Instead, he insisted she use a burner phone to contact her analyst. Just like he didn't want Alan Welch tracking his phone, he didn't want Mossad tracking Marla's phone. It was either that or get Alan and the CIA involved and right now, he didn't think he could trust Alan Welch. The CIA had been behind the power curve on this whole Wolfe issue. To the point where all the other actors had more current information on Matthew Wolfe than the CIA did. And to add insult to injury, Wolfe was a former American intelligence officer.

There was something else eating at him. Alan's lack of full disclosure and trickery. The more he rolled it around, the more obsessed he became and the more determined he was to get to Wolfe before the CIA did. There was something between Wolfe and the United States Intelligence Community that he couldn't put his finger on. Beyond him leaving the country and seeking exile as a whistleblower. Beyond the United States branding him a traitor and charging him with high crimes. He'd been in this business too long to accept Welch's simple explanation. This went deeper. Of course, there were plenty of foreign actors wanting to get their hands on Wolfe, that was obvious. Too obvious. Wolfe would know the Russians, Iranians, and even the Israelis would want the information he'd stolen from the U. S. Government. Even Wolfe would know he'd have to stay on the run from the bad actors.

What drove him out of Iceland where he had a good chance of not being extradited? And why France? If Wolfe got caught in France, they would extradite him back to the U.S. without hesitation. Then what would he do? He'd be facing a no-win trial…if the government even allowed him to make it to trial. In all probability they would not. What then? What was his incentive to be here? He had to be planning something.

But what?

His introspection interrupted when Marla nudged him with her elbow. She was still on the phone to her Mossad analyst and mouthed the words, *We found him* to Kaplan. She was scribbling on a note pad she found on Sophie's desk. A lot of scribbling. Page after page. Perhaps it was a good thing to let Mossad track Wolfe after all. She was speaking to her analyst in Hebrew, which Kaplan knew very little. Most Israelis spoke English. Or at least most of the ones with whom he'd had dealings in the past.

After she finally finished her call, she picked up the pad and walked over to where he and Moss were standing. "It took some doing," she said. "But my analyst was able to trace Wolfe's trail for quite some time. Turns out, like we speculated, he did take the train from Bayeux towards Paris, but instead of staying on the Paris train, he got off in Caen. There, Wolfe bought a bus ticket to Rennes and boarded a bus."

"We go to Rennes," Moss interrupted.

"Not so fast," she said. "He didn't get off in Rennes. In fact, he never made it to Rennes. He wasn't even on the bus when it arrived. Ari started backtracking each stop along the way. Wolfe actually got off the bus at Gare d'Avranches where he got a ride in a dark blue van. From there, we have no idea where he went. The van doesn't belong to any taxi or ride-share company and because of the camera angle, Ari wasn't able to read a plate number. Wolfe is good at elude and evade protocols. Good enough to keep from being followed."

"Where does that leave us?" Moss asked.

Marla looked at Kaplan. "Any ideas?"

He pulled up Google Maps on his iPhone and searched for Avranches, France. He studied the map and zoomed in and then zoomed out. Farther out and then something he remembered seeing in Bayeux struck him. He panned the screen to the left and zoomed in closer. Recalling the schedule he'd seen posted on the wall at the hotel in Bayeux, he knew P.A.P.A.CY. was slated to hold a protest, or *rally* as they referred to it, at Mont Saint Michel day after tomorrow. If Wolfe was still following the schedule of P.A.P.A.CY., then he had no idea of Sophie's fate. At least, he couldn't imagine a scenario where he did know and would still be putting himself in such a precarious position.

Kaplan knew better. He knew who the actors on stage were and their underlying motive—capture or kill Matthew Wolfe.

"Gregg?" Marla cut in. She raised her palms.

"Can your pilots get us to Avranches as soon as possible? I think I know where Wolfe is headed." He zoomed in on the small island Abbey of Mont Saint Michel and held his phone out for both of them to see.

"Of course," Moss said. "Mont Saint Michel. There is a P.A.P.A.CY. protest there in two days."

"You think he'd still go there?" Marla asked.

"What else would motivate him go in that direction? He knows someone must be after him, otherwise why go to so much trouble to make it hard to follow his tracks? He has some kind of interest in that particular P.A.P.A.CY. rally, I just don't know what it is yet."

Marla picked up the burner phone. "I'll get the pilots working on it." She walked back to Sophie's desk and sat down.

CHAPTER 45

The descent into the Dinard-Pluertuit-Saint-Malo Airport saw the last embers of sunset reflect off the Mossad's jet's wings. It was the closest airport capable of handling the jet's takeoff and landing requirements. There was an airport closer to Avranches, but it was currently closed due to flooding by the excessive tides from the Atlantic Ocean.

In this northwestern corner of France, the Celtic Sea and English Channel run past the Channel Islands and into the joint delta formed by the convergence of the Couesnon, La Sée and Sélune Rivers, an area prone to flooding during certain tidal events.

By the time the Mossad jet pulled next to the fixed base operator, or FBO, the sky was fully dark and the brightest of the stars were dotting the sky.

Brisk and windy from the passing cold front, each of them grabbed their gear and braved the cold as they headed inside the FBO. Kaplan had called ahead and had a rental car waiting for them at the Saint-Malo Jet Center. No more compact cars. He went with a high-end luxury sedan, an Audi A-8, and billed it to Alan Welch at the CIA station in Paris. He knew Welch wouldn't like it when he got the bill, but right now, he didn't give a shit.

When the trio walked out to the waiting Audi, even Kaplan was surprised at the extent of the luxury. Plush leather, top-of-the-line technology, state-of-the-art electronics and every bell and whistle available for an automobile. When he folded into the driver's seat and allowed the comfort to wrap around him, he glanced at his watch. Although it was dark, it was still early. Short days, long nights. The dead of winter in Northern France.

On the flight over, he garnered input from Marla and Moss and after reaching a consensus, he reserved three rooms for two nights in Avranches at La Boudrie Chambre d'Hôtes, a bed and breakfast situated near the heart of town.

Before he put the sedan in gear he asked, "Moss, You're always thinking a meal ahead, what does your stomach clock say? Eat here in Saint-Malo or wait till Avranches? 76 kilometers to the B&B, GPS says fifty-five minutes."

"I'm good. I had snacks on the plane."

"Marla?"

"Let's go on the Avranches and check-in. I'd like to clean up before we go out," she explained.

"Avranches it is."

An hour and ten minutes later, they checked in and each went to their respective rooms with plans to meet back downstairs in twenty minutes. The owner recommended a restaurant two blocks away called Le Montepego, which had a full-service menu with a wide variety of foods.

The trio spent the next two and a half hours at Le Montepego eating, drinking, and strategizing the next day's plan. The five-minute walk back to the B&B saw the trio relatively somber. It had been a long day. Hell, it had been a long several days for him and Moss.

All three rooms were upstairs. They planned to reconvene at breakfast in the morning. He went to his room, rummaged through his duffel and pulled out a change of clothes. He needed to unwind, and for him, that meant a hot shower. He turned on the hot water and let it run until steam clouded the mirror. He stepped in, adjusted the temperature and stood under the steady stream of cascading hot water and let the past few days purge from his system. He didn't move until his skin had turned pink from the near scalding water. When he felt his tension release, he twisted the handle to cold and let the sudden shock close his pores.

It also cleared his head. He felt refreshed and awake, his mind ready to focus on what was to come in his search for Matthew Wolfe. He slipped on his sweatpants and a t-shirt and plopped in the only chair in the room. He pulled out his burner phone and started studying the lay of the land trying to calculate Wolfe's next move.

Just as he thought he was putting the pieces together, there was a light rap on his door.

It was Marla.

She was wearing a terry cloth robe just like the one in his closet. The ones the B&B provided for guests to use. She had on the matching slippers as well. Her long dark hair draped evenly over both shoulders, rich brown eyes piercing. He shuddered at her beauty. She held both arms behind her back.

"I couldn't sleep," she whispered. "I saw your light on under the door. I guess you couldn't sleep either." She pulled one arm from behind her back. A bottle of Jameson Irish Whiskey, his favorite. "I thought this might help." She brought her other arm forward holding two glasses. "Snagged these from the kitchen."

"This isn't a good idea, Marla. We need to stay focused."

"You're right."

She pushed him aside and entered his room.

She placed the bottle and glasses on the dresser and walked over to where he was standing in front of an antique armoire.

She hooked his hands, pulling them around her waist and pushed herself against him. He felt her pulse pounding against his chest. His body responded when their lips touched. It was as if she knew what he wanted, what he needed. And to what degree of physicality.

She unbelted her robe and let it slide down her body. Her olive skin smooth. She kissed him deeply as her fingers found his shirt and cast it to the floor. She kissed his chest and slipped her hands lower, inside, until his clothes fell to the floor. He stepped out of them, lifted her up and carried her to the bed.

Afterwards, exhausted, he closed his eyes holding her tightly against him.

He fell asleep.

CHAPTER 46

The next morning Kaplan woke up alone.

Marla had slipped out during the night. He had fallen asleep shortly before midnight. After making love last night, he slept more deeply than he had in a long time. If he hadn't set the alarm on his phone, he might not have awakened in time for the early breakfast seating.

He had mixed emotions. A twinge of guilt that in some small way he had been unfaithful to Isabella, even though he knew that mindset was illogical. He and Isabella would never have a relationship again.

For the first time in years, he felt invigorated and ready to face the challenges ahead of him. Something he had been wanting but didn't realize how much until last night. Maybe Marla had helped him focus. Or maybe she helped him let go of Isabella a little bit more.

When the trio met in the breakfast room of the B&B, Marla played it cool, as if last night hadn't happened. He knew she would. Discretion was one of her strong suits and she played her cards well.

The breakfast room faced a rear garden. Plenty of windows and a slider that opened to the back yard. There were tables on the terrace, not in use this time of year. The morning broke with clear skies, wind rustling through leaf-barren trees. The sky was deep blue, and the bright yellow sun's heat penetrated through the wall of windows. Before he came down, he'd checked the weather—sunny and warmer with highs around 10°C or 50°F. Low humidity for the region, even with its proximity to the ocean.

Breakfast began with coffee, juices and pastries, fresh fruits, crepes and syrups. By the time they finished eating, the threesome's hunger was sated.

Climbing the stairs together, each went to their rooms and returned back downstairs within fifteen minutes as they agreed. The day's tasks would be daunting—find a man who didn't want to be found. And the only lead they had was that a dark blue van picked him up at the train station where the bus dropped him off yesterday afternoon.

Unless they had an unprecedented stroke of good luck, locating Wolfe might prove to be more difficult than he wanted to acknowledge. At breakfast, he ran his idea across the table about using the train station, Gare d'Avranches and the co-located bus terminal as their starting point for the morning. Moss and Marla agreed. Even though Ari, Marla's Mossad analyst had captured the video of Wolfe getting in the dark blue van, nothing beat a face-to-face chat with the locals.

The drive to the train station took less than ten minutes. Neither Gare d'Avranches nor the co-located bus terminal had much activity. As he found out later, they had arrived during a lull between train and bus arrivals, so with the exception of a lone man in line at the ticket counter inside the station and a couple sitting on a bench, the place was empty.

After the man purchased his ticket and left the counter, Kaplan approached the window. The attendant was younger, maybe mid to late twenties and sported a full beard. He had dark hair, blue eyes, and a mole to the side of his left eye. Kaplan pulled up a photo on his iPhone of the dark blue van Wolfe was seen riding off in and held it up for the man to see. "Reconnaissez-vous ce van?" *Do you recognize this van?*

"Oui, monsieur," the attendant said. "Il appartient à la société de location de voitures." *It belongs to the car rental company.*

He sensed Marla had moved up behind him. His mind wanted to relive last night's escapades, but he fought it off. He threw a smile over his shoulder and looked back at the attendant. "Quelle société de location de voiture?" he asked. *What car rental company?*

"Europcar Avranches sur Rue Victor Lemarchand." *Europcar Avranches on Victor Lemarchand Street.* The attendant reached behind the counter and handed Kaplan a business card for EuropCar Avranches.

"Merci," He and Marla walked over to the bench where Moss was sitting.

Moss stood and asked, "Anything?"

"Not much," he said as he held up the business card. "But it's a lead."

"Better than nothing," Marla added. "Van belongs to a rental car company. Some kind of courtesy pickup and drop off for rental car customers."

"What are we waiting for?" Moss said. "Let's go check it out."

The fastest route according to Google Maps took them 11 minutes to reach Europcar Avranches. It was literally on the other side of town from the train station. It was a dull gray metal building with a green *Europcar* sign above the main entrance. To the left of the lobby door was an open gate that led to a back lot where all the cars were kept as there were no vehicles parked in the front. He wheeled the black Audi into a parking spot next to the fence to his far left.

From the outside, the lobby appeared small. Moss

volunteered to wait outside and keep an eye out while Kaplan and Marla went inside to inquire about Wolfe's rental.

"Bonjour, monsieur," Kaplan said as he entered.

"Good morning," the man said in English catching both Kaplan and Marla by surprise. "How may I help you?"

"How did you know I wasn't French?"

The man replied, "Your French is very good, but your accent, it is not French. And you look American." He turned to Marla. "You, not so much."

The man behind the counter reeked of cigarette smoke and his teeth stained yellow from nicotine.

Kaplan slipped out his phone and brought up a picture of Matthew Wolfe. "Your courtesy van picked this man up at the train station yesterday afternoon. We are looking for him and I need a description of the car he rented from you."

The man leaned back. "So sorry, monsieur, I am not at liberty to release that type of information about our customers. That would be against company policy—"

"Company policy or not," Kaplan said. "It's urgent we find this man as soon as possible."

"I am sorry, I cannot give you that information."

Kaplan leaned over the counter. "I'm afraid I must insist."

The man reached for the phone. "If you do not leave at once, I shall call the police."

Kaplan reached into his pocket and pulled out the business card Colonel Pernille Skouboe gave him. "Tell you what, why don't you call this woman instead and explain why you're hindering her investigation."

He held up the card. "Gendarmerie? I-I don't think there is any need for them to be involved." The man paused while he studied Skouboe's card. "If you're working with the GIGN, then I see no reason why we can't cooperate." He turned to his computer. "What is this man's name?"

"Curtis Benoit."

The man typed in the name. "I am sorry, no one by that name has rented a vehicle from us."

"This was yesterday afternoon, he came from the bus station, train station, whatever. How many rentals did you have yesterday afternoon?"

The man counted. "Looks like six. Two were women, we can rule those out."

The door opened and Moss walked in and stood next to Marla. "Any luck?"

"Getting closer," she responded.

"What about Matthew Wolfe?" Kaplan asked.

"No. Got another name?" the man said.

Kaplan was stumped. There was no list of aliases in Wolfe's dossier other than Curtis Benoit. "Can we see the names?"

The man hit *Print Screen* and handed the sheet to Kaplan. He studied it, but nothing stood out. Three of the names were Anglo and one was clearly Middle Eastern. He pointed to the Middle Eastern name. "Do you remember this guy?"

"Oui."

"Describe him."

"Tall, long black hair, dark complexion." He pointed to Marla then Moss. "Much darker than her, not as dark as him. Had a long black beard."

Kaplan took a pen off the counter and lined the name off the list. He tapped the first name on the list. "What time did this guy rent his car?"

He clicked on his keyboard. "2:30 yesterday afternoon."

"Too early," Marla said. "It would have been at least 3:30

or closer to 4:00 before he could have possibly gotten here."

Kaplan lined the name off the list. "That leaves two. What times did these guys pick up the vehicles?"

"4:15 and 4:27. I believe they were both in here at the same time for a few minutes," the man explained.

Kaplan scanned the area. "Do you have security cameras?"

"In this town? No, we do not. This is a slow branch office. Europcar doesn't think the expense of security cameras is warranted in a branch this size. Besides, we've never had a break-in or theft since we've been here."

Kaplan handed the sheet to Marla. "Anything stand out?"

She shook her head and handed the sheet over to Moss.

Moss studied the sheet. He tapped the paper with his fingers and mumbled something under his breath.

"What Moss?" Kaplan said. "You see something or not?"

"Bob Woolsey," Moss finally said aloud. "Is his full name Robert?" Moss was looking at the man behind the counter.

The man looked down at the screen. "Yes. Robert James Woolsey."

Moss put the paper on the counter and said, "That's the guy. I'm sure of it."

Kaplan looked at him in awe. "How can you be sure?"

"Simple, I had to do a case study in my Poly-Sci class in college and I was assigned Robert James Woolsey Jr as my case study subject. At the time, Woolsey was the current Director of Central Intelligence. Unless this guy is bald and like 80 years old or so, this is our guy."

The man behind the counter chimed in. "I scanned his driver's license into our computer if you want to see his picture."

The trio were shell-shocked.

Kaplan spoke first. "Why didn't you tell us this earlier?'

"Sorry, it just now occurred to me." He swiveled the monitor on its base so the trio could see. "Is this the guy you're looking for?"

On the computer monitor was a picture of Matthew Wolfe.

CHAPTER 47

Dalton's superior had come through. He was able to track the private jet's tail number and get the details of its flight plan from Paris to Saint-Malo. Since he was still in Bayeux, he was able to make it to the Saint-Malo airport in plenty of time before the Mossad jet landed.

He followed Kaplan, Moss and the Israeli woman as they drove to Avranches and spent the night. Now, they were inside a rental car agency, for what reason he didn't know. Nor care. That wasn't his job. Yet.

His mission was still the same.

Track and report.

CHAPTER 48

Other than the name Robert James Woolsey, the other information they gleaned from the rental car attendant were the make, model, color of the car, plate and VIN number. Late model Citroen C3, white with a red roof and red side mirrors. A common color scheme for this manufacturer that model year.

"One last question," Kaplan said to the attendant. "Does the car have a GPS tracker?"

"Europcar is a large company," the man explained. "Our entire fleet has GPS trackers. We need to know where our vehicles are from time to time. Especially if they are stolen… or in an accident."

"Can you locate it for us?"

"No. That is only done through the corporate office in Paris. I have no access to that system from here. I report it, the main office locates it and contacts the authorities."

"Merci," Kaplan said as they walked out the door to their car.

"Now what?" Moss asked over the roof of the Audi before anyone got inside. "Wolfe could be anywhere and we can't start chasing every little white car we see with a red roof."

"You're right," Marla said. She reached inside her coat pocket, fished out the burner phone Kaplan gave her and held it against her ear. "But I can see if Ari can hack into Europcar's system and locate Wolfe using their GPS tracker."

Kaplan opened his door and said. "Sounds good." Then he slipped into the driver's seat and started the engine.

Moss crawled in the passenger seat and closed the door while Marla stood outside on the phone. "Mossad is doing a lot of favors for us. You think that's a wise move? No offense to your friend, but I don't believe Mossad is doing this out of the kindness of their heart. Her people could beat us to Wolfe while she leads us around in circles. Plus, she talks to him in some other language. Do we have any clue what she's telling her contact? Or are we just going to take her word for it?"

Kaplan hesitated to answer. He'd already thought of the ramifications of what Moss proposed. Of course, he didn't want to think Marla would betray him, especially in light of what happened between them last night. But Moss was right, Marla and her Mossad analyst were indeed the holders of most of the intel. She could be playing them. The only viable alternative at this point was getting Alan Welch involved…and he wasn't ready to make that call yet.

"Hebrew is the language. And yes, the thought has crossed my mind," he said to Moss. He had been trusting of Marla. "The time for mistrust isn't here yet. We need her intel and resources. If I think we're being played, I'll put an end to it."

"You sure you can do that? I've seen how you two look at each other. If I didn't know better, I'd swear you were sleeping with her."

"What if I am?" He noticed Marla slip her phone back in her coat pocket and walk toward the car. "I'm just not ready to bring the CIA back in yet and Mossad is all we've got."

Marla opened the rear passenger-side door, and got in. "Ari's going to try to locate the car. He said Europcar's system was easy to get into but the company that monitors the GPS trackers would be much harder to hack."

"So now we just wait?" Moss tossed the question out.

Kaplan put the Audi in reverse, backed out of the parking spot and drove in the direction from which they came.

"Yes," he said. "We'll wait back at the hotel."

CHAPTER 49

Mont Saint Michel Abbey

Bishop Jean Paul Renault exited the shuttle at the base of the island fortress. He had been in the area for several days making preparations for the upcoming Papal visit tomorrow. Until yesterday, there had not been much security on the island except for the normal staffing of Gendarmerie outside the gate at the base of the fortress. Around midday yesterday Vatican security arrived and the Abbey turned into a beehive.

Renault was a tall man in his seventies with a fringe of grey-white hair circling his mostly bald scalp. His face had aged with wrinkles boring deeply into his skin, something he blamed on being forced into the Catholic Church's political spectrum and overburdened with the negative publicity the Church had been receiving over its handling of sexual abuse by predator priests around the globe. A problem no one it seemed, including the Pope, wanted to take a hard public stance against. In Renault's opinion, it was because the problem was so pervasive it affected an extremely large number of priests.

This was not what he wanted to see, but it was what he was tasked to defend. And defend it he did. Publicity-wise and legally. As one of a handful of licensed attorneys who joined the priesthood, his advocacy stood out among his peers. He likened his fierce lawyer-style tenacity as part of the reason he was elevated to the level of Bishop.

Until today, security at Mont Saint Michel had let him drive his own vehicle to the main gate in order to unload the preparatory supplies for the Pope's visit. Now, security required he park on the mainland with the hordes of tourists and take the same shuttle. At 5:00 p.m. today, the Abbey would close its doors to the public and not reopen until the day after tomorrow.

No one on or off the island for two hours prior to and after the Pope's arrival and departure. And the Pontiff's visit had been a logistical nightmare for Renault. The Pontifical Swiss Guard made sure of that. Twenty plain-clothes Swiss Guards invaded the Abbey and had scattered themselves into every nook and cranny evaluating the entire island for security issues.

It wasn't supposed to be such a massive security nightmare until the United States Government received what they deemed as a credible threat against the Pope's life at this first-ever Papal visit to Mont Saint Michel.

The long history of Mont Saint Michel dated back to 708 A.D. when Aubert, Bishop of Avranches, had a sanctuary built on Mont Tombe in honor of the Archangel Michael. The Abbey itself sat at the top of the mount and beginning in the 10th century, a village grew at its base as the Benedictines settled in. By the 14th century, the village had extended as far as the foot of the rock. Ramparts and fortifications were built around the base as an example of military-style architecture and it was used as an impregnable stronghold during the Hundred Years War.

Before the causeway was built Mont Saint Michel was accessible only at low tide. Because of its unique location in a delta convergence of three rivers, tidal changes were rapid. After the ramparts and garrisons were built invaders would cross at low tide only to be driven off or drowned by the swift incoming tides.

In its darker days Mont Saint Michel served as a prison. The same swift tides that kept invaders at bay also served to keep prisoners inside the walls. Up to 14,000 prisoners did time at Mont Saint Michel during the 19th century until Napoleon III shut the prison down in 1863.

Over time, the decaying fortress was restored and regained popularity due to its medieval heritage. Now, although still a fully functioning Abbey, it had been relegated mostly as a tourist destination.

Until the Swiss Guard arrived Renault wore street clothes, meaning no priest's collar while he worked to bring Papal supplies to the island and up the long winding path to the Abbey at the top of the mount. He viewed himself as a man in good physical shape but the toil of the past few days left his aging bones creaky and muscles sore.

The Papal visit would take several hours in duration, the finale being Mass in the Abbey Church followed by a ceremonial meal in the Refectory. Renault's controversy of the day was settling a dispute between the Abbey authorities and the Swiss Guard over the ingress and egress of the Pope.

Swiss Guard wanted the Pope flown in and out by helicopter to what would be a then secured island. Abbey officials didn't want a helicopter landing and taking off from the island at all, but instead preferred he land at a secure site off the island and be transported by Swiss Guard to and from the island via Pont Passerelle, the 2.5-kilometer causeway connecting the mainland and the island.

In reality, there was no safe place for a helicopter to land and takeoff from the island except at the island end of Pont Passerelle next to the main gate. And even then, there were the preponderance of lamp posts to contend with.

Another concern of Renault's was the P.A.P.A.C.Y. rally planned for tomorrow during the Papal visit. This was no coincidence. The advocacy group had been making a deliberate progression toward Mont Saint Michel with the sole purpose of expressing their views in plain sight of the Pope.

Renault had received a Papal mandate to make sure that never happened.

But it would happen. He couldn't legally stop the rally.

P.A.P.A.C.Y. would get the chance to air their grievances.

And Renault would allow them their rally. Their single opportunity to voice their complaints. And he would urge the Pope to meet with them face to face.

CHAPTER 50

Saint-Malo, France

M atthew Wolfe had never used the alias *Robert James Woolsey* before, but he had used the names of former CIA and NSA directors. A taunt to see if his old colleagues at the respective spy agencies would ever catch on. Woolsey though, was the first name he'd used of someone still living. He got the idea for the aliases from thriller author Lee Child whose protagonist, Jack Reacher, used the names of old baseball icons as aliases. It was a clever concept, he thought, one that had so far proven useful as he ran from the United States Government.

When he arrived in France, he chose the name Curtis Benoit because it was a French name and he spoke fluent French with no perceived accent. It was good cover, until it was blown. He chose the economy car deliberately, since most French don't drive large expensive vehicles and he needed to blend in, not draw undue attention.

After he rented the Citroen C3, he tucked away the fake identification and returned to his French alias Curtis Benoit, simply because that was the name they knew him by at P.A.P.A.C.Y. He would make an appearance at the rally tomorrow because he had to find out what happened in Bayeux and to Sophie.

That incident disturbed him. He considered running again, disappearing without a trace, but there was something about his feelings for Sophie that wouldn't let him do it. Before Sophie he would have seized the opportunity to run. He'd always been clever at making women believe he cared for them when in fact he only used them to get what he wanted. When he got bored or the woman expressed any semblance of seriousness toward their relationship, he bolted.

He thought he felt that way about Sophie as well, even after she was thrown into the van in Bayeux. As his norm he bolted, with every intention of returning to Paris, gathering his belongings and disappearing. That lasted all of one stop on his way to Paris. That was how long it took him to realize how much he cared for Sophie.

It wasn't totally a spur of the moment decision to come to Mont Saint Michel to rejoin P.A.P.A.C.Y. He had business he wanted to see completed. Business that involved Sophie's younger brother, Pierre.

Over the course of the past few months, he'd grown quite fond of Pierre. After witnessing firsthand the trauma and suffering the young man endured as a result of the sexual abuse inflicted on him by his childhood priest, he understood Sophie's passion for the cause of P.A.P.A.C.Y.

Pierre's bouts of depression could come on at a moment's notice and linger anywhere from hours to days. He'd even been put on suicide watch twice after two failed overdose attempts.

Pierre could go from happy-go-lucky to the epitome of darkness in a matter of minutes.

Wolfe couldn't stand idly by and watch the young Bouquet self-destruct. He knew the debilitating power of depression. He'd suffered bouts as a child trying to deal with his unaffectionate parents who dismissed his angst as growing pains. They didn't care about his suffering, certainly not in the same way that Sophie cared for Pierre's. She had made it her pain too.

His passion for Pierre's cause grew as did his uncharacteristic fondness for Sophie. It was time to right a wrong. To avenge Pierre from his abuser. And Wolfe knew how. He was familiar with the workings of the underground. Hell, he was part of it now and knew who to contact. He put measures in place.

That's why he had to go to Mont Saint Michel. The Pope would be there. This P.A.P.A.C.Y. rally was guaranteed to draw the largest of crowds. It was their highest exposure event yet. His chance to ensure Pierre's plight was heard and didn't go unaccounted for. To ensure the Catholic church got the message loud and clear—the abuse had to stop. And ensure all the victims like Pierre, were compensated for decades of denial and negligence by the church. This would be his ultimate support for Sophie's cause.

He had heard people say there was someone for everyone, but he thought that mantra was bullshit…until now. Perhaps Sophie was the one for him. He'd tried calling her cell phone, even though she had dropped it in Bourges, shattering the glass, and couldn't get it to power back on. It went straight to voicemail, as did Pierre's when he tried calling him. He didn't know where the rally volunteers were staying tonight, but he did know where they would be tomorrow. In the meantime, he'd lay low and out of sight.

Yesterday, after he rented the Citroen, he drove to Saint-Malo and found a cheap hotel near the waterfront between the marina and the ocean, inside the ramparts. Parking inside the ramparts was a problem since most small hotels had no parking facilities, so he ended up parking at the Saint-Malo public parking lot next to *The Great Gate*, the main entrance to the interior of the ramparts.

Although it was quite chilly this morning, he planned to spend time on the beach since the forecast called for clear skies and mid-fifties. Maybe cross over the rocks and walk up to Le Fort National, a military fortress, now historical monument built in 1689 to protect the port of Saint-Malo. Or maybe, if the tides worked in his favor, walk across Passage des Bés to the small isles of Grand Bé and Petit Bé. Another plus for him, Saint-Malo had no shortage of restaurants.

Tomorrow morning, he would get up early, check out of the hotel and drive to Mont Saint Michel where he would meet up and join the P.A.P.A.C.Y. rally.

† † †

Avranches, France

The three of them had been waiting for over an hour in the common area of the B&B, La Boudrie, when Marla answered the burner phone. Kaplan could tell by the quick glance she gave him the caller was her Mossad analyst, Ari. They were speaking Hebrew, of course, of which he knew exactly three phrases, *Shalom*—hello, goodbye, peace. *Todah*— Thanks. And *Mazal Tov*, which was a phrase used to mean congratulations. Other than that, he was clueless.

She was writing on a notepad as she listened to the caller, the same one she lifted from Sophie's desk. In less than two minutes she disconnected the call. She got up and walked over to where Kaplan and Moss were seated. "We got him," she said with a broad grin. "His car is in Saint-Malo. It hasn't moved since it got there yesterday evening."

"We just came from there yesterday," Moss blurted out. "Bet we passed that bastard on the highway and didn't even know it."

Marla held up the notepad. "I have the exact coordinates if you want them."

"Hold on to them," Kaplan said. "We'll enter them into the Audi's GPS after we get on the road." He stood. "Everyone grab all your bags in case we don't return here tonight"

The trio bounded up the stairs.

CHAPTER 51

Saint-Malo, France
11:30 A. M.

From Avranches, Kaplan drove the major highways toward Saint-Malo avoiding the smaller towns and villages in order to save time. Time needed to locate Matthew Wolfe. When they approached the walled city on highway D126, a shipyard and marina appeared on their right and the ocean on their left. Kaplan had been to the area before and was somewhat familiar with its history.

"Hey Kaplan," Moss said. "Look to the right. Those cranes remind you of anything?"

It did remind him of the time he and Moss busted a criminal ring and chased an assassin at the Newark, New Jersey shipyard. That happened shortly after he and Moss first teamed up together.

"Moss, try to stay out of the line of fire next time."

"You got my promise on that one, cause I'm tired of protecting your sorry ass."

They shared a pissed off look for a few seconds and then burst out laughing.

"Why are you guys laughing?" Marla said in an exasperated tone. "Getting shot is no laughing matter."

Kaplan glanced in the rear-view mirror at Marla. Both men were still chuckling. "Guess you had to be there."

"You two have a perverse sense of humor, you know that?"

"You'll have to get Kaplan to tell you about it one day,"

Moss said.

"I already did." Kaplan slowed as they reached the walled city. "Hey Moss, I'm thinking you should steer clear of red-headed women, first Valkyrie then Tatyana."

"Oh my God," she said. "*You're* the man Valkyrie shot, aren't you?"

"Afraid so," Moss replied.

"Teach you to hang out with Kaplan. One day it might be worse than your leg."

Kaplan was about to respond when the GPS chimed in.

Your destination is ahead on the right.

He pulled into the Saint-Malo parking lot at the traffic circle in front of La Grande Porte de Saint-Malo otherwise known as The Great Gate. As he turned in, there were cars parked in both directions, to the right and to the left. Ahead and across the waters of the small yacht basin was the marina with dozens of sailboats and yachts tied up in their slips. The GPS indicated the coordinates were slightly to the left. "Look for a white Citroen C3 with a red roof and red mirrors."

As they progressed behind the rows of cars next to the marina, Moss said, "Like that one?" He pointed ahead and to Kaplan's left.

Marla checked her notepad. "Plates match. Let me out and I'll check the VIN to verify."

Marla hopped out of the car and scurried over to the front windshield of the Citroen. He saw her hovering her finger over a spot where the VIN should be mounted on the dash. She gave a thumbs up and returned to the car.

"Bingo. It's Wolfe's rental," she said as she got back into

the car.

Moss gave him the *Yeah, now what?* look.

"I'll disable his car so he can't go anywhere and then we scour the town looking for him. It stands to reason if his car was parked here overnight and hasn't moved, then he is either staying in the old town or on a boat. And since he's parked here," he pointed across the water toward a building," and not over at the marina access, my money is on him being within these walls."

† † †

Wolfe had checked the tide charts during breakfast and found low tide would be around 2:00 p.m. He decided to take a lunch and eat on Petit Bé since the winds were calm and forecast to remain that way until evening. He stopped by a crêperie near the hotel and placed a take-out order. He stuffed it into his backpack along with a small blanket from the hotel room. On the way out he picked up a tourist guide pamphlet of the Bé isles.

While the tide was ebbing he made his way across the still wet walkway toward the first isle, Grand Bé. He noted that workers must have had to prep and lay all this stonework during low tides, including the mortar work between the stones. At low tide, it became a prepared stone path all the way from the walled city of Saint-Malo out to the farthest isle of Petit Bé, where a Vauban-designed fort was built in 1689 to ward off British and Dutch fleets.

At Petit Bé, he climbed the trail to the fort itself and wandered through the main building, now a museum of sorts documenting the historical facts of the fort including mockups of life in the fort during its operation. It documented the dining hall, if you could call it that, and the compact bunk room with tiny bunk beds. He roamed out onto the grassed terrace behind the museum building. Mock cannons were stationed along the horseshoe-shaped crenelated battery to show how the fort operated as protection from invaders seeking to land at Saint-Malo.

The fort itself offered little protection from the elements save for the main building. He could see how attackers would not be able to penetrate the fort's walls, even at low tide. The rocky outcroppings from the isle itself would prevent an enemy ship from getting close to the ramparts without suffering major damage to its hull.

Wolfe expected to see others who had made the low-tide trek to the isle, but after he arrived, he found himself alone.

That suited him just fine.

He spread the blanket out across a patch of dormant grass and gathered the food he'd purchased earlier from the crêperie and spread it out on the blanket.

Peace and quiet of the tranquil day was interrupted only by the distant sound of waves crashing against the rocks and the squawking of a sea gull as it flew overhead in hopes he might toss it a morsel of his food. Inside the battery there was no wind at all and it felt much warmer than mid-fifties. In no time, he found himself shedding his windbreaker and over shirt in lieu of the single cooler t-shirt he wore underneath. After eating, he worked his way to the battery wall and gazed mindlessly out over the ocean and back toward the walled town of Saint-Malo.

With his binoculars, he saw a few stragglers wandering aimlessly along the beach and a half dozen or so following the stone pathway out to the isles. The stone pathways were only visible during lower tides. Among those on the pathway from Bon-Secours beach at Saint-Malo walking toward the first isle, Grand Bé, he noticed an odd trio, a well-built man with black hair, a large Black man wearing a beanie cap the same color as his skin, and an attractive olive-skinned woman with long dark hair.

There was nothing particularly significant about this trio other than the large Black man in the middle. It was Deja-vu, like he'd seen this man somewhere before.

As they drew closer, he refocused his binoculars on the trio, in particular the large Black man in the middle, who had now swapped positions with the woman. The three were walking up the rocky path on Grand Bé. There was really nothing of interest atop Grand Bé except the gravesite of writer François René Chateaubriand, and even that was unremarkable at best in his opinion. Nothing but a tomb adorned with a stone cross overlooking the ocean.

He followed the trio. They stopped and looked at the tomb.

He heard people talking and saw that two other couples had found their way onto Petit Bé and had joined him inside the battery. The couples walked together and obviously were friends. They were older. Sixties he guessed. They didn't pay him any attention, so he turned his focus back to the trio at Grande Bé. *Where'd they go?* He swept his binoculars across the area. He should see them somewhere, coming or going. Then he reacquired them. They had crossed down the rocky slope of Grand Bé and found the stone walkway leading them toward Petit Bé. He quickly adjusted the eyepiece to zoom in closer. Especially on the Black man.

His Deja vu turned into panic.

CHAPTER 52

After they entered the ramparts of Saint-Malo, Kaplan had them split up to cover the streets of the small walled city. With the above average warmth of the winter day, he told Marla and Moss to concentrate mainly on the outdoor areas to start with, then they were to rendezvous at 1300 hours at Porte des Bés, the gate on the west side of the city about midway along the western wall.

When they gathered at the gate, they discussed what they'd seen while each had scoured their designated sections of the walled city. No one had seen anyone who resembled Wolfe. Their task was easy since it was the off-season and then the recent cold snap and snowfall, now melted, had rendered Saint-Malo more a ghost town than a bustling center of tourism. After they compared notes, they walked the beach, first south and then north, checking out the limited number of people out on this day. Indeed, the off season had left most of the heavily traveled tourist towns in France painfully empty. Which worked in their favor, not as many faces to rule out.

"You seem to know where you're going," said Moss. "You been here before?"

He threw Marla a quick glance. "Years ago, on a mission assignment with Isa—a previous partner."

"It's okay," she said. "I get it. That was before her...medical issue, right?"

"It was." He swallowed hard and motioned to the north. "In the summer, all these beaches around Saint-Malo are wall-to-wall bodies. You can't walk up and down the beach without stepping on someone."

He waved their attention to Passage des Bés. "While it's low tide, let's check out these two islands. Grand Bé and Petit Bé. When the tide comes in, it won't be possible."

"Shouldn't we search the city some more?" Moss asked.

"As warm as it is right now, if I were Wolfe, I'd be outside. This mild weather is an anomaly."

"Looks like a long walk."

Kaplan started walking toward the stone walkway. "Let's go."

Moss's grumbling stopped after they reached Grand Bé. He appeared to be in awe of the beauty of the ocean and rocky islands. "Almost reminds me of that island near Martinique, but on a much smaller scale," he said.

There was no one on Grand Bé, so they quickly moved toward Petit Bé along the stone pathway, climbed the rocky steps and into the fort. Kaplan checked his watch—1345. "Low tide is at 1400 hours. We have to be out of here no later than 1500. Once the tide shifts, it comes in fast around these islands."

"No problem," said Moss. "Quick look around and we're outta here, right?"

They separated and each searched a third of the main building and met back at the entrance. As they entered the terrace inside the battery, two couples passed by them on their way back toward Saint-Malo. He heard them speaking. Americans. Two of them, a short bald guy and a blonde woman were clearly from the South. And as a fellow Southerner, he recognized the accents. The other couple, a white-haired man and a brunette were from somewhere up north. His guess was Michigan because they sounded just like Isabella's friends.

Kaplan and Moss moved aside allowing the couples to exit. When they entered the grassy terrace, there was only one other person up there. A man feverishly stuffing items into his backpack. He pulled on a shirt and then a jacket. He wore a baseball cap and kept his head tilted so the brim shielded his face from view. Beneath it, Kaplan could see sunglasses.

Marla spoke up. "What's the phrase you Americans like to say when you get lucky? Pay dirt?"

"Huh?" Moss said.

"She's right," Kaplan watched the man get to his feet and hurry toward the exit. Kaplan moved to cut off the man's retreat. "Wolfe?" he asked.

The man took off running.

"Matthew Wolfe. Stop." Kaplan hollered.

All four in a foot race for the exit. Marla was closest and had the jump on Wolfe. Kaplan, a close second. And Moss wasn't even a contender.

Right before Marla and Kaplan closed in there was a loud gunshot blast. A booming voice yelled, "Freeze, mother fucker."

Matthew Wolfe stopped dead in his tracks.

Moss grinned.

CHAPTER 53

Kaplan shoved Matthew Wolfe against the Petit Bé battery wall next to one of the nineteen embrasures for guns along the wall. Terror ran through the man's eyes. It was the four of them alone inside the fort and now they had finally nabbed Wolfe.

They'd all put their lives on the line more than once, just to be the first to locate Wolfe. And they'd done it…but not without cost. Three Russian lives. Actually, four when he factored in Spike, whose life was lost in Beaune. There were innocent people murdered. Wolfe's girlfriend in Iceland, the first innocent life lost. And now, Sophie Bouquet.

He glared at Wolfe. The traitor likely didn't know of Sophie's fate yet. Wolfe was the one responsible for putting Sophie Bouquet in the line of fire. Her blood was on his hands.

When Kaplan approached, Wolfe trembled, eyes begging not to be harmed. He grabbed Wolfe by the shirt and shoved him into the terrace leaving Moss, Marla and him between Wolfe and the only exit from the fort.

Wolfe held his hands up in surrender. "Are…are you going to kill me?" he stammered.

"Depends. I want answers," said Kaplan.

Marla stepped forward and shoved Wolfe in chest. He stumbled back two steps. She moved closer and shoved him again, this time harder and he fell backwards landing on his backside. She hovered over him and demanded, "Why did you drag Sophie Bouquet into your web of deceit?"

Kaplan had never seen Marla so angry.

"Why, asshole, why?" Marla's face turned red. "Why her? If

you hadn't come into her life, she would be alive today."

"What? Sophie's dead?" Wolfe had trouble catching his breath.

Marla kicked him in the ribs. "She died in my arms. You didn't even have the courage to come after her when she was kidnapped. She told me you were inside the coffee shop. Inside. Safe, while she was taken. You bastard."

Wolfe's head dropped against his chest. Marla swung her arm and slapped him hard against the face. "Look at me you coward." She slapped him again, and again till Kaplan caught her arm in midair.

Wolfe started crying, rolled to his side and curled into the fetal position. "Oh my God. What have I done?" he wailed.

Moss said, "I say we toss his sorry ass over the wall and let the sea gulls have him."

"Just let the prick cry it out," he said to Moss. He looked at Marla. "And you stay away from him," Kaplan said and pushed Marla away.

Then he walked over to the battery wall and gazed out over the ocean. There were clouds forming in the distance. Another change in the weather coming. The wind picked up. An ill wind. An omen of bad things on the horizon. He squinted down at the water lapping against the rocks below. The tide had changed. Waves were starting to roll over the prepared stone walkway leading back to shore.

He turned. Moss and Marla were staring at him. "Tides coming in, we got to go." He walked over to Wolfe. "You're lucky I don't let them kill you." What he really meant was Wolfe was lucky he didn't kill him himself.

Wolfe didn't move.

"I don't have time to argue." He bent down, snatched

Wolfe's arm and yanked the man to his feet. He reached beneath his jacket, got his gun and shoved it into Wolfe's lower back. Wolfe's eyes bulged. "You do what I tell you or I'll put a bullet in you. Now, start walking."

He motioned for Moss and Marla to take the lead, while he pulled up the rear. Wolfe was in the middle with Kaplan's gun barrel shoved hard in his back. They made their way from the island of Petit Bé toward the ramparts of Saint-Malo.

As the foursome passed Grand Bé, halfway back to shore, another gust of wind blew across Kaplan's back.

The ill wind blew harder.

His alarm bells went into high gear.

CHAPTER 54

Sitting atop the ramparts of Saint-Malo, Dmitry Gagarin was now the GRU's last level of backup.

His boss, Igor Nevsky, head of the Second Directorate of the GRU, had told him to personally ensure backup levels were in place in case their number one asset, Tatyana Kazakov, failed. The implied meaning was that he, Gagarin, *was* that backup level.

In his earlier days as an asset with the GRU, he was a sniper, one of the best in the world, especially with the long shot. But the modern GRU didn't have much use for a sniper, their methods were different, up close and personal, devious and sinister. And deadly. But on occasion his sniping skills were still needed. Especially when a target had to be executed from a distance, typically high-profile targets with strong security in place. There was no getting close to those targets. When GRU assets couldn't get close, they called Gagarin.

Tatyana Kazakov's man in training had failed his mentor and Gagarin ordered his termination. Tatyana personally handled that mandate in Beaune. She didn't make excuses for her trainee's failure, simply took care of business. As expected. It also gave her incentive not to fail knowing her fate would be the same if she did.

That left him to make sure Tatyana didn't fail, but she did. Through his scope, he saw the incident in Bayeux unfold. Tatyana and her two men had captured Matthew Wolfe's girlfriend and taken her inside an empty house to learn the location of Wolfe. Within minutes, three others arrived, two men and a woman, and entered the same abandoned home.

Seconds later, Gagarin heard gunshots and a bloody Tatyana ran from the house and scaled the wall to a cemetery, all the while being chased by one of the men who entered earlier.

Tatyana Kazakov had failed.

It was then up to him to accomplish the two-fold task for the GRU—deal with Kazakov's failure and locate Matthew Wolfe.

When Tatyana Kazakov stopped in the cemetery and was confronted by the man chasing her, Gagarin fulfilled one of his tasks. He squeezed off the 100-meter shot with his sniper rifle, the bullet found her chest dead center.

Tatyana Kazakov was dead.

At the sight of her chest exploding, the man searched the area where he had fired. It was only then Gagarin got a good look at the man's face through his scope. He recognized the man. An American. He had seen that face in several GRU files. He was the one responsible for the scar on Tatyana's neck. As much as he wanted to take out the American, he did not want the weight and fury of the CIA to come down on him nor the GRU. That could wait for another time and another place.

Dmitry Gagarin disassembled his rifle, packed it in its case and returned to his vehicle. Igor Nevsky would not be happy hearing the news of Tatyana's failure. But he knew he must inform his boss.

It took some doing, but he was able to pick up the trail of Matthew Wolfe by following the three who foiled Kazakov's attempt to extract information from Sophie Bouquet. He had to enlist help from his associates in Russia. He lost them in Caen when they boarded a private jet and flew to Paris. He was afraid he had failed. But a few hours later, the same associate informed him the jet was flying west to Saint-Malo. He was able to arrive at the Saint-Malo airport as the jet landed. It was indeed the same three people who foiled Tatyana's plan and killed two GRU men. From that point on, it was a matter of following the Audi the dark-haired man rented. One night in Avranches and now, back to Saint-Malo.

Perched on the rampart above the northwest gate of Porte des Champs-Vauvert, through his high-powered binoculars he watched the trio traverse the low-tide stone walkway out to the two islands sitting off the western shore. His attention piqued after he heard a blast coming from Petit Bé. He waited and saw four figures emerge from the fort's entrance…and one of them was Matthew Wolfe.

CHAPTER 55

Jasmine Habibi disconnected her call-in with Iranian Intelligence Minister Qasem Khatami. She knew he would be upset with her update, but she was not expecting a death threat. If his support people hadn't given her bad intel about Matthew Wolfe's whereabouts, then she wouldn't have had the run-in with the CIA operative, his friend and the Mossad operative in Sophie Bouquet's apartment.

She knew both Khatami and MOIS were under pressure from his nemesis at the Revolutionary Guard, but she shouldn't be held accountable for Khatami's support failure. Her success hinged on the accuracy of information his people provided her while she was in the field. They failed, thus she failed. This was on him, not her, and she resented being told that if the mission failed, she would not return to Iran alive. The more she thought about it, the angrier she became.

Of course, there was the added pressure put on Khatami from the Supreme Leader. If this mission failed, it wasn't just her life that hung in the balance, but his as well. Thus, the threat on her life. As the Americans were fond of saying, *shit rolls downhill.* And she sat pretty close to the bottom.

Her MOIS handler claimed they tracked the Mossad jet to Saint-Malo and she, along with her team, were dispatched there immediately. Jasmine thought they had lost the trail for good when she had a stroke of luck. She spotted the CIA operative, Gregg Kaplan, who she'd had a skirmish with before, driving a black Audi into the parking lot outside the ramparts of Saint-Malo. She and her team were back in the game. This time if

Kaplan, his friend or Marla Farache got in her way, she would kill them all.

Jasmine and her men covertly followed them through the streets of Saint-Malo until the trio wandered onto the beach. She and her men found their way to the Tower Bidouane, which was a fortified section of the rampart that jutted out from the northwest corner, formerly used as a weapons battery, now a raised spot for tourists to view the ocean and the islands of Grand Bé and Petit Bé to the west and Fort National to the northeast.

From this vantage point, she observed Kaplan, Marla Farache and Kaplan's friend, Pete Moss, walk out to Petit Bé along the low-tide stone walkway. Using her binoculars, she panned the surrounding area. Then she suddenly stopped panning, focusing on another face she recognized to the south of her. Standing on the ramparts, also using binoculars to look out over Petit Bé was Dmitry Gagarin, the right-hand man of Igor Nevsky of the GRU. He was accompanied by three men. His presence could mean only one thing, Tatyana Kazakov was dead.

Through the lenses Jasmine saw Gagarin perk up at the sound of a blast coming from Petit Bé. She panned her sights out toward the smaller island where Kaplan and his team had disappeared earlier, and she saw it.

Three people went out to the island and now there were four returning.

The fourth person was Matthew Wolfe.

CHAPTER 56

"Stop." Kaplan called to Moss and Marla. "Move back toward me."

Moss and Marla spun around and shared a bewildered look. He shoved the barrel of his gun hard in Wolfe's back. "You too."

"What's wrong?" Marla asked.

"Something's not right," he said.

"I sense it too," Moss added.

"What's going on?" Wolfe asked.

"We know the Russians were here…searching for you. Might still be. And the Iranians. Also, a third party we haven't identified yet. "Plus," he said while focusing on Marla. "She's Mossad. There are a lot of people on the hunt for you. Some have orders to kill on sight. Some want to take you back to their home country, torture, interrogate, then kill you. No one plans on keeping you alive but us. You need to understand that right now. We are your only chance of survival. Am I making myself clear?"

Wolfe gave a stiff nod.

"Good." He looked past Wolfe to Moss and Marla. "I have a gut feeling we're walking into an ambush. I don't know how, when or where but I'm pretty damn sure we're being watched and assessed."

"Maybe you're wrong," Wolfe said to Kaplan.

Moss shot back, "If Kaplan says we're in danger, you better fucking listen and do what he says. Because if it comes down to your life or ours, you're a dead man walking."

"Anyone got binoculars?" Kaplan asked.

Marla shook her head. So did Moss.

"Wolfe?" said Kaplan.

"Yes. In my backpack," the man answered.

Kaplan threw the backpack to Marla. She caught the bag in her hands. "Get them out and scan the area.

Kaplan shot Moss a look. "Marla knows who or what to look for. She's been in the business a long time. The world of espionage is small. We know most of the players."

Marla dug out the binoculars, put them against her eyes and swept the ramparts of Saint-Malo. "Nothing out of the ordinary," she said.

"Let's move ahead, but keep your eyes peeled for anything suspicious. Or anyone."

The foursome moved at a slow pace. Kaplan looked behind him. In the distance he could see the incoming tide rippling across the walkway from Grand Bé to Petit Bé. An inch or two, at most. For now.

They were about a hundred feet from the shoreline when Moss held up a hand. "Stop."

"I see him," Kaplan added. "Two o'clock. Moving down the ramp with three men."

"No," Moss said insistently. "Ten o'clock. Two men and a woman with long dark hair."

"Marla, check it out," Kaplan ordered.

"Moss is right. Ten o'clock, Jasmine and her two pals. Two o'clock is...is, oh my God." She handed the binoculars back to Kaplan. "I think it's Dmitry Gagarin. GRU. And another Russian goon squad."

Kaplan found the man in the sights, it was indeed Gagarin, the right-hand man to Igor Nevsky, head of the Second Directorate of the GRU. The pieces fell in place. He was the next level of backup. And probably the last. He was also a former sniper, which meant he was probably the trigger man who took out Tatyana Kazakov. And his goon squad, as Marla put it, were just like Kazakov's—all brawn, no brain.

He panned left to ten o'clock and confirmed it was Jasmine Habibi and her two thugs. The same ones they bested in Paris at Sophie's apartment. He remembered his promise to Jasmine— *if I see you again in France, I won't give you a warning. I will kill you first and then your two thugs.*

If there was any doubt that there were other actors following them, it had now evaporated. He lowered the binoculars.

Matthew Wolfe was gone.

"What the...?"

Moss and Marla spun around at the same time.

Moss said, "Where'd he go?"

"Dammit. That stupid asshole," barked Kaplan.

Marla spotted him and pointed.

Matthew Wolfe was in an all-out sprint back toward Petit Bé, splashing water when his shoes landed with each step along the flooded Passage des Bés.

Kaplan hadn't come this far to let Wolfe get away. And he wasn't too keen on having a shoot-out right here on the beach with the Iranians and the Russians. At least in the fort on Petit Bé he could hold off their assault, if there was one. The night would get cold but there was shelter indoors...kind of. The bastions of the fort could provide shelter and defense. Although the opposition could wait them out, it would give them a chance to regroup and formulate a new plan. And he could keep Wolfe out of harm's way.

"Retreat."

With that command, the trio ran back toward the fort on Petit Bé.

CHAPTER 57

After the four of them reached the safety of the fort, Moss pulled Kaplan to the side, out of earshot of Wolfe and Marla. "Okay buddy, I for one, am not too enthused about this last turn of events."

He wasn't too enthused about their predicament either, but he'd been in worse. Shit, they'd been in worse. He saw Marla eyeing him and Moss. He waved her over.

When she huddled with them, Kaplan said, "We don't have many options, so let's throw everything we can think of on the table. Who wants to start?"

Marla spoke up, "I can call in Mossad reinforcements. Probably take a couple of hours for them to get here."

"If I call Alan," Kaplan added. "It'll be about the same time frame."

"We can fight," Moss said.

"Seven of them to four of us," Marla said.

In unison, the trio looked at Matthew Wolfe sitting against the battery wall just inside the entrance to the terrace.

"Three of us," she corrected.

Wolfe blurted, "I'm not totally worthless, you know. I can shoot a gun. I had excellent scores at the range."

Moss moved close to Wolfe and glared at him. "This ain't target practice, shithead. This is real life. Ever shot a person before? Ever shot *at* a man before? How about at a somebody who's shooting back at you? Huh, Wolfe? There's a big difference between a firing range with or without moving targets and killing another human being." Moss motioned toward the shoreline. "Those people out there, they'll kill you…and they won't lose a moment's sleep doing it either."

Moss continued to stare, not saying a word, as if waiting for Wolfe to answer. Finally, he did.

"No." Wolfe's voice weak.

"What's that?" Moss deepened his voice.

"No," Wolfe fired back. "No, I haven't shot at a person before. Satisfied?"

"No, I'm not satisfied, prick. If it weren't for you, none of us would be in this predicament to start with. If you hadn't betrayed our country, stole secrets, and run off. If you had just worked your issues internally through the system and didn't have such a big ass ego to assume that only *you* can judge what's in the public's best interest, then we wouldn't be here right now. And one more thing little man." Moss gestured toward Kaplan. "You see that man over there, his job is to find you, protect you, and take you into custody. But that's not my job. I don't give two shits whether you live or die. I do care what happens to him and to her, so if you do another thing, and I mean one single thing to jeopardize our situation, or you get in our way, I'll kill you."

Moss walked back and stood next to Kaplan and Marla.

Wolfe shouted, "You gonna let him threaten me?"

Kaplan aimed his silenced weapon and fired a shot into the battery wall about three feet from Wolfe and head high.

Kaplan lowered his voice and said to Moss, "Why'd you go so easy on him?"

"Just my nurturing demeanor."

They all smiled and cut the tension of the moment.

Kaplan said, "Back to ideas. I'm not in favor of calling in either Mossad or the CIA. If we call either, we lose control of the situation. They'll want to take over."

He dug into his coat pocket and removed a business card. "This is the contact info for the GIGN colonel. I could call her. I'm sure the Gendarmerie have people a lot closer than Paris. But again, I'm sure they would insist on taking control."

"Since when do you ever call in the cavalry?" Moss asked.

"The enemy has the advantage," Marla said. "They can wait us out. And they have us outnumbered over two to one."

It was Kaplan's turn to speak. "Tide's coming in fast now, so we're stuck out here at least until the next low tide."

"Which means they are stuck on shore until the next low tide," Marla said.

"I wish that were true." He swiveled his head looking at the sky then he glanced at his watch. "It'll be dark in an hour or so and the weather will take a turn for the worse tonight. Fortunately, we have the high ground and built-in protection from the fort. After it gets dark, one or both parties will make their move."

Moss asked, "What if they join forces?"

"Then we're screwed."

CHAPTER 58

Dmitry Gagarin watched the group run back toward the farthest island. The one with the fort. First, Wolfe, followed by the others, either chasing him or joining him. The stone walkway, Passage des Be's, was rapidly disappearing with the incoming tide. Soon the tide would swallow it completely.

His prey would be trapped. Actually, they were already trapped.

He signaled to his men and said one word in Russian, "Go."

He followed as his men ran toward Grand Bé, the first island. At first the water barely hit the soles of his boots. Halfway to Grand Bé, it was mid-calf then shallowed as he and his men got closer to the larger island. Soon they were on dry land. Rock actually. He stood on a perch and observed his men wading toward Petit Bé, only to abandon near the halfway point when water got chest-high and wind-driven waves crashed over their heads. They slogged their way back to him on Grand Bé. Now he had to plan his next move. He didn't blame them and he wasn't angry. At least one of them, he knew, couldn't swim. Plus, the water was frigid. Just the small amount of water that seeped into his boots was ice cold and his toes were already feeling numb. But his men were younger, much younger, all in their twenties. Stronger and in better physical shape. He'd have them build a fire with the island's shrubs to warm them and help dry their clothes.

As Igor Nevsky's right-hand man, Gagarin sat at his desk most days, and not in the field. Until Tatyana failed.

He hated terminating Tatyana Kazakov. She had been a superior asset for over a decade. A sleeper agent in America who found legitimate occupation that included extensive travel, or at least that was the impression the Russian government spent decades building. A Russian owned company shielded by numerous levels of shell corporations to mask its true identity and purpose—spy on America and provide a base for their agents.

But Tatyana made mistakes. Her first being her over-confidence in the trainee she thought was ready for field duty and clearly wasn't. He was easily caught by the Americans. For that, his punishment was death...by her hand. Her second mistake was in Bayeux.

If Gagarin failed, his life might be spared by Nevsky, but he would likely be exiled to some remote location, like Siberia, and never heard from again. If he too was captured by the Americans like Tatyana and her trainee, he would receive the same death sentence. It was the way Russia handled failure.

He would not let that happen, though. He would never be captured alive by the Americans.

He would eat a bullet first.

† † †

Jasmine Habibi recognized the Russian as soon as she spotted him walking down the ramp with his men toward Passage des Bés and the fleeing Americans and Mossad agent.

Mossad agent.

Marla Farache, the niece of Eli Levine, director of Mossad. She'd dealt with Marla Farache before, but never like this. Never in an instance where it boiled down to kill or be killed. And that was what this was. Her orders were clear cut—under no circumstances allow Matthew Wolfe to fall into the hands of Mossad. Abandon capture, kill on sight. Now, Wolfe was on the small island with a known CIA operative, another man who seemed to be working for or with the CIA and Mossad operative Marla Farache. Her mission now was to kill Matthew Wolfe.

Gagarin and his men only made it as far as the first island before the incoming tides and crashing surf drove them back. She had never met Dmitry Gagarin, but certainly knew his reputation. Although not in an official capacity, for all intents and purposes Gagarin was the GRU's second-in-command. He had spent his entire career with the GRU, molded and prepped from a young age. He rose the ranks as he became the trusted confidant of Igor Nevsky. Gagarin did the dirty work Nevsky needed done to advance his own political career. As Nevsky moved up the GRU ladder, he brought along Gagarin.

In his day, Gagarin was a ruthless GRU operative. But his heyday was decades ago. Now in his sixties, Gagarin only oversaw the GRU's missions from a distance—unless he was needed in the field to ensure a younger operative did not fail a mission. And his presence here explained the sudden disappearance of Tatyana Kazakov and her men.

Jasmine's men followed her to the beach. She used her binoculars to scan both islands. No one was seen on the small island farthest from shore. Clearly Gregg Kaplan and friends were tucked away inside the fort. But, on the larger island, Gagarin and his men were huddled on top near the Tomb of Francois René Chateaubriand, no doubt strategizing how they could get to the smaller island and capture Wolfe.

There was one skill Gagarin possessed that Jasmine could use to fulfill her mission. He was the GRU's legendary sniper of old who still kept his skills sharp—and she needed Wolfe killed.

CHAPTER 59

Kaplan studied the unfolding situation with the Russians and the Iranians with renewed interest. Dmitry Gagarin and his three men waded to Grand Bé and then abandoned their attempt to reach the smaller island. Now they were camped at the top of Grand Bé, literally. He could see wisps of smoke where the men were huddled in a small circle around the amber glow of a fire.

On shore he saw Jasmine Habibi and her two men. And for her, a promise he had yet to fulfill.

Unfortunately, the four of them were trapped on Petit Bé. Passage des Bés had all but completely disappeared beneath the dark blue waters now creeping closer to the ramparts of Saint-Malo. The channel between the two islands was the deepest portion and the first to disappear with the incoming tide. Conversely, it would be the last to reappear with the outgoing tide. He used his burner phone to search for the Saint-Malo tide charts. The next low tide was in a little less than five hours. The average tidal shift from low tide to high tide was close to forty feet. That explained the swiftness of the tidal currents.

A reef of clouds raced across the sky, rolling in almost as fast as the tide did. The wind picked up and the temperature dropped. He could feel the change in humidity in the air. With the increase in winds and the incoming tide, a misting of sea spray off the rocks found its way over the battery wall.

Within minutes, rain moved in from the north, dimming the ocean in the offing, clicking against the stone ramparts. Wind-driven droplets stung his face.

Dusk came fast and so did nightfall. Much faster than usual when clear skies prevailed. Now, Grand Bé was just a shadow looming in the distance. All he could see of Saint-Malo were lights inside the ramparts and spotlights on the beach.

On Petit Bé, only darkness.

Tonight, darkness would be his friend.

CHAPTER 60

Kaplan summoned Marla and Moss to follow him inside the fort. He wasn't worried about Wolfe, that man wasn't going anywhere. There was nowhere to go.

During their downtime, he had decided the only way they were going to get out of there alive was if they took the offensive. If he took the offensive. He laid out his plan.

"I don't like it," Moss said. "Like I told Alan, you go, I go."

"I need you here, Moss. If the Russians or Iranians get here before I get back, I need you to fend them off. Can you do that?"

"Sure, but you need your partner. Two against four is a hell of a lot better than one against four."

"I can fend them off," she said.

"I know you can Marla and I need you to help Moss if they get past me."

"You need me, Kaplan," Moss insisted.

"Not this time, Moss. Besides you don't like to swim and this water is frigid." He glanced at his watch using his penlight. "High tide in 30 minutes. I want to use the last of the incoming and slack tide to get positioned. Jasmine and her men will come for us when the tide goes out. About three hours from now. By then, Grand Bé should be all clear. And Moss, if you haven't heard from me by then, come get me." He turned to Marla. "And you should call the GIGN."

Kaplan went in the bunkroom of the fort and started shedding his clothes. He needed to be as light as possible for the swim over and he'd need dry, warm clothes when he reached the island or hypothermia could and would set in fast. Moss and Marla followed him into the bunkroom.

"Let me get this straight," Moss said. "You're going to swim over…in your skivvies…in this cold water…holding your clothes over your head. And then get dressed and geared up?"

"Something like that, yeah."

"Stupid," Moss said. "Ballsy, but stupid. Ever done anything like this before?"

"Sort of. Back then I had a dry-bag and the water temperature wasn't this cold."

Marla pivoted and left the bunkroom.

"Come on, man," Moss argued. "Don't try to do this shit alone. I know you're capable and all, but going alone is too dangerous, not to mention foolish."

"I appreciate what you're saying, Moss. I need to better our chances."

Moss tried to interrupt but Kaplan continued, "Listen to me, Moss. If for some reason I don't get these guys, I need you to make sure those two are safe and Wolfe gets into CIA custody."

"You're pig headed. If you need help, you damn well better call me."

"Deal."

There were reasons Kaplan worked alone. When working with a team, or a single partner for that matter, it was difficult to do so covertly. When a team moved, especially a larger team, it usually could not be done in secrecy, but when one man moved alone, stealth was easier to accomplish.

Marla came back in the bunkroom holding Wolfe's backpack. She dumped all his belongings on one of the dusty old bunks. "It's not a dry-bag, but it might make it easier to swim and keep dry if everything is in one bag."

"Thanks, Marla." He continued stripping clothes and stuffing them in the backpack in the reverse order he would need to put them on. Moments later he was standing in his boxer-briefs, socks and boots.

Moss walked out.

Marla pushed next to him and gently kissed his cheek. "Be careful," she whispered in his ear.

He nodded and tried hard to show no concern for how he really felt.

† † †

Gregg hadn't been gone ten minutes when she walked in the bunkroom and found Moss stripping off his clothes. She turned feigning embarrassment.

"What do you think you're doing? Gregg told you to stay put."

"Kaplan's not my boss, Marla. I'm not going to sit out here and let my friend get killed. And I don't think you want that either. You want him to stay safe as much as I do...maybe more."

She couldn't argue with anything Moss said except that Gregg was adamant he should do this alone. And she'd seen him in action before. He was capable of handling this by himself. And more. He was lethal and didn't stop until the job was done. But she also knew these types of operations always had hiccups. She hadn't seen the two of them in action together. Maybe Moss was right. Maybe tonight Kaplan needed his partner.

"Marla?"

Moss and Gregg both have extensive experience handling their weapons. They were an odd pairing, but it had already become evident the kind of working relationship and friendship they have. All the digs at each other just fuels their immature sides, then at a moment's notice, they're all business. Her thoughts were interrupted when Moss placed his hand on her shoulder.

"Earth to Marla."

She jerked. "Oh, I'm sorry. What were you saying?"

"I said, don't you dare warn Kaplan I'm coming. He'll know when I get there."

"I won't, I promise. But like I told him. Be careful. And you need to let him know you're on the island the moment you get there or he might shoot you by mistake."

"Good thinking," Moss said.

He laid his tactical pants inside his parka with his weapons on top, folded the top and bottom of the parka on top of them and cinched it closed with the sleeves. It looked like an oversized hobo bag. Like Gregg, he was down to socks, boots, boxer-briefs, although Moss kept his t-shirt over his massive torso.

"Don't look so worried. Kaplan and I have been down this road before." He gave her a big toothy grin and then quickly disappeared into the darkness.

† † †

Kaplan could handle cold water, but he also knew the dangers that being submerged in cold water had on the body. Hypothermia occurred when body temperature fell below 95 degrees Fahrenheit, which could happen in minutes in cold water. A body lost heat 25 times faster in cold water than it did in cold air. In January in Northern France, the ocean water was likely around 40 degrees, giving him a window of 30 to 90 minutes before death. He had no intention of being in the water that long. 10 to 15 minutes, tops. It wasn't far from Petit Bé to Grand Bé and he had the help of the incoming tide to speed up the swim.

When he hit the water, he made an involuntary gasp called a torso reflex. He knew the process all too well from his Special Forces training. First, skin cooled. Then the body constricted surface blood vessels to conserve heat for the vital organs. Blood pressure and heart rate increased. Muscles tensed causing shivers to produce more heat. Dexterity and motor control diminished the longer in the water. As hypothermia set in, blood pressure, heart rate and respiration decreased. Rational thought diminished and confusion set in. Eventually leading to organ failure, cardiac and respiratory failure. The colder the water, the quicker death knocked on the door. Body fat played a role in time to hypothermia too. As did physical fitness. He wasn't as lean now as he was in the Army, but his BMI was still low compared to most people. Plus, he kept himself in excellent physical condition. Everyone was different and so was their time to hypothermia and death.

The wind and waves drove him toward a lone rocky outcropping between the islands. His feet found purchase on the shallowing water keeping him from crashing into the rocks.

When he neared Grand Bé, he could feel the incoming tide weaken.

He wanted to swim freestyle but he needed to keep the bag dry and also knew freestyle might make too much noise. He couldn't run the risk of being heard by Gagarin and company. He continued with his one-arm breaststroke method, not allowing his swimming arm to break the surface all the while holding the backpack above his head. When his arm cramped, he swapped swimming arms.

As the shadow of Grand Bé loomed larger in the darkness, he felt his feet hit the rocky bottom. The shivers started less than five minutes into his swim.

They were much worse now.

CHAPTER 61

The swim to Grand Bé took less than ten minutes. Traversing the rocky shore to the north side of the island took longer than Kaplan wanted. By the time he eased out of the water, he was shaking uncontrollably. Keeping the backpack above the water wasn't difficult at first, but almost impossible by the time he crawled from the surf.

He wasted no time getting dressed.

Quickly and quietly, he slipped on layer after layer, warming his body with each extra layer. After he was fully dressed, the only things not warm were his feet. Wet socks and wet boots. He knew from experience they would warm when he started moving. Fortunately, they were tactical boots with a self-purging foot bed for instances exactly like this. No water sloshing around inside. He tucked the backpack under a rock to keep it from blowing away in the now blustery cold wind.

He double-checked his gear and weaponry. All good.

He keyed his comm system. "On site. Check in."

Marla voice was first to speak. "Loud and clear. Awaiting instructions."

Moss's voice was next. He was panting and breathless. "Ditto."

"Moss, where are you?"

"I walked down the rocks to take a piss. I'm climbing back up now."

"Roger that," Kaplan replied with a smile.

Typical.

The climb up the north face of Grand Bé was treacherous and steep. He assumed Gagarin and his men would be looking toward Petit Bé or the mainland and not toward the east. His plan was to crest the cliff at the site of the tomb, giving him more cover when he reached the top. Then he could locate each of the four men and assess his options.

When he reached the cliff's edge, he caught sight of a small fire. Gagarin was seated in front of the fire warming his hands with his back to the tomb. His three men were scattered across the apex of the isle with guns in hands. Each keeping watch on his assigned sector. One looking and guarding west toward Petit Bé, one facing south toward shore where Habibi and her goons were no doubt waiting for the change in tide. And the third on patrol and constantly moving. That man could be a problem.

The three men were dressed alike, all young and fit. They had blocky features, not unlike Spike, who was killed in Beaune. Large shoulders and bulky physiques of men who spent several hours a day in the gym.

Gagarin barked an order in Russian and the man facing west tucked his gun in his belt and went down the western slope only to return moments later with branches in hand that he placed next to the fire. It appeared Gagarin was settling in and waiting for the next low tide. Probably with the intention of storming the fort once they could navigate Passage des Bés again.

The same one of Gagarin's men who gathered the firewood said something to Gagarin. The boss nodded and the man turned toward the tomb and moved in Kaplan's direction. Kaplan ducked low as the man came to the cliff's edge and stopped no more than ten feet away. He unzipped his fly and urinated. When he returned to the fire, Gagarin barked off the same order he heard before and the man again disappeared down the western slope.

Gagarin gave the same order to the man on patrol and directed the man's attention to the southern slope. The second man came Kaplan's way and walked down a path that led back toward Saint-Malo at low tide.

Kaplan moved from his perch, Ka-Bar knife in hand, and followed the Russian, paralleling him but staying just clear of the path. The Russian was larger than the other two, larger than Kaplan, and content there was no danger lurking about.

He was wrong.

Kaplan worked his way behind the Russian who was bent over next to a rock wall to break off a branch from a bush. He cupped his hand over the man's mouth with one hand and in one swift movement sliced the man's throat with his Ka-Bar blade. He held the man tight as he bled out. He squirmed for a few seconds before his life force left him.

Then Kaplan heard the sound on the far side of the isle. One of the Russians was in trouble, hollering out in pain. The night air burst in sounds of gun fire.

More yelling atop the isle and scrambling of feet.

Another blast.

Kaplan knew he was a sitting duck if Gagarin or one his men came in search of their comrade.

He lowered the dead man to the ground and wiped his bloody blade clean on the man's pant leg. After returning the Ka-Bar to its sheath, he used his pen light to search the man. The young face of the dead Russian, eyes still wide open was haunting.

Kaplan bent low to a half-squat and cautiously moved back to the crest of the island.

When he reached the site of the tomb, the third man was

looking over the western slope and calling a man's name. Gagarin was next to him, looking in the same direction, crouched as if they had seen something...or someone. Both men had weapons drawn and aimed down the slope.

Gagarin yelled over his shoulder. Probably calling the man Kaplan had just executed. He could hear the rising tension in Gagarin's voice. Almost panic.

Then Kaplan's comm crackled in his ear.

He wasn't alone.

CHAPTER 62

"Kaplan, location?"

It was Moss's voice in his ear.

"South of the tomb on the lower path. One hostile down. Don't know what's happening up top. Several gunshots and a lot of yelling."

"Make that two hostiles down."

"Moss, don't tell me you're here?"

"Northwest corner. Came out of the water and surprised a Russki."

"Dammit, Moss. I told you not to follow."

"You go, I go."

This was unexpected, but not unwelcome. Although he'd never tell Moss how he felt. If he took out one and Moss took out one, the odds were now even. Only thing was Gagarin and his man had the high ground. He and Moss were down and at a clear disadvantage. Although they knew roughly where Moss was, their thinking was the battle was against one gunman not two. And that gave him and Moss an edge. Specifically, that gave Kaplan an edge.

Kaplan belly-crawled in the darkness to the apex of the island. Or as far as he dared without giving away his position.

Gagarin had moved away from his other man to a location that allowed him to protect two directions at once—west and south. His man was perched in the northwest corner and could protect the west and north sectors. There was no one watching the east. The east side was as close to a sheer cliff as the small isle offered, but it was the way Kaplan had originally accessed the isle. Gagarin periodically turned and yelled for the man Kaplan killed. It wouldn't take him long to realize the odds had changed and he was up against more than one invader.

"Kaplan, what's happening?" Marla's voice over the comm system.

"All good," Kaplan replied.

"Moss?" she asked.

"Cold and wet."

"Can you move?" Kaplan asked Moss.

"Negative. I'm pinned behind a small boulder next to the water's edge. Seriously, I'm bigger than this damn rock. I can't even get dressed without that Russki having a clear shot at me. If I move, I'm toast."

Kaplan's mind raced to figure out his options. Actually, their options. He needed to create a diversion. Something that would give Moss a chance to reposition. But he had to be careful. Gagarin might not have a sniper's rifle on him, but he was still a ringer with any firearm. Moving target or not.

He had an idea and hoped like hell it would work.

"Moss, can you stay put for a while?"

"Do I have a choice?"

† † †

Marla Farache heard the gunshots echo in the air and faint, frantic voices in the distance. Matthew Wolfe sat next to her on the steps of the fort's entrance. They had both been sitting and waiting anxiously without a word between them. She had been listening to the comms and all was quiet until the first shots rang out. Moss didn't announce his arrival to Gregg when he got there, but after his quick explanation, it was clear he didn't have an option.

"What's happening?" Wolfe asked, his voice edgy.

His silhouette was clear but no features visible. Although her eyes had adjusted to the darkness, it was simply too dark for such clarity.

She hesitated to respond. "Shut up so I can hear," she finally said.

She watched the light of the fire in the distance slowly dim as time passed. At first, it was bright enough that she could see figures moving around the island's mesa top. Now she could not see anything.

"I'm sorry about Sophie. I thought maybe an anti-protester took her. I never meant for her to be harmed," Wolfe confessed.

"She was murdered, you bastard." She paused and then said, "If you don't shut up, you could end up with the same fate."

Gregg and Moss had been gone over an hour and it had been twenty minutes since the last gunshot. Wolfe's head dropped into his hands. He began softly whimpering. She couldn't take it any longer. "Why'd you do it, Wolfe? Why did you abandon your country and turn traitor?"

Wolfe raised his head and sniffed, wiping his nose on his sleeve. "I didn't abandon anything. I was in a position to see what was happening around the world. The renewed threat of global nuclear annihilation."

"Yeah, right. You were just out to save the world. What a noble person you must think you are."

"What I'm telling you is the truth. Nuclear war wouldn't happen in the conventional way most people think about. It won't happen when a major country misinterprets what another country does as a threat and fires off a nuke, then the other major country says, *"Watch this,"* and fires off more nukes until it escalates to mutual destruction. No, that's not how it will happen. There's a lot more going on out there." He pointed up to the sky. "And up there. More than most people realize. If the world only knew, there would be a global outcry."

"That's a little vague, Wolfe."

"It isn't the superpowers that will start self-destruction, but they will finish it. To each other's demise. It's the rogue country you don't expect that will start the process."

He now had her attention. "Like Iran?"

"Possibly. Let me give you a rudimentary example. One you might relate to."

"Tell me."

"We both know that Saudi Arabia hates Iran and also has its own secret nuclear weapons program, right?"

"In the works."

"Not in the works, Ms. Farache, done. Completed and ready to deploy."

"If that were true, my country would know."

"Believe it or not, it's true. That was my job, to know every country's capabilities. For instance, let's say the Saudis covertly fire off a nuke at Israel, your country, but made it look like it was Iran that attacked Israel. How would Israel react?"

"We would unload on Iran."

"Exactly. And who would come to Iran's defense?"

She glanced out to the larger island and back at Wolfe. "The Russians."

"And what would happen if Russia attacks Israel?"

"I see where this is going. The United States would defend Israel by attacking the Russians, the Russians would retaliate and then you have your mutually assured destruction." She paused a beat. "I don't believe that would happen."

"It's one of many possible scenarios. I have volumes of possible scenarios involving many countries. Some you've never heard of or would suspect. All of them much more complex than the one I used. Starting with simple destabilizations of governments but all leading to the same thing—MAD. Start small and insignificant in surface appearance, but with tentacles reaching out to the major powers. A simple rock tossed in the water has a ripple effect across an entire lake. This isn't much different. What might seem to most people as a simple, harmless event could be part of an intricate plan. And who's the real winner? No one."

"If you believe this then why betray your country? Why not stay and keep them safe?"

"That's the thing, I didn't betray my country. They're just as guilty of secret programs as all the other countries. Perhaps more than most. This is information the whole world needs to know, not just governments. All the world's people. Global change is necessary…or we're all doomed."

"Where's your proof?"

"Hidden away where no one can get to it."

"What if I kill you right now? What happens to your proof?"

"I have fail-safe measures in place. If certain criteria are not met periodically, like if you killed me and threw me in the ocean, then all the data on all the countries will be publicly released through the world's media outlets. It will be broadcast over the internet. Posted for the whole world to see."

"Why didn't you just send it to Wikileaks?"

"I don't trust Julian Assange. He's too self-serving. No telling what he would do with the information. How did that work out for Edward Snowden, huh? Not too well. He's still hiding in Russia."

She raised her head toward the sky. "And up there? What did you mean?"

"The Bible talks about fire raining down from the heavens. That has yet to happen...but could at any moment."

"Now you want me to think you are a religious man." She chuckled.

"No. I'm not religious. The fire raining down from the heavens is man-made. Decades ago, Ronald Reagan had his Strategic Defense Initiative, aka Star Wars. In 1993, Clinton renamed it Ballistic Missile Defense Organization. In 2002, it was renamed again to Missile Defense Agency. Ms. Farache, Star Wars is real. Satellites armed with nuclear weapons just waiting to be deployed on hostile enemies on Earth. Satellites designed to destroy other satellites. All the major powers have them. Even some non-super powers. Israel, your home country, has the Iron Dome. Think about the technology involved in that. You know what I'm saying is not only possible but true. Frightening, but still true."

Marla was quiet while she processed what Wolfe had just revealed. It sounded more science fiction to her than fact, but he sounded convincing. Finally, she said, "I am authorized to offer you asylum in Israel. You will be safe. No more people trying to kill you...or capture you."

"In return for what?"

"In return for your cooperation with our defense program against Iran."

CHAPTER 63

Hesitation could get Moss killed.

Kaplan had to make his move. Any move. And now.

Enough of a distraction to get Gagarin's man away from his perch allowing Moss time and opportunity to find suitable cover and get out of harm's way.

He had mixed emotions about Moss ignoring his instructions and swimming over after him. It was reckless and dangerous. On the flip side, he did even the odds.

Atop the mesa of Grand Bé were the ruins of an old fort. Actually, nothing left but a footprint of where *some* of the walls used to be. It was flat and spread out. Gagarin had found a perch on the northeast corner in what looked like an old cannon battery. It gave him high ground and a fox hole to dig into. It was like he was sitting in a tower looking down. Any attempt to breach his stronghold would be suicide. At least from three sides. The safest angle of attack was from the west, but that was covered by his man who had taken up position at the edge of the mesa about 70 feet away. Since Moss was pinned down, the only way Kaplan could get to Gagarin's man was to stay below the mesa, navigate the treacherous east side of the island and scale the north face of the cliff beneath the tomb.

Any other angle would leave him exposed to Gagarin or his man.

Kaplan started his trek around the east side of the island next to the water's edge. At first, it was relatively flat as he hopped from rock to rock. Then the terrain changed to cliffs with precarious footholds. Any false move and he was in the ocean. He remembered where he came ashore and that was his destination. He'd scaled the cliff once to the tomb from below, he could do it again.

He reached his marker, Wolfe's backpack under the rock, and knew where to go from there. No more circumnavigation, now it was all uphill. All the way to the tomb of François René Chateaubriand, which sat slightly below the main mesa and on a small rock outcropping.

He scaled the northern cliff face, trying to retrace his steps from earlier, and doing it as quietly as possible. One errant step and he could slip, not only tumbling down the cliff, but giving away his position as well.

He didn't.

His tactical boots clung tight to the rocks with each step. When he crested the cliff to the mesa, he was exactly where he wanted to be—behind the tomb and out of sight of Gagarin. A quick glance over the tomb platform and he noticed the campfire had died down to glowing red embers. No more light. Another added bonus.

He couldn't see Gagarin, nor could Gagarin see him.

"You okay, Moss?"

"Freezing my ass off."

"On my mark take a couple of pot shots to draw their attention."

Kaplan situated himself to make the crouched sprint from the tomb across the clearing and behind the knoll between him and Gagarin's last man.

"Now," Kaplan commanded.

He waited ten seconds, fifteen seconds and nothing happened. "Moss?"

Nothing.

"Dammit, Moss. Answer."

There were quite a few reasons why Moss couldn't answer or fire, none put Kaplan's mind at ease. With renewed purpose, he glanced in Gagarin's direction and could vaguely make out the Russian's silhouette against the flood lights lining the ramparts of Saint-Malo. The man wasn't moving, almost stiff.

Unexpectedly, two rapid fire blasts emanated from Petit Bé. Followed by two more. Then, two pings hit the island. It was the diversion he needed. He darted from the refuge of the tomb, crossed the open mesa and took cover behind the knoll. On top of the knoll were more of the shrubs the Russians used for firewood. He crept along the north side of the knoll, keeping below Gagarin's sight line until he reached the spot where he estimated the other Russian was hiding. From that point on, there were no more shrubs only rock. Without cover, he got down and used elbows, knees and toes to advance toward his target. Slow, steady and quiet.

When he reached the top of the rock knoll, he located his target below. He had a sight line on where Moss should be hiding. It was brighter on this side of the island, the southwest side, since flood lights from Saint-Malo emitted enough of a glow to make out the water and shoreline. If Moss was down there, the Russian could see him move.

He had two choices. Each had its pros and cons. First, he could use his silenced weapon. Quick and easy and the third hostile Russian would be dead. He had a good bead on him. The shot would be easy. The con—Gagarin would hear the round and see the flash. Even a sound suppressor wasn't totally quiet. With no other background noise other than the wind and the gentle surf of the now outgoing tide, a suppressed shot would give away his position. Alternatively, he could take the quiet approach, sneak up behind the Russian and slit his throat with his Ka-Bar as he did the first Russian. If it worked, Gagarin would never know. The con—there was twenty feet of open space between him and the Russian. One false step, one loose rock and he'd be a dead man. The Russian held his gun ready. Kaplan could not cover that much ground and not be shot or, as a minimum, shot at.

Moss was somewhere down there, wet and cold. He might have already succumbed to the cold. Marla had obviously heard Kaplan calling Moss and when the big man didn't answer, she provided the distraction he needed to make his move. If Moss was down, he needed to end this now.

Kaplan lined up his shot at the Russian's head and squeezed off a round.

Even in the darkness, Kaplan could the see the man's head explode. Two seconds later Gagarin fired. The round struck close enough that the ricochet off the rock peppered him with rock fragments.

He rolled hard right and fell off the cliff.

CHAPTER 64

Kaplan hit the ledge hard, knocking his firearm from his hand. He heard it bounce from the ledge and crash toward the sea. And then a splash. A sharp pain shot through his torso and knocked the breath from his lungs. Gasping for air, his first thought was he broke a rib from the fifteen-foot drop. Maybe two. At a minimum, it would leave one hell of a bruise. He didn't know which was worse, the pain in his ribcage or the claustrophobic feeling of being unable to breathe.

He heard rustling below him but was unable to move.

He struggled pushing himself to his feet. *Breathe, dammit.* The rustling sounds below him continued.

Above him he heard Gagarin yelling, "Anton. Anton." The man's voice was urgent…and futile at the same time. Nevsky's right-hand man was alone and knew it. All his men had been eliminated.

Kaplan's breathing returned, shallow and broken…each breath painful. Each inhale was accompanied by a sharp pain. He pressed his hands against his ribcage and pushed. *Not broken ribs.* He'd had them before, he remembered that pain. And the discomfort that seemed to last for weeks. This was much less, and would pass soon enough.

More rustling below and then it stopped.

Now, footsteps.

Coming his way.

He whipped out his Ka-Bar and readied himself.

A shadow moved directly below him, advancing up the rocky slope.

Then he heard it.

A voice in his earpiece.

"Kaplan, is that you?"

He relaxed and sank into the ledge. "Son of a bitch, Moss. I was about to slit your throat."

"That's makes us even, I was about to blow your head off," Moss answered. "You okay?"

"I'm fine. Gagarin's still up top."

Moss came into view. He was fully dressed. He pushed a handgun at Kaplan. "I think you dropped this."

"Where did you find it?

"Fished it out of the drink where you dropped it."

"Thanks." He took the gun and tucked it in his parka.

"Don't look now," Moss said. "But we got bigger problems."

Kaplan lifted his head and surveyed the area. The flurry of activity on the shoreline of Saint-Malo couldn't be overlooked. Police cars and flashing lights lit up the area. Men were running their way. Some splashing in the cold ocean water. The tide was going out fast and most of the Saint-Malo side of the Passage des Bés was clear of deep water.

From atop the mesa on Grand Bé, a single gunshot rang out. He and Moss flinched at the sound. The storming police dove for cover and returned to the beach. Kaplan knew they weren't in danger. It was over. Gagarin had ended it. Better to die in the field than to return to Mother Russia a disgraced failure.

Kaplan studied the swarming police when they regrouped on shore. When they came, they'd come strong and hard. He and Moss would not be safe on the island.

This would not end well.

They were going to jail. Along with Marla and Wolfe.

Alan Welch might have been able to cover what happened in Bayeux, but he would be useless here. This was between French law enforcement and them.

Kaplan said, "Let's get off this island. Back to the fort before one of these trigger-happy cops spots us."

Moss was already moving toward water's edge.

Part of the passage to the fort was already exposed, but he knew the deep channel in the middle would be at least waist high and the current was swift through that section.

The two men never spoke, linked arms, with Moss on the up-current side, and waded into deeper waters. When they hit the channel, the water level was higher than he'd guessed—chest high. Moss a bit lower. Both men leaned hard against the outgoing tide fighting the fast-moving cold water.

"Marla, we're on our way back."

"Looks like you're bringing trouble with you," she replied.

"Of course."

Bad luck and trouble.

His curse continued.

The two men struggled to cross the channel. Kaplan's ribcage ached with each step. Then the passage shallowed, and the water's pounding pressure lightened. A minute later they were climbing the steps to the fort. Both men soaked and cold.

Marla and Wolfe met them at the fort's entrance.

"Let me see the binoculars," Kaplan said.

Wolfe pointed at Marla. She tossed them to Kaplan.

He studied the shoreline and what he could see on Grand Bé. On shore, he counted eight uniformed officers and a man in an overcoat. On the larger island he could only see shadows with flashlights swarming the isle's mesa. Lights of Saint-Malo served as the backdrop. If he had to gander a guess, he'd say at least twenty officers total. Time now for damage control. There would no doubt be serious blowback from tonight's happening. A lot of explaining. Some of this shit storm would roll uphill. Another deadly encounter with the Russians, the first cleaned up by the CIA. This one won't be so easy to sweep under the rug. Too many involved. Too many witnesses. Too many cops. He needed help. The higher up the food chain it came from, the better.

He glanced at his watch. 0100 hours. Anyone he called was likely asleep.

He dug the binocular sights deep into his eye sockets, studied the man on shore in the overcoat. He wasn't a uniformed cop and his mannerisms and gait seemed somewhat familiar.

Then the light splashed across the man's face and revealed his identity. He knew now who he needed to contact in order to cover their asses…or at least prevent them from being shot on sight.

What were the odds?

Capitaine Travers Heuse.

CHAPTER 65

The situation in Saint-Malo was ominous. Reports of a fire out on the larger of the two Bé islands, followed by a barrage of gunfire. He normally would not be involved except Skouboe had sent him and his team to Mont Saint Michel to cover the Pope's arrival and they were staying in a Saint-Malo hotel. Between his team and the local police force, he had over twenty men under his command. And he was in charge, the highest-ranking officer by far and the locals were more than happy to hand over command to the GIGN Capitaine.

When they arrived at the hotel the day before, Heuse did what he always did, he informed the local police commander of GIGN presence in his town. He also needed to enlist a few extra officers to volunteer for tomorrow's assignment at the Abbey. When he received the call from the commander about the situation on Grand Bé, he and his men were activated.

He had to wake his boss, Colonel Pernille Skouboe, to report the incident. Her orders were simple, "Contain the situation and report back."

He didn't even know what the situation was yet. Could be as simple as a few mischievous teenagers out for a night of fun. Drinking and shooting firearms. Or maybe not firearms, perhaps simply fireworks.

Or the situation could be a lot worse. Could be some sort of criminal activity. When the first wave of officers ran toward the larger island, a single blast was heard. Thinking they were under fire, the officers scattered and returned to the safety of shore.

Since then, all had been quiet. He was given binoculars

by the local commander and he studied both islands. In the darkness, he saw nothing suspicious. It had started misting an hour ago when they arrived on the beach. Now it was windy and rainy.

And cold.

His phone vibrated. He pulled it from his jacket. Not a number he recognized. "Heuse," he said when he answered the call.

"Capitaine. Gregg Kaplan."

"I should have known."

When the man identified himself, the situation went from unknown to dire. He didn't need an explanation. He knew what had happened here. He knew, by the sheer fact this man was calling him, that he was involved. That there were dead bodies. Somewhere.

The man continued, "Capitaine, tell your men they are safe. No one will be shooting at them."

"Where are you?" Heuse asked already pretty certain of the answer.

"Petit Bé. In the fort."

"What happened on Grand Bé?"

"Russians."

"Is Wolfe with you?"

"You know about him, huh?" Kaplan paused then answered, "Yes, Wolfe is with me. As well as Moss and a third party."

"Monsieur Kaplan, why is it whenever you come to France, people die?" He didn't expect an answer, but the American spy gave him one.

"Someone usually dies. Better them than me."

"What will I find on Grand Bé?"

"Four down, one self-inflicted…Gagarin."

"Merde." *Shit.* "Monsieur Kaplan, you should have taken the Colonel's advice and left France."

"Capitaine, you knew that wouldn't happen and so did she. Can we talk?"

"What do you have in mind?"

"I would appreciate it if you would come out to Petit Bé so we can talk face to face. Preferably alone."

"And if I refuse?"

"We'll stay holed up until the CIA and Mossad get here."

Heuse didn't want either of those agencies involved if he could help it. It would only complicate matters even more than they already were. These things happened from time to time, assets from foreign spy agencies got tangled up with their adversaries inside France's borders. Typically, it was handled discreetly and without public knowledge. He wasn't sure how this could be kept low-key, but he'd try.

"Relax Monsieur Kaplan, I will walk out when the passage is clear. No need to bother the CIA or Mossad."

✝ ✝ ✝

Dalton's notebook was filling up fast, especially since his last report to his superior. So much had happened that needed to be called in. Using his high-powered NVG binoculars from his perch on the ramparts of Saint-Malo, he had a bird's eye view of what had transpired on the two small islands west of the city walls.

Kaplan, Moss and the Israeli woman had found his target, but there was much more. Jasmine Habibi showed up but was never able to make her move as the legendary Russian asset, Dmitry Gagarin, showed up and went after the exiled whistleblower.

On one island, the big one closest to shore, Gagarin and his death squad were involved in a shootout with Kaplan and Moss.

The Russians lost.

Gagarin's presence meant only one thing. He was to pick up where Tatyana Kazakov failed. Now all the Russians had failed. That left only the Iranians, Israelis and Americans.

His odds were getting better.

CHAPTER 66

Kaplan knew it was a long shot, but he didn't want to involve Alan Welch and the CIA until after he'd had a chance to have an extensive one on one talk with Matthew Wolfe. He still wasn't sure of his feelings about how Wolfe had handled his grievances. In his mind, there were better ways to handle internal issues, even with spy agencies and the Intelligence Community. The I.C. frowned on rogue actions, especially when they were borderline treason...and perhaps not even borderline. There were laws protecting whistleblowers in the United States, as with many countries, the difference lay in what was considered whistleblowing versus what crossed the line to treason.

Wolfe had crossed that line. And by going rogue and exiling himself, he'd created a problem for the United States I.C. He should have known, and probably did, that foreign powers would come after him. His actions had endangered lives and cost lives. Several innocent lives that got tangled in Wolfe's deceit. Such as his girlfriend in Iceland and Sophie Bouquet. And if Pierre Bouquet didn't survive his wounds, that was on Wolfe too. In a sense, the lives of seven Russians were on him as well. This could have all been prevented if he had done what Moss chastised him about and worked his issues internally.

It took a big ego to think he alone knew what was best for the country and the world. Wolfe possessed knowledge he felt the world should know. Big fucking deal. There were ways to handle it internally and still ensure his own personal safety...

if that was even a concern. Measures could have been put in place, legal measures, to protect him from any perceived threat he might be concerned about. Stealing government secrets was not his best choice. Running from the sanctity of his own country's borders was not the smart choice either. All his exile did was pique the interest of foreign powers who felt that if they had the knowledge and information Wolfe possessed, they could get an edge up on their enemies. And in some instances, their allies.

Wolfe had come to Kaplan earlier with a plea to attend the P.A.P.A.C.Y. rally at Mont Saint Michel, stating it was Sophie's biggest event as the Pope would be there. It was the special interest group's biggest opportunity to get their message to the leader of the Catholic Church. Wolfe seemed humbled by everything that had happened, but why should Kaplan believe him? He was an intelligence officer, an analyst, he knew how to lie. He promised not to try anything and agreed for Kaplan to accompany him at all times. He wanted to see this rally through for Sophie's sake. Then he would take Kaplan to where he had hidden the hard drive and let the CIA take him into custody. Letting Wolfe attend the rally might be the quickest way to put an end to this.

But it wasn't important to Kaplan. He saw it as another stall tactic by Wolfe. Another opportunity for other actors, bad actors, to take a shot at Wolfe. And he knew somewhere out there were Jasmine Habibi and her two goons. As long as Marla was here representing Mossad, Habibi would not leave. Sooner or later, she would make her move on Wolfe.

He and Marla had not discussed her role here. She had been a valuable asset thus far, but what exactly was Mossad's real intent? Was Marla going to betray them and make a move to recruit Wolfe? Or was Mossad's interest merely to keep Wolfe out of the hands of the Iranians? Could be either. Could be both. He wanted to trust Marla. On the other hand, he wouldn't put blind faith in her motives either. With her, he needed to proceed with caution.

There was mention of an unknown actor after Wolfe. But who? China? North Korea? Saudi Arabia? Any of those seemed unlikely, but these were strange times and the North Korean dictator was a wild card when it came to nuclear weaponry. He had struggled to build a viable long-range missile capable of reaching mainland United States. He could certainly benefit from the information Wolfe stole.

And so could the Chinese. Their arms race was much farther advanced than North Korea's. Any move the Chinese made on Wolfe could have serious adverse economic implications. The Chinese methodology was different. Although not out of the question, it would be unusual for China to get involved.

Saudi Arabia? He knew of their supposed *secret* nuclear weapons program. It was no secret in the I.C. Wolfe knew of it intimately. If the Saudis were the other actor, an assassination order was issued for Wolfe.

Who else did that leave?

His introspection was broken when Marla's frantic voice rang out. "We have a visitor." She was staring through the binoculars.

"Frenchman in an overcoat?"

"A man in an overcoat, yes."

"Is he alone?"

"As far as I can tell. I see no one else," she said.

"Let him in. I asked him to come out and talk to me."

Moss walked over to him. "You asked that GIGN man to

come out? Were you going to let us in on it?"

"I did."

"When was that?"

"Just now."

"That's not how partners work together." Moss raised his finger. "That's not how *we* work together."

A rain soaked Heuse walked up the steps to the fort. Kaplan greeted him at the top and beckoned him to follow. "Thank you for coming alone."

"Monsieur Kaplan, you have put me in a compromising position, something that has happened a lot lately. Now, please tell me what it is you want from me."

CHAPTER 67

Capitaine Heuse made a phone call, presumably to Colonel
Skouboe, then spoke into his handheld radio and a swarm
of officers marched toward the smaller island where Kaplan,
Moss, Marla and Wolfe had spoken with the Capitaine. With
them, the officers brought lanterns and flashlights.

On the larger island, he could see Heuse's men searching
the island. He heard the occasional yell and saw the men form
a group and then fan out again. Another body. There were
winners and losers in this world. In Kaplan's world, the losers
left in body bags. Tonight was no different.

The night sky was black and bitter cold. Windswept rain
battered the walls of the fort. The tide was fully out, roughly
twelve hours from when they walked out yesterday afternoon,
but the conditions were much different.

Heuse spoke into his handheld again in French. "Status
report?"

Kaplan understood the response that came back in French.
"Four bagged. All the bagged were armed. Still counting brass.
One backpack tucked under a rock."

He knew the count too. Four dead, four weapons and a lot
of empty shell casings."

"The backpack is mine," he said to Heuse in French.
"Actually, it's Wolfe's but I used it."

Heuse instructed Kaplan and crew to gather their
belongings and he would escort them back across Passage des
Bés to Saint-Malo where they could get warm and change into
dry clothes.

The five of them walked toward the lights of Saint-Malo without a word exchanged amongst them. Moss nudged Kaplan with his elbow wanting to know what was going on. All Kaplan would do was signal *later.* It was best for all parties involved to remain silent for now.

His discussion with Heuse was in French and sometimes heated, but never unfriendly. He'd learned a few lessons long ago about dealing with law enforcement types and Heuse was no exception. His problem was this was a serious incident that could not go unreported. It took some wheeling and dealing to get Heuse to not only let them go, but to let them keep their weapons, once confiscated by the GIGN and then returned by Welch. His gut told him he had just made a deal with the devil. One he felt Heuse would collect on soon enough.

When they reached the beach, Heuse pulled Kaplan aside. He motioned to Porte des Bés, the closest gate to enter the rampart-lined city, and said in French, "Monsieur Kaplan, if I don't see you in Mont Saint Michel at the rally by noon, I will personally track you down and lock you up for the rest of your life."

"Don't worry, Capitaine. We'll be there...all of us."

CHAPTER 68

The Refectory
Mont Saint Michel, France
7:30 A.M.

Sister Aimee Dubois received a text early this morning with
the itinerary and the location of the landing spot of the
Pope, a clearing a half kilometer north of the Barrage du Mont
Saint Michel dam in La Caserne, France on the east side of
the causeway road. Ironically, just a short walk north of the
approved site of the P.A.P.A.C.Y. rally scheduled for noon in
the north lawn of the Le Relais Saint-Michel hotel. North of
that, the 2.5-kilometer causeway was closed. No one allowed
until two hours after the Pope left for the Vatican.

Securing a room at the hotel was impossible as Papal
security had booked every room in all hotels in La Caserne
for security reasons. That certainly added an unplanned
complexity to her task, but not a showstopper.

And a show it would be.

Papal security also added an extra layer of difficulty by
prohibiting all non-essential vehicular traffic no farther north
than the Mont Saint Michel tourist parking lots on the south
side of town. Even that had been planned for and resolved.

According to the text, the Pope's helicopter was scheduled
to land at 1:00 p.m. That matched the Pope's tour schedule
posted inside the Abbey dwellings. The regular scheduled
chanting this morning was cancelled and all the nuns were
given stations to prepare for the Pope's tour.

The ides of January in Northern France was hardly the best time of year for a Papal visit, the weather being so unpredictable, but according to Abbey administration, it was the only negotiated time that worked under the constraints of the Pope's busy schedule that also didn't interfere with the Abbey's heavy tourist season.

Sister Aimee's transfer papers arrived less than a week ago and she had been busy trying to learn the routine expected of her at Mont Saint Michel. Of course, that learning had been hampered with the flurry of extra duties surrounding the Pope's visit. But she was catching on to most matters. Ingress and egress to the Abbey was simple, one road in winding all the way to the top and the same cobblestone road winding down and out to the exit. It was the inner chambers of the Abbey itself that proved challenging. Three levels, lower, middle and upper, sharing roughly the same footprint, but with radically different floor plans. There was the standard guided tour route, which wasn't too difficult to master. It was the inner workings of the Abbey that confused her. Back doors, secret doors and passageways the general public wasn't made aware of and weren't included in any of the tour books.

In a sense, all the mystery surrounding the passages was intriguing, but it was an added pressure she didn't appreciate at the moment. Especially after getting lost several times in those hidden corridors. She had duties to perform on different levels of the Abbey and had taken the wrong passage on more than one occasion. It had taken days of careful study but now she was feeling comfortable with her knowledge of the floor plans.

There seemed to be a lot of stress amongst the administrators of the Abbey pertaining to the Pope and his visit. Short tempers and the occasional flareup happened on a regular basis, even in such a setting as this. Although the bottom rung nuns, like herself, really didn't experience much of the stress, only witnessing the fallout with their superiors. In some sort of perverse way, it was almost comical watching the religious leaders attempt to throttle their emotions and then lose control of their tempers. It went to show that no one was immune.

Sister Aimee knew in five hours the entire Abbey would be in its height of activity. Abbey security, Vatican security and a contingent of the Swiss Guards, both uniformed and plain-clothed, had saturated the Pope's route through the Abbey. She hadn't seen any security in the back passageways, but she knew, odds were, some had found their way in there. Surely Abbey security, which was a contingent of the Gendarmerie, knew their way through the back corridors.

Before she made her way to the Abbey this morning, she dressed in the conforming habits all the Sisters were instructed to wear. She tucked her blonde hair, not her natural color, beneath her coif and veil. Because of the cold, wind and rain, she wore street clothes beneath her habit since many of her duties were outside, a minor violation of Abbey dress code.

All she had to do now was wait and do her job when the time came. Her duties and duty stations for the Pope's tour were all laid out and memorized. She had practiced her movements and timed them, honing her pattern for maximum efficiency...and safety. There was a lot that could go wrong with her assignment and matters could take a turn at any point, especially with a Pontiff who had a tendency to make changes at the last minute.

CHAPTER 69

La Caserne
2.5 Kilometers south of Mont Saint Michel
1030 Hours

Kaplan followed Heuse's GIGN vehicle from Saint-Malo to Mont Saint Michel. It was nothing more than a police escort. Behind his black Audi were several other vehicles belonging to the GIGN, all en route to the landing spot of the Papal helicopter. Heuse changed his mind about allowing Kaplan to meet him in La Caserne, opting instead to escort the foursome. He never let any of them out of his sight or the sight of a GIGN officer. He knew that order came down from Skouboe.

Heuse cleared the caravan through the roadblock south of the village, through the village and north to the roadblock at the south end of the causeway. That was the end of the road for everyone.

Ahead and to the right, in an open field north of the northernmost hotel, was a sea of yellow shirts, jackets and banners.

P.A.P.A.C.Y.

The rally was scheduled to start in an hour and a half and should be going strong by the time the Pope arrived. According to Wolfe, that was the plan. The protest group wanted visibility near the landing site. They wanted the Pope to see and understand the support for their cause. How else could P.A.P.A.C.Y. get their message across?

The media was making a small circus out of the event. Satellite vans lined the streets leading into La Caserne. Reporters with their videographers swarmed P.A.P.A.C.Y. trying to get a scoop on how the advocacy group felt about the Papal visit. He noticed a smile creep across Wolfe's face when he saw the amount of publicity the group was getting from the press.

Wolfe had expressed his passion for the cause and his regret that his presence in France had cost Sophie Bouquet her life. He had explained how he felt about Sophie and especially Pierre's tragic childhood. He explained how he'd seen Pierre try to deal with his demons and fail. Drug abuse, addiction all caused from depression. He had empathy for the young man's torment and admired how devoted Sophie was to her brother. Kaplan wondered if something had occurred in Wolfe's life that helped him identify with Pierre's suffering.

Heuse waved them out of the car and ordered all four to follow him. As they approached the Le Relais Saint-Michel hotel's north lawn and the rally, he noticed two familiar faces—Colonel Pernille Skouboe and Paris CIA Deputy Chief of Station Alan Welch.

Farther to the north of the rally site was a security checkpoint. It appeared to be the location chosen for the Pope's helicopter to land. Vatican security had cordoned off the area with red tape. The guards were well-armed with handguns on their belts and assault-style rifles in their hands. They all had comm systems as evidenced by the curled wires leading from the ear-fobs down inside their collars.

Standing in the midst of the security detail was a holy man. He wore lavish ceremonial clothing. More so than a simple priest might wear. Kaplan made the assumption this was the

Pope's Vatican advance-man.

Skouboe stepped up to Heuse while the rest followed Kaplan toward the rally where Welch was left standing alone.

At the sight of Wolfe, Welch said, "I'll deal with you in a minute." Then he guided Kaplan away from Moss, Marla and Wolfe.

"Guess Heuse informed you we'd be here?" Kaplan asked Welch.

He held up a folder and tapped it with his forefinger. "Nope. Just came to assist Colonel Skouboe. But I kinda figured you'd be here."

"How so?"

"Simple, you leave a trail of bodies everywhere you go. Beaune, Bourges, Bayeux, Saint-Malo. You're a regular one-man wrecking ball. Honestly, I'm surprised the GIGN didn't lock you and Moss up and throw away the key."

Kaplan said nothing.

Welch followed Kaplan's eyes then lifted the folder. "Credible threat against the Pope. Today." He pointed to the Abbey at the north end of the causeway. "Out there." He handed the folder to Kaplan. "An assassin you've dealt with before. It's why I'm here."

He unclasped the folder, took out the papers and read them. An assassin he'd tracked in the past, and not too long ago. A master of disguise and slippery as an eel. Code named *Chameleon*. The CIA had given this assassin the name due to similar characteristics to the animal. Chameleon was a loner and moved undetected, victims never saw an attack coming. A master of illusion. One who could pass for any ethnicity and blend in with the surroundings regardless of locale. Chameleon was a fitting code name.

His encounter with the assassin was in Murren, Switzerland, a hit on an American tourist with known ties to a mafia boss in New Jersey. The assassin's escape was unique— paragliding off the mountain top to the valley below. By the time law enforcement could respond, Chameleon had dumped the chute and escaped in a waiting vehicle.

The folder held many photos, all believed to be photos of Chameleon, but nothing confirmed. None of the photos had similarities that facial recognition software could match. A composite photo was created by the agency's software and sketch artist drawings that was rudimentary at best.

He knew if he saw Chameleon again face to face, he would recognize the assassin. It was something in the eyes that stood out in his mind. He needed to see Chameleon again, up close and personal.

"And what?" he said to Welch. He looked quickly across the causeway to the island. "You think Chameleon is out there at the Abbey? Waiting in hiding for the Pope?"

"Something like that, yeah."

He handed the folder back to Welch. "What assistance are you giving the GIGN?"

Welch looked him in the eyes. "You."

"Alan, now you're piling on and I don't appreciate it. First you trick me into coming to France, have me arrested under false pretenses only to be set free to fulfill your hidden agenda and capture Matthew Wolfe. I've had to battle Russian assets, Iranian assets, and now you throw this shit at me? Go after another assassin?"

"Call this your next assignment, Gregg. You and Moss have completed your first assignment. Wolfe is here, in CIA custody." Welch looked at Wolfe, Moss, and Farache. "Now, we're doing a favor for the French government—you're doing me a favor. I owe them this one. You could earn some kudos yourself...and Gregg, you need all you can get after the past three days."

"Sorry, Alan, I'm throwing the bullshit flag on that one. If I...we," he said while he glanced at Moss. "Had been given up to date information then we wouldn't have been playing catch-up. How is it our enemies and even allies had better intel than the CIA? Quite frankly, it's embarrassing. We should have been leading the charge. Hell, there never should have been a charge. The agency should have pinched Wolfe months ago. Dammit, Alan, we're better than this. You're better than this."

"I admit we were behind the eight-ball on this one, but thanks to you and Moss, Wolfe has been apprehended and is in CIA custody."

"At what cost, Alan? Don't forget, Jasmine Habibi is still out there and we still don't have the hard drive yet. Actually, we have no idea where Wolfe hid the damn thing. And if you think Jasmine has given up just because Wolfe is in your hands now, you've underestimated her. That could be a deadly mistake."

"I have some intel on that too, by the way. It seems an insider has been leaking intel back to Director Reed about your movements here in France. On top of that, the instructions I'm getting from Reed are counter-intuitive to what you're doing."

"Wait, Reed knows I'm here? Working for you?"

"That's what my source indicated. What makes it worse is that Reed hasn't mentioned it to me at all. He knows but won't call me on it."

"You think Reed might be setting you up? How does he even know I'm here? I thought you did this on the down-low."

"I did keep your presence here hush-hush. And yes, it does look like *we're* being set up. My source tells me you're being tailed and I am being deliberately fed bad intel. At first I didn't know what to make of this, but now I believe Reed has a personal vendetta and wants you to fail so he can fire you."

"And since you never told him you activated me, he wants your head on the chopping block too." Kaplan shook his head. "We have Wolfe in custody, but I need to see this to the end. I need to recover that hard drive. "

"You're officially out. The CIA will take over with Wolfe."

"No, I cut a deal with him while we were in Saint-Malo."

"What deal?"

"If I protect him and let him attend this P.A.P.A.C.Y. rally, he'll take me to where he stashed the hard drive. If not, then it will be released to the press."

"Shit. You made this more complicated. I've already persuaded Colonel Skouboe to sweep this under the rug...the Saint-Malo incident, I mean. If Reed caught wind of it, we're all history."

"From what you just told me, we're already history. Who's tailing me? Do you know?"

"Not definitively, but I have my suspicions."

"Dalton Palmer, I bet. Reed's personal pit bull and clean-up man."

"That would be my guess too."

"Dalton's a fucking weasel."

"Agreed. If Dalton is here, there's more at stake than simply catching Wolfe. Reed wants that hard drive, too. I don't trust Reed any farther than I can toss his 200-pound ass."

"How did you get Skouboe to sweep Saint-Malo?"

"Like I told you, I agreed for you to accompany Capitaine

Heuse onto Mont Saint Michel ahead of the Pope's arrival.
You're to personally check every person on the island, man,
woman, and child, until you've found Chameleon or positively
ruled out this assassin's presence. Do you understand?"

Kaplan noticed Skouboe and Heuse in a heated
conversation. It didn't take a genius to figure that one out.
Personally, he wasn't keen on the idea either.

"Kaplan," Alan said with ire in his voice.

"What about Moss? Is he coming with me?"

"No. Just you and Heuse. I'll have Moss and Farache stay
here while we guard Wolfe. You better be right that he'll tell us
where the hard drive is hidden."

"You tell Moss he's not going with me," Kaplan warned.
"He won't be happy."

"I can handle Moss."

"We'll see."

CHAPTER 70

Kaplan and Heuse rode in the back seat of the Abbey security cart from the staging area on the mainland to the island Abbey. The 2.5-kilometer ride took less than five minutes. When they arrived at the main gate, they were met by the Abbey-based Gendarmerie. The ranking officer snapped to attention when Capitaine Heuse showed his credentials. The officers acquiesced to Heuse's authority and never questioned Kaplan's lack of credentials. Or the fact that he was armed.

As midday rolled past, the weather turned windy and cold. The sky grew overcast with high clouds thick enough to keep the day dreary.

He wondered how Welch had handled Moss and his *He goes, I go* attitude. He also wondered how Welch had handled Marla Farache. She would in no way take orders from Alan Welch, CIA Deputy Chief of Station or not. He had no authority over her. The only person on the mainland who might have any authority with Marla was GIGN Colonel Pernille Skouboe. And even then, Skouboe wasn't likely to risk a chance of ruffling Mossad's feathers.

He followed Heuse into the Gendarmerie office where comprehensive floor plans were scattered on a large table. Every room, every nook and cranny, every door, and every window was marked and labeled from the main gate outside the Gendarmerie office all the way to the top floor of the Abbey itself. Also mapped were the Abbey's private corridors and stairways.

According to the officer, Vatican security had cleared all

hotels, restaurants and retail businesses from the main gate to the Abbey and given the all-clear. All staff and maintenance personnel not belonging to the Abbey itself were required to leave the island until after the Pope's departure, roughly six hours after his arrival. They could then return and ready the establishments for the next day's business. He also informed Heuse that he and Kaplan were on foot for the remainder of the uphill walk to the Abbey and to check in with the Gendarmerie officer at the entrance to the Abbey.

After leaving the small police headquarters, Heuse asked Kaplan, "Ever been here before?"

"Once. Several years ago."

"Lucky for you, Monsieur Kaplan, with the exception of his Mass service for Abbey personnel, he's doing the same walking route as tourists. But you'll get to see more of the Abbey this time. A behind the scenes look if you will."

"Can't wait." Heuse gave him an *if looks could kill* glance at Kaplan's sarcasm.

The steep walk up through the village to the Abbey left Heuse winded. He had to stop at the base of the Grand Degré Extérieur or the Great Outer Stairs, the staircase leading to the Abbey gateway, to rest. The walls of the Abbey rose high above the stairs, giving the impression the Abbey was a fortress.

Heuse's breathing slowed and he suddenly found the strength to press on. They climbed the remainder of the steps to the gateway and the guard house. As informed earlier, the Swiss Guard had set up a command post at the guard house and both Heuse and Kaplan had to wait to be cleared into the Abbey. He could tell Heuse found the ordeal insulting. After all, he was a law officer with the French GIGN and had been for decades. Now he had to submit to the ordeal of a security check by a foreign security force before entering a French Abbey. As Heuse's frustration with the stall by the Swiss Guard escalated, Kaplan began to feel the same. The decision to allow the Swiss Guard such authority was made well above Capitaine Heuse's pay grade...Colonel Skouboe's as well. What should have been a joint security effort had turned into Vatican security boondoggle.

They waited a long ten minutes for clearance before being allowed inside the Abbey itself. It gave Heuse a chance to rest before the next flight of steps—the climb from the guard house up the Interior Grand Degré to the Saut-Gaultier terrace on the west end of the complex. This put them in a passageway between the church on the right and Abbey buildings on the left. It was built as an added level of defense to the Abbey entrance.

As they passed through the corridor, two lofty corbeled turrets jutted from the main wall with a set of crenels designed for firing arrows at intruders and machicolations through which boiling liquids and stones could be dropped on attackers. An impregnable stronghold during the Hundred Years War, these ramparts and fortifications resisted all the English assaults and, as a result, Mont Saint Michel became a symbol of national identity.

The west terrace offered views of the bay and overlooked the causeway back toward the mainland. Views somewhat obscured by the cloudy, misty day. He wondered if the P.A.P.A.C.Y. rally had started and if Wolfe's driving desire to make the advocacy group's agenda known to the Pope would come to fruition.

As he thought it, he felt it. The familiar thump of an approaching helicopter reverberating through his body. Then he heard it. He gazed across the causeway and spotted the approach of the Papal helicopter.

Heuse gave him a nudge. "We must keep moving, Monsieur Kaplan." Heuse said in rapid French.

"You can drop the *monsieur*. Kaplan is fine." His replied in the same language.

"No monsieur, that would not be proper." Heuse switched to English.

On the terrace stood two monks. Kaplan's memory sharpened. From a distance he had already ruled them out as a threat. Neither was Chameleon. Not size-wise or shape. For the sake of thoroughness, he approached the men for a closer visual inspection. When he was certain his original assessment was correct, he and Heuse moved toward the next locale—the Abbey Church.

The entrance to the Abbey Church was flanked by two Swiss Guards. Each man, as with all the Swiss Guard he'd seen at Mont Saint Michel, wore plain clothes and had earbud comm systems, wires snaking from their ears and disappearing into their shirts. They were young with overly serious faces. He recalled that in 1527 almost all of the Swiss Guard were killed in the Sack of Rome while defending the Pope from the army of Holy Roman Emperor Charles V. The Swiss Guards had sworn the Oath of Loyalty to the Pope and would defend and sacrifice their life to defend him. Just like himself, he knew they were well trained and had their observational skills on high alert.

Stepping inside the Abbey Church, he marveled again at the elegant stonework which had undergone several waves of restoration to reveal the medieval complex. The first time he was here it was crowded with tourists. Today the room was empty and quiet, which made more of an impression. The usual light, airy space appeared stygian due to the gloomy skies that prevented sunlight from gleaming through the windows. But at least it was warm. The first warm spot since arriving on the island.

The nave of the Abbey Church had an elevation on three levels—arches, galleries and tall windows. He knew from his previous visit the nave sat directly on the rock at eighty meters above sea level and had a platform eighty meters long from front to rear. The nave was the main area for worshippers along with the side aisles and transepts or the transverse portion of the Abbey that crossed the main body. At the far end of the nave was the chancel, the area around the altar.

By design, the basic floor plan was shaped like a cross. In the Abbey Church were two nuns and two monks, all dressed in traditional garb. Monks in robes, nuns in habits. There were two more Swiss Guards stationed at each side of the transept. Unlike the guards at the entrance to the church, these wore their traditional colorful Vatican uniforms.

Heuse's radio chirped and Colonel Skouboe's voice rang out in French. "The Pope has landed. He and the Bishop are on their way to the Abbey." It was the only sound in the hushed sanctuary and drew the looks of the nuns, monks, and guards.

Heuse acknowledged.

Now he knew who the holy man was standing with the security detail at the landing site—a Bishop. If the Pope was on his way, he and Heuse needed to speed things up.

Welch's orders were to scrutinize every person he saw on the island—*man or woman*. The two uniformed Swiss Guards were easy eliminations, no way either could be Chameleon. From experience he knew Chameleon was short, not much taller than five four, but being the master of disguise that Chameleon was, it would be easy to appear taller with lifters or platform shoes.

One nun and one monk flanked each side of the altar. He gave a general inspection to the monks first and ruled one out immediately. The facial structure was wrong, and the eyes set too far apart. What hair he could see under the man's hood was silver. The man was the right height, but he knew this was not Chameleon. The other monk was tall, too tall but had the right build and facial features. He ruled this man out as well. The monk's robe was too short for his height and exposed his feet from the ankle down. Bare feet in sandals. No lifters.

One nun was too short to be Chameleon, however the other bore closer inspection. He walked over and stood face to face. Shape and size, she was a match, but not in the face. The eyes were all wrong too. Wrong shape. Wrong color, bright blue, although that was an easy disguise. Beneath her coif and veil was red hair. Her pale face was spotted with freckles. This nun was not Chameleon either.

Heuse's radio chirped again. Skouboe. "Switch to channel nine," she said. "The Pope has arrived on the island."

CHAPTER 71

The announcement that the Pope had officially arrived on Mont Saint Michel made Heuse nervous. The Capitaine fumbled with his radio switching the radio to the selected channel of Papal security and the Swiss Guard. Kaplan wasn't sure what to think of the Capitaine's attempt to calm himself. It was out of character for a man with as many years in the GIGN to let the Pope's arrival get him rattled.

"Capitaine," Kaplan whispered and gestured to a door. "We should move on."

Heuse nodded. "Of course, monsieur."

The Cloister was an open-air gallery used as a place for prayer and meditation. All he observed was wind, rain and biting cold. Although it wasn't raining hard, the driving wind made each droplet sting his face. Built around the Cloister were a double row of small columns, slightly out of line. From the Cloister were access points to the Refectory, the kitchen, back to the Abbey Church, from which they just came, the monk's dormitory, and a few stairways leading to other points unknown to him within the complex. The Cloister was empty. No guards. No monks. No nuns. No threat on the Cloister so he and Heuse braved the elements and headed for their next stop, the Refectory.

The Refectory was where the monks ate their meals in silence while one of them read from the pulpit on the far wall. Tables with benches lined the length of the Refectory with a small aisle down the middle leading to the pulpit. It had an arched roofline and a cross mounted on the wall behind the pulpit.

The first thing that caught his attention was the lack of guards or security personnel in the Refectory, only nuns and monks, four each. They were preparing several of the tables closest to the pulpit for the Pope to share a meal with the nuns and monks after mass. He and Heuse walked toward the pulpit. One nun exited through a small door on the west wall next to the pulpit. That left only three nuns and four monks for him to scrutinize.

Heuse's radio chirped and the man's voice indicated that the Pope was in the Abbey Church.

"He won't stay there long," Heuse said. "His schedule has him completing the tour, then holding Mass in the Abbey Church. After Mass, he and all the nuns and monks will return here for a meal together while Bishop Jean Paul Renault reads scripture. You can bet this place will be crawling with Papal security by then. The Pope has three moving teams accompanying him. One ahead of him, one with him, and one behind him. According to the head of Papal security, there is virtually no chance an intruder can get to him."

Kaplan made his assessments of all seven individuals in the Refectory and ruled them out as Chameleon. All of the sudden the Pope's lead security team was entering the Refectory. Time for him and Heuse to move on to the next stop.

Right before they left the Refectory for the Guests' hall, he glanced at the door the nun exited earlier and wondered where it led.

A stairway guided them directly below the Refectory to the Guests' hall, a room designed for receiving royalty and nobility. There was one guard, plain clothed, no monks, no nuns.

Next was the Great Pillared Crypt. Built to support the

Gothic chancel of the Abbey Church, the room was empty. Each pillar was massive in diameter. A reinforced pedestal and oversized column all built with the same stone extending upward to an arched entablature as it reached the ceiling. A literal maze of support pillars.

From there, Saint Martin crypt. A small room in comparison, and also empty. Next, they entered the monk's Ossuary and only one guard was visible. In the second bay of the Ossuary was a large wooden wheel installed in 1820 to hoist food via a funicular for the prisoners during the period Mont Saint Michel was used as a penitentiary. He heard a shuffle of footsteps and swiveled to check the source.

It was the nun from the Refectory who earlier left through the small door. After seeing him, she hung her head down and moved swiftly in the direction she had come from.

"Stop her," he yelled to the guard. But the man cut his eyes at Kaplan and didn't move.

Kaplan chased after her with Heuse steps behind. From the Ossuary, he followed the escaping nun through the Chapel of Saint Etienne where two other nuns and two monks were standing. Neither of whom moved from their assigned stations. He paid them no attention. He knew who he was chasing. Although she appeared heavier than he remembered, he recognized her gate and body language. He had dealt with her before.

He had found Chameleon.

The assassin was disguised as a nun.

Clever.

But she had failed. Papal security would put a tight net around the Pope. There was no way she could get to him now.

He shouted over his shoulder to Heuse. "It's her, Chameleon, call it in. We're looking for a nun."

She ran up the north-south stairs, bounding several steps at a time holding her habit above her knees with both hands. She wore jeans and running shoes. A quick-change artist ready to make her transition from nun to average person. But she was trapped on this island and there was no way off as an average person in street clothes. Either Papal security or Abbey security would see to that. Kaplan would see to it. By now, he was certain the Abbey was locked down like a prison.

She rounded a corner and vanished into what opened up as a long room with a double nave—Notre Dame Sous Terre.

But he had a problem.

A big problem.

The room was empty.

Chameleon was nowhere in sight.

CHAPTER 72

Sister Aimee Dubois spotted the familiar face in the Refectory before he could get a good look at her and escaped out the west door. Its use was off-limits except for Abbey personnel and was cordoned off during tourist visiting hours. His was a face she never forgot. They were on opposite sides of the law back then, as they were now, except here, he was in France where he should have no legal jurisdiction. Especially with all the law enforcement already on the island. Therefore, what exactly was his mission here?

She wondered if she could have been betrayed by her employer. But, why would he spend that kind of money for a hit and then try to scuttle it? No, this man's presence wasn't her employer's doing, but it might have something to do with her employer. As with all her contracts, she did her homework. Her employer was a wanted man.

Her previous encounter with this operative was in Switzerland. He was intuitive and somehow saw through her disguise, but not until after she had completed her hit. They were together in the same room when he figured out her ruse, but she managed to escape unscathed, but recognized. Thanks to him, she assumed, there were composites of her likeness distributed to Interpol and they were a dead ringer for her actual appearance. Somehow, he'd found her again and now he was pursuing her through the Abbey.

She was captive on this island, but it wasn't a scenario she hadn't factored in her planning. She would go AWOL from her Abbey duties. She had to at this juncture. During her prior planning she discovered a 3D scan of the Abbey using photogrammetry. The digitization provided information on the passageways hidden inside the thick walls and a plethora of hiding spaces throughout the island fortress. Thick stone crypts constructed under the transept of the church. It was easy to disappear with all the hidden corridors and passageways. She could stay on the island for days without being discovered. As a precaution, she'd already stashed supplies in several of the better ones for such an instance. A contract killer had to have backup plans. And she had several. That's why she'd never been caught. That's why she wouldn't get caught this time either.

When the man spotted her the second time in the monk's Ossuary, she knew she'd been made. And the chase ensued. She had a pre-planned and practiced escape route. Fool proof in her opinion. The operative was fast, but she could hold her own. She knew the Abbey and all its secrets. He did not. And that worked to her advantage when she took the steps on the north-south stairway three at a time.

When she rounded the corner into the Church of Notre Dame Sous Terre, she had a good forty-foot lead on the operative and that was all she needed to disappear behind the wall through the hidden passage. By the time he found the recessed wall, *if* he could find it, she would be tucked away in a secure location.

That was, until she needed to move on her target. Then she would slink back to the spot she knew the target would be and fulfill her contract.

And there was nothing this operative could do to stop her.

CHAPTER 73

Pete Moss was miffed that CIA Paris Deputy Chief of Station Alan Welch double-crossed him. At least that was how he perceived it. Welch sent Kaplan off to the island Abbey to track down an assassin to prevent an attempt on the Pope's life. Both he and Kaplan had made it clear they were a team, each had the other's back, but Welch had other ideas. Or he did when it came to this assignment.

He was willing for them to work together to locate and capture Matthew Wolfe, but not this? No. Welch said it was important for him to stay close and keep an eye on Wolfe. It didn't seem to matter that he had three other men from his Paris station already assigned to that duty. He sent Kaplan off with Capitaine Heuse and ordered Moss and Marla to stay on the mainland.

That didn't sit well with Marla either. At first he thought she was anxious and upset because she wasn't with Kaplan in tracking down an assassin, but there was something else going on with her. She made several phone calls and was visibly upset with the conversations. He wished he understood Hebrew. All he could interpret from her voice was she wasn't happy. When he asked her if she was okay, she lied and told him it was nothing. Then she forced a tense smile. Welch didn't seem to notice nor did Colonel Skouboe. As a matter of fact, the only thing those two were interested in was monitoring the radio.

The Pope had landed and was whisked away by his security detail. His Holiness was accompanied to the island in a caravan of covered vehicles. Assassination attempt or not, it wasn't going to happen on the open causeway. Even a long-range assassin wouldn't have a clean shot out there. And when the wind and rain were factored in, it would be a damn near impossible shot even for the best snipers. According to Skouboe and Welch, the small village of La Caserne had been locked down for two days, meaning the assassin couldn't be a sniper. It would have to be a close up kill. Also meaning the assassin was already on the island. And Papal security had failed to thoroughly secure it.

How Welch and the CIA found out about a planned attempt on the Pope's life puzzled him, but as a man left out of the loop, he guessed it was some top-secret spy eavesdropping bullshit some computer geek like Wolfe had uncovered.

He kept his eyes on the P.A.P.A.C.Y. stage where Wolfe was standing. He was chatting with several group members about who knows what. Close by were Welch's men, communication fob wires dangling from their ears and disappearing into their jackets. Anything but discreet. The comms Kaplan had acquired for them to use, now those were discreet. Hidden wireless comms with hidden voice-activated mics. Top-notch stuff. He had to admit his partner had connections. Good ones.

When he noticed Welch and Skouboe's demeanor change, he inched closer. Within earshot. The radio communication was in French as was their conversation with each other.

After a few minutes, he couldn't take it any longer, he approached Welch. "What's going on out there?"

Welch looked away and ignored him for a second. Then he faced him and said, "Kaplan identified Chameleon. She's disguised as a nun in full habit. He chased her through the Abbey and said she disappeared. Not surprising for someone who knows her way through the back passages of the Abbey."

He shifted his attention to Skouboe then back at Moss. "According to the colonel, there are a preponderance of secret corridors, passageways and hidden stairwells. She has Abbey security combing through employee records to find out which nun is missing."

While he spoke, Skouboe's expression hardened, eyebrows furrowed. She motioned Welch to her side. Moss followed, Skouboe apparently didn't mind. She spoke in English. "There is one nun unaccounted for after they ran a personnel check. Her name is Sister Aimee Dubois. Records indicate she was transferred to Mont Saint Michel Abbey a week ago from Paris. A call was placed back to Paris and the description of our Dubois here and the Dubois from Paris aren't even close. We have no idea what happened to the real Sister Aimee Dubois. The other nuns on the Abbey said Dubois kept to herself and did her assigned duties in silence, which is not terribly unusual. I sent some of my men in Paris to interview the convent and check the morgues. My hunch is our assassin killed the real Dubois in order to steal her identity. She must have obtained insider information and somehow found out about the transfer."

Moss looked at the P.A.P.A.C.Y. stage, Wolfe was chatting with some guy with a long blond ponytail.

CHAPTER 74

Bishop Jean Paul Renault received a rare accolade from the Pope for his arrangements of the first ever Papal tour of Mont Saint Michel. Even though the Pope was getting the standard tourist version, the Abbey staff had added a few extras for the Pope's benefit. With the pending threat against the Pope's life hanging in the balance, Papal security, the security teams of the Abbey, along with France's GIGN, the Pontiff was surrounded at all times by men well trained for a threat such as this.

The Pope moved slowly, which aided in security efforts. No one got close to the Pope except those individuals that had been extensively vetted. But there had been a glitch, one of the nuns previously vetted for the Pope's visit was indeed *not* a nun, but rather an assassin. Or so the Gendarmerie had told him. An American operative had also been brought in to help identify and capture the woman. And he had done part of this already—he had identified her, but she evaded capture inside the Abbey. This actually altered the Pope's route through the Abbey. The advance team of the Swiss Guard cleared every room before he and the Pope reached them. This kept the Pope moving and safe. The only moments when the Pope would be physically idle for any duration of time would be when he held Mass in the Abbey Church and then again for the special ceremonial meal and prayer in the Refectory. Those would also be the only times he wasn't by the Pope's side.

Renault had been staying in La Caserne for the past week making sure all arrangements were in place, including security, meals, and everything necessary for communion during Mass.

He had spent months preparing for this event, writing and rewriting checklists so that nothing would be missed.

And nothing was missed.

He had submitted the names of all personnel who would be on the island months in advance so Papal security could run background checks and fully vet them all. No one else was allowed on the island until two hours after the Pope's departure. It was security's oversight that the imposter of Sister Aimee Dubois was here and had cleared the security ID check. Security was out of his hands and being handled by Papal security. The traveling squadron of Swiss Guards' job was protecting the Pope.

How the imposter slipped through security was their problem.

When he first learned of the impending threat, he tried to convince the Pope to cancel this visit and reschedule another date, but the Pontiff refused, claiming the Swiss Guard would protect him. There were always impending threats against his life and the Pope insisted he could not do his duty to God and his followers if he hid from every threat.

And if the Pope didn't want to reschedule the visit to Mont Saint Michel, then neither did the Swiss Guard. They were adamant the Pope would be safe at all times. As with Secret Service protecting the President of the United States, the Swiss Guard would take a bullet for the Pope.

His concern was what if it wasn't a bullet? Again, the Swiss Guard refused to budge. If anything happened to the Pope, heads would roll.

He'd see to it personally.

CHAPTER 75

Kaplan and Heuse regrouped at the last known sighting of Chameleon—Notre Dame Sous Terre. Along with them were a small contingent of Swiss Guards in plain clothes and the head of Papal security. In all there were ten men inside the 16 meters by 12 meters double nave church. A double semi-arched wall separated the two parallel naves.

The Church of Notre Dame Sous Terre was the oldest building on Mont Saint Michel. It was the Abbey's heart and was believed to be the spot of Saint Aubert's original shrine. It was also the original Abbey Church. The name translates to *Our Mother Underground*. After the Abbey Church was built, Notre Dame Sous Terre was forgotten and covered by multiple expansions of the Abbey. The walls were nearly six-feet thick. The outer walls dated back to the late 10th century. In the 19th and 20th centuries, it was restored to its pre-Roman architecture.

It was somewhere in this room that Chameleon disappeared and so far, no one had been able to identify where. The room looked solid except for a small door above a ledge over one of the altars. But Kaplan knew there was no way Chameleon could have escaped through that door without being seen by him. He was too close. There simply wasn't enough time for her to enter the church, reach the altar, climb to the ledge and escape through the door. But it was the only scenario the Swiss Guard would entertain, so while the Pope's advance team reached the Church of Notre Dame Sous Terre, the Swiss Guard placed a guard on the ledge above the altar to ensure Chameleon couldn't come out of that door and make an attempt on the Popes life. They also insisted he and Heuse move forward with their search.

Together the two men walked through the Knight's Hall to the Merveille. Kaplan shook his head. "Idiots," he mumbled in a low voice.

"Sometimes, Monsieur Kaplan, resistance is futile. The Swiss Guard is not to be challenged."

"I was too close. There was no way she climbed above the altar. I want to go back for a closer look. The Swiss Guard are too hind-sighted, too regimented, too locked into tradition. They won't see their mistake until it's too late."

"Perhaps, monsieur, but we have our orders. It is best we follow them."

"Best for whom? The Swiss Guard? The Pope? I think not. If we don't get back in there and find out how Chameleon escaped, then the Pope is as good as dead."

"I hope for all our sakes, monsieur, that you are mistaken."

CHAPTER 76

Kaplan and Heuse did as the Capitaine insisted and pushed ahead. The remainder of the tour route was empty of any personnel with the singular exception of one room at the end of the tour route—the gift shop. There was one person in the shop, a man, not Chameleon.

Heuse had been monitoring the radio closely and giving him updates as they progressed through the Abbey. The Pope was behind schedule and his event coordinator, Bishop Jean Paul Renault, rerouted him back to the Abbey Church so the Pontiff wouldn't be late for Mass.

His Mass.

Now he and Heuse were free to return to Notre Dame Sous Terre so he could continue to search for Chameleon's escape portal. But the Capitaine, apparently being Catholic himself, wanted to hear the Pope give Mass so they backtracked all the way to the Abbey Church. The return route took them back through the old twin-nave church and Kaplan insisted on one last quick search of the space.

Kaplan studied the church and everything within a five-second dash from the door. He determined that was the time it took Chameleon to reach her escape portal before he entered the room. At the pace of her run though, a five-second distance covered a lot of ground. He visually surveyed the room again and again. Nothing. Not one thing stood out and Heuse was growing impatient and insisted they move on.

"The Pope is no longer in here, Monsieur. We are wasting time," said Heuse.

If he could find the escape route then he could follow it. He needed more time for a thorough hands-on search of the room, but Heuse wouldn't allow it. Nor would he allow Kaplan to remain in the twin-nave church alone, so they made their way back to the Abbey Church.

When they reached the Abbey Church, the Abbey's nuns, monks and priests lined the rows of benches in the church's transept, all facing the altar. The Pope and Bishop were huddled behind the altar transfixed in a private conversation.

Kaplan took the opportunity, while all the nuns were gathered together, to give each one a closer inspection. None were Chameleon. The head of Papal security stepped forward and indicated there was one nun missing for Mass—Sister Aimee Dubois—and proceeded to lecture Kaplan on the highly capable and thorough skills of the Swiss Guard and Papal security. According to him, their belief was that since Chameleon's presence and identity had been revealed, she would hide out until it was safe for her to leave the island. Because she knew they were on to her, she would not make an attempt on the Pope's life. According to their Papal brain-trust, she was no longer a threat.

He knew Chameleon. He knew what she was capable of and how determined she was to fulfill her contract.

No, Chameleon was still a threat. He doubted she was still dressed as a nun. She had likely morphed into another Abbey character, like a monk...or a priest.

He made a nonchalant pass between the altar and the transept benches. He studied not only the nuns faces again, but also the monks and priests. He felt sure Chameleon was not in here.

Not yet.

He stood by Heuse next to the Abbey Church door from where they just entered. Without delay, the Bishop processed to the altar. Mass had begun.

This was the first time he'd ever attended a Catholic worship service. Hell, this was the first time he'd been in any church since he was a teenager. He grew up in a Jewish household. His parents were devout, but he didn't share their religious beliefs and would find any excuse to avoid the Synagogue. Eventually they gave up trying and left him alone.

And now, maybe he'd taken too many lives and seen too much to believe in organized religion. In his business he had learned that with power and money, there was crime. And the Church had a lot of power and a lot of wealth.

Early afternoon had transitioned to late afternoon. The skies darkened as the cloudy weather clung to the heavens. Rain had stopped but the dampness remained, making the musty Abbey smell even more so.

Mass was abbreviated due to the lateness of the day and the fact there was one more item on the Pope's agenda, sharing a meal with the Abbey personnel in the Refectory.

When the Pope gave his final prayer, the head of security signaled them to follow him to the Refectory.

When they entered the Refectory, the only people in there were security personnel. They were making one last sweep of the dining hall. Tables and benches had been set up for the meal. Kitchen personnel had set the tables and placed silver carafes of water on each table along silver goblets. The multi-colored tiled Refectory floor was the most elaborate he'd seen since he'd entered the Abbey. At the far end of the Refectory was the door Chameleon slipped through earlier…before he knew who she was.

There was a guard posted next to it.

† † †

Chameleon shed her habit, coif and veil. Her bleached blonde hair now covered with a short brunette wig. Her complexion darker and brown contacts removed. Fake chin and nose, gone. No one would recognize her as Sister Aimee Dubois now. She had also shed her body suit, all designed to make her look heavier than she actually was.

Swiss Guard and Papal security wouldn't stand a chance of catching her. If they were anything, they were predictable. Their policing style regimented and unwavering. They were cops with a cop's mentality.

Her concern was the operative she knew as Kaplan. He knew her tactics. There was the strong possibility he'd see through her new disguise. She had evaded his capture years ago in Switzerland and was determined to do it again. With any luck at all, she would complete her contract and escape through the bowels of the Abbey using the incoming tide to wash her to shore.

And all in the cover of darkness.

CHAPTER 77

The Refectory
1700 Hours

Nightfall was now complete. It hadn't rained in a couple of hours and the wind had dried most of the exterior walkways. The temperature had dropped outside, the Abbey's heat was turned up and the Refectory was bordering on toasty.

Bishop Jean Paul Renault was at the pulpit reading from the Bible. He prefaced his read with scripture and verse, but Kaplan wasn't listening. He knew Chameleon's timetable was running out. If she was going to make a move, she'd have to do it soon. After the meal, the Pope, who sat at the head table along with two priests, would be escorted out of the Abbey, down the streets of Mont Saint Michel village, into his waiting caravan and taken back to the mainland where his helicopter would be ready to fly him to his waiting jet in Saint-Malo.

He had surveyed the narrow village streets on his way to the Abbey and with all the buildings emptied and locked and the Swiss Guard posted every few meters, it was unlikely Chameleon would or could make her move in the open. In order to assassinate the Pope, his bet was that she would do it somewhere in the Abbey. That's where he would do it.

He did now what he always did when tracking a target—think like the adversary.

The Refectory wasn't an ideal spot since it didn't have many avenues for escape. Back outside in the Cloister would have been better. From the Cloister there were many doors from which to lurk. Refectory, kitchen, church dormitory as well as several stairways. That's where he would be.

But there was still the door Chameleon used earlier when he first arrived. At the time, he didn't think anything of a nun slipping out the narrow door. In retrospect, he should have known...or at least suspected and investigated where the door led. And that tidbit of information was still a mystery to him.

The guard who was previously posted next to the door had been repositioned by the entrance to the Refectory from the Cloister.

If Chameleon tried to use that door to kill the Pope, she would have to open it all the way to get a shot off and that would leave her completely exposed to security, who would easily be able to take her down before she could acquire the firing angle she needed to kill the Pope.

While he stared at the Bishop reading from his Bible and his proximity to the door, a strange thought occurred to him. What if the Pope wasn't the actual target? What if a hit on the Pope was a diversion from the real target? What if the Intelligence Community was duped into believing the hit was on the Pope in order to lower their awareness for a different target? If that were the case, who would the target be?

He studied the layout of the Refectory, where everyone was seated, who would be a viable target. The Pope was safe. No angle from any door. Plus, he was surrounded by Swiss Guard. Who was exposed that could be a viable target?

In his mind he ran through all the possibilities as if a homicide investigator had sketched it out in perfect detail. Right now, there was only one possible target. And Chameleon would have a clear line of sight to take the kill shot.

Bishop Jean Paul Renault.

And if the Bishop was the target, he knew who hired Chameleon.

† † †

Chameleon studied the live-feed video on her phone from the three micro cameras she'd hidden in the Refectory. Her target was standing in place behind the pulpit and the door was unguarded.

As planned.

The Pope had all the attention, security wise, and Bishop Jean Paul Renault was a forgotten soul. She'd bet they never even gave his safety a second thought.

Leaking intel about a hit on the Pope was a brilliant idea. One that came from and was handled by her employer. It ensured all attention would be diverted from the real target. And the plan had worked.

She made her way down the back stairwell that connected the Refectory via a recessed hallway. The same route she used the first time she saw and recognized the CIA operative. Once behind the walls and in the secret corridors, she had a multitude of options. Her favorite was the dark and dank passageway's connection to the Church of Notre Dame Sous Terre. It was quick, quiet and secure. No one used it. Most didn't even know it existed. The monks and nuns didn't like the corridors because they weren't kept clean and were overrun with rats. That kept everyone in the main halls, rooms, and stairways. Plus, they were discouraged from exploring the back recesses of the Abbey.

She, on the other hand, liked maneuvering through the hidden passages.

She made her way next to the door. On the other side, the Refectory. The door had to open at least three inches to give her a clean shot. Hinges already oiled because old doors were prone to squeak. She had thought of everything.

On one of the video feeds, she saw Kaplan studying the Refectory, every angle, then his eyes locked on the Bishop. And then on the door she was standing behind.

He knew.

She was out of time.

She readied her weapon, eased the door ajar with her free hand just enough to slip the silencer through the slot. She fired three rounds in quick succession.

The first bullet struck the left side of the Bishop's chest. His white robe exploded in a sea of crimson. Screams filled her ears. The bullet torqued his body to his left. The second blast, dead center chest. The Bishop froze, disbelief filled his face for an instant before the third round bore into his forehead. A pink mist spewed in the air.

Footsteps pounded her way.

She jerked the door closed and tried to latch it but there was a tug from the other side. Strong. Too strong.

She let go and ran.

CHAPTER 78

Kaplan recognized the situation as it unfolded. He bolted from where he stood toward the door next to the pulpit.

Bishop Jean Paul Renault showed alarm by his sudden movement as did the Swiss Guard. When Kaplan sped toward the door, the Bishop turned to follow. The rest seemed to happen in slow motion.

The door opened a few inches. It wasn't the opening of the door that first caught Kaplan's attention. It was what he saw sticking out. A silencer.

He shouted and waved at the door, "Get down."

A guard moved to cut off his angle but stopped at the sound of the first pop.

It was too late.

Blood mushroomed from the Bishop's robe. His sanguine fluid spattered across the pulpit.

A second round fired into the Bishop's chest. He staggered backward but remained on his feet, eyes bulged in horror and disbelief.

A third shot caused the Bishop's head to recoil backward, and the robed man dropped to the floor. A pink mist blew from the back of his head and seemed to suspend in mid-air before sinking to the tile floor.

Bishop Jean Paul Renault was dead.

Chameleon had fired off all three shots in less than two seconds and attempted to close the door. Before she could secure the door, Kaplan grabbed the handle. There was resistance at first, then there was none.

He yanked the door opened and saw nothing but the faint outline of stone steps leading upwards…somewhere into the darkness.

With his weapon drawn he took off, sprinting into the dark void, tripping on the first step and stumbling forward. Behind him he heard a growing cacophony of voices—yelling and screaming. As he bounded up the stairs, the sounds trailed away.

He was alone.

No Heuse.

No Swiss Guard.

Just him and Chameleon.

And this time, she wasn't getting away.

His Beretta Px4 Storm .45 in one hand, holding his other in front of him for protection from anything unseen in the dark stairwell. He rushed upward through the darkness.

The hunt was on.

His prey on the run.

He could hear her footsteps above him. She was light on her feet, running up the stairs like she did in the earlier chase, several steps at a time. Faster than him. And she had the advantage—she knew the passage. He did not and kept bumping walls when the steps made a turn. He lost his footing twice when his shoes found wet surface and he had to slow to keep from falling. When he found purchase, he sped up, two steps at a time.

Suddenly the stairwell stopped. Almost like he'd run into a cul-de-sac. He ran his hands along the walls until he found a small gap. Through the gap, a faint light. Just enough to see his hand in front of his face, but it was the only way out.

He followed the passageway until it ended. He was at a

recessed wall behind another wall. Notre Dame Sous Terre. *This was how Chameleon got away.*

When he entered the old twin-nave church, Chameleon was nowhere in sight. With only two exits, he knew which way she wouldn't go—back toward the Swiss Guard.

Never losing a stride, he sped toward the remaining exit. Running faster than before. He blasted through the doorway and spotted her at the far end of a corridor, not the route he had taken earlier with Heuse. She was in street clothes and hurdled a roped off area like a track star and vanished down a stairwell.

When he reached the stairwell, it forked left and right. He paused to catch a sound. She went left. He followed her footfalls, bounding down four or five steps at a time.

Her sounds grew louder. He was closing in. She was in sight again but still had a good lead. The stairwell was now rectangular, dropping fifteen steps a flight then turning 180 degrees left. Another flight of fifteen, another 180 degrees left. It was lit, not well, but good enough for him to see without falling.

He was tiring, breathing heavy, but refused to slow. He looked down the stairwell, it ended four flights below. Shit. Chameleon had a two-flight advantage.

Chameleon exited through a door on the bottom flight.

He followed.

The door opened onto an elevated courtyard at upper village level and just above a small cemetery. The sky was dark, but the island fortress was brightly lit. Spotlights shot light daggers into the night sky illuminating the base of the clouds above. An angry wind howled through the nooks and crannies of Mont Saint Michel. His subconscious mind registered the distant beat of helicopter rotors.

To his left, Chameleon fled toward a ramp leading down toward the village. She kept running, past the main road, until she reached the rampart sea wall and turned down the rampart passage.

He'd walked this before, many years ago. A sunset stroll with Isabella. The rampart passage was well lit. He remembered where it went and where it ended—at the base of the village near the main gate. The village was secured with Swiss Guard. Chameleon was trapped.

She had to go through them…or him.

She was slowing. She craned a look over her shoulder. He was closing the gap fast and she knew it. Her options were few. She abruptly stopped and he knew where this encounter was headed.

She spun around, handgun rising in her left hand to meet him.

His Beretta already trained on her and he'd eased the slack out of the trigger. She was one squeeze away from oblivion. He stopped, facing her, twenty feet away.

"Drop it." His tone forceful and commanding, allowing him to be heard over the wind and surf. He cautiously advanced. One step at a time.

She stopped lifting her weapon. "You," she yelled back at him.

"Yep. This time you won't get away."

Without another word, she took her right hand and removed her brunette wig revealing her long blonde hair. She tossed the wig over the rampart and her eyes followed it. He noticed the strong wind carried the hairpiece away like a feather. She shook her head letting her long hair unfurl in the wind.

"I said drop it."

"No," she shouted back in defiance. "You'll have to kill me."

"Is that what you want?"

"I won't be taken alive. I won't go to prison."

He saw the fiery eyes, he remembered them well. This was indeed Chameleon. "It doesn't have to end this way."

"Unless you're letting me go, it does."

"That won't happen."

It had come down to this. A virtual standoff, but this time he had the edge. Other than dropping her weapon, any move she made now was suicide. He knew it. She knew it.

"Who hired you?" Kaplan asked.

She smiled.

"That won't do you any good now."

She raised her weapon.

He felt it coming, saw it coming, and was ready. Before her barrel lifted, he fired, striking her left arm just above the elbow. At this distance how could he miss? For him, point blank range. Her gun dropped and landed on the stone rampart passage. She clamped her wounded arm, blood oozing through her fingers where the 45-caliber round found its mark.

He sprung forward and tackled her. He rolled her to her stomach and pinned her down. Reaching behind his back he removed the flex cuffs from his parka and secured her hands, then her ankles. He rolled her to her back. She was kicking and cursing. He pulled out his field first aid kit, the one Frederic acquired for him in Bayeux, and bandaged her arm with a tight wrap to stop the bleeding.

"Now, I'll ask again. Who hired you?"

✝ ✝ ✝

The news of the murder of Bishop Jean Paul Renault blared through the radio and spread through the crowd like wildfire. A few from P.A.P.A.C.Y. cheered, while most showed some semblance of sorrow.

Moss had to get Welch to explain what was happening as the tension rose around them into a furor of chaos. The media had gone into a frenzy. Lights shown on reporters as they took their message on-air live.

"What about the Pope?" Moss asked Welch.

"Apparently not the target. Either that or Chameleon shot the wrong person," Welch replied.

"What about Chameleon? Where's she?"

"Kaplan's chasing her while we speak."

"I should have been there with him," Moss insisted. "I should have had some skin in the game."

"Sorry, Moss. Couldn't let you do it. Besides, I doubt Papal security would have bought into it. We had enough trouble getting Kaplan out there."

Moss stared out at the island Abbey, lit up like a bright city. Lights reflecting off the water surrounding the fortress. The Papal helicopter now en route to the Abbey. The crew took off in such a rush that the downwash of the helicopter's blades gathering lift blew over a portion of the P.A.P.A.C.Y stage. Volunteers were scrambling to keep the overhead banners from falling on spectators.

Moss felt dejected, regardless of what Alan Welch said. He should have been out there with Kaplan. Now all he could do was wait. And he hated waiting.

He stood next to Welch and Colonel Skouboe as he heard more reports come across the radio.

"English, please," he said to Skouboe.

"Your friend has shot and detained the assassin. She is now in the custody of Capitaine Heuse and the GIGN."

The radio blared again. Skouboe handed it to Moss. "Monsieur Kaplan wishes to speak to you."

He took the radio and keyed the mic. "Moss."

"Moss, you and Marla need to find and secure Wolfe."

Moss hesitated too long to answer.

"Is there a problem?" Kaplan asked.

"Marla left the rally site hours ago."

"Left? Did she say why?"

"No. She was here one minute and gone the next."

"Okay, you do it alone. Sit on Wolfe till I get there."

"Sure thing. By the way, nice going out there."

Moss handed the radio back to Skouboe and headed toward the P.A.P.A.C.Y. stage. He searched the area.

Matthew Wolfe was gone.

CHAPTER 79

Kaplan arrived back on the mainland to a frenzy of activity. The men Welch had assigned to keep track of Matthew Wolfe had failed and the traitor had eluded his captors during the bedlam.

Welch was fuming, face red, as he barked orders to his men. Moss was standing to the side of Welch, who was visibly angry. Another government SNAFU. As federal employees with top-secret security clearances, he had seen it too many times to count.

Moss saw him approaching, walked away from Welch and his men and angled toward Kaplan.

"How did Wolfe get away?" Kaplan asked Moss.

"Those clowns of Welch's dropped the ball and let their guard down after the announcement of the Bishop's death. It turned into a media circus with all the lights and cameras. The Pope's security teams took over pushing crowds away from the causeway and then the helicopter fired up, took off and landed over on the island. I assume to pick up the Pope and get him out of here and to a safe location. I imagine when the helicopter blew over the stage, Wolfe took advantage of the distraction and made his getaway."

"Now that you mention it, I remember hearing a chopper while I was involved with Chameleon on the rampart walkway."

"Involved?"

"Chasing her through the Abbey, damn near shooting her arm off, cuffing her and bandaging what was left of her arm then hauling her ass down to the Gendarmerie building."

"Just another day in the life of Gregg Kaplan."

He could see Alan Welch was still barking orders to his men. "How much of a head start does Wolfe have?"

"Fifteen, maybe twenty minutes. Nothing insurmountable."

The advocacy group members were breaking down the stage and packing up protest materials. The show was over.

P.A.P.A.C.Y. had their chance to get the Pope's attention and failed. Or maybe they didn't fail. Perhaps they accomplished their mission with an outcome they couldn't have foreseen or wanted. It wasn't likely anyone would forget this day anytime soon. Especially with an incident that would dominate international news for a week or so.

"Tell me something, Moss. Have you ever had a gut feeling about something that didn't make sense? One where you had absolutely no rhyme or reason to suspect something? Nothing concrete to go on."

"Or damn near impossible? Hell yeah, I have. A lot of times when I had to apprehend fugitives. A guy once told me *never buck your gut*. What's your long shot hunch?"

"Remember what Wolfe told us about Sophie's brother Pierre? About how he'd been repeatedly abused by a priest when he was young and how that had devastated his adult life? How he would do anything to avenge Pierre if he could?"

Moss's face lit up. "You mean like use some of that top-secret underworld knowledge he learned at the NSA and CIA to hire an assassin to take out the priest who abused Pierre? What are the odds Bishop Jean Paul Renault was that priest?" He paused. "I don't know, Kaplan, sounds too convenient an explanation. I think Chameleon just screwed up and killed the wrong person."

"I realize that's a lot of speculation, but it could explain

Wolfe's sudden disappearance," Kaplan added, "Maybe we were set up and this was part of his plan all along."

"That's giving that weasel too much credit. Maybe he simply saw a window of opportunity and seized it knowing full well the CIA was about to haul his sorry traitor ass back to the United States for trial."

"Did you notice if he was chummier with any one of those in the P.A.P.A.C.Y. group more than others?"

"He spent most of his time chatting with that guy over there, the one with the blond hair in a ponytail."

He motioned for Moss to follow. "Let's go talk to him."

He and Moss flanked the young man and marched him away from the P.A.P.A.C.Y. staging area. Ponytail started to protest when Kaplan jabbed him in the ribs with his knife. "Make a sound and it'll be your last," Kaplan said in French. The two men marched Ponytail to the back of the Le Relais Saint-Michel hotel, through the back door into a dimly lit atrium where he was shoved into a chair. "Where's Matthew Wolfe?" Kaplan asked.

"Qui?" *Who?*

"Matthew Wolfe."

The man shook his head. "Je ne sais pas." *I don't know.*

"Curtis Benoit," Moss chimed in.

Kaplan could see it on Ponytail's face. Recognition...and guilt. "Où est Benoit?" *Where is Benoit?*

Moss seized the back of Ponytail's neck, catching a handful of hair in his clutches. The man's face full of fear. Kaplan pulled back his parka, exposing his Beretta for Ponytail to see.

"I won't ask again."

Ponytail glanced at Moss, back to Kaplan. "Please, no

harm," he said in English. "I loaned Curtis my car. He told me it was an emergency. He had to check on Pierre. He said he owed it to Sophie. Pierre has no one now, Sophie was his only living relative. Now she's gone." Ponytail started to cry.

"When was he going to return your car?"

"At our next rally. In Beaune."

Moss's face lit up. "Hear that, Kaplan? Beaune. Back where we started."

Kaplan didn't answer.

"Did Curtis give you his route to Bourges?"

"Oui."

Kaplan plucked a notepad and pen from the hostess desk. "Write it down."

There was something else on his mind. Or rather someone. And that someone would never let Wolfe get to Bourges where Pierre was a patient in the hospital. She was out there somewhere. Watching. Waiting for her chance to get to Wolfe.

"Write down make, model, color and plate number too," he ordered Ponytail.

After Ponytail complied, they hurried back where Alan Welch was huddled with Colonel Pernille Skouboe and Capitaine Heuse.

"What's the rush?" Moss asked.

"We've got to get to Wolfe before she does?"

"Who? Marla?"

"No. Jasmine Habibi."

CHAPTER 80

Paris Deputy Chief of Station Alan Welch stood next to GIGN Colonel Pernille Skouboe and Capitaine Travers Heuse as the trio watched Kaplan and Moss speed away in the black Audi. Nothing but taillights, but he knew it was Kaplan's rental car. Welch shook his head.

"Where is Monsieur Kaplan going?" Skouboe asked. "The GIGN is not finished with him yet."

"Where do you think he's going, Colonel?" Welch answered. "To recapture Matthew Wolfe."

"Does he think he has a better chance than we do? The GIGN and CIA combined forces should have him located in no time."

"Kaplan and Moss certainly have a better chance than we do, even with our combined forces."

"He knows something we don't," Heuse chimed in.

"Of course, he does," Welch agreed. "Why else would he tear out of here without a word? Wolfe has a head start, but soon that gap will close."

Skouboe looked at Heuse. "Check the crowd, I want to know what Kaplan knows. The GIGN will beat Messieurs Kaplan and Moss to Wolfe."

"Oui, Colonel."

"I applaud your tenacity Colonel, but if you don't mind, I will leave now and return to Paris."

Skouboe nodded. "Nothing left for you here. I appreciate the CIA's assistance in capturing Chameleon. You have fulfilled your debt to me, Alan. The slate is clean."

Welch was pleased Skouboe wiped out his debt. Glad Kaplan came through for him. The past few days had been tense, but he'd learned from his mistakes. He'd also learned to never underestimate Gregg Kaplan and his ability to accomplish the damn-near impossible. In his opinion, his operative had always been the best asset the agency had even if the DCI didn't see it that way. Even if Reed wanted to fire him.

The DCI wanted *yes men* in his new and improved CIA. Welch was not a yes man. Reed was slowly removing the old ways of doing the business of espionage, even when they were the most effective. If it didn't fit the mold of his ideals, he opted for removal. Kaplan was one of those old school operatives and that stuck in the DCI's craw. That and Kaplan's insubordinate refusal to obey the DCI's orders. But in this day and age, someone had to do the dirty work. Lies and deceit could be useful when needed. There was only one man Welch trusted to get Wolfe—Gregg Kaplan.

He looked at the blonde Skouboe and forced a smile. "Colonel, please don't take this the wrong way, but it would be best for all of us if we left Kaplan and Moss alone to do what they do best."

He walked off before Skouboe could respond.

† † †

Kaplan plugged the route Ponytail gave him into the Audi's GPS system and left La Caserne in a hurry. He thought about bringing Welch into the loop but didn't want the oversight. Not from the CIA. Not from the GIGN. He and Moss could handle this. All he wanted to do was get to Wolfe before Jasmine Habibi. Besides, it was best if Welch didn't know what they were up to. Plausible deniability Welch might need to save his job.

The route Wolfe chose was not on the major highways, he opted instead for back roads at the expense of extra driving time. Wolfe could have shaved off close to an hour had he chosen the major highways. But even in darkness, major highways could get him caught.

By now, Colonel Skouboe might know most of what Kaplan knew and might know the make and model of the car he was chasing. And if so, a watch bulletin for Wolfe had no doubt been issued. He doubted Welch would pursue Wolfe any further, instead opting to let Kaplan finish the task.

Wolfe had a twenty-minute lead on them, so he pressed the accelerator increasing his speed in hopes of catching Wolfe. Moss was visibly uncomfortable with his speed on the small roads, especially on curves and while passing, but the big man didn't say a word. Kaplan's urgency to catch Wolfe was obvious.

Another concern was Marla's sudden disappearance. Did she give up and return to Israel? Or was she still in France? Perhaps waiting her own opportunity to get Wolfe. Then again, she had her chance. She was on the small island in Saint-Malo alone with Wolfe for several hours. She'd had plenty of time to make a play on Wolfe, talk him in to going back with her to Tel Aviv. But she didn't. Or if she did, he refused.

Why up and leave without a word?

Then another thought occurred to him, perhaps she was ordered to go after Jasmine. To keep Habibi away from Wolfe. That would certainly be doing them all a favor. But he could shoot holes in that theory too. Deep down inside he knew, Marla had no reason to stay in France any longer. Wolfe was already in CIA custody. She couldn't predict this turn of events. That he would be called out to Mont Saint Michel to stop an assassin from killing the Pope...only to realize too late the Pope wasn't the target. The Bishop was. She couldn't have known Wolfe would make a break for it during a subsequent media frenzy.

No, Marla must have returned to Israel. He was certain of it.

Kaplan slowed to the speed limit when they approached small towns and villages, but when the road opened up in the barren countryside, he pushed the limits. On more than one occasion he noticed Moss was white-knuckling the dashboard and side grab-bar.

"Doing okay over there?" Kaplan smirked at Moss when he asked.

"Keep driving. I'll let you know if I have to puke. I want to catch up to Wolfe as much as you do. I'm just glad you're comfortable on these narrow roads at these speeds. I know I'm not."

"Comes with experience. This is my favorite European country." Kaplan paused for a beat. "Helps to know the language too."

"I've noticed. What are you going to do when we catch him?"

"If Jasmine Habibi hasn't killed him, then I might."

"No, seriously?" Moss pressed.

"I told him to stay put and he didn't."

"How about you let me have a go at him first. I mean before you shoot him."

"Got to get him to tell me where he hid the hard drive first."

"So, that's the deal you cut with him. I wondered why you let him go to the rally." Moss smiled. "You're a sneaky bastard, I'll give you that."

He noticed the night sky was clearing and saw the first twinkling of stars through the windshield. Tomorrow would be a better day, he thought. He was weary and his energy draining. Moss had yawned a few times too. No sleep last night and with another four hours of driving left to Bourges, no sleep tonight either. He was running on fumes. Both of them were.

If he were alone, he would've kept driving, but instead of continuing east on the N12 bypass around Fougères, he turned into town. He had seen the sign for McDonald's and knew he could spend minimum time getting food and coffee. He needed something to power him through and as much as he despised fast food, this was his best alternative. A five-minute or so detour and they were back on the road again.

The line was short, and he and Moss ordered two large coffees each and a bagful of burgers and fries.

"You know this shit'll kill ya?" Moss said to Kaplan with a chuckle.

"Gotta die of something, I guess. Better than eating a bullet."

"A bullet is quicker."

CHAPTER 81

O nce again, he'd proven the incompetence of the CIA. Without any real difficulty, his plan was pulled off without a hitch.

Matthew Wolfe had to admit the darkness helped, so did the media with all its lights and commotion. It created the perfect disruption to elude his captors, especially when the Papal helicopter blew the stage over.

There were times when he thought he wouldn't get away from Kaplan and Company and if the CIA operative hadn't been dispatched to Mont Saint Michel Abbey, he might still be in custody. The man had a heightened awareness he'd never seen in any operative before—a full comprehension of the *big picture*. Unlike the new hires at the agency, Kaplan didn't operate by the normal rules, he operated on instinct. He could get in the head of the person he was tracking. He was indeed a dangerous man.

That explained how he captured Chameleon so quickly. And now that Chameleon was in the custody of the French GIGN, he could only wonder if it would be safe to stiff her the final payment for the hit on Bishop Jean Paul Renault. It didn't matter. The money she had received came from the coffers of the United States Government. Money he'd redirected from CIA Black Ops accounts to his own anonymous offshore accounts.

Regardless, Bishop Renault was dead and Pierre Bouquet had been avenged.

Sophie's advocacy group would likely come under scrutiny

but would be exonerated in the long run. There was no evidence linking them to the Bishop's death. That was his doing and he went to extreme measures to ensure there was nothing that could lead authorities to P.A.P.A.C.Y. or himself. When he got to Bourges, he would let Pierre know about Renault's fate. He'd leave out the part where it was him who arranged the hit.

He wondered how Sophie's younger brother was recovering. And if he knew about Sophie's death. When Kaplan captured him on Petit Bé, he was told about Sophie and Pierre. Actually, the Mossad woman told him about Sophie. Sophie's death came as a surprise, but even though he didn't want to accept it, deep down he knew something bad had happened to her. When she was abducted in front of his eyes, he panicked and ran. He hoped to catch up with Pierre at the Mont Saint Michel rally, that was before he knew about what happened to him.

A dark despair swept over him.

What had he done?

He had brought all this on Sophie and Pierre. The only two people he ever really cared about had their lives ruined because of his actions. If he hadn't met Sophie on the train and become involved with her, none of this would have happened. His on-the-lam lifestyle had taken its toll on the innocent, like it always did. But this time it cost someone their life. Actually, two lives. He had almost forgotten about what happened to Serena in Iceland. With all that had happened since, it seemed so long ago. He never loved her though. Not like Sophie. He was simply using Serena. Nothing more.

That was the way it started with Sophie too. She was end to his means. Yet Sophie had a quality none of the others had—devotion to a cause. To help keep others from being harmed, like her own brother. Sophie was selfless. She was a giver. She dearly loved her brother and cared for Pierre during his bouts with depression. It was that tender side he'd never encountered with other women.

Before, he'd only wanted shallow relationships with no commitment. Sophie changed him. Those womanizing desires had left him. Now he understood the true meaning of love… and he pissed it away because he was a coward.

He ran.

Sophie died.

In retrospect, he wished he had charged out of the coffee shop and let the red-headed Russian take him instead. It was him she was after anyway. He knew what she wanted, the same thing they all wanted—something he possessed.

When the time was right, he'd release everything on the internet for the whole world to see. At least the free world anyway. He would expose not only his country's secrets, but all the great world powers. Their nuclear stockpiles and locations, their advanced weaponry, and most importantly, their secret satellite programs.

It was the newest Cold War. The one most the world didn't know existed.

At least not yet.

Satellites in orbit with only one purpose, disable or destroy other satellites, making way for the ultimate weapon— satellites armed with nuclear weapons ready to rain death and destruction down on the Earth leaving a victim country with no chance to defend itself.

By the time the vulnerable country knew what was happening, it was too late to do anything about it. Too late to defend itself. Too late to retaliate.

As he approached the town of Tours, France, it was after

midnight. He didn't get enough sleep last night out on Petit Bé with all the wind and rain, but he did get some after they got off the island.

He needed a break from driving. He wouldn't be able get in to see Pierre until morning anyway and it wasn't that far from Tours to Bourges. He could find food and take a well-deserved nap in the car. He was sure he wasn't being followed. He'd taken precautionary measures. Plus, he'd made his friend Julien swear not to tell anyone he'd borrowed the car or where he was going.

In the morning, he'd check on Pierre and tell him about Sophie and Bishop Jean Paul Renault. He hoped the news of the Bishop's demise would bring the young man a little peace of mind.

††††

Jasmine Habibi and her two men had been following Matthew Wolfe at a safe distance for nearly four hours when the man took a turn into a town called Tours. There hadn't been an opportunity to take down Wolfe on the highway, but now it was getting late and traffic had thinned.

It was a stroke of luck that one of her men saw Wolfe get away from the men who were guarding him in La Caserne. Something had happened and the place turned into a frenzy of activity. That was when Wolfe melted into the crowd and got away. They had been following him ever since he headed southeast on back roads. He was smart, she thought, he kept his speed inconspicuous—only two or three kilometers per hour over the posted speed limit. Always less than five.

With headlights in the distance behind her, she and her

men hadn't had an opportunity to take him down.

Wolfe cruised through downtown, frequently braking as he approached diners and cafes, but none were open at this hour. She knew what he was doing, she was hungry too. As were her men. Last night they staked out Saint-Malo, waiting to see the outcome of what happened on those two small islands. There was a shootout on one of them and then the French authorities showed up. That put her into a covert surveillance mode. Her men took turns watching while she tried to rest. It was an all-night affair.

Then Wolfe and his captors were escorted by the GIGN, in marked Gendarmerie vehicles, to Mont Saint Michel. She had yet to find an opportunity to get to Wolfe. She saw that Mossad bitch leave when her men picked her up outside of the barricades in La Caserne. She left and never returned.

Good riddance.

Mossad had stepped out of the picture leaving MOIS a chance to get to Wolfe without Israeli interference. Wolfe possessed secret intel that could give Iran an advantage over the evils of Israel and the West. She had dealt with Marla Farache once before, but not in the field. Farache wasn't a field agent anymore, at least not until now, although she did know of Marla's reputation.

What a chance for advancement it would have been for her to capture Wolfe and covertly kill the Mossad agent during the same mission. She would have found favor with the Supreme Leader and been able to write her own ticket for the rest of her life.

Wolfe was within arm's reach and it shouldn't be long before they captured him.

CHAPTER 82

Marla Farache had been following the two cars for over four hours keeping an inconspicuous distance behind the trailing car.

In the first car, Matthew Wolfe.

In the second car, Jasmine Habibi and her two thugs. They were mindless men with no capacity to do anything other than what they were directly ordered to do. Independent thought wasn't a skillset.

She had given up on Wolfe until she spotted Habibi on the southern outskirts of La Caserne. She couldn't leave knowing Habibi was lying in wait. Her mission was still ongoing and to chance Habibi getting her hands on Wolfe would be negligent on her part. It was one thing for the CIA to capture and contain Wolfe, it was another for Habibi and Iran's MOIS to get their hands on him. If that were to happen, she could never face her uncle. It would be a failure of epic proportion and that had yet to happen to her. Success was a Mossad tenet.

She wondered how Gregg had taken her sudden and unexplained disappearance. She picked up her phone thinking a quick call could resolve any potential conflict that might arise between them. Alienation from Kaplan was the last thing she wanted. Perhaps not the last thing, she *did* have a job to do and now all the pieces were falling into place.

She put her phone down after she watched the hatchback Wolfe was driving deviate from the main road and head toward town center of Tours. Habibi's sedan followed Wolfe. She and her men, both pilots of her uncle's jet, followed in the van they rented in Saint-Malo. One of the pilots was driving, the other in the front passenger seat. She sat center seat behind them.

How conspicuous could they all be? Cruising slowly through downtown in the middle of the night? If Wolfe didn't make Habibi's tail or Habibi make Marla's tail, then no one was paying attention.

But she wasn't backing off. Wolfe needed her protection from the Iranians. And Israel needed her protection from the Iranians. So what if Habibi knew she was being followed. Perhaps it would discourage her from making a move on Wolfe.

"Looks like we got company," the pilot who was driving said. "And coming up behind us fast."

Marla craned her neck to see headlights in the not too far distance. As they entered Tours, the car was gaining on them.

"You think it's the police?" she asked.

"Perhaps. Hard to tell from this distance. We'll know soon enough."

She twisted back around and watched Wolfe and Habibi cruise toward downtown. Wolfe would slow, hit the brakes, then speed up again. He only seemed to slow at diners or cafes. She guessed what he was doing—looking for food and a restroom.

They crossed the Loire River and followed Wolfe through downtown. Just north of the Le Cher River, he pulled into an open nightclub called Bar le Corsaire.

She checked traffic behind her vehicle.

The car had caught up to them.

It was a black Audi.

She saw the silhouettes of two men through the windshield. Then when they passed beneath a bright streetlight, she caught a glimpse of their faces.

Gregg Kaplan and Pete Moss.

When Wolfe got out of the hatchback, Habibi and her men pulled up behind his vehicle and all three Iranians jumped out with weapons in hand. The black Audi whizzed past her and screeched to a stop behind Habibi.

Kaplan and Moss bolted from the Audi.

Weapons raised.

Before she knew it, they were in the middle of a war zone.

†††

Kaplan caught sight of Wolfe's white hatchback only moments before the man turned off the highway and headed toward Tours town center. There were two other vehicles between them. He planned to pass both as soon as he had the opportunity. There were a few cars on the road at this early morning hour, but not many. Every city in nearly every country he'd been to had night owls. It was rare when he didn't see people out and about in medium and larger cities and at all hours of the night. He knew, because those were the hours he usually conducted his missions.

Between him and Wolfe were a silver sedan and a dark blue van. Moss indicated it looked like the van that picked up Marla. Kaplan drove up on the van fast and considered himself lucky to have located the white hatchback before he circumvented the Tours downtown district. If he'd been a few minutes later, he'd have missed Wolfe altogether. There was an old saying he was fond of— *I'll take luck over skill any day.*

Today, he had both.

He watched as Wolfe slowed and expected the two other vehicles to go around him. But they didn't. When Wolfe slowed, they slowed. When Wolfe sped up, they sped up. When Wolfe turned, they turned. Whether Wolfe knew it or not, he was being followed, but followed by whom?

It was unlikely that the GIGN or the CIA could have caught up with him by now, but not impossible. Both had the necessary resources at their disposal to do so. The most likely scenario was Wolfe was seen leaving La Caserne and was being tailed by a hostile. And whoever it was had a big advantage, they outnumbered Wolfe. The sedan could hold four hostiles and the van could hold up to eight.

Wolfe was as good as dead or captured if he stopped.

And then he did.

Wolfe took a right into an open nightclub. The sedan followed. The van pulled to the curb half a block away.

Three people jumped out of the sedan. Three he recognized.

Moss raised his voice and said, "It's her. That Iranian bitch."

Kaplan jammed the gas pedal, jumped the curb and screeched toward the two parked vehicles. Out of the corner of his eye he saw no movement from anyone in the van. With one hand steering the car he used his free hand to get his gun. Moss already had his drawn.

He hit the brakes so hard the Audi skidded, fishtailed and corrected at a dead stop in front of Jasmine Habibi and her two thugs.

Both of Habibi's men were out of the vehicle.

"Freeze," he yelled as soon as he and Moss had jumped out of the Audi, using the car doors for protection.

Habibi's face twisted. "Kaplan. I should have known."

"Jasmine, I made you a promise, drop your weapons or die."

"You take her," Moss said. "I got the other two."

"Drop them now. You're not walking out of—"

Before Kaplan could finish, he heard a loud pop from behind him. Jasmine Habibi legs bent, and she crumpled to the ground. A crimson flood gushing from her chest. He pivoted to see where the gunshot came from.

Marla Farache.

† † †

Things were getting better for Dalton.

The Israeli woman killed the Iranian woman. Then Kaplan and Moss eliminated the other Iranian men. Unlike the Russians, the Iranians didn't send backup.

What had started as many had whittled down to three. He liked his odds. It was now a matter of waiting for the right moment to present itself.

And when it did, Kaplan and Moss would go down.

And the Israeli woman along with them.

CHAPTER 83

At the sound of gunfire, Wolfe dove behind a sign next to the nightclub's entrance. He didn't appear to comprehend what had just transpired until he saw Kaplan. A sudden epiphany flashed across the man's face. He'd been followed and never knew it.

From a crouched position, Wolfe pushed himself to his feet and walked over to where Kaplan was hovering over the three dead Iranian bodies.

"Who were they?" Wolfe asked, his voice unsteady.

"Iranians. They work for MOIS...*worked* for MOIS."

"And they were following me?"

Marla interrupted, "Yes, for nearly four hours. Do you not *ever* look in your rearview?"

Wolfe's face rigid with tension. "Thanks for saving my life. I'm exhausted. I guess I got careless."

Moss pushed Wolfe hard in the chest, knocking him three steps back. "Listen here you fucking little weasel, you think you had a rough night? How much sleep you think *we* got last night?" He gestured to Kaplan, Marla and then himself. "If you'll remember, we were the ones out there in the cold trying to save your sorry ass last night." He said to Kaplan, "I told you we should've let the Russians have him." He directed his ire to Wolfe. "I oughta beat the shit out of you for trying to escape."

"Enough," Kaplan interrupted Moss's tirade. He addressed Wolfe, "Why'd you leave?"

"I wanted to check on Pierre," he explained. "I owe it to Sophie to watch after him. I want to be the one to tell him about her, not someone he doesn't know. He needs to hear it from me."

"You think it will make a difference who it comes from?" Marla asked. "He'll be devastated either way. Tell the truth, Wolfe, you're doing this to satisfy your guilty conscience for being responsible for Sophie's death, not out of some misplaced compassion for Pierre."

"That's not true. I do care for Pierre and I don't care what you think." His voice cracked and tears welled in his eyes.

Marla balled her fist and stepped toward him. Kaplan caught her around her waist. "Easy. He'll get plenty of ass whippings where he's going. That is if they ever let him see the light of day again."

"What's that supposed to mean?" Wolfe asked.

It was his turn to take a shot at Wolfe. "It means I'll be turning you over to CIA Deputy Chief of Station Alan Welch. Remember him, you met him this afternoon…make it yesterday afternoon…outside Mont Saint Michel? After that, who knows where they'll lock you up. Gitmo maybe, I don't have a clue. You'll be charged with more crimes. Hell, you worked for the agency, you know better than I do where they'll find a hole to throw your sorry ass in."

Wolfe looked down and stayed silent.

"But I can guarantee you one thing," Kaplan continued. "If you try to escape again." He pointed to the dead Iranians. "You'll end up like them. I'll see to it personally."

In the distance he heard klaxons wailing. Someone from inside the bar must've called the cops. "Moss, you mind driving Wolfe's hatchback? I'm not letting Wolfe out of my sight again."

"No, I guess not. Where're we going?"

"Bourges. I'll have Alan pick him up at the hospital." He

shoved Wolfe's chin up forcing him to look him in the eye. "I'm not doing this for you, asshole, but for Pierre. He needs to be able to look you in the eye when he learns the truth."

"The truth. Is that what's important to you, Mr. Kaplan? Because the truth is whatever your government wants it to be. That's why I did what I did. Otherwise, the truth would never be heard."

Kaplan shook his head in disgust and let out a grunt. He said to Marla, "You're with me. Send your pilots back to Saint-Malo. I'll let you know later where they can pick you up tomorrow."

She nodded. "I'll go tell them." She headed back to the van.

A small group of people stood outside the nightclub's door.

"And hurry, the cops will be here soon." He turned to Moss and said, "Stay on this road until A85, it's like an interstate. Go east toward Bourges. Just follow the signs. I'll catch up to you in a few." He held up his phone. "If you see a good place to stop, call me."

"Roger that." Moss grabbed his bag from the Audi, tossed it behind the seat and folded into the hatchback and drove off.

Marla returned. "All set."

"Get in," he ordered. "Wolfe in the back. Marla, up front with me."

He engaged the rear-door child locks so Wolfe couldn't get out without one of them opening the door for him. "One more thing," he said to Wolfe before he closed the car door. "We had an agreement. The rally for the hard drive. Don't try anything else or I'll kill you before you can get to that hard drive and let the chips fall where they may. Understood?" He slammed the door before Wolfe could answer.

Kaplan fired up the engine and drove away from the

nightclub.

He glanced at Marla. She was already looking at him. Streetlights flashed across their faces as he drove south toward A85.

There was an awkward silence.

Finally, he said, "Maybe now you can tell me why you left without saying a word to anybody."

CHAPTER 84

Jacques Coeur Hospital Center
Bourges, France—0900 Hours

Kaplan entered the ground floor hospital room first.
Pierre Bouquet was no longer in ICU. He was sitting
up in his hospital bed. Hair up in his standard man-bun style.
An IV bag hung from a rod next to his bed, the clear plastic line
winding down to Pierre's arm. His heart monitor sounded its
rhythmic cadence like a metronome set to 60 beats per minute.
A semi-private room, but there was no one in the other bed.
He looked much better than the last time Kaplan saw him a
couple of days ago when he was unconscious and bleeding
on his living room floor. He had one black eye, right side,
where Tatyana Kazakov had bashed him over the head. A large
bandage covered the contusion on his forehead.

The nurse at the station had given Kaplan an update on
Pierre's condition. He was improving rapidly. The wound was
minor, as minor as a gunshot wound could be, and struck
nothing vital. Mostly his issue was blood loss. The transfusions
corrected that. His youth and overall good physical health
prior to the attack had done wonders for his speedy recovery
time. His prognosis was full recovery with a planned hospital
release in a day or so. What the nurse didn't know was that the
news they were about to deliver would no doubt send Pierre
into a deep dark spiral of depression.

The young man's face lit up when he saw Wolfe, but it was
short-lived. His eyebrows furrowed. A concerned look took

over. "Curtis," Pierre said. Then in French, "How was the rally at Mont Saint Michel? Did the Pope show up?" He craned his neck and looked at the door as Moss and Marla followed Wolfe into the room. "Did Sophie come with you?"

Wolfe didn't answer.

"She couldn't make it," Marla answered for him in French.

Pierre looked at Kaplan then at Moss. "Have we met? You look familiar."

Wolfe interrupted, "These are the two men who found you. They called emergency rescue. If it weren't for them, you might have died."

He raised his hand and extended it toward Kaplan and Moss. "Merci, merci."

Kaplan and Moss took turns shaking Pierre's hand. "De rien," Kaplan said. *You're welcome.*

Pierre said in English, "Curtis, tell me about the rally. Was Renault there?" His eyes narrowed. A dark expression washed across his face.

Kaplan grabbed Wolfe by the arm and shoved him at Moss. "Take him outside. I want to talk to Pierre alone." He glanced at Marla. "You too, please."

It was exactly what he'd explained to Moss earlier about the unexplained strange feeling he had about Renault and Pierre and Wolfe. And now it had all but been confirmed by one innocent question from Pierre. His expression told him everything he needed to know.

When the room was empty Pierre said, "What is this about?"

"I was at the rally in Bourges. I heard what you said about your experiences with abuse from a priest. Was Bishop Jean Paul Renault that priest? Is he the man who abused you as a child?"

"What does it matter to you?" His voice full of disdain.

Kaplan changed his tone. The pleasantness had evaporated. "Was he…or wasn't he?"

Pierre hesitated, then lowered his head. "Yes. He was only a priest back then."

"That's what I thought."

"Why do you ask?" Pierre questioned.

"Because Bishop Jean Paul Renault was assassinated yesterday at the Abbey. In front of the Pope. Did you have the Bishop killed?"

Kaplan didn't need an answer. It was written on Pierre Bouquet's face.

"No, of course not."

The young man was telling the truth. If Kaplan was certain about anything, he was certain of this. Pierre Bouquet knew nothing about Renault's assassination until this moment.

"Why would you ask me that?"

"Because if anyone had a motive for killing Renault, it was you. I captured the assassin but couldn't get a name from her."

"Her?"

"Assassins come in both genders and all colors."

"Mister, who are you?"

"Someone who is trying to get to the truth."

"What is Curtis' involvement in this?" Pierre asked.

"You'll have to ask him yourself." He turned toward the door. "Moss, Marla, bring Wolfe in here."

"Wolfe? Who is Wolfe?" The trio entered and stood next to Pierre's bed. "What's he talking about Curtis? Who is Wolfe?"

After a few awkward moments of silence Moss prodded Wolfe in the back. "Tell him the truth. You owe him that."

"My name is not really Curtis Benoit. That's an alias. My real name is Matthew Wolfe."

"I don't understand, Curtis...or whatever your name is. Why would you lie?" Then Pierre seemed to have a moment of enlightenment. "Wait a minute. I've heard that name before. Matthew Wolfe, isn't that the name of the NSA analyst who stole secrets and exiled from the United States? You mean... that's you?"

Wolfe answered in a solemn voice, "Yes, Pierre. It is."

Pierre said, "The rest of you are spies, yes?"

"It's not that simple," Kaplan chimed in.

"Yes, it is," Wolfe said. "You're CIA, she's Mossad..." He looked back at Moss. "And I don't know what the hell he is."

"Where's my sister, Curtis or whoever you are?" his voice frantic. "Tell me, where is Sophie?"

Wolfe opened his mouth several times, but nothing came out.

Pierre's eyes moistened. "You must tell me, where is my sister? Is Sophie okay?"

Marla stepped forward and sat on the edge of the hospital bed. She gently held Pierre's hand. "I'm sorry, Pierre. Sophie was murdered by the Russian woman who did this to you."

CHAPTER 85

It was times like these Kaplan hated.

Pierre Bouquet was an innocent bystander and tragedy showed him no mercy. Ten minutes ago, he was cheerful and now his world had crashed around him. He took the news of Sophie's demise as hard as anybody who lost a loved one. He had lost Isabella, not in death but in life. Sophie was her brother's anchor and now that was gone. Both he and Pierre had been set adrift at sea. He knew how hard it would be for the young man to come to grips with the finality of it all and move on.

Tears flowed nonstop for twenty minutes. Pierre wailed so hard at times he couldn't talk. All anyone could do was watch the pain rip the young man apart as reality set in.

Delivering bad news was one thing. Delivering devastating news was another. As cold hearted as he thought he could be, Kaplan genuinely felt Pierre's anguish.

And it pissed him off.

When Pierre was composed enough to speak, Moss brought Wolfe back in the room. Pierre wiped his eyes and blew his nose several times. "This is all your fault, isn't it, Matthew Wolfe? The Russian woman...the one who did this to me, the one who killed Sophie, she was after you, wasn't she?"

Wolfe lowered his head.

"You brought all this on. You are responsible for killing my sister." Pierre's bloodshot eyes welled up again. "Why couldn't you just stay out of our lives. Look what you have done."

Pierre's eyes burning with hatred, all aimed at Wolfe. "Did

you have Renault killed?"

"Does it matter?" Wolfe raised his head and responded, "The man who abused you is dead. He can never hurt another person. I thought you'd be happy."

"Happy?" Pierre shouted, face turning red. "I hated Renault, despised everything the man stood for. What he'd done to me. What he'd done to others. But I never wanted him dead...I... wanted him punished. I wanted him in prison. I wanted someone to do to him what he did to me. Death was too good for Renault. He needed to suffer, know what it was like to have someone humiliate him. Make him live out the rest of his days realizing firsthand how it felt. But no, you took matters into your own hands. You decided what was best for me."

"How can you be certain it was Wolfe who had the Bishop assassinated?" Marla asked.

Pierre looked at Marla. A tear rolled down his cheek. He wiped it with the back of his hand. "Because the only people who knew the priest's name were my parents and sister. My parents have been dead for years. Sophie must have told him." Pierre glared at Wolfe. "And Sophie would never have him killed. She knew how I felt. She had been trying for years to get him arrested. Mont Saint Michel was the chance she was waiting for. Her chance to confront Renault personally and hopefully bring it to the attention of the Pope."

"But Pierre—" Wolfe started to speak.

Pierre cut him off. "I hate you. This is all your fault. I don't ever want to see your face again." Pierre sobbed. "Get out. Get out," he shouted at Wolfe.

Wolfe blinked, fighting back tears, but it was no use, the tears streamed down his face. "I'm sorry Pierre. Truly, I am sorry."

"I'll take Wolfe out in the hall," said Moss.

Kaplan knew what Moss wanted to do. Moss never had a good poker face. He wanted to rough him up and he didn't care except now wasn't the time and this wasn't the place.

Marla spoke up, "I'll keep watch on Wolfe till Alan gets here."

Kaplan agreed, "Just don't take your eyes off that son of a bitch."

As soon as the door closed Kaplan placed the call. "Where are you?" Welch asked.

"Bourges. Pierre Bouquet's hospital room. Send someone for Wolfe...before Moss or I kill the bastard." Kaplan told him which hospital and room number. "When I hand him over, I'm done. We're done. He'll be your problem then. Let him take you to the hard drive."

"I'll be there in a little over an hour," Welch said. "Gregg, something else has come up. We can talk when I get there." Welch disconnected the call without any other explanation.

Kaplan tucked his cell phone in his parka. This whole ordeal had been a goat-rope from the beginning and he was tired of it. Tired of being misled. Tired of cleaning up other people's messes. In a word, he was just plain tired. There once was a time when he enjoyed the thrill of the hunt. Believing he was ridding the world of the bad guys. At times, he wondered if maybe somewhere along the line, he had become the bad guy. He'd spent decades tracking down terrorists and killing them, typically alone and in the middle of the night. No witnesses. No partners. He was a rogue assassin. He went in, found and eliminated his target, and got out. Clean, simple, fast.

The new DCI took the agency in a different direction. He was separated from his handler, Alan Welch, and left to his own devices. Assignments slowed to a crawl. When they did come, they weren't like before and the rationale behind them confusing or just abysmal. It was as if the United States had become a kinder, gentler nation and the CIA's hard line approach to terrorism softened. The agency became politically correct and the methods he used were frowned upon. The next thing he knew, he had been ostracized. Now he found out from Welch that the new director wanted him fired but Welch intervened somehow and saved his job. He didn't even know he had a job any more until Welch explained the facts to him a few days ago. Now, he wasn't sure he wanted the job any longer.

At least they had captured Matthew Wolfe. Wolfe knew more about the world's nuclear and satellite defenses than anyone. Wolfe had not, at least not yet, released what he had stolen. Wolfe was a threat to national security. In many ways, more so than the terrorists Kaplan was so fond of eliminating.

Someday Wolfe might be viewed by some as a hero, a patriot who placed his nation above his personal safety. To others he was a traitor. A man who had risked the lives of people around the world by his irresponsible actions. But he had not yet reached that level of notoriety. And he had not leaked sensitive information to any foreign power or to the media. But he could at any given moment. Wolfe told him he had failsafe measures in place in the event of his capture or death. That's why Kaplan cut a deal with him. Wolfe could go to the rally and in return hand over the hard drive and remove the failsafe. Why he believed the traitor, he wasn't sure. But now that would be his superior's problem to get the location of the hard drive. He had done what he does best, field operations. He had taken all the personal risks he was going to take on this operation.

He would be glad to hand this traitor over to Alan Welch. Happy to never hear the man's name mentioned again. He'd made a threat moments ago to Welch on the phone, but he knew it was an idle threat. He was peeved at Welch, but he wasn't done. There was too much injustice in the world. Too much evil. Too many bad guys who needed to be eliminated. But he knew he could no longer be effective with the status quo. Something had to give. And give in a big way.

Pierre interrupted Kaplan's thoughts, "Messieurs, I owe you my life. I want to repay you."

Moss spoke up, "If you could get Wolfe to tell us where he hid the hard drive that would help. Think you could convince him?"

"This hard drive is crucial, yes?"

"It's a matter of life and death," said Kaplan. He knew if he could get that hard drive, then he'd have leverage over Reed.

"I will do my best to help you."

"Are you sure you're up to it?" asked Kaplan.

Pierre wiped his nose with a tissue and nodded.

"Moss, get Wolfe in here."

Moss left the room. He could hear him yelling and heavy footfalls echoing in the hall. Kaplan stuck his head out the door searching. What was going on? No Moss, no Wolfe, no Marla. Within a few seconds, he saw Moss bounding down the hall in a panic.

"It's Wolfe," Moss said out of breath. "He's gone. And so is Marla."

CHAPTER 86

Dalton Palmer had learned the best way to defeat most opponents was to let all the players fight it out amongst each other until only one remained. Stay out of sight. Always observe. The remaining player was the one he would pursue. In this case, it was Kaplan and his friends. But Kaplan had no idea he was even involved.

And that was an advantage for Dalton.

He stalked in the shadows, watching, learning.

Kaplan had battled the Russians, technically two sets of Russians in two separate engagements, and then the Iranians. He had come out victorious over both. And now that he felt his mission was over, he let his guard down.

Like his dark-skinned body, Dalton's face was lean and weathered. Eyes deep-set. Hair cut short, black and graying. Old battle wounds and scars marred his torso and limbs from too many hand-to-hand engagements. As one of the covert operatives of the Central Intelligence Agency's *Kill Squad*, formerly known as *Staff D*, these wounds came with the territory. His superior called him a small man, topping out at only 5'8" in height, but it worked to his advantage. It made him an unsuspecting figure.

Staff D was an obscure department of the CIA consisting of a small band of professional assassins. They were equipped with the latest in weaponry and gadgetry with orders to kill those persons considered a threat to the national security of the United States. Gregg Kaplan was once one of those operatives. But now, CIA Director Lucas Reed considered Kaplan a threat to his agenda…along with his handler, Alan Welch. Dalton worked directly under Reed and answered to no one but Reed. His orders were to track Matthew Wolfe, retrieve the stolen data, then eliminate him. His next targets were Kaplan and Welch. In that order.

The laws of the United States had become too left leaning for his taste. Inside the U.S., the FBI had strict legal limits on intelligence gathered within their country. Their court system would not allow any intelligence they deemed illegally gathered to prosecute criminals or spies. And the CIA was prohibited by executive order from collecting intelligence inside the U.S. Although they did anyway.

Dalton didn't abide by those constraints. He gathered any intelligence he wanted, utilizing any means he wanted. His targets would never see the inside of a courtroom. He would carry out their death sentence himself.

Dalton had been on Kaplan's trail for days, starting in Bourges, France. Now, by a strange twist of fate, he and Kaplan were back in Bourges. But Kaplan had failed and didn't even know it yet. The man he was holding had escaped with the help of the Israeli woman.

And they were in the white hatchback 400 meters in front of him, Wolfe behind the wheel.

† † †

"Shit," was the only response Kaplan had at the moment. "How the hell did that happen?"

"I don't know," Moss said. "I still have the keys to the hatchback in my pocket."

"Let me see."

Moss dug the key out of his pocket and held it up."

"That son of a bitch. Ponytail must have given him two keys at the rally. Wolfe gave you one and kept the other."

After Kaplan had repeatedly warned Wolfe not to try anything, the man did it anyway. Again. As disappointing as it was, Marla must have cut a deal with Wolfe. Now, he'd have to follow through on Wolfe. Welch or no Welch, failsafe plan or not, Wolfe was as good as dead.

He'd handle Marla's betrayal later.

† † †

Betrayal to him was almost as bad as taking a bullet. Had Marla's sole purpose all along been to take Wolfe back to Israel? Did she sleep with him to make him believe she wanted to help him? He didn't want to believe that was the case.

Not yet anyway.

He and Moss settled into the black Audi. He had all the information on Wolfe's borrowed car, but had no clue which direction Marla had gone. He doubted she would leave the country and take Wolfe to Israel without the hard drive. Where would Wolfe hide the drive?

He looked at Moss. "How much of a jump do you think they have on us?"

"Ten minutes maybe. Fifteen at the most."

"Guess I'll read Alan back in to help us locate Marla and Wolfe."

"Why would you do that?" Moss asked.

"Because I don't believe Marla would leave the country without the hard drive. Until she has it, she'll stay in France. And that weasel could have stashed it anywhere. I don't have a clue which way to go."

Kaplan fished out his phone. With one hand on the steering, he used his other to start thumbing through his contact list.

Moss put a hand on Kaplan's arm. "Hold on, I got a better idea."

"What?"

"Just give me your phone."

Kaplan handed it to Moss. "I don't understand—"

Moss tapped Kaplan's phone. "It worked," Moss exclaimed. "We got him."

"How?" Kaplan was confused at Moss's cheerful mood.

"When we got here, I left my gear bag on the floorboard behind the driver's seat. Didn't think I'd need it inside the hospital. In my bag is my personal phone. Not the burner. And it's turned on. Remember what you had us do on the plane ride over here?"

"Set up the *Find My* app. Moss you're brilliant. Which way is he headed?"

"Looks like due north. App says 18 kilometers. Highway D940. He's coming up on a town called...Hell, I can't pronounce it. Here." He shoved the phone in Kaplan's face.

Kaplan studied the map. "My guess is they're headed to Paris."

"What makes you think that?"

"Where would you go if you needed to get lost in a crowd? Paris is a huge city. Matthew Wolfe speaks fluent French. Sophie lived there. He could be tricking Marla into believing that's where the hard drive is hidden. Maybe it is. Maybe she cut him a deal that once she has the hard drive in hand, he could disappear. A deal with the devil. Then he could use another one of those fake identities he's tucked away in his back pocket. He could hide in plain sight for years…maybe forever. It would be the proverbial needle in the haystack."

"Then I guess we better stop him before he hands over the hard drive or before she hauls his ass to Israel."

Kaplan nodded, put the Audi in gear and made his way to D940. He plugged his phone into the Audi's USB jack and put the *Find My* app in the vehicle's GPS screen. This was almost a repeat of last night's chase from La Caserne to Bourges, only with the luxury of daylight.

This time though, there was no one to intervene. No one trying to kill Wolfe. No one chasing after the self-proclaimed whistleblower but them. Marla and Wolfe's guard would be down. They wouldn't know they were being tracked. Both Marla and Wolfe would believe they had given Kaplan and Moss the slip with no way of figuring out which direction they were headed. Marla might suspect he'd contact Welch for assistance, but he doubted it. She'd think that's the last thing he'd do since he wouldn't want Welch to know she had tricked him. Kaplan bet Marla had calculated that he would wait her out at the airport to catch them before they could board.

And that was what Kaplan was counting on.

CHAPTER 87

There was a time in every man's life when he had to face his own demons. When he had to take a hard look at himself and decide if the man in the mirror was the man he wanted to be. Or if somewhere along the journey he had veered down the wrong path.

For Matthew Wolfe, pain and death had become a too frequent occurrence, and all of it caused by his own doings.

It was too late to turn over a new leaf. Too late to start over. Pierre Bouquet's troubled life would never be the same. All Wolfe had done was add more pain and grief to it. Pierre was all alone. His guardian angel sister was dead.

All because of me.

And now, Wolfe was on the run again. This time with an Israel operative. The CIA had come close to capturing him. No, they had captured him. Twice. He outsmarted them. Twice. He'd learned something about himself over the past few days, something that made him despise the man in the mirror even more.

He was a coward.

A womanizing, scamming, cheating, lying coward.

In the back of his mind he always suspected he might be some of those things, now he knew it was the truth. Now he knew he was no different than the man who raised him—his father. His father was never faithful to his mother. His mother traveled a lot on business. An only child, he grew up secretly wishing he had a sibling like Sophie. A sibling who would stand by him. Those were painful years. He vowed to be different than his father and yet, he turned out to be a carbon copy.

As an adult he reasoned there were plenty of bad people in this world, people worse than him. People with no values, no compassion, no conscience. At least, he thought, he had some compassion and conscience. He genuinely felt bad for what had happened to Sophie and Pierre. The Bishop, though, he had it coming to him. The man who claimed to be a Man of God had committed the ultimate sin. Sexually abusing children.

He had hoped Pierre would be happy and relieved to hear the Bishop was dead, especially after all the years of depression and torment Pierre had endured. Instead, Pierre was upset and wanted the man alive and in prison. Pierre was one of many who Jean Paul Renault had abused. A quick internet search had brought up numerous allegations against the man spanning nearly three decades. The priest had his victims call him *Uncle Jean*. There were so many people out there suffering because of this man. Renault thought he was more important than his victims. He never realized, or never cared, that he had destroyed hundreds of lives. Not just his victims but the families as well. Wolfe had no remorse for that demon's death. He deserved what he got.

All Wolfe had to do now was give Marla the hard drive. In return, she had promised to let him go so he could disappear again.

Not as Matthew Wolfe.

Not as Curtis Benoit.

Not as Robert James Woolsey.

But as Rémy Girard. A name taken from the French-Canadian actor who, for the most part, was unheard of in France. And now, it was time for Wolfe to assume his new identity. A quick stop outside the Montparnasse train terminal in Paris where he would retrieve his documents, give the hard drive to Marla and make his transition to Rémy Girard. It wasn't the way he had originally planned it, but he had no choice.

After he picked up his new credentials—passport, driver's permit, credit cards, money—he would start his old pattern all over again. Find another unsuspecting woman to charm, to provide a roof over his head and fulfill his needs and desires. Someone who liked to live low-key so he could do the same and hide in relative anonymity.

Maybe she won't be as annoying as Serena. Perhaps more like Sophie. Loving, trusting, intelligent. But he wouldn't make the same mistake he did with Sophie. He would shelter his feelings. Put up a wall, not allow any emotional attachment.

Back to his old self. The self he was comfortable with.

He could do this. After all, he did have many years of practice and Sophie Bouquet was his only failure.

He knew the routine.

He'd perfected this art of deceit.

Like father, like son.

CHAPTER 88

20 Kilometers South of Paris-Orly Airport
Late Afternoon

D alton had been following his target for several hours.
He was no longer in the track and report mode. Reed had given him the green light to execute the targets with only one stipulation — no witnesses. Dalton was ordered to take down the Israeli woman first and then Matthew Wolfe *after* he had the hard drive in his possession.

The rationale behind the order was rather simple—Wolfe knew too much. No one except Dalton and Reed were to know that the data Wolfe stole had been recovered. Reed had made other arrangements for the data. Arrangements he told Dalton would make them both rich beyond their wildest imagination. Dalton knew what Reed's intentions were but kept those suspicions to himself. He'd deal with Reed when the time came.

Dalton knew by using the *Google Maps* app on his phone Wolfe was taking a route toward Paris. Thus far, he'd been able to keep a safe distance behind his target. But Paris was a big city with an immense amount of traffic congestion. Eventually he knew he'd have to follow closer, running the risk of being made. If he didn't, he ran the risk of losing the hatchback in traffic and failing his assignment.

Wolfe veered off N20 and followed the signs toward the Paris-Orly Airport. He was sure the Israeli woman had her weapon trained on him. He wondered if she was taking Wolfe and leaving the country. He knew she had a private jet. Last he knew, though, it and the crew were in Saint-Malo. A quick phone call from Bourges and the woman could have the aircraft waiting for her at the airport.

If that were the case, Dalton would have to act fast, he couldn't allow Wolfe to get on the jet. If he did, Dalton would lose him for good.

And failure was not an option.

† † †

W olfe took the Paris-Orly Airport exit. As did the car that had been following him for such a long distance. Kaplan did too.

The closer they got to Paris, the more the weather improved. It was still cold out, but the heavy clouds in Bourges had turned to a cirrus overcast where he could see blue skies above.

Kaplan and Moss watched the small beige sedan in front of them tail Wolfe's white hatchback. Even though he couldn't see Marla in the vehicle, Moss said he caught sight of her a few times. She had Wolfe drive. But where was Wolfe taking her?

Moss asked, "You think they're leaving the country?"

"Hope not. If Marla got her pilots to move the jet from Saint-Malo to the Paris-Orly Airport, then we've got big problems. We'll have to get Alan and his GIGN colonel buddy involved to lockdown the airport."

"I can't believe she did this to us." Moss said. "I liked her."

Kaplan's memories started flashing back to the last time he made love to Marla. It made him feel so alive. Now he was hurt and angry. "Let's just focus on getting Wolfe."

"Who do you think is following Wolfe?"

"I can't wait to find out," Kaplan said. "Whoever it is, is damned determined. Been on his tail longer than we have. Maybe it's the third hostile Marla said was involved."

"I kinda thought Chameleon was the other player."

"So did I, Moss. So did I."

Both men watched while Wolfe pulled into the P2 terminal parking lot. The beige sedan followed. Trailing farther behind was the black Audi, a car Marla or Wolfe might recognize if they got too close. Kaplan stayed back and turned toward a parallel parking row and parked a good hundred meters away from Wolfe and the beige sedan that parked almost next to him.

Kaplan directed, "You go that way. I'll go this way."

"Roger. Wish we had our comm systems."

"Me too. If you need me," Kaplan said holding his burner out, "call. I'll do likewise. Let's see where Wolfe takes us."

"What about our uninvited guest?"

"Guess we'll worry about him when the time comes."

The two men split up, flanking the outer parking spaces of the P2 parking lot and keeping Wolfe and his stalker on the interior spaces. Kaplan caught a good glimpse of the man who climbed out of the beige sedan. Dark-skinned, small frame, black hair.

Familiar.

And the pieces fell into place.

Upon closer inspection, the stranger was Dalton Palmer, DCI Lucas Reed's one-man kill squad, just like he and Welch had speculated. He knew why Reed sent Dalton. And he knew what would happen to Wolfe when Dalton cornered him alone. Dalton would threaten him. If that didn't work, he'd torture him until Wolfe handed over the hard drive containing the terabytes of stolen data. Wolfe, being the chickenshit bastard that he was, wouldn't hold out for long before he spilled his guts. Perhaps literally.

As he pondered the possibilities, a man and woman followed by another man in front of him entered the terminal. First Wolfe and Marla. Then Dalton. Kaplan followed with Moss behind him about fifty feet. *Keep your distance, Moss.* As if he sent the message telepathically, Moss skirted to the outside wall of the terminal keeping well clear of Wolfe, Marla and Dalton.

Wolfe acted nervous. Marla had her arm locked around his arm. She was sweeping the area. He thought about rushing them but there were too many people around. Marla would resist. She was a big problem. They weren't headed for an airside terminal, instead they entered the Metro terminal.

Now another challenge, following Wolfe and Marla on the train without being made or losing them at a station along the way when they disembarked. Or being made by Dalton Palmer.

The kiosk wasn't a problem for him, but he knew Moss would have trouble. He bought two passes, gave Moss a chin nod. Moss understood. Kaplan held a ticket behind his back while he stood at the kiosk. Moss briskly came up from behind, snagged the ticket and pushed his way through the turnstile. Kaplan followed twenty feet back.

Wolfe and Marla got in the short line at one of the middle rail cars, so did Dalton. Moss went one car behind Wolfe and Marla while Kaplan made his way to the car forward. It was nice working with Moss. Nothing to explain. Nothing to verbalize. Even now, in a foreign country where Moss didn't speak the language, he and Moss could silently communicate. It was the same silent communication that brought them together as friends after their first meeting in Virginia several years ago.

The doors to the train closed and the waiting game began.

CHAPTER 89

Many operatives in Kaplan's line of business never seemed to grasp the art of patience. They wanted to move in quickly and make the kill. Granted, sometimes, that was exactly what needed to be done. But many times, if not most times, patience was the best option. The younger operatives had not learned that waiting was, in and of itself, a skillset. And one that needed to be perfected. Hours of boredom interrupted by moments of sheer terror was a saying he'd coined to describe his job. Actually, there was a lot of truth to that statement.

Kaplan found a spot on the train that didn't give him an unencumbered view of Wolfe, Marla or Dalton, but rather he used the reflection in the car's forward window to monitor all three of them. Moss, he wasn't able to see but knew where he was sitting. He wondered where Wolfe was taking Marla.

Wolfe's body language was smug. He wondered if he planned to trick Marla. Not a wise decision. Perhaps Wolfe's over confidence was because in his mind, he'd outsmarted his pursuers. He had been tracked by the Russians, the Iranians, the CIA and had evaded them all. Except Mossad. And Dalton. Did Marla sense the man sitting across the aisle from them was an operative after Wolfe? Dalton was a master of waiting and patience. And he had balls. He was calm and never flinched facing any highly trained operative. Wolfe had no idea how close to danger he truly was. How close to death he might be. Marla would fight but Dalton had the element of surprise on his side.

When the train slowed for the Denfert-Rochereau station,

Wolfe and Marla stood, and holding the seat-back rails, worked their way to the car door.

Dalton rolled up the magazine he pretended to have been reading and followed. If the passenger car had been empty, Wolfe and Marla might already be dead, if that was Dalton's intention, but the car was well over half full. Too many witnesses. He was sure the first part of Dalton's mission was to get Wolfe alone and make him tell him where the hard drive was located. He was also sure Dalton would take out Marla first. He couldn't warn Marla because he didn't know how much Wolfe had told her. Did she already have the drive? He wanted to make sure Dalton didn't harm Marla. Wolfe needed to stay alive too because there was no way he would let Reed, or his personal pit bull possess what Wolfe had stolen. After Dalton's threat was neutralized, he'd deal with Reed personally. One way or another, he'd get that job done.

Brakes squealing, the train came to a stop, Wolfe, Marla and Dalton disembarked onto the platform and walked forward. Kaplan was forced to wait inside the car until after Dalton passed by, so he didn't get a chance to recognize him. A warning sounded, the doors were closing, Kaplan jumped onto the platform ten feet behind Dalton. He checked down the platform toward the rear of the train.

No Moss.

Where could the big man be?

He turned around, Wolfe, Marla and Dalton were getting too far away. With or without Moss, he had to move and move now. He caught up to them near the escalator. After the train started to roll down the track toward the next station, he spotted Moss.

In the window.

Still sitting.

And oblivious he'd missed their exodus from the train.

He couldn't dwell on Moss's mistake. They would eventually locate each other, but not using the *Find My* app. Moss's personal phone was still in the white hatchback at the Paris-Orly Airport. Now their only communication would be through the burners. He'd send Moss a text later, after he eliminated Dalton and put the finger on Wolfe. He and Moss working together to capture Wolfe had just come to a screeching halt.

He followed his prey to the Metro level where Marla, keeping a tight grip on Wolfe's arm, stood side-by-side with Dalton on another platform waiting for the Line 4 subway heading north toward Porte De Clignancourt. Neither Wolfe nor Marla had any idea the man standing next to them in line was planning on killing them.

Line 4 also made a stop at Montparnasse, only two stops ahead. Kaplan was certain that was Wolfe's destination, but he'd be a fool to go back to Sophie's apartment. Welch for sure, and possibly the GIGN, would have her apartment staked out with round the clock surveillance. The only reason Wolfe would chance going to Sophie's apartment would be if he hid the hard drive there. But something told Kaplan it wasn't in her apartment. He'd be paranoid leaving the hard drive in her apartment after what happened to Serena. After she was murdered, the attacker ransacked the apartment looking for the hard drive.

There was another reason Wolfe was going to Montparnasse and Kaplan had a good idea what it was.

† † †

W hat would motivate Wolfe to return to the Montparnasse area where he certainly knew he stood a chance of being caught?

To retrieve something of value.

And where was the safest place that didn't require an ID to store something of value?

A luggage locker at the train station. Kaplan had used the tactic numerous times. Find an empty locker, put your belongings inside, take the key or type in an access code, no money needed until accessing the locker. No bank safety deposit box. No gym locker. In a train station, thousands upon thousands of people go in and out every day. It was an easy and safe way to store something for an indeterminate amount of time.

Why Montparnasse? Simply because it was the closest available spot near Sophie's apartment. Less than a ten-minute walk. Easy, quick access and away from the prying eyes of a roommate. Wolfe had polished his tactics. And they were good ones, unless pursued by someone who knew them and had used them. Then, they were obvious.

Understanding the mindset of his prey allowed Kaplan to concentrate on the bigger obstacle in his way—Dalton Palmer.

He pulled out his burner phone and typed out a text to Moss's burner.

When you wake up from your nap, get to Montparnasse train station ASAP.

His next move was one he'd put off long enough. He didn't really want to make the call, but it was time. He dialed the number and waited for an answer.

"Alan Welch," the voice said on the other end.

"Turncoat's in Paris. Expect a message with location." Kaplan disconnected the call.

His phone vibrated. It was Moss returning his text.

CHAPTER 90

Gare Montparnasse

He had the right idea, just the wrong location.

Kaplan knew, or at least strongly suspected, that Wolfe was headed for a luggage storage locker inside the train station. But when the traitor and Marla exited Gare Montparnasse and crossed the street, that theory was debunked…partially. He didn't have a luggage locker *inside* the train station but rather at a private luggage locker storage company called *Bag Sitter-Paris* across the street from the station where he was able to secure a locker for an extended time period rather than pay the standard 10€ per day fee inside the terminal.

The late afternoon had long passed dusk and darkness had settled on downtown Paris. A slight breeze blew through the well-lit streets. He jammed his hands in his pockets when he walked into the cold night. The clouds had given way to clear skies once again. When he paced down the steps, he turned right and crossed Avenue du Maine, keeping his distance from Marla, Wolfe and Dalton, To his left, Montparnasse Tower, the tallest building in Paris.

His burner phone vibrated.

An incoming text from Alan Welch

It simply read—*Shutdown Turncoat.*

In his world of espionage, codes words mattered. And he and Welch had their own. In this case, the manner of spelling and punctuation made the difference between life and death when instructions were in writing. *Shut down*, two words, meant one thing and *Shutdown,* one word, meant something entirely different. Shut down, two words, meant abandon the operation. Shutdown, one word, meant eliminate the target. A single tap of the spacebar radically changed the meaning of the message.

This took him by surprise and knotted his stomach at the same time. A far departure from his previous orders, which were to capture Wolfe alive. Now Welch had just ordered him to kill Matthew Wolfe. Where did that order come from? Reed? He doubted Welch unilaterally made this decision. It was a reversal of his previous instructions and one he wondered if he could follow through on, even though he'd threatened to. That threat was more out of frustration than sincerity. Matthew Wolfe was scum and Kaplan disapproved of the methods the whistleblower had used, but he actually hadn't released any secret information to the world, he'd only threatened. Somewhere, someone had decided this man's fate. But Dalton's presence had already tipped Reed's hand.

It was a replay in his mind. His trouble with Reed had started in a similar manner when he refused to comply with an order of which he strongly disagreed. Wolfe deserved to feel the wrath of the law as it was enforced to its fullest extent, but an execution order was a different matter altogether. One he wasn't in total agreement with at the moment. And perhaps never would be. That would all depend on what Wolfe had to say after Kaplan eliminated the threat from Dalton.

With his new orders, he was expected to find an appropriate location, execute his target and make a call with an address so Welch's *janitors* could clean the scene. They would erase any evidence the man had ever existed. He would never be seen or heard from again. And no one would know the man's true fate. And since he had no family, no one would come looking for him later.

Wolfe and Marla entered the luggage locker company. Marla hesitated before entering, checking to see if she had been followed. If Dalton raised any red flags with her, she didn't show it. Perhaps her eyes were trained to spot him or maybe Moss. Her mistake. In reality, unless Kaplan intervened, both of them were only moments away from death at the hands of Dalton once that locker was opened and Dalton had possession of the hard drive.

Dalton waited till Marla and Wolfe entered then he paused at the door, scanned his surroundings and followed them inside.

Kaplan picked up his pace. If he didn't hurry, Wolfe and Marla would die.

When he entered the *Bag Sitter* building, he was surprised at how small it was and how so many lockers were jammed inside such a pocket-sized area. There were lockers to accommodate any size luggage, large or small, all electronic lockers with personally entered access codes. Simply find an empty locker the desired size, store your luggage inside, close the door and enter the code twice. The locker locked. The only way to access the locker after that was with the code and a credit card. Insert the credit card, enter the code. The credit card was charged and the locker unlocked. Amazing how simple it was.

To his right, the soft sound of shuffling shoes. He noticed a restroom door closing. There was no one else inside the building. Something didn't feel right. The emergency exit sign indicated it had an audible alarm, however no alarm had sounded. Wolfe and Dalton were still in the building. He heard a scream—a cry of pain. It was Marla's voice.

He eyed the restroom and bolted in that direction.

Kaplan burst into the room, weapon in hand, and found Dalton, backpack slung over one shoulder, holding Wolfe with a knife against the traitor's throat. Marla was on the floor groaning, a stab wound to her abdomen. She was clutching it with her blood-covered hand and writhing in pain. As much as he wanted to render aid, he focused on Dalton and Wolfe.

"Let him go, Palmer," Kaplan demanded. He thought he saw a sign of relief on Wolfe's face when he saw Kaplan. But it was short-lived when Dalton broke skin and blood trickled down Wolfe's neck.

Dalton said nothing, just held the knife pointed at Kaplan before returning the blade to Wolfe's neck.

"Palmer, I said let him go." Kaplan raised his barrel toward the man's head.

"I should have known you wouldn't give up," Dalton said. "Now, get out of my way or he dies." He pulled Wolfe between him and Kaplan using Wolfe as a shield.

Kaplan holstered his gun.

"I'm not leaving and you're not going to kill him." Then Kaplan taunted him. "Unless you kill me first."

Dalton didn't hesitate. He shoved Wolfe inside a toilet stall, dropped the backpack and took a defensive stance facing Kaplan.

"I've been waiting for this day, Kaplan. You'd be dead already, but Reed wanted that hard drive first." Dalton pointed toward Wolfe with the blade of his knife. "He'll be pleased to hear what I've done, retrieved the hard drive and killed you, the woman and Wolfe while doing so. One last hit and I can leave this country."

Kaplan already knew who the last hit was...Alan Welch.

"Only one problem with your plan, Palmer."

"Yeah, what's that?"

"You're about to die."

CHAPTER 91

He'd been in too many knife fights to count. And had hated every one of them. There could be an incredible amount of damage from a blade in mere seconds. Even in the hands of an amateur. Dalton wielded the knife liked a trained professional. Kaplan had never lost a knife fight, but in confined spaces, he would likely get cut. And the cut could be large and deep.

Statistically, his chances were better against a gun. When shooting at a moving target, people tend to miss more often than they hit. A bladed weapon within reach is deadly inside the arc. Veins, vessels, arteries, tendons, ligaments—easily sliced. The knife fight in this confined bathroom was going to be dangerous, personal, and bloody.

There was a certain skill in surviving a knife fight, especially when your opponent wanted you dead. When two opponents at similar skill levels squared off with daggers in hand, it became a matter of dexterity and cunning. Strength had little to do with it.

Dalton lunged at Kaplan who instinctively arched his body and jumped back, barely avoiding the sharp blade when Dalton made a wide slashing arc at his torso. The rogue operative kept attacking, feverishly slashing while Kaplan ducked and dodged waiting for his chance to strike.

Kaplan retreated and Dalton advanced. The man was using a lot of energy as he charged forward slashing at Kaplan. Wasting energy. Dalton lunged forward, knife first, with an extended arm.

An opportunity.

Kaplan evaded, knocking Dalton to the side with a fisted blow to the side of the man's head, but not before taking a slash across his upper arm, cutting through his parka and finding flesh. Warm, sticky blood oozed under the sleeve. With his elbow, he drove his opponent toward the wall.

Dalton crashed against the sink, his head shattering the mirror above sending shards of glass raining to the floor. Dalton wheeled around, forehead dripping blood, glass embedded in his skin, hand tightened on the shaft of the knife and his face like a rabid animal ready to pounce on his prey. Rational thought had evaporated and now the operative was driven by blind rage.

Dalton charged, aiming the blade straight at Kaplan's chest as a fencer would his épée.

Mistake.

Kaplan rotated, grabbed the man's wrist with one hand and placed his arm over Dalton's arm. Now they stood side by side. He jammed Dalton's wrist down into his upward moving knee, knocking the knife from his grip—shattering bones in the man's wrist and forearm.

With his leg extended, Kaplan shoved Dalton backward, landing him flat on his back. With his free hand, he picked up the man's knife, bent down and plunged it into Dalton's abdomen just below the navel. With a downward thrust, he arced the six-inch blade severing Dalton's intestines.

A brutal way to kill a man.

A painful way to die.

Dalton writhed on the bathroom tile floor, bleeding profusely while his entrails pulsed through the large gash in his abdomen.

Kaplan pulled the blade out of Dalton's gut and pushed himself to his feet. The man yelled at Kaplan.

Kaplan leaned over him, placed the tip of the blade between two ribs on Dalton's chest and said, "Just so you know, I'll tell Reed personally how you failed."

The man's eyes bulged with anger. Kaplan pushed the blade into the man's heart.

Kaplan slowly stood erect and looked at the dead Dalton Palmer, his blood spreading across the bathroom floor leaving islands of broken glass surrounded by a sea of crimson.

He walked over and opened the stall door where Dalton had shoved Wolfe earlier.

"Shit.

Wolfe was gone. And so was the backpack.

He kicked open all the stall doors.

Empty.

He hurried to Marla's side and dropped to one knee. Pulling at her bloody hand clutching her wound he said, "Let me take a look."

"Wolfe ran while you two were fighting." She cut her eyes toward the door. "He's getting away. Go after him...I'll be okay."

He jumped to his feet and ran into the luggage locker storage area.

No Wolfe.

Not again.

He had had enough of Wolfe. His never-ending attempts to escape. Welch just might get him to follow orders after all... and kill the ungrateful bastard.

He ran outside the building and skidded to a stop.

Moss.

"I think I found something of yours" Moss laughed. He

held a backpack in one hand and a hard drive in the other.

Prone on the sidewalk next to Moss's feet was Matthew Wolfe, nose bleeding, jaw reddened.

"Dammit man, how'd you get here so fast?"

"Don't ask cause you really don't want to know."

Both men laughed as they hovered over the unconscious Wolfe.

"Dipshit here has a bigger problem," Kaplan added.

"Oh yeah?"

"I just received a *kill order* from Alan." He made a slicing gesture with his thumb across his neck."

"Guess somebody had a change of heart. We were supposed to bring him in alive. You think the order came from Welch or higher up the chain?"

"Without a doubt above his pay grade. From Reed, I'm sure. The man we followed was Reed's personal kill squad. He was tasked to get the hard drive, then kill Wolfe. Then me, then Welch."

"How do you know all this?"

"Because I just killed Reed's pit bull. A slime ball named Dalton Palmer." Kaplan paused. "Besides, Alan wouldn't want to dirty his hands with this kind of thing on his own. Too political. He wants to keep his job here, maybe advance to Chief of Station one day. A rogue decision on his part, especially a wrong one, could put an end to his upward mobility. Alan's a company man, eyes on the top floor one day."

"And that might not happen," Moss said. "If Wolfe lives."

"Not if it somehow lands back in Alan's lap. I need to keep that from happening if I can."

Moss looked down at Wolfe. "So, you *are* going to kill him then?"

"Right now, I want to."

"As much as I despise this piece of shit traitor. And that's what he is by the way. I think killing him is crossing the line… my line anyway. Welch didn't give me the order. He gave it to you. Do what you think is best, I support you either way."

"Thanks, Moss. I appreciate your support. And for what it's worth, it crosses my line too."

"Let me ask you this, Kaplan, how are you going to leave Wolfe alive and not get Alan fired?"

"I have an idea, but I'm going to have to make a few phone calls first.

Capitaine Travers Heuse was at home when his cell phone rang. Not a number he recognized.

He accepted the call. "Heuse."

"Capitaine, Gregg Kaplan."

"Monsieur Kaplan, this is unexpected."

"I have a proposition for you."

"Oui, monsieur, I feel certain I won't like it."

"Capitaine, I feel certain you'll hate it."

†††

While they waited on the ambulance to come for Marla, Kaplan typed in the text message to Paris Deputy Chief of Station Alan Welch. Generic and non-committal wording, similar to the way Welch issued the kill order on Wolfe. Plausible deniability was what Welch would need and Kaplan was giving him plenty of it.

In war, sometimes a soldier had to jump on a grenade to save the lives of his fellow squad members. In a sense, what he was about to do now was tantamount to diving on a grenade for Welch.

But it had to be done. Welch didn't deserve to lose in this battle, he needed to come out on top. For the betterment of all.

Alan Welch was an honest man. Sure, he wasn't impervious to mistakes as this Wolfe debacle was proof. But his former handler was an asset to the CIA. One the company couldn't afford to lose. Certainly not at the doing of a weak-minded DCI and his utopic new direction for the CIA.

Welch was by far the best handler he'd ever had. A man who cared. A true patriot. Kaplan would do whatever it took to protect Welch and the future of the agency.

Kaplan's future was about to be written. He was writing it. If everything worked as planned, in a sense, he was penning his final chapter with the CIA. And writing it for the good of everyone involved.

It would mean a clean slate for him.

A new life.

A clean break from the past.

And unfortunately, from old friends.

CHAPTER 92

Bag Sitter Luggage Storage
Gare Montparnasse Branch

The first to arrive was Capitaine Travers Heuse. Without him Kaplan's entire plan would fall to pieces. It wasn't an easy sell, but the French GIGN officer understood and agreed. The killing had to stop. In many ways, through all their seeming differences, he and Heuse were much alike. Heuse was a man of true character. An asset for the GIGN. An asset for France. They both had strong convictions about right and wrong and a drive to fight injustices. A kill order on Matthew Wolfe was an injustice in both their minds.

While he placed a call to Alan Welch, Heuse called Colonel Pernille Skouboe. Both were en route to the scene. And so were the major Paris media and press outlets. Kaplan had called them first.

When Welch and Skouboe arrived, both were hounded as to what the *big* announcement was about. Neither knew until after entering Bag Sitter Luggage Storage. Once inside, all they could do was listen and acquiesce to the list of Kaplan's demands.

"Seems like you covered all the bases," Welch said to Kaplan. "The director will fire you for this, you know."

"It's better this way, Alan."

"Wolfe said he has a failsafe in place, do you know what it is?"

"You know what, Alan? Any failsafe Wolfe has in place is

not my problem. It's Reed's." He handed Welch a folded piece of paper. "Burn after reading."

Welch slipped the paper in his pants pocket and nodded.

Heuse slipped the handcuffs on Wolfe and paraded him outside the building to the waiting media frenzy. Skouboe and Welch shared center stage as they announced the remarkable joint effort of the French GIGN and the United States Government in capturing the elusive American traitor, Matthew Wolfe, and the recovery of the data stolen from the United States Intelligence Community.

While Welch and Skouboe took turns speaking to the press, Kaplan and Moss quietly slipped away from the crowd.

CHAPTER 93

Beaune, France
One week later

Pete Moss's journey was ending where it began.
He was returning to Chicago tomorrow.
Alone.

For whatever reason, his friend Gregg Kaplan was staying longer before he returned to D.C. for his face-to-face with the CIA Director Lucas Reed and Alan Welch. Kaplan seemed to already know that outcome. In a way, he had orchestrated it. Kaplan knew the system well, perhaps too well. That was one reason, Moss supposed, for the overwhelming media presence at the luggage locker.

When he and Kaplan left Bag Sitter Luggage Storage after handing over Matthew Wolfe to the French GIGN to be held in a French prison, Kaplan had some kind of transformation. If Moss didn't know better, he'd think his partner and friend had made peace with a decision he'd struggled to make. He was too tranquil, too quiet. More introspective than usual. Moss wanted to ask but decided to let it go.

While Welch and Skouboe were informing the press of Wolfe's capture, Kaplan led him back to Gare Montparnasse where they backtracked to the Paris-Orly Airport.

From there, Kaplan retrieved his belongings and returned his rented Audi. Then the two men located the white hatchback that Wolfe borrowed from Ponytail and drove in relative silence all the way to Beaune.

Somehow his friend managed to rent the same apartment they had when they first arrived in France.

The first night, both men crashed, catching up on much needed rest. When he thought back on all their adventures together, it was always this way. Full speed ahead until the job was done—then take time to recover later.

Since arriving back in Beaune, Kaplan had been the perfect tour guide for Moss. Although the weather was cold, it had been sunny, or mostly so, every day. His friend had taken him on two wine tastings beneath the surface streets of Beaune, his favorite was Patriarche. To that extent Moss, a self-proclaimed die-hard beer drinker, had a case of Grande CRU Cuvée shipped to his home in Chicago. It cost him a pretty penny, then again, he had just earned quite a lucrative paycheck compliments of the CIA.

Since their arrival back in Beaune Kaplan had been cordial and friendly, but nowhere near his normal smart-ass self. He missed his the old Kaplan but knew this too would pass. It was obvious Kaplan had something on his mind he didn't want to share. Perhaps it was Marla. She was treated and released from the hospital in Paris and as far as he knew, the two hadn't talked since the incident when Marla got stabbed.

For Moss, France was an adventure he wouldn't soon forget. He didn't get to see France like a tourist might, he got to see France like most people, certainly tourists, never would. He got a deeper look into the inner workings of Kaplan's world. Much like his old world with the U.S. Marshals Service, the CIA was saddled with too much bureaucracy. Something he despised as a Deputy U.S. Marshal and something he knew Kaplan abhorred as well. Kaplan wrote his new future. In his own words, Kaplan threw himself on the grenade.

Moss and Kaplan had become the best of friends, although those were words understood and never spoken. There wasn't anything they wouldn't do for one another. Again, understood.

Like always, tomorrow they would shake hands and say goodbye without setting any definitive plans to see each other again…or even talk for that matter. But they didn't need to.

Sooner or later he would hear from Kaplan.

Sooner or later, Kaplan would call.

And when he did, they would be off on another adventure.

† † †

Breaking into the mansion and eluding the man's security detail was much easier than he'd expected. The unknown was fear. To overcome it, meant preparation. And preparation was his forte. He'd acquired the floor plans to the mansion from the architect's office, including the intricate details of the high-end security system.

He knew hackers like Wolfe and Snowden. The agency's employee roster was full of them. And he knew which ones would discreetly provide him what he needed. The analyst he enlisted despised the target as much or more than he did. She had acquired the floor plans and obtained video from the indoor and outdoor security cameras along with cataloging the target's daily routines and patterns. She then forwarded that intel to Kaplan.

When his target arrived, Kaplan was already in place. Security monitors already running a previously taped loop. His target was a creature of habit. The same routine every day. A deadly mistake for a man at such a level in the Intelligence Community.

After his security detail escorted him to the door and were dismissed, all Kaplan had to do was wait. His prey would come to him. Patience and meticulous care were required.

When Lucas Reed descended the stairs to his basement, Kaplan was ready.

Reed, dressed in his workout attire, stepped on his treadmill and began his running regimen. Kaplan waited. Now was not the time.

Thirty minutes into Reed's run, after the man was in a full sweat, was the time.

Without hesitation Kaplan moved swiftly across the room toward the treadmill. Reed's head turned, his jaw dropped slightly staring at the 8-inch long tube in Kaplan's hand.

Click.

A vapor spurted from the tube, surrounding Reed's face.

"Kaplan, what the—" Reed stammered when he inhaled the fumes. He stumbled, grabbing the kill switch on the treadmill before collapsing to the floor. His face an unnatural purple color.

Kaplan tucked the tube into his back pocket and stood over Reed. "Sending Dalton was your first mistake. You sent a boy to do a man's job. His blood is on your hands. I want you to know one thing in your dying breaths—Dalton gave you up. He left out no details about your plan. You're a traitor to your country, worse than Matthew Wolfe. That will be your legacy. I'm not surprised you sent Dalton after me but I was surprised to learn you ordered Dalton to kill Alan Welch. Alan is a decent and honorable man—as forthright as they come in this business. You tried to kill Alan, and for that, you must die."

Reed's eyes were bulging as the toxin he inhaled was

carried through his arteries to his brain. He was motionless. The paralyzing effects took hold.

It took 67 seconds for Lucas Reed to take his last breath. An autopsy would certainly be done, but this toxin takes seconds to kill and minutes to disappear from the system. Tomorrow, his housekeeper would discover his body.

Ultimately, the coroner would rule his death a heart attack.

EPILOGUE

Burgundy, France
April

It was called a *brush pass*. A brief encounter, typically without speaking, between a case officer and an operative.

Except he was no longer an operative and the man wearing the tweed cap wasn't his case officer. He didn't officially have a case officer because he didn't officially have a job.

Not anymore.

He'd had a long run with the CIA. And a successful one.

But Gregg Kaplan's days as an operative under the employ of the United Stated Government had come to an end.

There was a new arrangement in place, one secretly funded by the U.S. Government's black budget and one he'd initiated with Alan Welch on the night Matthew Wolfe was captured. He made the offer on the folded piece of paper he passed to Welch before he and Moss disappeared.

After being officially relieved of duty, Welch contacted him with the details.

Relieved of duty wasn't the appropriate phrase. He wasn't fired, per se, instead given the opportunity to take an immediate retirement with the same full retirement benefits any federal employee was so entitled. That too, was part of his plan. With a little interference from Alan Welch. An offer extended to him by the new, acting director of the CIA after the untimely death of DCI Lucas Reed.

The brush pass seemed a lot like a reinstitution of Cold War, cloak and dagger, ways of doing things, but he and Welch couldn't have a face-to-face conversation for a long while. Alan had received a commendation for his success in capturing Matthew Wolfe and recovery of the stolen data. As it turned out, Matthew Wolfe had no failsafe in place and had just lied to keep everyone at bay and put the pressure on the United States Intelligence Community. In addition, Welch had been named acting Paris Chief of Station and was the front runner for the permanent assignment.

No electronic or digital communication either. Every move Welch made was scrutinized. Any suspicion he was communicating with Kaplan in any manner might mean the end of Welch's upward mobility within the CIA. Therefore, brush passes and dead drops had become his new norm.

Their new norm.

When the two men walked past each other on Pont Neuf, one of Paris's best-known bridges spanning the Seine River, the exchange of the envelope was unnoticeable even for the best trained eyes.

Kaplan walked north after the exchange, descended into the Metro station and boarded the subway line to Gare de Lyon where he boarded a TGV to Dijon.

Things had changed a lot after turning over Matthew Wolfe to the French GIGN. The traitor was locked in a French jail cell still awaiting extradition to the United States. The French government was stalling until written assurances were put in place that Wolfe would not suddenly disappear and would receive due process in the American judicial system.

Wolfe and what happened to him were issues he no longer cared to keep tabs on. His newfound trust in Capitaine Travers Heuse and Colonel Pernille Skouboe put his mind at ease that the French government would do the right thing by Wolfe. In the sense that the man would stay alive to face his day in court instead of vanishing, never to be seen again, locked away in some secret CIA black site.

Or dead.

Back in January when he and Moss returned the white hatchback to Ponytail at the P.A.P.A.C.Y. rally in Beaune, Pierre Bouquet was there. He was taking over his sister's role as the France director of the advocacy group. His face was still recovering from the beating. Coping with Sophie's death was an ongoing process, but the young man was managing. Taking over his sister's legacy had given him a newfound purpose in life.

He had not spoken with his friend Pete Moss since they parted ways three months ago. Welch assured him Moss got paid the full amount of the agreement as did he. Soon they'd talk, he promised himself.

When the time was right.

While the TGV sped toward Dijon, he read the contents of the envelope. Alan Welch had included the username and password to a new Google Gmail account they were to jointly use to communicate. The two had used this technique in the past and he knew the routine. No emails would ever be actually sent from the account, instead communications were accomplished by simply logging in and editing the same draft email. Not 100% secure but close and Welch would never log in from his office computer or from the Paris station.

After he was named permanent Chief of Station, if he was, then those safety protocols might relax. Although not for a long time.

Kaplan was now Alan Welch's secret weapon.

Only European assignments.

Which had necessitated a major change in Kaplan's life.

He had returned to the States in February and sold his Tysons Corner, Virginia home, all of his furniture and most of his possessions. He bought an older home in Meursault, France just a few kilometers outside of Beaune. Actually, it was an older chateau with its own vineyard that had gone out of business. The chateau itself had fallen into a state of disrepair and he'd spent the better part of the past three months having it restored and remodeled.

Meursault was his new base. Perhaps not the most convenient for last minute travel, but it was secure and isolated. A great place for him to live off the grid.

Before he had his Harley shipped to France he rode back to Grass Lake one last time. He walked to the front porch and rang the doorbell. Neither Jerry nor Clara were home. Isabella was alone. When he presented her with the rose, she smiled and thanked him. She didn't invite him in. He could see it in her eyes. There wasn't so much as a glimmer of recognition. Any vestige of him in the recesses of her brain had vanished.

He had been permanently erased.

All his doubts had now been resolved.

It was better that way, he told himself. Better for everyone.

He stared out the window of the TGV. This move was for the best he thought, plus his deal with Alan was lucrative. It was a new life in many ways. New location. New lifestyle. Same basic job function—kill the bad actors.

He read over his newest assignment, an American high value target in Marseille. The hit scheduled for next week.

As the TGV slowed for the Dijon station, he slipped the

envelope in his backpack. He'd read the rest after he got home.
Home.

It still felt strange to call France home or the chateau and he knew it would for a while, he mused as he left Gare de Dijon depot and walked to his Harley in the covered parking lot.

The forty-five-minute ride from Dijon to Meursault took closer to an hour, but he wasn't in a hurry, so he took a scenic route through several vineyards south of Beaune. The weather was warm, skies clear, and a beautiful spring day for a long ride.

† † †

W hen he heard the footfalls, it was almost too late. The door pushed open and she entered the bedroom he had converted to an office in his chateau. He had swiveled his chair and kept his back to her. He didn't have to turn and see who it was, he was expecting her.

"I thought you'd come sooner," he said.

"So, you knew I'd come?"

He spun the chair around and faced her.

"I did."

"Why didn't you visit me in the hospital?"

"I called. *Treated and released* were the terms they used. I heard you were going to be fine. How's the wound?"

"It's fine. It's my heart that is broken."

They locked eyes and did not speak for a moment. In her hands a bottle of Jameson Irish Whiskey and two glasses.

"I'm sorry Gregg. I shouldn't have betrayed you. Uncle Eli gave me strict orders to keep the Iranians away from Wolfe and to recover the hard drive at any cost."

"You followed orders. But, there was a cost."

"What do you mean? I told you, the knife wound is all healed."

"A greater cost." He glanced at the Jameson bottle then returned his stare to Marla. "It's too late for us Marla."

"We could try."

"It would only prolong the inevitable."

Moisture collected in her eyes. She walked to a table on the side of the room and put the whiskey and glasses down. "So, that's it?"

"Afraid so."

"Be careful out there, Gregg." She hesitated at the door. "And when you see Moss wish him well for me."

His eyes followed her out. He stared out the window until Marla drove away.

"You can come out now," he said.

The louvered closet door pushed open.

"That must have been hard on you," said the big man who stepped out of the closet.

"Not as hard as stuffing your big ass in my closet."

Moss grinned. "It was pretty tight in there."

"We got work to do, Moss. I'm glad you flew out when I called."

"Anything for you, Bro. Why'd you have me hide from Marla?"

"If she knew you were here, she wouldn't have been as honest. Plus, she'd know we were back on another assignment."

"Where to this time? Another HVT?"

"Marseille."

AUTHOR NOTES

Devil in the Wind was an exciting book to write in many ways since I was fortunate enough to have visited most of the locales depicted herein.

First things first—Acknowledgements: First and foremost, as always, the first read goes to my wife, Debi (author DJ Steele to many). She is an awesome fact-checker and her unfettered honesty always makes my books better. Once again, she claimed that Disruption, (and then again with Last Chance), would be the last book she would edit and, once again, I groveled, and she gave in—burying herself into Devil in the Wind. Her input is an integral part of my writing and editing process, one I'm not sure I could do without. One I certainly wouldn't want to do without. She keeps me on the straight and narrow and helps punch up many scenes, especially when it comes to character emotions. For that, I am eternally grateful.

With each new book I write, the list of acknowledgements typically grows. I am indebted to those who have graciously volunteered their time and energy to steer this author in the right direction. It's their occupational expertise and/or past experiences that have provided me, through interviews and discussions, with a rudimentary foundation to write about things of which I know nothing. My sincerest gratitude to each of those. Every author understands the true value of beta-readers. Not only are they extra eyes on your manuscript, they are readers who donate their time to provide honest, unbiased, and unabashed input. These are volunteers whose motivation is simply to help me make this the best book possible.

To those experts and volunteers, you have my upmost gratitude. Thank you to Debi Barrett, Alan Welch, Mike Catt, Early McCall, Cheryl Duttweiler, Terrence Traut, Nancy Mace, C.J. "Cos" Cosgrove, & Artie Lynnworth.

Lastly, I want to thank you, the reader. It is my genuine hope that you found this story entertaining and that those unexpected twists and turns along with down your throat action left you smiling...or cursing...either way, it works for me.

Is it fact or fiction? — This is something I've tried to include in the back of every novel for those of you who like to differentiate reality from this author's ... for lack of better words, exaggeration or editorial license.

The locations in this book are factual as is the history about them. Some extra details were added for the sake of the story. I will explain them now.

Beaune, France—A beautiful place I would recommend visiting. The light projectors used during Summer Festival of Lights are accurate; however, these projectors aren't typically out in the winter. The Clock Tower is correct, although I have not been inside. Therefore, the doors leading to the adjacent building are added for the sake of the story as are my depictions of the interior of that building. The exterior street exits are correct as are the security cameras in the alley behind the tower.

Bourges, France—Everything here is accurate. The cathedral and its physical footprint are larger than that of Notre Dame in Paris.

Bayeux, France and Saint Malo, France—All accurate.

Mont Saint Michel and surrounding area—I specifically wanted to depict this marvel as accurately as possible without getting into any painstaking historical minutia that would slow the pace of the story. It would have been too easy to do with all the history surrounding this island Abbey. Inside the Abbey are concealed passageways from the public. Since I obviously couldn't go exploring where each led, I took some editorial license and created my own maze of tunnels and corridors. The public portion is accurate.

P.A.P.A.C.Y. is a fictional entity. There are several organizations with the same mission in mind, hold the Church accountable for the abusive actions of its priests. As contentious as this issue is to many faithful Catholics, I kept it as light as I could. No facts were misrepresented or exaggerated, but the characters are, of course, fictitious as are their accounts of abuse.

Paris—If you've never been atop the Montparnasse Tower, you should go. And you should go at night when the skies are clear. There are several baggage/luggage storage businesses near Gare Montparnasse train station, however, Bag Sitters is my own fabrication.

I hope you enjoyed this story and keep reading!

CPSIA information can be obtained
at www.ICGtesting.com
Printed in the USA
BVHW080014150521
607367BV00001B/90